THE DEATH OF GULAH.

THE

BOY SLAVES

BY

CAPT. MAYNE REID,

AUTHOR OF "THE DESERT HOME," "THE OCEAN WAIFS," ETC.

With Illustrations.

Fredonia Books
Amsterdam. The Netherlands

The Boy Slaves

by
Capt. Mayne Reid

ISBN: 1-58963-452-7

Reprinted from the 1885 edition

Fredonia Books
Amsterdam, The Netherlands
http://www.fredoniabooks.com

CONTENTS.

CONTENTS.

THE BOY SLAVES.

CHAPTER I.

THE LAND OF THE SLAVE.

LAND of Ethiope! whose burning centre seems unapproachable as the frozen Pole!

Land of the unicorn and the lion, — of the crouching panther and the stately elephant, — of the camel, the camelopard, and the camel-bird! land of the antelopes, — of the wild gemsbok, and the gentle gazelle, — land of the gigantic crocodile and huge river-horse, — land teeming with animal life, and last in the list of my apostrophic appellations, — last, and that which must grieve the heart to pronounce it, — land of the slave!

Ah! little do men think while thus hailing thee, how near may be the dread doom to their own hearths and homes! Little dream they, while expressing their sympathy, — alas! too often, as of late shown in England, a hypocritical utterance, — little do they suspect, while glibly commiserating the lot of thy sable-skinned children, that hundreds — aye, thousands — of their own color and kindred are held within thy confines, subject to a lot even lowlier than these, — a fate far more fearful.

Alas! it is even so. While I write, the proud Caucasian, — despite his boasted superiority of intellect, — despite the whiteness of his skin, — may be found by hundreds in

the unknown interior, wretchedly toiling, the slave not only
of thy oppressors, but the slave of thy slaves!

Let us lift that curtain, which shrouds thy great Saära,
and look upon some pictures that should teach the son of
Shem, while despising his brothers Ham and Japhet, that
he is not yet master of the world.

. . . . .

Dread is that shore between Susa and Senegal, on the
western edge of Africa, — by mariners most dreaded of any
other in the world. The very thought of it causes the sailor
to shiver with affright. And no wonder: on that inhospitable seaboard thousands of his fellows have found a watery
grave; and thousands of others a doom far more deplorable
than death!

There are two great deserts: one of land, the other of
water, — the Saära and the Atlantic, — their contiguity ex
tending through ten degrees of the earth's latitude, — an
enormous distance. Nothing separates them, save a line
existing only in the imagination. The dreary and dangerous wilderness of water kisses the wilderness of sand, — not
less dreary or dangerous to those whose misfortune it may
be to become castaways on this dreaded shore.

Alas! it has been the misfortune of many — not hun
dreds, but thousands. Hundreds of ships, rather than hundreds of men, have suffered wreck and ruin between Susa
and Senegal. Perhaps were we to include Roman, Phoeni-
cian, and Carthaginian, we might say thousands of ships
also.

More noted, however, have been the disasters of modern
times, during what may be termed the epoch of modern
navigation. Within the period of the last three centuries,
sailors of almost every maritime nation — at least all whose
errand has led them along the eastern edge of the Atlantic
— have had reason to regret approximation to those shores,
known in ship parlance as the Barbary coast; but which

with a slight alteration in the orthography, might be appropriately styled "Barbarian."

A chapter might be written in explanation of this peculiarity of expression — a chapter which would comprise many parts of two sciences, both but little understood — ethnology and meteorology.

Of the former we may have a good deal to tell before the ending of this narrative. Of the latter it must suffice to say : that the frequent wrecks occurring on the Barbary coast — or, more properly, on that of the Saära south of it — are the result of an Atlantic current setting eastwards against that shore.

The cause of this current is simple enough, though it requires explanation : since it seems to contradict not only the theory of the "trade" winds, but of the centrifugal inclination attributed to the waters of the ocean.

I have room only for the theory in its simplest form. The heating of the Saära under a tropical sun ; the absence of those influences — moisture and verdure — which repel the heat and retain its opposite ; the ascension of the heated air that hangs over this vast tract of desert ; the colder atmosphere rushing in from the Atlantic Ocean ; the consequent eastward tendency of the waters of the sea.

These facts will account for that current which has proved a deadly maelstrom to hundreds — aye, thousands — of ships, in all ages, whose misfortune it has been to sail unsuspectingly along the western shores of the Ethiopian continent.

Even at the present day the castaways upon this desert shore are by no means rare, notwithstanding the warnings that at close intervals have been proclaimed for a period of three hundred years.

While I am writing, some stranded brig, barque, or ship may be going to pieces between Bojador and Blanco ; her crew making shorewards in boats to be swamped among the foaming breakers; or, riding three or four together upon some severed spar, to be tossed upon a desert strand, that each may wish, from the bottom of his soul, should prove *uninhabited!*

I can myself record a scene like this that occurred not ten years ago, about midway between the two headlands above named — Bojador and Blanco. The locality may be more particularly designated by saying: that, at half distance between these noted capes, a narrow strip of sand extends for several miles out into the Atlantic, parched white under the rays of a tropical sun — like the tongue of some fiery serpent, well represented by the Saära, far stretching to seaward; ever seeking to cool itself in the crystal waters of the sea.

CHAPTER II.

TYPES OF THE TRIPLE KINGDOM.

NEAR the tip of this tongue, almost within "licking" distance, on an evening in the month of June 18—, a group of the kind last alluded to — three or four castaways upon a spar — might have been seen by any eye that chanced to be near.

Fortunately for them, there was none sufficiently approximate to make out the character of that dark speck, slowly approaching the white sand-spit, like any other drift carried upon the landward current of the sea.

It was just possible for a person standing upon the summit of one of the sand "dunes" that, like white billows, rolled off into the interior of the continent — it was just possible for a person thus placed to have distinguished the aforesaid speck without the aid of a glass; though with one it would have required a prolonged and careful observation to have discovered its character.

The sand-spit was full three miles in length. The hills stood back from the shore another. Four miles was sufficient to screen the castaways from the observation of anyone who might be straying along the coast.

For the individuals themselves it appeared very improbable that there could be any one observing them. As far as eye could reach — east, north, and south, there was nothing save white sand. To the west nothing but the blue water. No eye could be upon them, save that of the Creator. Of His creatures, tame or wild, savage or civilized, there seemed not one within a circuit of miles: for within that circuit there was nothing visible that could afford subsistence either to man or animal, bird or beast. In the white substratum of sand, gently shelving far under the sea, there was not a sufficiency of organic matter to have afforded food for fish — even for the lower organisms of *mollusca*. Undoubtedly were these castaways alone; as much so, as if their locality had been the centre of the Atlantic, instead of its coast!

We are privileged to approach them near enough to comprehend their character, and learn the cause that has thus isolated them so far from the regions of animated life.

There are four of them, astride a spar; which also carries a sail, partially reefed around it, and partially permitted to drag loosely through the water.

At a glance a sailor could have told that the spar on which they are supported is a topsail-yard, which has been detached from its masts in such a violent manner as to unloose some of the reefs that had held the sail, thus partially releasing the canvas. But it needed not a sailor to tell why this had been done. A ship has foundered somewhere near the coast. There has been a gale two days before. The

spar in question, with those supported upon it, is but a frag-
ment of the wreck. There might have been other frag-
ments, — others of the crew escaped, or escaping in like
manner, — but there are no others in sight. The castaways
slowly drifting towards the sandspit are alone. They have
no companions on the ocean, — no spectators on its shore.

As already stated, there are four of them. Three are
strangely alike, — at least, in the particulars of size, shape,
and costume. In age, too, there is no great difference. All
three are boys: the oldest not over eighteen, the youngest
certainly not a year his junior.

In the physiognomy of the three there is similitude enough
to declare them of one nation, — though dissimilarity sufficient to prove a distinct provinciality both in countenance
and character. Their dresses of dark blue cloth, cut pea-
jacket shape, and besprinkled with buttons of burnished
yellow, — their cloth caps, of like color, encircled by bands
of gold lace, — their collars, embroidered with the crown
and anchor, declare them, all three, to be officers in the
service of that great maritime government that has so long
held undisputed possession of the sea, — midshipmen of the
British navy. Rather should we say, had been. They have
lost this proud position, along with the frigate to which
they had been attached; and they now only share authority
upon a dismasted spar, over which they are exerting some
control, since, with their bodies bent downwards, and their
hands beating the water, they are propelling it in the direction of the sand-spit.

In the countenances of the three castaways thus introduced, I have admitted a dissimilitude something more than
casual, — something more, even, than what might be termed
provincial. Each presented a type that could have been
referred to that wider distinction known as a nationality.

The three "middies" astride of that topsail-yard were
of course castaways from the same ship, in the service of

the same government, though each was of a different nationality from the other two. They were the respective representatives of Jack, Paddy, and Sandy, — or, to speak more poetically, of the Rose, Shamrock, and Thistle, — and had the three kingdoms from which they came been searched throughout their whole extent, there could scarcely have been discovered purer representative types of each, than the three reefers on that spar, drifting towards the sand-spit between Bojador and Blanco.

Their names were Harry Blount, Terence O'Connor, and Colin Macpherson.

The fourth individual — who shared with them their frail embarkation — differed from all three in almost every respect, but more especially in years. The ages of all three united would not have numbered his: and their wrinkles, if collected together, would scarce have made so many as could have been counted in the crowsfeet indelibly imprinted in the corners of his eyes.

It would have required a very learned ethnologist to have told to which of his three companions he was compatriot; though there could be no doubt about his being either English, Irish, or Scotch.

Strange to say, his tongue did not aid in the identification of his nationality. It was not often heard; but even when it was, its utterance would have defied the most accomplished linguistic ear; and neither from that, nor other circumstance known to them, could any one of his three companions lay claim to him as a countryman. When he spoke, — a rare occurrence already hinted, — it was with a liberal misplacement of "h's" that should have proclaimed him an Englishman of purest Cockney type. At the same time his language was freely interspersed with Irish "ochs" and shures"; while the "wees" and "bonnys," oft recurring in his speech, should have proved him a sworn Scotchman. From his countenance you might have drawn your own in-

ference, and believed him any of the three; but not from
his tongue.   Neither in his accent, nor the words that fell
from him, could you have told which of the three kingdoms
had the honor of giving him birth.

Whichever it was, it had supplied to the Service a true
British tar: for although you might mistake the man in
other respects, his appearance forbade all equivocation upon
this point.

His costume was that of a common sailor, and, as a matter of course, his name was "Bill."   But as he had only
been one among many "Bills" rated on the man-o'-war's
books,—now gone to the bottom of the sea,—he carried a
distinctive appellation, no doubt earned by his greater age.
Aboard the frigate he had been known as "Old Bill"; and
the soubriquet still attached to him upon the spar.

CHAPTER III.

THE SERPENT'S TONGUE.

THE presence of a ship's topsail-yard thus bestridden
plainly proclaimed that a ship had been wrecked, although no other evidence of the wreck was within sight.
Not a speck was visible upon the sea to the utmost verge
of the horizon: and if a ship had foundered within that
field of view, her boats and every vestige of the wreck must
either have gone to the bottom, or in some other direction
than that taken by the topsail-yard, which supported the
three midshipmen and the sailor Bill.

A ship *had* gone to the bottom — a British man-of-war —
a corvette on her way to her cruising ground on the Guinea
coast.   Beguiled by the dangerous current that sets towards

the seaboard of the Saära, in a dark stormy night she had struck upon a sand-bank, got bilged, and sunk almost instantly among the breakers. Boats had been got out, and men had been seen crowding hurriedly into them; others had taken to such rafts or spars as could be detached from the sinking vessel: but whether any of these, or the overladen boats, had succeeded in reaching the shore, was a question which none of the four astride the topsail-yard were able to answer.

They only knew that the corvette had gone to the bottom, — they saw her go down, shortly after drifting away from her side, but saw nothing more until morning, when they perceived themselves alone upon the ocean. They had been drifting throughout the remainder of that long, dark night, — often entirely under water, when the sea swelled over them, — and one and all of them many times on the point of being washed from their frail embarkation.

By daybreak the storm had ceased, and was succeeded by a clear, calm day; but it was not until a late hour that the swell had subsided sufficiently to enable them to take any measures for propelling the strange craft that carried them. Then using their hands as oars or paddles, they commenced making some way through the water.

There was nothing in sight — neither land nor any other object — save the sea, the sky, and the sun. It was the east which guided them as to direction. But for it there could have been no object in making way through the water; but with the sun now sinking in the west, they could tell the east, and they knew that in that point alone land might be expected.

After the sun had gone down the stars became their compass, and throughout all the second night of their shipwreck they had continued to paddle the spar in an easterly direction.

Day again dawned upon them, but without gratifying their eyes by the sight of land, or any other object to inspire them with a hope.

1 *

Famished with hunger, tortured with thirst, and wearied with their continued exertions, they were about to surrender to despair; when, as the sun once more mounted up to the sky, and his bright beams pierced the crystal water upon which they were floating, they saw beneath them the sheen of white sand. It was the bottom of the sea, and at no great depth, — not more than a few fathoms below their feet.

Such shallow water could not be far from the shore. Reassured and encouraged by the thought, they once more renewed their exertions, and continued to paddle the spar, taking only short intervals of rest throughout the whole of the morning.

Long before noon they were compelled to desist. They were close to the tropic of Cancer, almost under its line. It was the season of midsummer, and of course at meridian hour the sun was right over their heads. Even their bodies cast no shadow, except upon the white sand directly underneath them, at the bottom of the sea.

The sun could no longer guide them; and as they had no other index, they were compelled to remain stationary, or drift in whatever direction the breeze or the currents might carry them.

There was not much movement any way, and for several hours before and after noon they lay almost becalmed upon the ocean. This period was passed in silence and inaction. There was nothing for them to talk about but their forlorn situation, and this topic had been exhausted. There was nothing for them to do. Their only occupation was to watch the sun, until, by its sinking lower in the sky, they might discover its *westing*.

Could they at that moment have elevated their eyes only three feet higher, they would not have needed to wait for the declination of the orb of day. They would have seen land, such land as it was; but, sunk as their shoulders were almost to the level of the water, even the summits of the sand dunes were not visible to their eyes.

When the sun began to go down towards the horizon, they once more plied their palms against the liquid wave, and sculled the spar eastward. The sun's lower limb was just touching the western horizon, when his red rays, glancing over their shoulders, showed them some white spots that appeared to rise out of the water.

Were they clouds? No! Their rounded tops, cutting the sky with a clear line, forbade this belief. They should be hills, either of snow or of sand. It was not the region for snow: they could only be sand-hills.

The cry of "land" pealed simultaneously from the lips of all, — that cheerful cry that has so oft given gladness to the despairing castaway, — and redoubling their exertions, the spar was propelled through the water more rapidly than ever.

Reinvigorated by the prospect of once more setting foot upon land, they forgot for the moment thirst, hunger, and weariness, and only occupied themselves in sculling their craft towards the shore.

Under the belief that they had still several miles to make before the beach could be attained, they were one and all working with eyes turned downward. At that moment old Bill, chancing to look up, gave utterance to a shout of joy, which was instantly echoed by his youthful companions: all had at the same time perceived the long sand-spit projecting far out into the water, and which looked like the hand of some friend held out to bid them welcome.

They had scarce made this discovery before another of like pleasant nature came under their attention. That was, that they were *touching bottom!* Their legs, bestriding the spar, hung down on each side of it; and to the joy of all they now felt their feet scraping along the sand.

As if actuated by one impulse, all four dismounted from

the irksome seat they had been so long compelled to keep; and, bidding adieu to the spar, they plunged on through the shoal water, without stop or stay, until they stood high and dry upon the extreme point of the peninsula.

By this time the sun had gone down; and the four dripping forms, dimly outlined in the purple twilight, appeared like four strange creatures who had just emerged from out the depths of the ocean.

" Where next ? "

This was the mental interrogatory of all four: though by none of them shaped into words.

" Nowhere to-night," was the answer suggested by the inclination of each.

Impelled by hunger, stimulated by thirst, one would have expected them to proceed onward in search of food and water to alleviate this double suffering. But there was an inclination stronger than either, — too strong to be resisted, — sleep: since for fifty hours they had been without any; since to have fallen asleep on the spar would have been to subject themselves to the danger, almost the certainty, of dropping off, and getting drowned; and, notwithstanding their need of sleep, increased by fatigue, and the necessity of keeping constantly on the alert, — up to that moment not one of them had obtained any. The thrill of pleasure that passed through their frames as they felt their feet upon *terra firma* for a moment aroused them. But the excitement could not be sustained. The drowsy god would no longer be deprived of his rights; and one after another — though without much interval between — sank down upon the soft sand, and yielded to his balmy embrace.

WARE THE TIDE

CHAPTER IV.

'WARE THE TIDE.

THROUGH that freak, or law, of nature by which penin-
sulas are shaped, the point of the sand-spit was elevated
several feet above the level of the sea; while its neck,
nearer the land, scarce rose above the surface of the water.

It was this highest point — where the sand was thrown
up in a "wreath," like snow in a storm — that the castaways had chosen for their couch.   But little pains had been
taken in selecting the spot.   It was the most conspicuous,
as well as the driest; and, on stepping out of the water,
they had tottered towards it, and half mechanically chosen
it for their place of repose.

Simple as was the couch, they were not allowed to occupy
it for long.   They had been scarce two hours asleep, when
one and all of them were awakened by a sensation that
chilled, and, at the same time, terrified them.   Their terror
arose from a sense of suffocation : as if salt water was being
poured down their throats, which was causing it.   In short,
they experienced the sensation of drowning; and fancied
they were struggling amid the waves, from which they had
so lately escaped.

All four sprang to their feet, — if not simultaneously, at
least in quick succession, — and all appeared equally the
victims of astonishment, closely approximating to terror.
Instead of the couch of soft, dry sand, on which they had
stretched their tired frames, they now stood up to their
ankles in water, — which was soughing and surging around
them.   It was this change in their situation that caused
their astonishment; though the terror quick following sprang
from quite another cause.

The former was short-lived : for it met with a ready ex

planation. In the confusion of their ideas, added to their
strong desire for sleep, they had forgotten the tide. The
sand, dust-dry under the heat of a burning sun, had deceived
them. They had lain down upon it, without a thought of
its ever being submerged under the sea; but now to their
surprise they perceived their mistake. Not only was their
couch completely under water: but, had they slept a few
minutes longer, they would themselves have been quite
covered. Of course the waves had awakened them; and no
doubt would have done so half an hour earlier, but for the profound slumber into which their long watching and weariness
had thrown them. The contact of the cold water was not
likely to have much effect: since they had been already exposed to it for more than forty hours. Indeed, it was not
that which had aroused them; but the briny fluid getting
into their mouths, and causing them that feeling of suffocation that very much resembled drowning.

More than one of the party had sprung to an erect attitude, under the belief that such was in reality the case; and
it is not quite correct to say that their first feeling was one of
mere astonishment. It was strongly commingled with terror.

On perceiving how matters stood, their fears subsided almost as rapidly as they had arisen. It was only the inflow
of the tide; and to escape from it would be easy enough.
They would have nothing more to do, than keep along the
narrow strip of sand, which they had observed before landing.
This would conduct them to the true shore. They knew
this to be at some distance; but, once there, they could
choose a more elevated couch, on which they could recline
undisturbed till the morning.

Such was their belief, conceived the instant after they had
got upon their legs. It was soon followed by another, —
another consternation, — which, if not so sudden as the first.
was, perhaps, ten times more intense.

On turning their faces towards what they believed to be

the land, there was no land in sight, — neither sand-hills, nor shore, nor even the narrow tongue upon whose tip they had been trusting themselves! There was nothing visible but water; and even this was scarce discernible at the distance of six paces from where they stood. They could only tell that water was around them, by hearing it hoarsely swishing on every side, and seeing through the dim obscurity the strings of white froth that floated on its broken surface.

It was not altogether the darkness of the night that obscured their view; though this was of itself profound. It was a thick mist, or fog, that had arisen over the surface of the ocean, and which enveloped their bodies; so that, though standing almost close together, each appeared to the others like some huge spectral form at a distance!

To remain where they were, was to be swallowed up by the sea. There could be no uncertainty about that; and therefore no one thought of staying a moment longer on the point of the sand-spit, now utterly submerged.

But in what direction were they to go? That was the question that required to be solved before starting; and in the solution of which, perhaps, depended the safety of their lives.

We need scarce say perhaps. Rather might we say, for certain. By taking a wrong direction they would be walking into the sea, — where they would soon get beyond their depth, and be in danger of drowning. This was all the more likely, that the wind had been increasing ever since they had laid down to rest, and was now blowing with considerable violence. Partly from this, and partly by the tidal influence, big waves had commenced rolling around them; so that, even in the shoal water where they stood, each successive swell was rising higher and higher against their bodies.

There was no time to be lost. They must find the true direction for the shore, and follow it, — quickly too; or perish amid the breakers!

CHAPTER V.

A FALSE GUIDE.

WHICH way to the shore?

That was the question that arose to the lips of all.

You may fancy it could have been easily answered. The direction of the wind and waves was landward. It was the sea-breeze, which at night, as every navigator is aware. blows habitually towards the land, — at least, in the region of the tropics, and more especially towards the hot Saära.

The tide itself might have told them the direction to take. It was the in-coming tide, and therefore swelling towards the beach.

You may fancy that they had nothing to do but follow the waves, keeping the breeze upon their back.

So they fancied, at first starting for the shore; but they were not long in discovering that this guide, apparently so trustworthy was not to be relied upon; and it was only then they became apprised of the real danger of their situation. Both wind and waves were certainly proceeding landward, and in a direct line; but it was just this direct line the castaways dared not — in fact could not — follow; for they had not gone a hundred fathoms from the point of the submerged peninsula when they found the water rapidly deepening before them; and a few fathoms further on they stood up to their armpits!

It was evident that, in the direction in which they were proceeding, it continued to grow deeper; and they turned to try another.

After floundering about for a while, they found shoal water again, — reaching up only to their knees; but wherever they attempted to follow the course of the waves, they perceived that the shoal trended gradually downward.

This at first caused them surprise, as well as alarm. The former affected them only for an instant. The explanation was sought for, and suggested to the satisfaction of all. The sand-spit did not project perpendicularly from the line of the coast, but in a diagonal direction. It was in fact, a sort of natural breakwater — forming one side of a large cone, or embayment, lying between it and the true beach. This feature had been observed, on their first setting foot upon it; though at the time they were so much engrossed with the joyous thought of having escaped from the sea, that it had made no impression upon their memory.

They now remembered the circumstance; though not to their satisfaction; for they saw at once that the guide in which they had been trusting could no longer avail them.

The waves were rolling on over that bay — whose depth they had tried, only to find it unfordable.

This was a new dilemma. To escape from it there appeared but one way. They must keep their course along the combing of the peninsula — if they could. But their ability to do so had now become a question — each instant growing more difficult to answer.

They were no longer certain that they were on the spit; but, whether or not, they could find no shallower water by trying on either side. Each way they went it seemed to deepen; and even if they stood still but for a few moments, as they were compelled to do while hesitating as to their course — the water rose perceptibly upon their limbs.

They were now well aware that they had two enemies to contend with — time and direction. The loss of either one or the other might end in their destruction. A wrong direction would lead them into deep water; a waste of time would bring deep water around them. The old adage about time and tide — which none of them could help having heard — might have been ringing in their ears at that moment. It was appropriate to the occasion.

B

They thought of it; and the thought filled them with apprehension. From the observations they had made before sunset, they knew that the shore could not be near — not nearer than three miles — perhaps four.

Even with free footing, the true direction, and a clear view of the path, it might have been a question about time. They all knew enough of the sea to be aware how rapidly the tide sets in — especially on some foreign shores — and there was nothing to assure them that the seaboard of the Saära was not beset by the most treacherous of tides. On the contrary, it was just this — a tidal current — that had forced their vessel among the breakers, causing them to become what they now were, — castaways!

They had reason to dread the tides of the Saära's shore; and dread them they did, — their fears at each moment becoming stronger as they felt the dark waters rising higher and higher around them.

CHAPTER VI.

WADE OR SWIM?

FOR a time they floundered on, — the old sailor in the lead, the three boys strung out in a line after him. Sometimes they departed from this formation, — one or another trying towards the flank for shallower water.

Already it clasped them by the thighs; and just in proportion as it rose upon their bodies, did their spirits become depressed. They knew that they were following the crest of the sand-spit. They knew it by the deepening of the sea on each side of them; but they had by this time discovered another index to their direction. Old Bill had kept his "weath-

er-eye " upon the waves ; until he had discovered the angle
at which they broke over the " bar," and could follow the
"combing" of the spit, as he called it, without much danger
of departure from the true path.

It was not the *direction* that troubled their thoughts any
longer ; but the *time* and the *tide*.

Up to their waists in water, their progress could not be
otherwise than slow.   The time would not have signified
could they have been sure of the tide, — that is, sure of its
not rising higher.

Alas ! they could not be in doubt about this.   On the contrary, they were too well assured that it *was* rising higher ;
and with a rapidity that threatened soon to submerge them
under its merciless swells.   These came slowly sweeping
along, in the diagonal direction, — one succeeding the other,
and each new one striking higher up upon the bodies of the
now exhausted waders.

On they floundered despite their exhaustion ; on along
the subaqueous ridge, which at every step appeared to sink
deeper into the water, — as if the nearer to the land the
peninsula became all the more depressed.   This, however,
was but a fancy.   They had already passed the neck of the
sand-spit where it was lowest.   It was not that, but the fast
flowing tide that was deepening the water around them.

Deeper and deeper, — deeper and deeper, till the salt sea
clasped them around the armpits, and the tidal waves began
to break over their heads !

There seemed but one way open to their salvation, — but
one course by which they could escape from the engulfment
that threatened.   This was to forego any further attempt
at wading, to fling themselves boldly upon the waves, and
swim ashore !

Now that they were submerged to their necks, you may
wonder at their not at once adopting this plan.   It is true
they were ignorant of the distance they would have to swim

before reaching the shore. Still they knew it could not be
more than a couple of miles; for they had already traversed
quite that distance on the diagonal spit. But two miles
need scarce have made them despair, with both wind and
tide in their favor.

Why, then, did they hesitate to trust themselves to the
quick, bold stroke of the swimmer, instead of the slow, tim-
id, tortoise-like tread of the wader?

There are two answers to this question; for there were
two reasons for them not having recourse to the former alternative. The first was selfish; or rather, should we call
it *self-preservative*. There was a doubt in the minds of all,
as to their ability to reach the shore by swimming. It was
a broad bay that had been seen before sundown; and once
launched upon its bosom, it was a question whether any of
them would have strength to cross it. Once launched upon
its bosom, there would be no getting back to the shoal water
through which they were wading; the tidal current would
prevent return.

This consideration was backed by another, — a lingering
belief or hope that the tide might already have reached its
highest, and would soon be on the "turn." This hope,
though faint, exerted an influence on the waders, — as yet
sufficient to restrain them from becoming swimmers. But
even after this could no longer have prevailed, — even when
the waves began to surge over, threatening at each fresh
"sea" to scatter the shivering castaways and swallow them
one by one, — there was another thought that kept them together.

It was a thought neither of self nor self-preservation;
but a generous instinct, that even in that perilous crisis was
stirring within their hearts.

Instinct! No. It was a thought, — an impulse if you
will; but something higher than an instinct.

Shall I declare it? Undoubtedly, I shall. Noble emotions should not be concealed; and the one which at that moment throbbed within the bosoms of the castaways, was truly noble.

There were but three of them who felt it. The fourth could not: *he could not swim!*

Surely the reader needs no further explanation?

CHAPTER VII.

A COMPULSORY PARTING.

ONE of the four castaways could not swim. Which one? You will expect to hear that it was one of the three midshipmen; and will be conjecturing whether it was Harry Blount, Terence O'Connor, or Colin Macpherson.

My English boy-readers would scarce believe me, were I to say that it was Harry who was wanting in this useful accomplishment. Equally incredulous would be my Irish and Scotch *constituency*, were I to deny the possession of it to the representatives of their respective countries, — Terence and Colin.

Far be it from me to offend the natural *amour propre* of my young readers; and in the present case I have no fact to record that would imply any national superiority or disadvantage. The castaway who could not swim was that peculiar hybrid, or *tribrid*, already described; who, for any characteristic he carried about him, might have been born either upon the banks of the Clyde, the Thames, or the Shannon!

It was "Old Bill" who was deficient in natatory prowess: Old Bill the sailor.

It may be wondered that one who has spent nearly the

whole of his life on the sea should be wanting in an accom
plishment, apparently and really, so essential to such a call
ing. Cases of the kind, however, are by no means uncom-
mon; and in a ship's crew there will often be found a large
number of men, — sometimes the very best sailors, — who
cannot swim a stroke.

Those who have neglected to cultivate this useful art,
when boys, rarely acquire it after they grow up to be men;
or, if they do, it is only in an indifferent manner. On the
sea, though it may appear a paradox, there are far fewer
opportunities for practising the art of swimming than upon
its shores. Aboard a ship, on her course, the chances of
" bathing" are but few and far between; and, while in port,
the sailor has usually something else to do than spend his
idle hours in disporting himself upon the waves. The sail-
or, when ashore, seeks for some sport more attractive.

As Old Bill had been at sea ever since he was able to
stand upon the deck of a ship, he had neglected this useful
art; and though in every other respect an accomplished
sailor — rated A.B., No. 1 — he could not swim six lengths
of his own body.

It was a noble instinct which prompted his three youthful
companions to remain by him in that critical moment, when,
by flinging themselves upon the waves, they might have
gained the shore without difficulty.

Although the bay might be nearly two miles in width
there could not be more than half that distance beyond their
depth, — judging by the shoal appearance which the coast
had exhibited as they were approaching it before sundown.

All three felt certain of being able to save themselves;
but what would become of their companion, the sailor?

" We cannot leave you, Bill!" cried Harry: "we will
not!"

" No, that we can't: we won't!" said Terence.

" We can't, and won't," asseverated Colin, with like em-
phasis.

These generous declarations were in answer to an equally generous proposal: in which the sailor had urged them to make for the shore, and leave him to his fate.

" Ye must, my lads !" he cried out, repeating his proposition. " Don't mind about me; look to yersels ! Och ! shure I 'm only a weather-washed, worn-out old salt, 'ardly worth savin'. Go now — off wi' ye at onest ! The water 'll be over ye, if ye stand 'eer tin minutes longer."

The three youths scrutinized each other's faces, as far as the darkness would allow them. Each tried to read in the countenances of the other two some sign that might determine him. The water was already washing around their shoulders ; it was with difficulty they could keep their feet.

" Let loose, lads !" cried Old Bill ; " let loose, I say ! and swim richt for the shore. Don't think o' me ; it bean't certain I shan't weather it yet. I 'm the whole av my head taller than the tallest av ye. The tide may n't full any higher ; an' if it don't I 'll get safe out after all. Let loose, lads — let loose I tell ye !"

This command of the old sailor for his young comrades to forsake him was backed by a far more irresistible influence, — one against which even their noble instincts could no longer contend.

At that moment, a wave, of greater elevation than any that had preceded it, came rolling along ; and the three midshipmen, lifted upon its swell, were borne nearly half a cable's length from the spot where they had been standing.

In vain did they endeavor to recover their feet. They had been carried into deep water, where the tallest of them could not touch bottom.

For some seconds they struggled on the top of the swell, their faces turned towards the spot from which they had been swept. They were close together. All three seemed desirous of making back to that dark, solitary speck, pro

truding above the surface, and which they knew to be the
head of Old Bill. Still did they hesitate to forsake him.

Once more his voice sounded in their ears.

"Och, boys!" cried he, "don't thry to come back. It 's
no use whatever. Lave me to my fate, an' save yersels
The tide 's 'ard against ye. Turn, an' follow it, as I tell ye.
It 'll carry ye safe to the shore; an' if I 'm washed afther
ye, bury me on the bache. Farewell, brave boys, — fare
well!"

To the individuals thus apostrophized, it was a sorrowful
adieu; and, could they have done anything to save the
sailor, there was not one of the three who would not have
risked his life over and over again. But all were impressed
with the hopelessness of rendering any succor; and under
the still - further discouragement caused by another huge
wave, that came swelling up under their chins, they turned
simultaneously in the water; and, taking the tidal current
for their guide, swam with all their strength towards the
shore.

CHAPTER VIII.

SAFE ASHORE.

THE swim proved shorter than any of them had anticipated. They had scarce made half-a mile across the
bay, when Terence, who was the worst swimmer of the
three, and who had been allowing his legs to droop, struck
his toes against something more substantial than salt water

"I' faith!" gasped he, with exhausted breath, "I think
I 've touched bottom. Blessed be the Virgin, I have!" he
continued, at the same time standing erect, with head and
shoulders above the surface of the water.

"All right!" cried Harry, imitating the upright attitude of the young Hibernian. "Bottom it must be, and bottom it is. Thank God for it!"

Colin, with a similar grateful ejaculation, suspended his stroke, and stood upon his feet.

All three instinctively faced seaward — as they did so, exclaiming —

"Poor Old Bill!"

"In troth, we might have brought him along with us!" suggested Terence, as soon as he had recovered his wind; "might we not?"

"If we had but known it was so short a swim," said Harry, "it is possible."

"How about our trying to swim back? Do you think we could do it?"

"Impossible!" asserted Colin.

"What, Colin, you are the best swimmer of us all! Do you say so?" asked the others, eager to make an effort for saving the old salt, who had been the favorite of every officer aboard the ship.

"I say impossible," replied the cautious Colin; "I would risk as much as any of you, but there is not a reasonable chance of saving him, and what's the use of trying impossibilities? We'd better make sure that we're safe ourselves. There may be more deep water between us and the shore. Let us keep on till we've set our feet on something more like terra firma."

The advice of the young Scotchman was too prudent to be rejected; and all three, once more turning their faces shoreward, continued to advance in that direction.

They only knew that they were facing shoreward by the inflow of the tide, but certain that this would prove a tolerably safe guide, they kept boldly on, without fear of straying from the track.

For a while they waded; but, as their progress was both

2

slower and more toilsome, they once more betook themselves to swimming. Whenever they felt fatigued by either mode of progression, they changed to the other; and partly by wading and partly by swimming, they passed through another mile of the distance that separated them from the shore. The water then became so shallow, that swimming was no longer possible; and they waded on, with eyes earnestly piercing the darkness, each moment expecting to see something of the land.

They were soon to be gratified by having this expectation realized. The curving lines that began to glimmer dimly through the obscurity, were the outlines of rounded objects that could not be ocean waves. They were too white for these. They could only be the sandhills, which they had seen before the going down of the sun. As they were now but knee-deep in the water, and the night was still misty and dark, these objects could be at no great distance, and deep water need no longer be dreaded.

The three castaways considered themselves as having reached the shore.

Harry and Terence were about to continue on to the beach, when Colin called to them to come to a stop.

" Why?" inquired Harry.

" What for?" asked Terence.

" Before touching dry land," suggested the thoughtful Colin, " suppose we decide what has been the fate of poor Old Bill."

" How can we tell that?" interrogated the other two.

" Stand still awhile; we shall soon see whether his head is yet above water."

Harry and Terence consented to the proposal of their comrade, but without exactly comprehending its import.

" What do you mean, Coley?" asked the impatient Hibernian.

" To see if the tide's still rising," was the explanation given by the Scotch youth.

"And what if it be?" demanded Terence.

"Only, that if it be, we vill never more see the old sailor in the land of the living. We may look for his lifeless corpse after it has been washed ashore."

"Ah! I comprehend you," said Terence.

"You're right," added Harry. "If the tide be still rising, Old Bill is under it by this time. I dare say his body will drift ashore before morning."

They stood still, — all three of them. They watched the water, as it rippled up against their limbs, taking note of its ebbing and flowing. They watched with eyes full of anxious solicitude. They continued this curious vigil for full twenty minutes. They would have patiently prolonged it still further had it been necessary. But it was not. No further observation was required to convince them that the tidal current was still carried towards the shore; and that the water was yet deepening around them.

The data thus obtained were sufficient to guide them to the solution of the sad problem. During that interval, while they were swimming and wading across the bay, the tide must have been continually on the increase. It must have risen at least a yard. A foot would be sufficient to have submerged the sailor: since he could not swim. There was but one conclusion to which they could come. Their companion must have been drowned.

With heavy hearts they turned their faces toward the shore, — thinking more of the sad fate of the sailor than their own future.

Scarce had they proceeded a dozen steps, when a shout, heard from behind, caused them to come to a sudden stop.

"Avast there!" cried a voice that seemed to rise from out the depths of the sea.

"It's Bill!" exclaimed all three in the same breath.

"'Old on my 'arties, if that's yerselves that I see!' continued the voice. "Arrah, 'old on there. I'm so tired wadin', I want a short spell to rest myself. Wait now, and I'll come to yez, as soon as I can take a reef out of my tops'ls."

The joy caused by this greeting, great as it was, was scarce equal to the surprise it inspired. They who heard it were for some seconds incredulous. The sound of the sailor's voice, well known as it was, with something like the figure of a human being dimly seen through the uncertain mist that shadowed the surface of the water was proof that he still lived; while, but the moment before, there appeared substantial proof that he must have gone to the bottom. Their incredulity even continued, till more positive evidence to the contrary came before them, in the shape of the old man-o'-war's-man himself; who, rapidly splashing through the more shallow water, in a few seconds stood face to face with the three brave boys whom he had so lately urged to abandon him.

" Bill, is it you ? " cried all three in a breath.

" Auch ! and who else would yez expect it to be ? Did yez take me for 'ould Neptune risin' hout of the say ? Or did yez think I was a mare-maid ? Gee me a grip o' yer wee fists, ye bonny boys. Ole Bill warn't born to be drowned ! "

" But how did ye come, Bill ? The tide 's been rising ever since we left you."

" Oh ! " said Terence, " I see how it is, the bay isn't so deep after all : you've waded all the way."

" Avast there, master Terry ! not half the way, though I've waded part of it. There's wather between here and where you left me, deep enough to dhrown Phil Macool. I did n't crass the bay by wading at all — at all."

" How then ? "

" I was ferried on a nate little craft — as yez all knows of — the same that carried us safe to the sand-spit."

" The spar ! "

"Hexactly as ye say. Just as I was about to gee my last gasp, something struck me on the back o' the head, making me duck under the wather. What was that but the tops'l yard. Hech! I was na long in mountin' on to it. I've left it out there afther I feeled my toes trailin' along the bottom. Now, my bonny babies, that's how Old Bill's been able to rejoin ye. Flippers all round once more; and then let's see what sort o' a shore we've got to make port upon."

An enthusiastic shake of the hands passed between the old sailor and his youthful companions; after which the faces of all were turned towards the shore, still only dimly distinguishable, and uninviting as seen, but more welcome to the sight than the wilderness of water stretching as if to infinity behind them.

CHAPTER IX.

UNCOMFORTABLE QUARTERS.

THE waders had still some distance to go before reaching dry land; but, after splashing for about twenty minutes longer, they at length stood upon the shore. As the tide was still flowing in they continued up the beach; so as to place themselves beyond the reach of the water, in the event of its rising still higher.

They had to cross a wide stretch of wet sand before they could find a spot sufficiently elevated to secure them against the further influx of the tide. Having, at length, discovered such a spot, they stopped to deliberate on what was best to be done.

They would fain have had a fire to dry their dripping

garments: for the night had grown chilly under the influence of the fog.

The old sailor had his flint, steel, and tinder — the latter
still safe in its water-tight tin box; but there was no fuel
to be found near. The spar, even could they have broken
it up, was still floating, or stranded, in the shoal water —
more than a mile to seaward.

In the absence of a fire they adopted the only other
mode they could think of to get a little of the water out of
their clothes. They stripped themselves to the skin, wrung
out each article separately; and then, giving each a good
shake, put them on again — leaving it to the natural warmth
of their bodies to complete the process of drying.

By the time they had finished this operation, the mist
had become sensibly thinner; and the moon, suddenly
emerging from under a cloud, enabled them to obtain a better view of the shore upon which they had set foot.

Landward, as far as they could see, there appeared to be
nothing but white sand — shining like silver under the light
of the moon. Up and down the coast the same landscape
could be dimly distinguished.

It was not a level surface that was thus covered with
sand, but a conglomeration of hillocks and ridges, blending
into each other and forming a labyrinth, that seemed to
stretch interminably on all sides — except towards the sea
itself.

It occurred to them to climb to the highest of the hillocks. From its summit they would have a better view of
the country beyond; and perhaps discover a place suitable
for an encampment — perhaps some timber might then come
into view — from which they would be able to obtain a few
sticks.

On attempting to scale the " dune," they found that their
wading was not yet at an end. Though no longer in the
water, they sank to their knees at every step, in soft yielding sand.

The ascent of the hillock, though scarce a hundred feet high, proved exceedingly toilsome — much more so than wading knee-deep in water — but they floundered on, and at length reached the summit.

To the right, to the left, in front of them, far as the eye could reach, nothing but hills and ridges of sand — that appeared under the moonlight of a whiteness approaching to that of snow. In fact, it would not have been difficult to fancy that the country was covered with a heavy coat of snow — as often seen in Sweden, or the Northern parts of Scotland — drifted into "wreaths," and spurred hillocks of every imaginable form.

It was pretty, but soon became painful from its monotony; and the eyes of that shipwrecked quartette were even glad to turn once more to the scarce less monotonous blue of the ocean.

Inland, they could perceive other sand-hills — higher than that to which they had climbed — and long crested "combings," with deep valleys between; but not one object to gladden their sight — nothing that offered promise of either food, drink, or shelter.

Had it not been for their fatigue they might have gone farther. Since the moon had consented to show herself, there was light enough to travel by; and they might have proceeded on — either through the sand-dunes or along the shore. But of the four there was not one — not even the tough old tar himself — who was not regularly done up, both with weariness of body and spirit. The short slumber upon the spit — from which they had been so unexpectedly startled — had refreshed them but little; and, as they stood upon the summit of the sand-hill, all four felt as if they could drop down, and go to sleep on the instant.

It was a couch sufficiently inviting, and they would at once have availed themselves of it, but for a circumstance that suggested to them the idea of seeking a still better place for repose.

The land wind was blowing in from the ocean; and, according to the forecast of Old Bill — a great practical me-
teorologist, — it promised ere long to become a gale. It was
already sufficiently violent — and chill to boot — to make
the situation on the summit of the dune anything but comfortable. There was no reason why they should make their
couch upon that exposed prominence. Just on the land
ward side of the hillock itself — below, at its base — they
perceived a more sheltered situation; and why not select that
spot for their resting place?

There was no reason why they should not. Old Bill
proposed it; there was no opposition offered by his young
companions, — and, without further parley, the four went
floundering down the sloping side of the sand-hill, into the
sheltered convexity at its base.

On arriving at the bottom, they found themselves in the
narrowest of ravines. The hillock from which they had descended was but the highest summit of a long ridge, trending
in the same direction as the coast. Another ridge, of about
equal height, ran parallel to this on the landward side. The
bases of the two approached so near, that their sloping sides
formed an angle with each other. On account of the abrupt
acclivity of both, this angle was almost acute, and the ravine
between the two resembled a cavity out of which some great
wedge had been cut, — like a section taken from the side of
a gigantic melon.

It was in this re-entrant angle that the castaways found
themselves, after descending the side of the dune, and where
they had proposed spending the remainder of the night.

They were somewhat disappointed on reaching their
sleeping-quarters, and finding them so limited as to space
In the bottom of the ravine there was not breadth enough
for a bed, — even for the shortest of the party, — supposing
him desirous of sleeping in a horizontal position.

There were not six feet of surface — nor even three —

that could strictly be called horizontal. Even longitudinally, the bottom of the "gully" had a sloping inclination: for the ravine itself tended upwards, until it became extinguished in the convergence of its inclosing ridges.

On discovering the unexpected "strait" into which they had launched themselves, our adventurers were for a time nonplussed. They felt inclined to proceed farther in search of a "better bed," but their weariness outweighed this inclination; and, after some hesitation, they resolved to remain u the "ditch," into which they had so unwillingly descended. They proceeded therefore to encouch themselves.

Their first attempt was made by placing themselves in a half-standing position — their backs supported upon the sloping side of one of the ridges, with their feet resting against the other. So long as they kept awake, this position was both easy and pleasant; but the moment any one of them closed his eyes in sleep, — and this was an event almost instantaneous, — his muscles, relaxed by slumber, would no longer have the strength to sustain him; and the consequence would be an uncomfortable collapse to the bottom of the "gully," where anything like a position of repose was out of the question.

This vexatious interruption of their slumbers happening repeatedly, at length roused all four to take fresh counsel as to choosing a fresh couch.

Terence had been especially annoyed by these repeated disturbances; and proclaimed his determination not to submit to them any longer. He would go in search of more "comfortable quarters."

He had arisen to his feet, and appeared in the act of starting off.

"We had better not separate," suggested Harry Blount. "If we do, we may find it difficult to come together again."

"There's something in what you say, Hal," said the young

2 *   o

Scotchman. "It will not do for us to lose sight of one another. What does Bill say to it?"

"I say, stay here," put in the voice of the sailor. "It won't do to stray the wan from the t' other. No, it won't. Let us hold fast, thin, where we 're already belayed."

"But who the deuce can sleep here?" remonstrated the son of Erin. "A hard-worked horse can sleep standing; and so can an elephant, they say; but, for me, I'd prefer six feet of the horizontal — even if it were a hard stone — to this slope of the softest sand."

"Stay, Terry!" cried Colin. "I've captured an idea."

"Ah! you Scotch are always capturing something — whether it be an idea, a flea, or the itch. Let's hear what it is."

"After that insult to ma kintree," good-humoredly rejoined Colin, "I dinna know whuther I wull."

"Come, Colin," interrupted Harry Blount, "if you've any good counsel to give us, pray don't withhold it. We can't get sleep, standing at an angle of forty-five degrees. Why should we not try to change our position by seeking another place?"

"Well, Harry, as you have made the request, I'll tell you what's just come into my mind. I only feel astonished it didn't occur to any of us sooner."

"Mother av Moses!" cried Terence, jocularly adopting his native brogue; "and why don't you out with it at wanse? — you Scatch are the thrue *rid-tape* of society."

"Never mind, Colly!" interposed Blount; "there's no time to listen to Terry's badinage. We're all too sleepy for jesting; tell us what you've got in your mind."

"All of ye do as you see me, and, I'll be your bail, ye'll sleep sound till the dawn o' the day. Good night!"

As Colin pronounced the salutation he sank down to the bottom of the ravine, where, stretched longitudinally, he might repose without the slightest danger of being awakened by slipping from his couch.

On seeing him thus disposed, the others only wondered they had not thought of the thing before.

They were too sleepy to speculate long upon their own thoughtlessness; and one after the other, imitating the example set them by the young Scotchman, laid their bodies lengthwise along the bottom of the ravine, and entered upon the enjoyment of a slumber from which all the kettledrums in creation would scarce have awaked them.

CHAPTER XI.

'WARE THE SAND !

AS the gully in which they had gone to rest was too narrow to permit of them lying side by side, they were disposed in a sort of lengthened chain, with their heads all turned in the same direction. The bottom of the ravine, as already stated, had a slight inclination; and they had, of course, placed themselves so that their heads should be higher than their feet.

The old sailor was at the lower end of this singular series, with the feet of Harry Blount just above the crown of his head. Above the head of Harry were the heels of Terence O'Connor; and, at the top of all, reclined Colin, — in the place where he had first stretched himself.

On account of the slope of the ground, the four were thus disposed in a sort of *échelon* formation, of which Old Bill was the base. They had dropped into their respective positions, one after the other, as they lay.

The sailor had been the last to commit himself to this curious couch; he was also the last to surrender to sleep. For some time after the others had become unconscious of outward impressions, he lay listening to the "sough" of the sea, and the sighing of the breeze, as it blew along the smooth sides of the sandhills.

He did not remain awake for any great length of time. He was wearied, as well as his young comrades; and soon also yielded his spirit to the embrace of the god Somnus.

Before doing so, however, he had made an observation,— one of a character not likely to escape the notice of an old mariner such as he. He had become conscious that a storm was brewing in the sky. The sudden shadowing of the heavens;— the complete disappearance of the moon, leaving even the white landscape in darkness;— her red color as she went out of sight;— the increased noise caused by the roaring of the breakers; and the louder "swishing" of the wind itself, which began to blow in quick gusty puffs; all these sights and sounds admonished him that a gale was coming on.

He instinctively noted these signs; and on board ship would have heeded them,— so far as to have alarmed the sleeping watch, and counselled precaution.

But stretched upon terra firma — not so very firm had he but known it — between two huge hills, where he and his companions were tolerably well sheltered from the wind, it never occurred to the old salt, that they could be in any danger; and simply muttering to himself, "the storm be blowed!" he laid his weather-beaten face upon the pillow of soft sand, and delivered himself up to deep slumber.

The silent prediction of the sailor turned out a true forecast. Sure enough there came a storm; which, before the castaways had been half an hour asleep, increased to a tempest. It was one of those sudden uprisings of the elements common in all tropical countries, but especially so in the desert tracts of Arabia and Africa,— where the atmosphere, rarefied by heat, and becoming highly volatile, suddenly loses its equilibrium, and rushes like a destroying angel over the surface of the earth.

The phenomenon that had broken over the arenaceous couch, — upon which slept the four castaways, — was neither more nor less than a "sandstorm;" or, to give it its Arab title, a *simoom.*

The misty vapor that late hung suspended in the atmosphere had been swept away by the first puff of the wind; and its place was now occupied by a cloud equally dense, though perhaps not so constant, — a cloud of white sand lifted from the surface of the earth, and whirled high up towards heaven, — even far out over the waters of the ocean.

Had it been daylight, huge volumes, of what might have appeared dust, might have been seen rolling over the ridges of sand, — here swirling into rounded pillar-like shapes, that could easily have been mistaken for solid columns, standing for a time in one place, then stalking over the summits of the hills, or suddenly breaking into confused and cumbering masses; while the heavier particles, no longer kept in suspension by the rotatory whirl, might be seen spilling back towards the earth, like a sand-shower projected downward through some gigantic "screen."

In the midst of this turbulent tempest of wind and sand — with not a single drop of rain, — the castaways continued to sleep.

One might suppose — as did the old man-o'-war's-man before going to sleep — that they were not in any danger; not even as much as if their couch had been under the roof of a house, or strewn amid the leaves of the forest. There were no trees to be blown down upon them, no bricks nor large chimney-pots to come crashing through the ceiling, and crush them as they lay upon their beds.

What danger could there be among the "dunes?"

Not much to a man awake, and with open eyes. In such a situation, there might be discomfort, but no danger.

Different however, was it with the slumbering castaways
Over them a peril was suspended — a real peril — of which
perhaps, on that night not one of them was dreaming — and
in which, perhaps, not one of them would have put belief, —
but for the experience of it they were destined to be taught
before the morning.

Could an eye have looked upon them as they lay, it would
have beheld a picture sufficiently suggestive of danger. It
would have seen four human figures stretched along the bottom of a narrow ravine, longitudinally aligned with one another — their heads all turned one way, and in point of
elevation slightly *en échelon* — it would have noted that these
forms were asleep, that they were already half buried in
sand, which, apparently descending from the clouds was still
settling around them ; and that, unless one or other of them
awoke, all four should certainly become "smoored."

What does this mean ? Merely a slight inconvenience
arising from having the mouth, ears, and nostrils obstructed
by sand, which a little choking, and sneezing, and coughing
would soon remove.

Ask the Highland shepherd who has imprudently gone to
sleep under the "blowin' sna'" ; question the Scandinavian,
whose calling compels him to encamp on the open "fjeld" ;
interrogate Swede or Norwegian, Finn or Lapp, and you
may discover the danger of being "smoored."

That would be in the snow, — the light, vascular, porous,
permeable snow, — under which a human being may move,
and through which he may breathe, — though tons of it may
be superpoised above his body, — the snow that, while im-
prisoning its victim, also gives him warmth, and affords him
shelter, — perilous as that shelter may be.

Ask the Arab what it is to be "smoored" by sand ; question the wild Bedouin of the Bled-el-jereed, — the Tuarick
and Tiboo of the Eastern Desert, — they will tell you it is
danger often *death !*

Little dreamt the four sleepers as they lay unconscious under that swirl of sand, — little even would they have suspected, if awake, — that there was danger in the situation.

There was, for all that, a danger, great as it was imminent, — the danger, not only of their being "smoored," but stifled, suffocated, buried fathoms deep under the sands of the Saära, for fathoms deep will often be the drift of a single night.

The Arabs say that, once "submerged" beneath the arenaceous "flood," a man loses the power to extricate himself. His energies are suspended, his senses become numbed and torpid — in short, he feels as one who goes to sleep in a snow-storm.

It may be true; but, whether or no, it seemed as if the four English castaways had been stricken with this inexplicable paralysis. Despite the hoarse roaring of the breakers, despite the shrieking and whistling of the wind, despite the dust constantly being deposited on their bodies, and entering ears, mouth, and nostrils, — despite the stifling sensation one would suppose they must have felt, and which should have awakened them, — despite all, they continued to sleep. It seemed as if that sleep was to be eternal!

If they heard not the storm that raged savagely above them, if they felt not the sand that pressed heavily upon them, what was there to warn, what to arouse them from that ill-starred slumber?

CHAPTER XII.

A MYSTERIOUS NIGHTMARE.

THE four castaways had been asleep for a couple of hours, — that is, from the time that, following the example of the young Scotchman, they had stretched themselves along the bottom of the ravine. It was not quite an hour, however, since the commencement of the sand-storm; and yet in this short time the arenaceous dust had accumulated to the thickness of several inches upon their bodies; and a person passing the spot, or even stepping right over them, could not have told that four human beings were buried beneath, — that is, upon the supposition that they would have lain still, and not got startled from their slumbers by the foot thus treading upon them.

Perhaps it was a fortunate circumstance for them, that by such a contingency they might be awakened, and that by such they *were* awakened.

Otherwise their sleep might have been protracted into the still deeper sleep — from which there is no awaking.

All four had begun to feel — if any sensation while asleep can be so called — a sense of suffocation, accompanied by a heaviness of the limbs and torpidity in the joints, — as if some immense weight was pressing upon their bodies, that rendered it impossible for them to stir either toe or finger It was a sensation similar to that so well known, and so much dreaded, under the name of *nightmare*. It may have been the very same; and was, perhaps, brought on as much by the extreme weariness they all felt, as by the superincumbent weight of the sand.

Their heads, lying higher than their bodies, were not so deeply buried under the drift; which, blown lightly over their faces, still permitted the atmosphere to pass through i

Otherwise their breathing would have been stopped altogether; and death must have been the necessary consequence.

Whether it was a genuine nightmare or no, it was accompanied by all the horrors of this phenomenon. As they afterwards declared, all four felt its influence, each in his own way dreaming of some fearful fascination from which he could make no effort to escape. Strange enough, their dreams were different. Harry Blount thought he was falling over a precipice; Colin that a gigantic ogre had got hold of and was going to eat him up; while the young Hibernian fancied himself in the midst of a conflagration, a dwelling house on fire, from which he could not get out!

Old Bill's delusion was more in keeping with their situation, — or at least with that out of which they had lately escaped. He simply supposed that he was submerged in the sea, and as he knew he could not swim, it was but natural for him to fancy that he was drowning.

Still, he could make no struggle; and, as he would have done this, whether able to swim or not, his dream did not exactly resemble the real thing.

The sailor was the first to escape from the uncomfortable *incubus;* though there was but an instant between the awakening of all. They were startled out of their sleep, one after another, in the order in which they lay, and inversely to that in which they had lain down.

Their awakening was as mysterious as the nightmare itself, and scarce relieved them from the horror which the latter had been occasioning.

All felt in turn, and in quick succession, a heavy crushing pressure, either on the limbs or body, which had the effect, not only to startle them from their sleep, but caused them considerable pain.

Twice was this pressure applied, almost exactly on the same spot, and with scarce a second's interval between the applications. It could not well have been repeated a third time with like exactness, even had such been the design of whatever creature was causing it; for, after the second squeeze, each had recovered sufficient consciousness to know he was in danger of being crushed, and make a desperate effort to withdraw himself.

The exclamations, proceeding from four sets of lips, told that all were still in the land of the living; but the confused questioning that followed did nothing towards elucidating the cause of that sudden and almost simultaneous uprising.

There was too much sneezing and coughing to permit of anything like clear or coherent speech. The *shumu* was still blowing. There was sand in the mouths and nostrils of all four, and dust in their eyes. Their talk more resembled the jibbering of apes, who had unwisely intruded into a snuff shop, than the conversation of four rational beings.

It was some time before any one of them could shape his speech, so as to be understood by the others; and, after all had at length succeeded in making themselves intelligible, it was found that each had the same story to tell. Each had felt two pressures on some part of his person; and had seen, though very indistinctly, some huge creature passing over him, — apparently a quadruped, though what sort of quadruped none of them could tell. All they knew was, that it was a gigantic, uncouth creature, with a narrow body and neck, and very long legs; and that it had feet there could be no doubt: since it was these that had pressed so heavily upon them.

But for the swirl of the sand-storm, and the dust already in their eyes, they might have been able to give a better description of the creature that had so unceremoniously stepped over them. These impediments, however, had hindered them from obtaining a fair view of it; and some animal, — grotesquely shaped, with a long neck, body, and legs, — was the image which remained in the excited minds of the awakened sleepers.

Whatever it was, they were all sufficiently frightened to stand for some time trembling. Just awaking from such dreams, it was but natural they should surrender themselves to strange imaginings; and instead of endeavoring to identify the odd-looking animal, if animal it was, they were rather inclined to set it down as some creature of a supernatural kind.

The three midshipmen were but boys, not so long from the nursery as to have altogether escaped from the weird influence which many a nursery tale had wrapped around them; and as for old Bill, fifty years spent in "ploughing the ocean" had only confirmed *him* in the belief, that the "black art" is not so mythical as philosophers would have us think.

So frightened were all four, that, after the first ebullition of their surprise had subsided, they no longer gave utterance to speech, but stood listening, and trembling as they listened. Perhaps, had they known the service which the intruder had done for them, they might have felt gratitude towards it, instead of the suspicion and dread that for some moments kept them, as if spell-bound, in their places. It did not occur to any of the party, that that strange summons from sleep — more effective than the half-whispered invitation of a *valet-de-chambre*, or the ringing of a breakfast-bell — had in all probability rescued them from a silent, but certain death.

They stood, as I have said, listening. There were several distinct sounds that saluted their ears. There was the "sough" of the sea, as it came swelling up the gorge; the "whish" of the wind, as it impinged upon the crests of the ridges; and the "swish" of the sand as it settled around them.

All these were the voices of inanimate objects, — phenom

ena of nature, easily understood. But, rising above them, were heard sounds of a different character, which, though they might be equally natural, were not equally familiar to those who listened to them.

There was a sort of dull battering, — as if some gigantic creature was performing a Terpsichorean feat upon the sand-bank above them; but sharper sounds were heard at intervals, — screams commingled with short snortings, both proclaiming something of the nature of a struggle.

Neither in the screams nor the snortings was there anything that the listeners could identify as sounds they had ever heard before. They were alike perplexing to the ears of English, Irish, and Scotch. Even old Bill, who had heard, sometime or other, nearly every sound known to creation, could not classify them.

"Divil take thim!" whispered he to his companions, "I dinna know what to make av it. It be hawful to 'ear 'em!"

"Hark!" ejaculated Harry Blount.

"Hish!" exclaimed Terence.

"Wheesh!" muttered Colin. "It's coming nearer, whatever it may be. Wheesh!"

There could be no doubt about the truth of this conjecture; for as the caution passed from the lips of the young Scotchman, the dull hammering, the snorts, and the unearthly screams were evidently drawing nearer, — though the creature that was causing them was unseen through the thick sand-mist still surrounding the listeners. These, however, heard enough to know that some heavy body was making a rapid descent down the sloping gorge, and with an impetuosity that rendered it prudent for them to get out of its way.

More by an instinct, than from any correct appreciation of the danger, all four fell back from the narrow trench in which they had been standing, — each, as he best could, retreating up the declivity of the sand-hill.

Since they were able to obtain footing in their new position, when the sounds they had heard not only became louder and nearer, but the creature that had been causing them passed close to their feet, — so close that most of them could have touched it with their toes.

For all that, not one of the party could tell what it was; and after it had passed, — on its way down the ravine, — and was once more lost to their view amid the swirling sand, they were not a bit further advanced in their knowledge of the strange creature that had come so near crushing out their existence with its ponderous weight!

All that they had been able to see was a conglomeration of dark objects, — resembling the head, neck, body, and limbs of some uncouth animal, — while the sounds that proceeded from it were like utterances that might have come from some other world; for certainly they had but slight resemblance to anything the castaways had ever heard in this — either upon sea, or land!

CHAPTER XIII.

THE MAHERRY.

FOR some length of time they stood conjecturing, — the boys with clasped hands, — Old Bill near, but apart.

During this time, at intervals, they continued to hear the sounds that had so astonished them — the stamping, the snorts, and the screaming, though they no longer saw the creature that caused them.

The sand gully opened towards the sea, in a diagonal direction. It could not be many yards to the spot, where it debouched upon the level of the beach; and the creature that had caused them such a surprise — and was still continuing to occupy their thoughts — must have reached this level surface: though not to suspend its exertions. Every now and then could be heard the same repetition of dull noises, — as if some animal was kicking itself to death, — varied by trumpet-like snorts and agonizing screams, which could be likened to the cry of no animal upon earth.

But that the castaways knew they were on the coast of Africa, — that continent renowned for strange existences, — they might have been even more disposed to a supernatural belief in what was near them; but as the minutes passed, and their senses began to return to them, they became more inclined to think that what they had seen, heard, and *felt*, might be only some animal — a heavy quadruped — that had trampled over them in their sleep.

The chief difficulty in reconciling this belief with the actual occurrence was the odd behavior of the animal. Why had it gone up the gorge, apparently *parenti passu*, to come tumbling down again in such a confused fashion? Why was it still kicking and stumbling about at the bottom of the ravine, — for such did the sounds proclaim it to be doing?

No answer could be given to either of these questions; and none was given, until day dawned over the sand-hills. This was soon after; and along with the morning light had come the cessation of the simoom.

Then saw the castaways that creature that had so abruptly awakened them from their slumbers, — and, by so doing, perhaps, saved their lives. They saw it recumbent at the bottom of the gorge, where they had so uneasily passed the night.

It proved to be — what from the slight glimpse they had got of it, they were inclined to believe — an animal, and a quadruped; and if it had presented an uncouth appearance, as it stepped over them in the darkness, not less so did it appear as they now beheld it, under the light of day.

It was an animal of very large size, — in height far exceeding a horse, — but of such a grotesque shape as to be easily recognizable by any one who had ever glanced into a picture-book of quadrupeds. The long craning neck, with an almost earless head and gibbous profile; the great straggling limbs, callous at the knees, and ending in broad, wide splitting hooves; the slender hind-quarters, and tiny, tufted tail, — both ludicrously disproportioned, — the tumid, misshapen trunk; but, above all, the huge hunch rising above the shoulders, at once proclaimed the creature to be a dromedary.

"Och! it's only a kaymal!" cried Old Bill, as soon as the daylight enabled him to get a fair view of the animal. "What on hearth is it doin' 'ere?"

"Sure enough," suggested Terence, "it was this beast that stepped over us while we were asleep! It almost squeezed the breath out of me, for it set its hoof right upon the pit of my stomach."

"The same with me," said Colin. "It sunk me down nearly a foot into the sand. Ah, we have reason to be thankful there was that drift-sand over our bodies at the time. If not, the great brute might have crushed us to death!"

There was some truth in Colin's observation. But for the covering of sand, — which acted as a cushion, — and also from that which formed their couch yielding beneath them, the hoof of the great quadruped might have caused them a serious injury. As it was, none of them had received any hurt beyond the fright which the strange intruder had occasioned them.

The singular incident was yet only half explained. They saw it was a camel that had disturbed their slumbers; that the animal had been on its way up the ravine, — perhaps seeking shelter from the sand-storm; but what had caused it to return so suddenly back down the slope? Above all,

why had it made the downward journey in such a singular
manner? Obscure as had been their view of it, they could
see that it did not go on all-fours, but apparently tumbling
and struggling, — its long limbs kicking about in the air, as
if it was performing the descent by a series of somersaults.

All this had been mysterious enough; but it was soon explained to the satisfaction of the four castaways, who, as
soon as they saw the camel by the bottom of the gorge, had
rushed down and surrounded it.

The animal was in a recumbent position, — not as if it had
lain down to rest, but in a constrained attitude, with its long
neck drawn in towards its forelegs, and its head lying low
and half-buried in the sand !

As it was motionless when they first perceived it, they
fancied it was dead, — that something had wounded it
above. This would have explained the fantastic fashion in
which it had returned down the slope, — as the somersaults
observed might have been only a series of death struggles.

On getting around it, however, they perceived that it was
not only still alive, but in perfect health; and its late mysterious movements were accounted for at a single glance.
A strong hair halter, firmly noosed around its head, had got
caught in the bifurcation of one of its fore-hoofs, where a
knot upon the rope had hindered it from slipping through
the deep split. This had first caused it to trip up, and tumble head over heels, — inaugurating that series of struggles
which had ended in transporting it back to the bottom of
the ravine, — where it now lay with the trailing end of the
ong halter knotted inextricably around its legs.

CHAPTER XIV.

A LIQUID BREAKFAST.

MELANCHOLY as was the situation of the self-caught camel, it was a joyful sight to those who beheld it. Hungry as they were, its flesh would provide them with food; and thirsting as they were, they knew that inside its stomach would be found a supply of water!

Such were their first thoughts as they came around it.

They soon perceived, however, that to satisfy the latter appetite it would not be necessary for them to kill the camel. Upon the top of its hump was a small, flat pad or saddle, firmly held in its place by a strong leathern band passing under the animal's belly. This proved it to be a "maherry," or riding camel, — one of those swift creatures used by the Arabs in their long rapid journeys across the deserts; and which are common among the tribes inhabiting the Saära.

It was not this saddle that gratified the eyes of our adventurers, but a bag, tightly strapped to it, and resting behind the hump of the maherry. This bag was of goatskin, and upon examination was found to be nearly half-full of water. It was, in fact, the "Gerba," or water-skin, belonging to whoever had been the owner of the animal, — an article of camel equipment more essential than the saddle itself.

The four castaways, suffering the torture of thirst, made no scruple about appropriating the contents of the bag, and, in the shortest possible time, it was stripped from the back of the maherry, its stopper taken out, and the precious fluid extracted from it by all four, in greedy succession, until its light weight and collapsed sides declared it to be empty.

Their thirst being thus opportunely assuaged, a council was next held, as to what they should do to appease the other appetite.

3   D

Should they kill the camel ?

It appeared to be their only chance ; and the impetuous Terence had already unsheathed his midshipman's dirk, with the design of burying it in the body of the animal.

Colin, however, more prudent in counsel, cried to him to hold his hand, — at least until they should give the subject a more thorough consideration.

On this suggestion they proceeded to debate the point between them. They were of different opinions, and equally divided. Two, — Terence and Harry Blount, — were for immediately killing the maherry, and making their breakfast upon its flesh ; while the sailor joined Colin in voting that it should be reprieved.

" Let us first make use of the animal to help carry us somewhere," urged the young Scotchman. " We can go without food a day longer. Then, if we find nothing, we can butcher this beast."

" But what 's to be found in such a country as this ? " inquired Harry Blount. " Look around you ! There 's nothing green but the sea itself. There is n't anything eatable within sight, — not so much as would make a dinner for a dormouse ! "

" Perhaps," rejoined Colin, " when we 've travelled a few miles, we may come upon a different sort of country. We can keep along the coast. Why should n't we find shellfish, — enough to keep us alive? See, — yonder 's a dark place down upon the beach. I should n't wonder if there 's some there."

The glances of all were instantly directed towards the beach, — excepting those of Sailor Bill. His were fixed on a different object ; and an exclamation that escaped him — as well as a movement that accompanied it — arrested the attention of his companions, causing them to turn their eyes upon him.

" Shell-fish be blow'd," cried Bill, " here 's something better for breakfast than cowld oysters. Look ! "

" The sailor, as he spoke, pointed to an oval-shaped object, something larger than a cocoa-nut, appearing between the hind legs of the maherry.

" It 's a shemale!" added he, " and 's had a calf not long ago. Look at the ' eldher,' and them tits. They 're swelled wi' milk. There 'll be enough for the whole of us, I warrant yez."

As if to make sure of what he said, the sailor dropped down upon his knees by the hind-quarters of the prostrate camel; and, taking one of the teats in his mouth, commenced drawing forth the lacteal fluid which the udder contained.

The animal made no resistance. It might have wondered at the curious " calf" that had thus attached himself to its teats; but only at the oddness of his color and costume; for no doubt it had often before been similarly served by its African owner.

" Fust rate!" cried Bill, desisting for a moment to take breath. " Ayqual to the richest crame; if we 'd only a bite av bred to go along wi' it, or some av your Scotch porritch, Master Colin. But I forgets. My brave youngsters," continued he, rising up and standing to one side, " yez be all hungrier than I am. Go it, wan after another: there 'll be enough for yez all."

Thus invited, and impelled by their hungry cravings, the three, one after another, knelt down as the sailor had done, and drank copiously from that sweet " fountain of the desert."

Taking it in turns, they continued " sucking," until each had swallowed about a pint and a half of the nutritious fluid when, the udder of the camel becoming dry, told that her supply of milk was, for the time, exhausted.

CHAPTER XV.

THE SAILOR AMONG THE SHELL-FISH.

IT was no longer a question of slaying the camel. That would be killing the goose that gave the golden eggs Though they were still very hungry, the rich milk had to some extent taken the keen edge off their appetites; and all declared they could now go several hours without eating.

The next question was: where were they to go?

The reader may wonder that this was a question at all Having been told that the camel carried a saddle, and was otherwise caparisoned, it will naturally be conjectured that the animal had got loose from some owner, and was simply straying. This was the very hypothesis that passed before the mind of our adventurers. How could they have conjectured otherwise?

Indeed it was scarce a guess. The circumstances told them to a certainty that the camel must have strayed from its owner. The only question was: where that owner might be found.

By reading, or otherwise, they possessed enough knowledge of the coast, on which they had been cast away, to know that the proprietor of the "stray" would be some kind of an Arab; and that he would be found living — not in a house or a town — but in a tent; in all likelihood associated with a number of other Arabs, in an "encampment."

It required not much reasoning to arrive at these conclusions; and our adventurers had come to them almost on that instant, when they first set eyes on the caparisoned camel.

You may wonder that they did not instantly set forth in search of the master of the maherry; or of the tent or en-

campment from which the latter should have strayed.   One
might suppose,- that this would have been their first movement.

On the contrary, it was likely to be their very last; and
for sufficient reasons, — which will be discovered in the conversation that ensued, after they had swallowed their liquid
breakfasts.

Terence had proposed adopting this course, — that is, to
go in search of the man from whom the maherry must have
wandered.   The young Irishman had never been a great
reader, — at all events no account of the many "lamentable
shipwrecks on the Barbary coast" had ever fallen into his
hands, — and he knew nothing of the terrible reputation of
its people.   Neither had Bill obtained any knowledge of it
from books; but, for all that, — thanks to many a forecastle
yarn, — the old sailor was well informed both about the
character of the coast on which they had suffered shipwreck,
and its inhabitants.   Bill had the best of reasons for dreading the denizens of the Saäran desert.

"Sure they 're not cannibals?" urged Terence.   "They
won't eat us, any how?"

"In troth I 'm not so shure av that, Masther Terry," replied Bill.   "Even supposin' they won't ate us, they 'll do
worse."

"Worse!"

"Aye, worse, I tell you.   They 'd torture us, till death
would be a blissin'."

"How do you know they would?"

"Ach, Masther Terry!" sighed the old sailor, assuming
an air of solemnity, such as his young comrades had never
before witnessed upon his usually cheerful countenance; "I
could tell yez something that 'ud convince ye of the truth
av what I 've been sayin', an' that 'll gie ye a hidear av what
we 've got to expect if we fall into the 'ands av these feero
cious Ayrabs."

Bill had already hinted at the prospective peril of an encounter with the people of the country.

"Tell us, Bill. What is it?'

"Well, young masthers, it beant much, — only that my own brother was wrecked som'ere on this same coast. That was ten years agone. He never returned to owld Hengland."

"Perhaps he was drowned?"

"Betther for 'im, poor boy, if he 'ad. No, he 'ad n't that luck. The crew, — it was a tradin' vessel, and there was tin o' them, — all got safe ashore. They were taken prisoners as they landed by a lot o' Ayrabs. Only one av the tin got home to tell the tale; and he would n't a 'ad the chance but for a Jew merchant at Mogador, that found he had rich relations as 'ud pay well to ransom him. I see him a wee while after he got back to Hengland; and he tell me what he had to go through, and my hown brother as well: for Jim, — that be my brother's name, — was with the tribe as took 'im up the counthry. None o' yez iver heerd o' cruelties like they 'ad to put up with. Death in any way would be aisy, compared to what they 'ad to hendure. Poor Jim! I suppose he 's dead long ago. Tough as I be myself, I don't believe I could a stood it a week, — let alone tin years. Talk o' knockin' about like a Turk's head. They were knocked about, an' beat, an' bullied, an' kicked, an' starved, — worse than the laziest lubber as ever skulked about the decks o' a ship. No, Masther Terry, we must n't think av thryin' to find the owner av the beest; but do everythink we can to keep out o' the way av both him and his."

"What would you advise us to do, Bill?"

"I don't know much 'bout where we be," replied the sailor; "but wheresomever it is, our best plan are to hug by the coast, an' keep within sight o' the water. If we go innard, we 're sure to get lost one way or t' other By keep-in' south'ard we may come to some thradin' port av the Portagee."

"We'd better start at once, then," suggested the impatient Terence.

"No, Masther Terry," said the sailor; "not afore night. We musn't leave 'eer till it gets dark. We'll 'ave to thravel betwane two days."

"What!" simultaneously exclaimed the three midshipmen. "Stay here till night! Impossible!"

"Aye, lads! an' we must hide, too. Shure as ye are livin' there'll be somebody afther this sthray kaymal, — in a wee while, too, as ye'll see. If we ventured out durin' the daylight, they'd be sure to see us from the 'ills. It's sayed, the thievin' schoundrels always keep watch when there's been a wreck upon the coast; an' I'll be bound this beest belongs to some av them same wreckers."

"But what shall we do for food?" asked one of the party; "we'll be famished before nightfall! The camel, having nothing to eat or drink, won't yield any more milk."

This interrogative conjecture was probably too near the truth. No one made answer to it. Colin's eyes were again turned towards the beach. Once more he directed the thoughts of his comrades to the shell-fish.

"Hold your hands, youngsthers," said the sailor. "Lie close 'eer behind the 'ill, an' I'll see if there's any shell-fish that we can make a meal av. Now that the sun's up, it won't do to walk down there. I must make a crawl av it."

So saying, the old salt, after skulking some distance farther down the sand gully, threw himself flat upon his face, and advanced in this attitude, like some gigantic lizard crawling across the sand.

The tide was out; but the wet beach, lately covered by the sea, commenced at a short distance from the base of the "dunes."

After a ten minutes' struggle, Bill succeeded in reaching

the dark-looking spot where Colin had conjectured there might be shell-fish.

The old sailor was soon seen busily engaged about something; and from his movements it was evident, that his errand was not to prove fruitless. His hands were extended in different directions; and then at short intervals withdrawn, and plunged into the capacious pockets of his pea-jacket.

After these gestures had been continued for about half an hour, he was seen to "slew" himself round, and come crawling back towards the sand-hills.

His return was effected more slowly than his departure; and it could be seen that he was heavily weighted.

On getting back into the gorge, he was at once relieved of his load, which proved to consist of about three hundred "cockles," — as he called the shell-fish he had collected, — and which were found to be a species of mussel.

They were not only edible, but delicious, — at least they seemed so to those who were called upon to swallow them.

This seasonable supply did a great deal towards allaying the appetites of all; and even Terence now declared himself contented to remain concealed, until night should afford them an opportunity of escape from the monotony of their situation.

CHAPTER XVI.

KEEPING UNDER COVER.

FROM the spot, where the camel still lay couched in his "entetherment," the sea was not visible to one lying along the ground. It was only by standing erect, and looking over a spur of the sand-ridge, that the beach could be seen, and the ocean beyond it.

There would be no danger, therefore, of their being dis-

THE OLD SAILOR SUCCEEDS IN GATHERING SOME SHELL-FISH.

covered, by any one coming along the strand — provided
they kept in a crouching attitude behind the ridge, which,
sharply crested, like a snow-wreath, formed a sort of parapet
in front of them. They might have been easily seen from
the summit of any of the "dunes" to the rear; but there
was not much likelihood of any one approaching them in
that direction. The country inward appeared to be a labyrinth of sand-hills — with no opening that would indicate a
passage for either man or beast. The camel, in all probability, had taken to the gorge — guided by its instincts —
there to seek shelter from the sand-storm. The fact of its
carrying a saddle showed that its owner must have been
upon the march, at the time it escaped from him. Had our
adventurers been better acquainted with Saäran customs,
they would have concluded that this had been the case : for
they would have known that, on the approach of a "shuma"
— the "forecasts" of which are well known — the Bedouins at once, and in all haste, break up their encampments; and put themselves, and their whole personal
property, in motion. Otherwise, they would be in danger
of getting smoored under the settling sand-drift.

Following the counsels of the sailor — whose desert
knowledge appeared as extensive as if it, and not the sea,
had been his habitual home — our adventurers crouched
down in such a way as not to be seen by any one passing
along the beach.

Scarcely had they placed themselves in this humble attitude, when Old Bill — who had been keeping watch all the
while, with only the upper half of his head elevated above
the combing of the sand-wreath — announced, by a low exclamation, that something was in sight.

Two dark forms were seen coming along the shore, from
the southward; but at so great a distance that it was impossible to tell what sort of creatures they might turn out.

"Let me have a look," proposed Colin. "By good luck,
3 *

I 've got my glass. It was in my pocket as we escaped
from the ship; and I did n't think of throwing it away."

As the young Scotchman spoke, he took from the breast
of his dreadnought jacket, a small telescope, — which, when
drawn out to its full extent, exhibited a series of tubes, *en
echelon*, about half a yard in length.   Directing it upon the
dark objects, — at the same time taking the precaution to
keep his own head as low down as possible, — he at once
proclaimed their character.

"They 're two bonny bodies," said he, "dressed in all the
colors of the rainbow.   I can see bright shawls, and red
caps, and striped cloaks.   One is mounted on a horse; the
other bestrides a camel, — just such a one as this by our
side.   They 're coming along slowly; and appear to be staring about them."

"Ah, that be hit," said Old Bill.   "It be the howners of
this 'eer brute.   They be on the sarch for her.   Lucky the
drift-sand hae covered her tracks, — else they 'd come right
on to us.   Lie low, Masther Colin.   We may n't show our
heeds over the combin' o' the sand.   They 'd be sure to see
the size o' a saxpence.   We maun keep awthegither oot o'
sicht."

One of the old sailor's peculiarities — or, perhaps, it
may have been an eccentricity — was, that in addressing
himself to his companions, he was almost sure to assume
the national *patois* of the individual spoken to.   In anything like a continued conversation with Harry Blount,
his " h's " were handled in a most unfashionable manner;
and while talking with Terence, the Milesian came from
his lips, in a brogue almost as pure as Tipperary could
produce.

In a *tête-à-tête* with Colin, the listener might have sworn
that Bill was more Scotch than the young Macpherson himself.

Colin perceived the justice of the sailor's suggestion; and

immediately ducked his head below the level of the parapet
of sand.

This placed our adventurers in a position at once irksome
and uncertain. Curiosity, if nothing else, rendered them
desirous to watch the movements of the men who were approaching. Without noting these, they would not be able
to tell when they might again raise their heads above the
ridge; and might do so, just at the time when the horseman
and the rider of the maherry were either opposite or within
sight of them.

As the sailor had said, any dark object of the size of a
sixpence would be seen if presented above the smooth combing of snow-white sand; and it was evident to all that for
one of them to look over it might lead to their being discovered.

While discussing this point, they knew that some time
had elapsed; and, although the eyes they dreaded might
still be distant, they could not help thinking, that they were
near enough to see them if only the hair of their heads
should be shown above the sand.

They reflected naturally. They knew that these sons of
the desert must be gifted with keen instincts; or, at all events,
with an experience that would enable them to detect the
slightest " fault " in the aspect of a landscape, so well known
to them, — in short, that they would notice anything that
might appear " abnormal " in it.

From that time their situation was one of doubt and anxiety. They dared not give even as much as a glance over
the smooth, snow white sand. They could only crouch behind it, in anxious expectation, knowing not when that du-
bious condition of things could be safely brought to a close.

Luckily they were relieved from it, and sooner than they
had expected. Colin it was who discovered a way to get
out of the difficulty.

" Ha ! " exclaimed he, as an ingenious conception sprang

up in his mind. " I 've got an idea that 'll do.   I 'll watch
these fellows, without giving them a chance of seeing me.
That will I."

" How ? " asked the others.

Colin made no verbal reply ; but instead, he was seen to
insert his telescope into the sand-parapet, in such a way that
its tube passed clear through to the other side, and of course
commanded a view of the beach, along which the two forms
were advancing.

As soon as he had done so, he placed his eye to the glass,
and, in a cautious whisper, announced that both the horseman and camel-rider were within his " field of view "

CHAPTER XVII.

THE TRAIL ON THE SAND.

THE tube of the telescope, firmly imbedded in the sand,
kept its place without the necessity of being held in
hand. It only required to be slightly shifted as the horseman and camel-rider changed place, — so as to keep them
within its field of view.

By this means our adventurers were able to mark their
approach and note every movement they made, without
much risk of being seen themselves. Each of them took
a peep through the glass to satisfy their curiosity, and then
the instrument was wholly intrusted to its owner, who was
.henceforth constantly to keep his eye to it, and observe the
movements of the strangers. This the young Scotchman
did, at intervals communicating with his companions in a
low voice.

" I can make out their faces." muttered he, after a time.

▪ and ugly enough are they. One is yellow, the other black He must be a negro, — of course he is, — he's got woolly hair too. It's he that rides the camel, — just such another as this that stumbled over us. The yellow man upon the horse has a pointed beard upon his chin. He has a sharp look, like those Moors we've seen at Tetuan. He's an Arab, I suppose. He appears to be the master of the black man. I can see him make gestures, as if he was directing him to do something. There! they have stopped, — they are looking this way!"

"Marcy on us!" muttered old Bill, "if they have speered the glass!"

"Troth! that's like enough," said Terence. "It'll be flashing in the sun outside the sand. That sharp-eyed Arab is almost sure to see it."

"Had you not better draw it in?" suggested Harry Blount.

"True," answered Colin. "But I fear it would be too late now. If that's what halted them, it's all over with us, so far as hiding goes."

"Slip it in, any how. If they don't see it any more, they may n't come quite up to the-ridge."

Colin was about to follow the advice thus offered, when on–taking what he intended to be a last squint through the telescope, he perceived that the travellers were moving on up the beach, as if they had seen nothing that called upon them to deviate from their course.

Fortunately for the four "stowaways," it was not the sparkle of the lens that had caused them to make that stop. A ravine, or opening through the sand-ridges, much larger than that in which our adventurers were concealed, *emboucheea* upon the beach, some distance below. It was the appearance of this opening that had attracted the attention of the two mounted men; and from their gestures Colin could tell they were talking about it, as if undecided whether to go that way or keep on up the strand.

It ended by the yellow man putting spurs to his horse, and galloping off up the ravine, followed by the black man on the camel.

From the way in which both behaved, — keeping their eyes generally bent upon the ground, but at intervals gazing about over the country, — it was evident they were in search of something, and this would be the she-camel that lay tethered in the bottom of the sand-gorge, close to the spot occupied by our adventurers.

"They've gone off on the wrong track," said Colin, taking his eye from the glass as soon as the switch tail of the maherry disappeared behind the slope of a sand-dune. "So much the better for us. My heart was at my mouth just a minute ago. I was sure it was all over with us."

"You think they haven't seen the shine of the lens?" interrogated Harry.

"Of course not; or else they'd have come on to examine it. Instead, they've left the beach altogether. They've gone inland, among the hills. They're no longer in sight."

"Good!" ejaculated Terence, raising his head over the ridge, as did also the others.

"Och! good yez may well say, Masther Terence. Jist look fwhot fools we've been all four av us! We never thought av the thracks, nayther wan nor other av us!"

As Bill spoke, he pointed down towards the beach, in the direction in which he had made his late crawling excursion. There, distinctly traceable in the half-wet sand, were the marks he had made both going and returning, as if a huge tortoise or crocodile had been dragging itself over the ground.

The truth of his words was apparent to all. It was chance and not their cunning that had saved them from discovery. Had the owner of the camel but continued another hundred yards along the beach, he could not have failed to see the double "trail" made by the sailor, and of course would have

followed it to the spot where they were hidden.   As it was,
the two mounted men had not come near enough to note the
sign made by the old salt in his laborious flounderings; and
perhaps fancying they had followed the strand far enough,
they had struck off into the interior, — through the opening
of the sand-hills, in the belief that the she-camel might have
done the same.

Whatever may have been their reason, they were now
gone out of sight, and the long stretch of desert shore was
once more under the eyes of our adventurers, unrelieved by
the appearance of anything that might be called a living
creature.

CHAPTER XVIII.

THE " DESERT SHIP."

THOUGH there was now nothing within sight between
them, they did not think it prudent to move out of the
gorge, nor even to raise their heads above the level of the
sand-wreath. They did so only at intervals, to assure themselves that the " coast was clear"; and satisfied on this
score, they would lower their heads again, and remain in this
attitude of concealment.

One with but slight knowledge of the circumstances — or
with the country in which they were — might consider them
over-cautious in acting thus, and might fancy that in their
forlorn, shipwrecked condition they should have been but
too glad to meet men.

On the contrary, a creature of their own shape was the
last thing they desired either to see or encounter; and for
the reasons already given in their conversation, they could
meet no men there who would not be their enemies,

worse than that, their tyrants, perhaps their torturers. Old Bill was sure of this from what he had heard. So were Colin and Harry from what they had read. Terence alone was incredulous as to the cruelty of which the sailor had given such a graphic picture.

Terence, however rash he was by nature, allowed himself to be overruled by his more prudent companions; and therefore, up to the hour when the twilight began to empurple the sea, no movement towards stirring from their place of concealment was made by any of the party.

The patient camel shared their silent retreat; though they had taken precautions against its straying from them, had it felt so inclined, by tying its shanks securely together. Towards evening the animal was again milked, in the same fashion as in the morning; and, reinvigorated by its bounti-ful yield, our adventurers prepared to depart from a spot, of which, notwithstanding the friendly concealment it had afforded them, they were all heartily tired.

Their preparations were easily made, and occupied scarce ten seconds of time. It was only to untether the camel and take to the road, or, as Harry jocosely termed it, "unmoor the desert ship and begin their voyage."

Just as the last gleam of daylight forsook the white crests of the sand-hills, and went flickering afar over the blue waters of the ocean, they stole forth from their hiding-place, and started upon a journey of which they knew neither the length nor the ending.

Even of the direction of that undetermined journey they had but a vague conception. They believed that the coast trended northward and southward, and that one of these points was the proper one to head for. It was almost "heads or tails" which of them they should take; and had they been better acquainted with their true situation, it might as well have been determined by a toss-up, for any chance they had of ever arriving at a civilized settlement

But they knew not that. They had a belief—the old sailor stronger than the rest—that there were Portuguese forts along the coast, chiefly to the southward, and that by keeping along shore they might reach one of these. There were such establishments it is true—still are; and though at that time there were some nearer to the point where their ship had been wrecked, none were near enough to be reached by the starving castaway, however perseveringly he might travel towards them.

Ignorant of the impracticability of their attempt, our ad venturers entered upon it with a spirit worthy of success,—worthy of the country from which they had come.

For some time the maherry was led in hand, old Bill being its conductor. All four had been well rested during the day, and none of them cared to ride.

. As the tide, however, was now beginning to creep up into the sundry inlets, to avoid walking in water, they were compelled to keep well high up on the beach; and this forced them to make their way through the soft yielding sand, a course that required considerable exertion.

One after another now began to feel fatigue, and talk about it as well; and then the proposal was made, that the maherry—who stepped over the unsure surface with as much apparent lightness as a cat would have done—should be made to carry at least one of the party. They could ride in turns, which would give each of them an opportunity of resting.

No sooner was the proposition made than it was carried into execution. Terence, who had been the one to advance it, being hoisted in the hump of the camel.

But though the young O'Connor had been accustomed to the saddle from childhood, and had ridden "across country" on many an occasion, it was not long before he became satisfied with the saddle of a maherry. The rocking, and jolting, and "pitching," as our adventurers termed it, from larboard to starboard, fore and aft, and alow and aloft, soon caused Terence to sing out "enough"; and he descended into the soft sand with a much greater desire for walking than the moment before he had had for riding.

Harry Blount took his place, but although the young Englishman had been equally accustomed to a hunting-saddle, he found that his experience went but a little way towards making him easy on the hump of a maherry; and he was soon in the mood for dismounting.

The son of Scotia next climbed upon the back of the camel. Whether it was that natural pride of prowess which oft impels his countrymen to perseverance and daring deeds, — whether it was that, or whether it arose from a sterner power of endurance, — certain it is that Colin kept his seat longer than either of his predecessors.

But even Scotch sinews could not hold out against such a tension, — such a bursting and wrenching and tossing, — and it ended by Colin declaring that upon the whole he would prefer making the journey upon " Shank's mare."

Saying this he slid down from the shoulders of the ungainly animal, resigning the creature once more to the conduct of Old Bill, who had still kept hold of the halter.

CHAPTER XIX.

HOMEWARD BOUND.

THE experience of his young companions might have deterred the sailor from imitating their example; more especially as Bill, according to his own statement, had never been " abroad " a saddle in his life. But they did not; and for special reasons. Awkward as the old salt might feel in a saddle, he felt not less awkward *afoot.* That is ashore, — on *terrâ firma.*

Place him on the deck of a ship, or in the rigging of one, and no man in all England's navy could have been more secure as to his footing, or more difficult to dispossess of it; but set sailor Bill upon shore, and expect him to go ahead upon it, you would be disappointed: you might as well expect a fish to make progress on land; and you would witness a species of locomotion more resembling that of a manatee or a seal, than of a human biped. As the old man-o'-war's-man had now being floundering full five weeks through the soft shore-sand, he was thoroughly convinced that a mode of progression must be preferable to that; and as soon as the young Scotchman descended from his seat, he climbed into it.

He had not much climbing to do, — for the well-trained maherry, when any one wished to mount him, at once knelt down, — making the ascent to his "summits" as easy as possible.

Just as the sailor had got firmly into the saddle, the moon shone out with a brilliance that almost rivalled the light of day. In the midst of that desert landscape, against the ground of snow-white sand, the figures of both camel and rider were piquantly conspicuous; and although the one was figuratively a ship, and the other really a sailor, their juxtaposition offered a contrast of the queerest kind. So ludicrous did it seem, that the three "mids," disregarding all ideas of danger, broke forth with one accord into a strain of loud and continuous laughter.

They had all seen camels, or pictures of these animals; but never before either a camel, or the picture of one, *with a sailor upon his back.* The very idea of a dromedary carries along with it the cognate spectacle of an Arab on its back, — a slim, sinewy individual of swarth complexion and picturesque garb, a bright burnouse steaming around his body, with a twisted turban on his head. But a tall camel, surmounted by a sailor in dreadnought jacket and sou'-wester, was a picture to make a Solon laugh, let alone a tier of midshipmen; and it drew from the latter such a cachin-nation as caused the shores of the Saära to echo with sounds of joy, perhaps never heard there before. Old Bill was not angry, he was only gratified to see these young gentlemen in such good spirits; and calling upon them to keep close after him, he gave the halter to his maherry and started off over the sand.

For some time his companions kept pace with him, doing their best; but it soon became apparent, even to the sailor himself, that unless something was done to restrain the im-petuosity of the camel, he must soon be separated from those following afoot.

This something its rider felt himself incapable of accom-plishing. It is true he still held the halter in his hand, but this gave him but slight control over the camel. It was not a mameluke bitt — not even a snaffle — and for direct-ing the movements of the animal the old sailor felt himself as helpless as if standing by the wheel of a seventy-four that had unshipped her rudder. Just like a ship in such a situation did the maherry behave. Surging through the ocean of soft sand, now mounting the spurs that trended down to the beach, now descending headlong into deep gullies, like troughs between the ocean waves, and gliding silently, gently forward as a shallop upon a smooth sea. Such was the course that the sailor was pursuing. Very different, however, were his reflections to those he would have indulged in on board a man-o'-war; and if any man ever sneered at that simile which likens a camel to a ship, it was Sailor Bill upon that occasion.

"Avast there!" cried he, as soon as the maherry had fairly commenced moving. "Shiver my old timbers! what do yez mean, you brute? Belay there! belay! 'Ang it, I must pipe all 'ands, an' take in sail. Where the deevil are ye steerin' tc? Be jabers, yez may laugh, ycung gentlemen, but this ain't a fair weather craft, I tell yez. Thunder an' ouns! it be as much as I can do to keep her to her course. Hulloo! she's off afore the wind!"

As the rider of the maherry gave out this declaration, the animal was seen suddenly to increase its speed, not only in a progressive ratio, but at once to double quick, as if impelled by some powerful motive.

At the same time it was heard to utter a strange cry, half scream, half snort, which could not have been caused by any action on the part of its rider.

It was already over a hundred yards in advance of those following on foot; but after giving out that startling cry, the distance became quickly increased, and in a few seconds of time the three astonished "mids" saw only the shadow of a maherry, with a sailor upon its back, first dissolving into dim outline until it finally disappeared behind the sand dunes that abutted upon the beach.

CHAPTER XX.

THE DANCE INTERRUPTED.

LEAVING the midshipmen to their mirth, which, however, was not of very long duration, we must follow Sailor Bill and the runaway camel.

In reality the maherry had made off with him, though for what reason the sailor could not divine. He only knew that it was going at the rate of nine or ten knots an hour, and going its own way; for instead of keeping to the line cf the coast, — the direction he would have wished it to take, — it had suddenly turned tail upon the sea, and headed towards the interior of the country.

Its rider had already discovered that he had not the slightest control over it. He had tugged upon the hair halter and shouted "Avast!" until both his arms and tongue were tired. All to no purpose. The camel scorned his commands, lent a deaf ear to his entreaties, and paid not the slightest heed to his attempt to pull up, except to push on in the opposite direction, with its snout elevated in the air and its long ungainly neck stretched forward in the most determined and provoking fashion.

There was not much force in the muscular efforts made to check it. It was just as much as its rider could do to balance himself on its hump, which, of course, he had to do Arab-fashion, sitting *upon* the saddle as on a chair, with his feet resting upon the back of the animal's neck. It was this position that rendered his seat so insecure, but no other could have been adopted in the saddle of a maherry, and the sailor was compelled to keep it as well as he could.

At the time the animal first started off, it had not gone at so rapid a pace but that he might have slipped down upon the soft sand without much danger of being injured. This for an instant he had thought of doing; but knowing that while "unhorsing" himself the camel might escape, he had voluntarily remained on its back, in the hope of being able to pull the animal up.

On becoming persuaded that this would be impossible, and that the maherry had actually made off with him, it was too late to dismount without danger. The camel was now shambling along so swiftly that he could not slip down without submitting himself to a fall. It would be no longer a tumble upon soft sand, for the runaway had suddenly swerved into a deep gorge, the bottom of which was thickly strewed with boulders of rock, and through these the maherry was making way with the speed of a fast-trotting horse.

Had its rider attempted to abandon his high perch upon the hump, his chances would have been good for getting dashed against one of the big boulders, or trodden under the huge hoofs of the maherry itself.

Fully alive to this danger, Old Bill no more thought of throwing himself to the ground; but on the contrary, held on to the hump with all the tenacity that lay in his well-tarred digits.

He had continued to shout for some time after parting with his companions; but as this availed nothing, he at length desisted, and was now riding the rest of his race in silence.

When was it to terminate? Whither was the camel conducting him? These were the questions that now came before his mind.

He thought of an answer, and it filled him with apprehension. The animal was evidently in eager haste. It was snuffing the wind in its progress forward; something ahead seemed to be attracting it. What could this something be but its home, the tent from which it had strayed, the dwelling of its owner? And who could that owner be but one of those cruel denizens of the desert they had been taking such pains to avoid?

The sailor was allowed but little time for conjectures; for almost on the instant of his shaping this, the very first one, the maherry shot suddenly round the hip of a hill, bringing him in full view of a spectacle that realized it.

A small valley, or stretch of level ground enclosed by surrounding ridges, lay before him; its gray, sandy surface interspersed by a few patches of darker color, which the moon, shining brightly from a blue sky, disclosed to be tufts of tussock-grass and mimosa bushes.

These, however, did not occupy the attention of the involuntary visitor to that secluded spot; but something else that appeared in their midst, — something that proclaimed the presence of human beings.

Near the centre of the little valley half a dozen dark objects stood up several feet above the level of the ground Their size, shape, and color proclaimed their character. They were tents, — the tents of a Bedouin encampment. The old man-o'-war's-man had never seen such before; but there was no mistaking them for anything else, — even going as he was at a speed that prevented him from having a very clear view of them.

In a few seconds, however, he was near enough to distinguish something more than the tents. They stood in a sort of circle of about twenty yards in diameter, and within this could be seen the forms of men, women, and children. Around were animals of different sorts, — horses, camels, sheep, goats, and dogs, grouped according to their kind, with the exception of the dogs, which appeared to be straying everywhere. This varied tableau was distinctly visible under the light of a full, mellow moon.

There were voices, — shouting and singing. There was music, made upon some rude instrument. The human forms, — both of men and women, — were in motion, circling and springing about. The sailor saw they were dancing.

He heard, and saw, all this in a score of seconds, as the maherry hurried him forward into their midst. The encampment was close to the bottom of the hill round which the camel had carried him. He had at length made up his mind to dismount *coute que coute;* but there was no time. Before he could make a movement to fling himself from the shoulders of the animal, he saw that he was discovered. A cry coming from the tents admonished him of this fact. It was too late to attempt a retreat, and, in a state of desponding stupor, he stuck to the saddle. Not much longer. The camel, with a snorting scream, responding to the call of its fellows, rushed on into the encampment, — right into the very circle of the dancers; and there amidst the shouts of men, the screeches of women, the yelling of children, the neighing of horses, the bleating of sheep and goats, and the barking of a score or two of cur dogs, — the animal stopped, with such abrupt suddenness that its rider, after performing a somersault through the air, came down on all-fours, in front of its projecting snout!

In such fashion was Sailor Bill introduced to the Arab encampment.

CHAPTER XXI.

A SERIO-COMICAL RECEPTION.

IT need scarce be said that the advent of the stranger produced some surprise among the Terpsichorean crowd, into the midst of which he had been so unceremoniously projected. And yet this surprise was not such as might have been expected. One might suppose that an English man-o'-war's-man in pilot-cloth, pea-jacket, glazed hat, and wide duck trousers, would have been a singular sight to the eyes of the dark-skinned individuals who now encircled them — dressed as all of them were in gay colored floating shawl-robes, slipped or sandalled feet, and with fez caps or turbans on their heads.

Not a bit of a singular sight: neither the color of his skin, nor his sailor-costume, had caused surprise to those who surrounded him. Both were matters with which they were well acquainted — alas! too well.

The astonishment they had exhibited arose simply from the *sans façons* manner of his coming amongst them; and on the instant after it disappeared, giving place to a feeling of a different kind.

4

Succeeding to the shouts of surprise, arose a simultaneous peal of laughter from men, women, and children ; in which even the animals seemed to join — more especially the maherry, who stood with its uncouth head craned over its dis: mounted rider, and looking uncontrollably comic !

In the midst of this universal exclamation the sailor rose to his feet. He might have been disconcerted by the reception, had his senses been clear enough to comprehend what was passing. But they were not. The effects of that fearful somersault had confused him ; and he had only risen to an erect attitude, under a vague instinct or desire to escape from that company.

After staggering some paces over the ground, his thoughts returned to him ; and he more clearly comprehended his situation. Escape was out of the question. He was prisoner to a party of wandering Bedouins, — the worst to be found in all the wide expanse of the Saäran desert, — the wreckers of the Atlantic coast.

The sailor might have felt surprised at seeing a collection of familiar objects into the midst of which he had wandered. By the doorway of a tent, — one of the largest upon the ground, — there was a pile of *paraphernalia*, every article of which was tropical, not of the Saära, but the sea. There were "belongings" of the cabin and caboose, — the 'tween decks, and the forecastle, — all equally proclaiming themselves the *débris* of a castaway ship.

The sailor could have no conjectures as to the vessel to which they had belonged. He knew the articles by sight, — one and all of them. They were the spoils of the corvette, that had been washed ashore, and fallen into the hands of the wreckers.

Among them Old Bill saw some things that had appertained to himself.

On the opposite side of the encampment, by another large tent, was a second pile of ship's equipments, like the first guarded by a sentinel who squatted beside it: the sailor looked around in expectation to see some of the corvette's crew. Some might have escaped like himself and his three companions by reaching the shore on cask, hoop, or spar. If so, they had not fallen into the hands of the wreckers; or if they had, they were not in the camp — unless, indeed, they might be inside some of the tents. This was not likely. Most probably they had all been drowned, or had succumbed to a worse fate than drowning — death at the hands of the cruel coast robbers, who now surrounded the survivor.

The circumstances under which the old sailor made these reflections were such as to render the last hypothesis sufficiently probable. He was being pushed about and dragged over the ground by two men, armed with long curved scimitars, contesting some point with one another, apparently as to which should be first to cut off his head!

Both of these men appeared to be chiefs; "sheiks" as the sailor heard them called by their followers, a party of whom — also with arms in their hands — stood behind each "sheik" — all seemingly alike eager to perform the act of decapitation.

So near seemed the old sailor's head to being cut off, that for some seconds he was not quite sure whether it still remained upon his shoulders! He could not understand a word that passed between the contending parties, though there was talk enough to have satisfied a sitting of parliament, and probably with about the same quantity of sense in it.

Before he had proceeded far, the sailor began to comprehend, — not from the speeches made, but the gestures that accompanied them, — that it was not the design of either party to cut off his head. The drawn scimitars, sweeping through the air, were not aimed at his neck, but rather in mutual menace of one another.

Old Bill could see that there was some quarrel between

the two sheiks, of which he was himself the cause; that the camp was not a unity consisting of a single chief, his family, and following; but that there were too separate leaders, each with his adherents, perhaps temporarily associated together for purposes of plunder.

That they had collected the wreck of the corvette, and divided the spoils between them, was evident from the two heaps being kept carefully apart, each piled up near the tent of a chief.

The old man-o'-war's-man made his observations in the midst of great difficulties: for while noting these particulars, he was pulled about the place, first by one sheik, then by the other, each retaining his disputed person in temporary possession.

From the manner in which they acted, he could tell that it was his person that was the subject of dispute, and that both wanted to be the proprietor of it.

CHAPTER XXII.

THE TWO SHEIKS.

THERE was a remarkable difference between the two men thus claiming ownership in the body of Old Bill. One was a little wizen-faced individual, whose yellow complexion and sharp, angular features proclaimed him of the Arab stock, while his competitor showed a skin of almost ebon blackness — a frame of herculean development — a broad face, with flat nose and thick lubberly lips — a head of enormous circumference, surmounted by a mop of woolly hair, standing erect several inches above his occiput.

Had the sailor been addicted to ethnological speculations,

he might have derived an interesting lesson from that contest, of which he was the cause. It might have helped him to a knowledge of the geography of the country in which he had been cast, for he was now upon that neutral territory where the true Ethiopian — the son of Ham — occasionally contests possession, both of the soil and the slave, with the wandering children of Japhet.

The two men who were thus quarrelling about the possession of the English tar, though both of African origin, could scarce have been more unlike had their native country been the antipodes of each other.

Their object was not so different, though even in this there was a certain dissimilation. Both designed making the shipwrecked sailor a slave. But the sheik of Arab aspects wished to possess him, with a view to his ultimate ransom. He knew that by carrying him northwards there would be a chance to dispose of him at a good price, either to the Jew merchants at Wedinoin, or the European consuls at Mogador. It would not be the first Saärian castaway he had in this manner restored to his friends and his country — not from any motives of humanity, but simply for the profit it produced.

On the other hand, the black competitor had a different, though somewhat similar, purpose in view. His thoughts extended towards the south. There lay the emporium of his commerce, — the great mud-built town of Timbuctoo. Little as a white man was esteemed among the Arab merchants when considered as a *mere* slave, the sable sheik knew that in the south of the Saära he would command a price, if only as a curiosity to figure among the followers of the sultan of some grand interior city. For this reason, therefore, was the black determined upon the possession of Bill, and showed as much eagerness to become his owner as did his tawny competitor.

After several minutes spent in words and gestures of mu

tual menace, which, from the wild shouts and flourishing of scimitars, seemed as if it could only end in a general lopping off of heads, somewhat to the astonishment of the sailor, tranquillity became restored without any one receiving scratch or cut.

The scimitars were returned to their scabbards; and although the affair did not appear to be decided, the contest was now carried on in a more pacific fashion by words. A long argument ensued, in which both sheiks displayed their oratorial powers. Though the sailor could not understand a word of what was said, he could tell that the little Arab was urging his ownership, on the plea that the camel which had carried the captive into the encampment was his property, and on this account was he entitled to the " waif."

The black seemed altogether to dissent from this doctrine; on his side pointing to the two heaps of plunder ; as much as to say that his share of the spoils — already obtained — was the smaller one.

At this crisis a third party stepped between the two disputants — a young fellow, who appeared to have some authority with both. His behavior told Bill that he was acting as mediator. Whatever was the proposal made by him, it appeared to satisfy both parties, as both at once desisted from their wordy warfare — at the same time that they seemed preparing to settle the dispute in some other way.

The mode was soon made apparent. A spot of smooth, even sand was selected by the side of the encampment, to which the two sheiks, followed by their respective parties, repaired.

A square figure was traced out, inside of which several rows of little round holes were scooped in the sand, and then the rival sheiks sat down, one on each side of the figure. Each had already provided himself with a number of pellets of camels' dung, which were now placed in the holes, and the play of " helga " was now commenced.

Whoever won the game was to become possessed of the single stake, which was neither more nor less than Sailor Bill.

The game proceeded by the shifting of the dung pellets in a particular fashion, from hole to hole, somewhat similar to the moving of draughts upon the squares of a checker-board.

During the play not a word was spoken by either party, the two sheiks squatting opposite each other, and making their moves with as much gravity as a pair of chess-players engaged in some grand tournament of this intellectual game.

It was only when the affair ended, that the noise broke forth again, which it did in loud, triumphant shouts from the conquering party, with expressions of chagrin on the side of the conquered.

By interpreting these shouts, Bill could tell that he had fallen to the black; and this was soon after placed beyond doubt by the latter coming up and taking possession of him.

It appeared, however, that there had been certain sub-siding conditions to the play, and that the sailor had been in some way or another *staked against his own clothes ;* for before being fully appropriated by his owner he was stripped to his shirt, and his habiliments, shoes and sou'-wester in-cluded, were handed over to the sheik who had played second-best in the game of " helga."

In this forlorn condition was the old sailor conducted to the tent of his sable master, and placed like an additional piece upon the pile of plunder already apportioned !

CHAPTER XXIII.

SAILOR BILL BESHREWED.

SAILOR BILL said not a word. He had no voice in the disposal of the stakes, — which were himself and his "toggery," — and, knowing this, he remained silent.

He was not allowed to remain undisturbed. During the progress of the game, he had become the cynosure of a large circle of eyes, — belonging to the women and children of the united tribes.

He might have looked for some compassion, — at least, from the female portion of those who formed his *entourage*. Half famished with hunger, — a fact which he did not fail to communicate by signs, — he might have expected them to relieve his wants. The circumstance of his making them known might argue, that he did expect some sort of kind treatment.

It was not much, however. His hopes were but slight, and sprang rather from a knowledge of his own necessities, and of what the women *ought* to have done, than what they were likely to do. Old Bill had heard too much of the character of these hags of the Saära, — and their mode of conducting themselves towards any unfortunate castaway who might be drifted among them, — to expect any great hospitality at their hands.

His hopes, therefore, were moderate; but, for all that, they were doomed to disappointment.

Perhaps in no other part of the world is the "milk of human kindness" so completely wanting in the female breast, as among the women of the wandering Arabs of Africa. Slaves to their imperious lords, — even when enjoying the sacred title of wife, — they are themselves treated worse than the arimals which they have to manage and tend, —

even worse at times than their own bond-slaves, with whom they mingle almost on an equality. As in all like cases, this harsh usage, instead of producing sympathy for others who suffer, has the very opposite tendency; as if they found some alleviation of their cruel lot in imitating the brutality of their oppressors.

Instead of receiving kindness, the old sailor became the recipient of insults, not only from their tongues, — which he could not understand, — but by acts and gestures which were perfectly comprehensible to him.

While his ears were dinned by virulent speeches, — which, could he have comprehended them, would have told him how much he was despised for being an infidel, and not a follower of the true prophet, — while his eyes were well-nigh put out by dust thrown in his face, — accompanied by spiteful expectorations, — his body was belabored by sticks, his skin scratched and pricked with sharp thorns, his whiskers lugged almost to the dislocation of his jaws, and the hair of his head uprooted in fistfuls from his pericranium.

All this, too, amid screams and fiendish laughter, that resembled an orgie of furies.

These women — she-devils they better deserved to be called — were simply following out the teachings of their inhuman faith, — among religions, even that of Rome not excepted, the most inhuman that has ever cursed mankind. Had old Bill been a believer in their "Prophet," that false seer of the blood-stained sword, their treatment of him would have been directly the reverse. Instead of kicks and cuffs, hustlings and scratchings, he would have been made welcome to a share in such hospitality as they could have bestowed upon him. It was religion, not nature, made them act as they did. Their hardness of heart came not from *God*, but the *Prophet*. They were only carrying out the edicts of their "priests of a bloody faith."

In vain did the old man-o'-war's-man cry out "belay"

4 *

and "avast." In vain did he "shiver his timbers," and ap
peal against their scurvy treatment, by looks, words, and
gesture.

These seemed only to augment the mirth and spitefulness
of his tormentors.

In this scene of cruelty there was one woman conspicuous
among the rest. By her companions she was called *Fatima*.
The old sailor, ignorant of Arabic feminine names, thought
"it a misnomer," for of all his she-persecutors she was the
leanest and scraggiest. Notwithstanding the poetical no-
tions which the readers of Oriental romance might associate
with her name, there was not much poetry about the personage who so assiduously assaulted Sailor Bill, — pulling
his whiskers, slapping his cheeks, and every now and then
spitting in his face !

She was something more than middle-aged, short, squat,
and meagre; with the eye-teeth projecting on both sides, so
as to hold up the upper lip, and exhibit all the others in
their ivory whiteness, with an expression resembling that of
the hyena. This is considered beauty, — a fashion in full
vogue among her countrywomen, who cultivate it with great
care, — though to the eyes of the old sailor it rendered the
hag all the more hideous.

But the skinning of eye-teeth was not the only attempt
at ornament made by this belle of the Desert. Strings
of black beads hung over her wrinkled bosom; circlets of
white bone were set in her hair; armlets and bangles
adorned her wrists and ankles, and altogether did her costume and behavior betoken one distinguished among the
crowd of his persecutors, — in short, their sultana or queen.

And such did she prove; for on the black sheik appropriating the old sailor as a stake fairly won in the game, and
rescuing his newly-acquired property from the danger of being damaged, Fatima followed him to his tent with such dem-
onstrations as showed her to be, if not the "favorite," certainly the head of the harem.

CHAPTER XXIV.

STARTING ON THE TRACK.

A S already said, the mirth of the three midshipmen was brought to a quick termination. It ended on the instant of Sailor Bill's disappearance behind the spur of the sand-hills. At the same instant all three came to a stop, and stood regarding one another with looks of uneasiness and apprehension.

All agreed that the maherry had made away with the old man-o'-war's-man. There could be no doubt about it. Bill's shouts, as he was hurried out of their hearing, proved that he was doing his best to bring to, and that the "ship of the desert" would not yield obedience to her helm.

They wondered a little why he had not slipped off, and let the animal go. They could not see why he should fear to drop down in the soft sand. He might have had a tumble, but nothing to do him any serious injury, — nothing to break a bone, or dislocate a joint. They supposed he had stuck to the saddle, from not wishing to abandon the maherry, and in hope of soon bringing it to a halt.

This was just what he had done, for the first three or four hundred yards. After that he would only have been too well satisfied to separate from the camel, and let it go its way. But then he was among the rough, jaggy rocks through which the path led, and then dismounting was no longer to be thought of, without also thinking of danger, considering that the camel was nearly ten feet in height, and going at a pitching pace of ten miles to the hour. To have forsaken his saddle at that moment would have been to risk the breaking of his neck.

From where they stood looking after him, the mids could not make out the character of the ground. Under the light

of the moon, the surface seemed all of a piece, — all a bed
of smooth soft sand! For this reason were they perplexed
by his behavior.

There was that in the incident to make them apprehensive.
The maherry would not have gone off at such a gait, without some powerful motive to impel it. Up to that moment it
had shown no particular *penchant* for rapid travelling, but had
been going, under their guidance, with a steady, sober docil-
ity. Something must have attracted it towards the interior.
What could that something be, if not the knowledge that its
home, or its companions, were to be found in this direction?

This was the conjecture that came simultaneously into the
minds of all three, — as is known, the correct one.

There could be no doubt that their companion had been
carried towards an encampment; for no other kind of settlement could be thought of in such a place. It was even a
wonder that this could exist in the midst of a dreary, wild
expanse of pure sand, like that surrounding them. Perhaps,
thought they, there may be "land" towards the interior of
the country, — a spot of firm soil, with vegetation upon it;
in short, an *oasis*.

After their first surprise had partially subsided, they took
counsel as to their course. Should they stay where they
were, and wait for Bill's return? Or should they follow, in
the hope of overtaking him?

Perhaps he might *not* return. If carried into a camp of
barbarous savages, it was not likely that he would. He
would be seized and held captive to a dead certainty. But
surely he would not be such a simpleton, as to allow the maherry to transport him into the midst of his enemies.

Again sprang up their surprise at his not having made an
effort to dismount.

For some ten or fifteen minutes the midshipmen stood
hesitating, — their eyes all the while bent on the moonlit

opening, through which the maherry had disappeared. There were no signs of anything in the pass, — at least anything like either a camel or a sailor. Only the bright beams of the moon glittering upon crystals of purest sand.

They thought they heard sounds, — the cries of quadrupeds mingling with the voices of men. There were voices, too, of shriller intonation, that might have proceeded from the throats of women.

Colin was confident he heard such. He was not contradicted by his companions, who simply said, they could not be sure that they heard anything.

But for the constant roar of the breakers, — rolling up almost to the spot upon which they stood, — they would have declared themselves differently; for at that moment there was a chorus being carried on at no great distance, in a variety of most unmusical sounds, — comprising the bark of the dog, the neigh of the horse, the snorting scream of the dromedary, the bleat of the sheep, and the sharper cry of its near kindred the goat, — along with the equally wild and scarce more articulate utterances of savage men, women, and children.

Colin was convinced that he heard all these sounds, and declared that they could only proceed from some encampment. His companions, knowing that the young Scotchman was sharp-eared, made no attempt to question his belief; but, on the contrary, gave ready credence to it.

Under any circumstances it seemed of no use to remain where they were. If Bill did not return, they were bound in honor to go after him; and, if possible, find out what had become of him. If, on the other hand, he should be coming back, they must meet him somewhere in the pass, — through which the camel had carried him off. — since there was no other by which he might conveniently get back to them.

This point determined, the three mids, setting their faces for the interior of the country, started off towards the break between the sand-hills

CHAPTER XXV.

BILL TO BE ABANDONED

THEY proceeded with caution, — Colin even more than
his companions. The young Englishman was not so
distrustful of the "natives," whoever they might be, as the
son of Scotia; and as for O'Connor, he still persisted in the
belief that there would be little, if any, danger in meeting
with men, and, in his arguments, still continued to urge seeking such an encounter as the best course they could pursue.

"Besides," said Terence, "Coly says he hears the voices
of women and children. Sure no human creature that's
got a woman and child in his company would be such a
cruel brute as you make out this desert Ethiopian to be?
Sailors' stories, to gratify the melodramatic ears of Moll and
Poll and Sue! Bah! if there be an encampment, let's go
straight into it, and demand hospitality of them. Sure they
must be Arabs; and sure you've heard enough of Arab
hospitality?"

"More than's true, Terry," rejoined the young Englishman. "More than's true, I fear."

"You may well say that," said Colin, confirmingly. "From
what I've heard and read, — ay, and from something I've
seen while up the Mediterranean, — a more beggarly hospitality than that called Arab don't exist on the face of the
earth. It's all well enough, so long as you are one of themselves, and, like them, a believer in their pretended prophet.
Beyond that, an Arab has got no more hospitality than a
hyena. You're both fond of talking about skin-flint Scotch-
men."

"True," interrupted Terence, who, even in that serious
situation, could not resist such a fine opportunity for dis-
playing his Irish humor. "I never think of a Scotchman

without thinking of ais skin. 'God bless the gude Duke of Argyle!'"

"Shame, Terence!" interrupted Harry Blount; "our situation is too serious for jesting."

"He — all of us — may find it so before long," continued Colin, preserving his temper unruffled. "If that yelling crowd — that I can now hear plainer than ever — should come upon us, we 'll have something else to think of than jokes about 'gude Duke o' Argyle.' Hush! Do you hear that? Does it convince you that men and women are near? There are scores of both kinds."

Colin had come to a stop, the others imitating his example. They were now more distant from the breakers, — whose roar was somewhat deadened by the intervention of a sand-spur. In consequence, the other sounds were heard more distinctly. They could no longer be mistaken, — even by the incredulous O'Connor.

There were voices of men, women, and children, — cries and calls of quadrupeds, — each according to its own kind, all mingled together in what might have been taken for some nocturnal saturnalia of the Desert.

The crisis was that in which Sailor Bill had become a subject of dispute between the two sheiks, — in which not only their respective followers of the biped kind appeared to take part, but also every quadruped in the camp, — dogs and dromedaries, horses, goats, and sheep, — as if each had an interest in the ownership of the old man-o'-war's-man.

The grotesque chorus was succeeded by an interval of silence, uninterrupted and profound. This was while the two sheiks were playing their game of "helga," — the "chequers" of the Saära, with Sailor Bill as their stake.

During this tranquil interlude, the three midshipmen had advanced through the rock-strewn ravine, had crept cautiously inside the ridges that encircled the camp, and concealed by the sparse bushes of mimosa, and favored by the light of a full moon, had approached near enough to take note of what was passing among the tents.

What they saw there, and then, was confirmatory of the theory of the young Scotchman; and convinced not only Harry Blount, but Terence O'Connor, that the stories of Arab hospitality were not only untrue, but diametrically opposed to the truth.

There was old Bill before their faces, stripped to the shirt, — to the "buff," — surrounded by a circle of short, squat women, dark-skinned, with black hair, and eyes sparkling in the moonlight, who were torturing him with tongue and touch, — who pinched and spat upon him, — who looked altogether like a band of infernal Furies collected around some innocent victim that had fallen among them, and giving full play to their fiendish instincts!

Although they were witnesses to the subsequent rescue of Bill by the black sheik, — and the momentary release of the old sailor from his tormentors, — it did not increase their confidence in the crew who occupied the encampment.

From the way in which the old salt appeared to be treated, they could tell that he was regarded by the hosts into whose hands he had fallen, not as a guest, but simply as a "piece of goods," — just like any other waif of the wreck that had been washed on that inhospitable shore.

In whispers the three mids made known their thoughts to one another. Harry Blount no longer doubted the truth of Colin's statements; and O'Connor had become equally converted from his incredulity. The conduct of the women towards the unfortunate castaway — which all three witnessed — told like the tongue of a trumpet. It was cruel beyond question. What, when exercised, must be that of their men?

To think of leaving their old comrade in such keeping was not a pleasant reflection. It was like their abandoning him upon the sand-spit, — to the threatening engulfment of the tide. Even worse: for the angry breakers seemed less spiteful than the hags who surrounded him in the Arab camp.

Still, what could the boys do? Three midshipmen, — armed only with their tiny dirks, — what chance would they have among so many? There were scores of these sinewy sons of the Desert, —without counting the shrewish women, — each armed with gun and scimitar, any one of whom ought to have been more than a match for a "mid." It would have been sheer folly to have attempted a rescue. Despair only could have sanctioned such a course.

In a whispered consultation it was determined otherwise. The old sailor must be abandoned to his fate, just as he had been left upon the sand-spit. His youthful companions could only breathe a prayer in his behalf, and express a hope that, as upon the latter occasion, some providential chance should turn up in his favor, and he might again be permitted to rejoin them.

After communicating this hope to one another, all three turned their faces shoreward, determined to put as much space between themselves and the Arab encampment as night and circumstances would permit.

CHAPTER XXVI.

A CAUTIOUS RETREAT.

THE ravine, up which the maherry had carried the old man-o'-war's-man, ran perpendicularly to the trending of the seashore, and almost in a direct line from the beach to the valley, in which was the Arab encampment. It could not, however, be said to debouch into this valley. Across its mouth the sand-drift had formed a barrier, like a huge "snow-wreath," uniting the two parallel ridges that formed the sides of the ravine itself. This "mouth-piece" was not so high as either of the flanking ridges; though it was nearly a hundred feet above the level of the beach on one side, and the valley on the other. Its crest, viewed *en profile*, exhibited a saddle-shaped curve, the concavity turned upward.

Through the centre of this saddle of sand, and transversely, the camel had carried Bill; and over the same track the three midshipmen had gone in search of him.

They had seen the Arab tents from the summit of the "pass"; and had it been daylight, need have gone no nearer to note what was being there done. Even by the moonlight, they had been able to make out the forms of the horses, camels, men, and women; but not with sufficient distinctness to satisfy them as to what was going on.

For this reason had they descended into the valley, — creeping cautiously down the slope of the sand-wreath, and with equal caution advancing from boulder to bush, and bush to boulder.

On taking the back track to regain the beach, they still observed caution, — though perhaps not to such a degree as when approaching the camp. Their desire to put space between themselves and the barbarous denizens of the Desert, — of whose barbarity they had now obtained both ocular and auricular proof, — had very naturally deprived them of that prudent coolness which the occasion required. For all that, they did not retreat with reckless rashness; and all three arrived at the bottom of the sloping sand-ridge, without having any reason to think they had been observed.

But the most perilous point was yet to be passed. Against the face of the acclivity, there was not much danger of their being seen. The moon was shining on the other side. That which they had to ascend was in shadow, —

dark enough to obscure the outlines of their bodies to an eye looking in that direction, from such a distance as the camp. It was not while toiling up the slope that they dreaded detection, but at the moment when they must cross the saddle-shaped summit of the pass. Then, the moon being low down in the sky, directly in front of their faces, while the camp, still lower, was right behind their backs, it was not difficult to tell that their bodies would be exactly aligned between the luminary of night and the sparkling eyes of the Arabs, and that their figures would be exhibited in conspicuous outline.

It had been much the same way on their entrance to the oasis; but then they were not so well posted up in the peril of their position. They now wondered at their not having been observed while advancing; but that could be rationally accounted for, on the supposition that the Bedouins had been, at the time, too busy over old Bill to take heed of anything beyond the limits of their encampment.

It was different now. There was quiet in the camp, though both male and female figures could be seen stirring among the tents. The *saturnalia* that succeeded the castaway had come to a close. A comparative peacefulness reigned throughout the valley; but in this very tranquillity lay the danger which our adventurers dreaded.

With nothing else to attract their attention, the occupants of the encampments would be turning their eyes in every direction. If any of them should look westward at a given moment, — that is, while the three mids should be "in the saddle," — the latter could not fail to be discovered.

What was to be done? There was no other way leading forth from the valley. It was on all sides encircled by steep ridges of sand, — not so steep as to hinder them from being scaled; but on every side, except that on which they had entered, and by which they were about to make their exit, the moon was shining in resplendent brilliance. A cat could not have crawled up anywhere, without being seen from the tents, — even had she been of the hue of the sand itself.

A hurried consultation, held between the trio of adventurers, convinced them that there was nothing to be gained by turning back, — nothing by going to the right or the left. There was no other way — no help for it — but to scale the ridge in front, and "cut" as quickly as possible across the hollow of the "saddle."

There *was* one other way; or at least a deviation from the course which had thus recommended itself. It was to wait for the going down of the moon, before they should attempt the "crossing." This prudent project originated in the brain of the young Scotchman; and it might have been well if his companions had adopted the idea. But they would not. What they had seen of Saäran civilization had inspired them with a keen disgust for it; and they were only too eager to escape from its proximity. The punishment inflicted upon poor Bill had made a painful impression upon them; and they had no desire to become the victims of a similar chastisement.

Colin did not urge his counsels. He had been as much impressed by what he had seen as his companions, and was quite as desirous as they to give the Bedouins a "wide berth." Withdrawing his opposition, therefore, he acceded to the original design; and, without further ado, all three commenced crawling up the slope.

CHAPTER XXVII.

A QUEER QUADRUPED.

HALF way up, they halted, though not to take breath. Strong-limbed, long-winded lads like them — who could have "swarmed" in two minutes to the main truck of a man-o'-war — needed no such indulgence as that. Instead of one hundred feet of sloping sand, any one of them could have scaled Snowdon without stopping to look back.

Their halt had been made from a different motive. It was sudden and simultaneous, — all three having stopped at the same time, and without any previous interchange of speech. The same cause had brought them to that abrupt cessation in their climbing; and as they stood side by side, aligned upon one another, the eyes of all three were turned on the same object.

It was an animal, — a quadruped It could not be anything else if belonging to a sublunary world; and to this it appeared to belong. A strange creature notwithstanding; and one which none of the three remembered to have met before. The remembrance of something like it flitted across their brains, seen upon the shelves of a museum; but not enough of resemblance to give a clue for its identification.

The quadruped in question was not bigger than a "San Bernard," a "Newfoundland," or a mastiff: but seen as it was, it loomed larger than any of the three. Like these creatures, it was canine in shape — lupine we should rather say — but of an exceedingly grotesque and ungainly figure. A huge square head seemed set without neck upon its shoulders; while its fore limbs — out of all proportion longer than the hind ones — gave to the spinal column a sharp downward slant towards the tail. The latter appendage, short and "bunchy," ended abruptly, as if either cut

or " driven in," — adding to the uncouth appearance of the
animal.   A stiff hedge of hard bristles upon the back continued its *chevaux de frise* along the short, thick neck, till it
ended between two erect tufted ears.   Such was the shape
of the beast that had suddenly presented itself to the eyes of
our adventurers.

They had a good opportunity of observing its outlines.   It
was on the ridge towards the crest of which they were advancing.   The moon was shining beyond.   Every turn of
its head or body — every motion made by its limbs — was
conspicuously revealed against the luminous background of
the sky.

It was neither standing, nor at rest in any way.   Head,
limbs, and body were all in motion, — constantly changing,
not only their relative attitudes to one another, but their
absolute situation in regard to surrounding objects.

And yet the change was anything but arbitrary.   The
relative movements made by the members of the animal's
body, as well as the absolute alterations of position, were
all in obedience to strictly natural laws, — all repetitions of
the same manœuvre, worked with a monotony that seemed
mechanical.

The creature was pacing to and fro, like a well-trained
sentry, — its "round" being the curved crest of the sand-
ridge, from which it did not deviate to the licence of an
inch.   Backward and forward did it traverse the saddle in
a longitudinal direction, — now poised upon the pommel, —
now sinking downward into the seat, and then rising to the
level of the coup, — now turning in the opposite direction,
and retracing in long, uncouth strides, the path over which
it appeared to have been passing since the earliest hour of
its existence!

Independent of the surprise which the presence of this
animal had created, there was something in its aspect calcu
lated to cause terror.   Perhaps, had the mids known what

kind of creature it was, or been in any way apprized of its
real character, they would have paid less regard to its presence. Certainly not so much as they did: for, instead of
advancing upon it, and making their way over the crest of
the ridge, they stopped in their track, and held a whispered
consultation as to what they should do.

It is not to be denied that the barrier before them presented a formidable appearance. A brute, it appeared as big as
a bull — for magnified by the moonlight, and perhaps a little
by the fears of those who looked upon it, the quadruped was
quite *quadrupled* in size. Disputing their passage too; for
its movements made it manifest that such was its design.
Backwards and forwards, up and down that curving crest,
did it glide, with a nervous quickness, that hindered any
hope of being able to rush past it — either before or behind
— its own crest all the while erected, like that of the dragon
subdued by St. George.

With all his English "pluck" — even stimulated by this
resemblance to the national knight — Harry Blount felt shy
to approach that creature that challenged the passage of
himself and his companions.

Had there been no danger *en arrière*, perhaps our adventurers would have turned back into the valley, and left the
ugly quadruped master of the pass.

As it was, a different resolve was arrived at — necessity
being the dictator.

The three midshipmen, drawing their dirks, advanced in
line of battle up the slope. The Devil himself could scarce
withstand such an assault. England, Scotland, Ireland,
abreast — *tres juncti in uno* — united in thought, aim, and
action — was there aught upon earth — biped, quadruped,
or *mille-pied* — that must not yield to the charge?

If there was, it was not that animal oscillating along the
saddle of sand, progressing from pommel to cantle, like the
pendulum of a clock.

Whether natural or supernatural, long before our adventurers got near enough to decide, the creature, to use a phrase of very modern mention, "skedaddled," leaving them free — so far as it was concerned — to continue their retreat unmolested.

It did not depart, however, until after delivering a salute, that left our adventurers in greater doubt than ever of its true character. They had been debating among themselves whether it was a thing of the earth, of time, or something that belonged to eternity. They had seen it under a fair light, and could not decide. But now that they had heard it, — had listened to a strain of loud cachinnation, — scarce mocking the laughter of the maniac, — there was no escaping from the conclusion that what they had seen was either Satan himself, or one of his Ethiopian satellites!

CHAPTER XXVIII.

THE HUE AND CRY.

AS the strange creature that had threatened to dispute their passage was no longer in sight, and seemed, moreover, to have gone clear away, the three mids ceased to think any more of it, — their minds being given to making their way over the ridge without being seen by the occupants of the encampment.

Having returned their dirks to the sheath, they continued to advance towards the crest of the transverse sand-spar, as cautiously as at starting.

It is possible they might have succeeded in crossing, without being perceived, but for a circumstance of which they had taken too little heed. Only too well pleased at seeing

the strange quadruped make its retreat, they had been less
affected by its parting salutation, — weird and wild as this
had sounded in their ears.   But they had not thought of the
effects which the same salute had produced upon the people
of the Arab camp, causing all of them, as it did, to turn
their eyes in the direction whence it was heard.   To them
there was no mystery in that screaming cachinnation.   Unearthly as it had echoed in the ears of the three mids, it fell
with a perfectly natural tone on those of the Arabs : for it
was but one of the well-known voices of their desert home,
recognized by them as the cry of the *laughing hyena*.

The effect produced upon the encampment was twofold.
The children straying outside the tents, — like young chicks
frightened by the swooping of a hawk, — ran inward ; while
their mothers, after the manner of so many old hens, rushed
forth to take them under their protection.   The proximity
of a hungry hyena, — more especially one of the *laughing*
species, — was a circumstance to cause alarm.   All the
fierce creature required was a chance to close his strong,
vice-like jaws upon the limbs of one of those juvenile Ish-
maelites, and that would be the last his mother should ever
see of him.

Knowing this, the screech of the hyena had produced a
momentary commotion among the women and children of
the encampment.   Neither had the men listened to it un-
moved.   In hopes of procuring its skin for house or tent
furniture, and its flesh for food, — for these hungry wanderers will eat anything, — several had seized hold of their
long guns, and rushed forth from among the tents.

The sound had guided them as to the direction in which
they should go ; and as they ran forward, they saw, not a
hyena, but three human beings just mounting upon the summit of the sand-ridge, under the full light of the moon.   So
conspicuously did the latter appear upon the smooth crest
of the wreath, that there was no longer any chance of con-

5   G

cealment. Their dark blue dresses, the yellow buttons on their jackets, and the bands around their caps, were all discernible. It was the costume of the sea, not of the Saära. The Arab wreckers knew it at a glance; and, without waiting to give a second, every man of the camp sallied off in pursuit, — each, as he started, giving utterance to an ejaculation of surprise or pleasure.

Some hurried forward afoot, just as they had been going out to hunt the hyena; others climbed upon their swift camels; while a few, who owned horses, thinking they might do better with them, quickly caparisoned them, and came galloping on after the rest; all three sorts of pursuers, — footmen, horsemen, and maherrymen, — seemingly as intent upon a contest of screaming, as upon a trial of speed!

It is needless to say that the three midshipmen were, by this time, fully apprised of the "hue and cry" raised after them. It reached their ears just as they arrived upon the summit of the sand-ridge; and any doubt they might have had as to its meaning, was at once determined, when they saw the Arabs brandishing their arms, and rushing out like so many madmen from among the tents.

They stayed to see no more. To keep their ground could only end in their being captured and carried prisoners to the encampment; and after the spectacle they had just witnessed, in which the old man-o'-war's-man had played such a melancholy part, any fate appeared preferable to that.

With some such fear all three were affected; and simultaneously yielding to it, they turned their backs upon the pursuit, and rushed headlong down the ravine, up which they had so imprudently ascended.

CHAPTER XXIX.

A SUBAQUEOUS ASYLUM.

AS the gorge was of no great length, and the downward incline in their favor, they were not long in getting to its lower end, and out to the level plain that formed the sea-beach.

In their hurried traverse thither, it had not occurred to them to inquire for what purpose they were running towards the sea? There could be no chance of their escaping in that direction; nor did there appear to be much in any other, afoot as they were, and pursued by mounted men. The night was too clear to offer any opportunity of hiding themselves, especially in a country where there was neither "brake, brush, nor scaur" to conceal them. Go which way they would, or crouch wherever they might, they would be almost certain of being discovered by their lynx-eyed enemies.

There was but one way in which they *might* have stood a chance of getting clear, at least for a time. This was to have turned aside among the sand ridges, and by keeping along some of the lateral hollows, double back upon their pursuers. There were several such side hollows; for on going up the main ravine they had observed them, and also in coming down; but in their hurry to put space between themselves and their pursuers, they had overlooked this chance of concealment.

At best it was but slim, though it was the only one that offered. It only presented itself when it was too late for them to take advantage of it, — only after they had got clear out of the gully and stood upon the open level of the sea-beach, within less than two hundred yards of the sea itself. There they halted, partly to recover breath and partly to hold counsel as to their further course.

There was not much time for either; and as the three stood in a triangle with their faces turned towards each other, the moonlight shone upon lips and cheeks blanched with dismay.

It now occurred to them for the first time, and simultaneously, that there was no hope of their escaping, either by flight or concealment.

They were already some distance out upon the open plain, as conspicuous upon its surface of white sand as would have been three black crows in the middle of a field six inches under snow.

They saw that they had made a mistake. They should have stayed among the sand-ridges and sought shelter in some of the deep gullies that divided them. They bethought them of going back; but a moment's deliberation was sufficient to convince them that this was no longer practicable. There would not be time, scarce even to re-enter the ravine, before their pursuers would be upon them.

It was an instinct that had caused them to rush towards the sea — their habitual home, for which they had thoughtlessly sped — notwithstanding their late rude ejection from it. Now that they stood upon its shore, as if appealing to it for protection, it seemed still desirous of spurning them from its bosom, and leaving them without mercy to their merciless enemies!

A line of breakers trended parallel to the water's edge — scarce a cable's length from the shore, and not two hundred yards from the spot where they had come to a pause.

They were not very formidable breakers — only the tide rolling over a sand-bar, or a tiny reef of rocks. It was at best but a big surf, crested with occasional flakes of foam, and sweeping in successive swells against the smooth beach.

What was there in all this to fix the attention of the fugitives — for it had? The seething flood seemed only to hiss at their despair!

And yet almost on the instant after suspending their flight, they had turned their faces towards it — as if some object of interest had suddenly shown itself in the surf. Object there was none — nothing but the flakes of white froth and the black vitreous waves over which it was dancing.

It was not an object, but a purpose that was engaging their attention — a resolve that had suddenly sprung up within their minds — almost as suddenly to be carried into execution. After all, their old home was not to prove so inhospitable. It would provide them with a place of concealment!

The thought occurred to all three almost at the same instant of time; though Terence was the first to give speech to it.

"By Saint Patrick!" he exclaimed, "let's take to the wather! Them breakers 'll give us a good hiding-place. I've hid before now in that same way, when taking a moonlight bath on the coast of owld Galway. I did it to scare my schoolfellows — by making believe I was drowned. What say ye to our trying it?"

His companions made no reply. They had scarce even waited for the wind-up of his harangue. Both had equally perceived the feasibility of the scheme; and yielding to a like impulse, all three started into a fresh run, with their faces turned towards the sea.

In less than a score of seconds, they had crossed the strip of strand; and in a similarly short space of time were plunging — thigh deep — through the water; still striding impetuously onward, as if they intended to wade across the Atlantic!

A few more strides, however, brought them to a stand — just inside the line of breakers — where the seething waters, settling down into a state of comparative tranquillity, presented a surface variegated with large clouts of floating froth.

Amidst this mottling of white and black, even under the bright moonlight, it would have been difficult for the keenest eye to have detected the head of a human being — supposing the body to have been kept carefully submerged; and under this confidence, the mids were not slow in submerging themselves.

Ducking down, till their chins touched the water, all three were soon as completely out of sight — to any eye looking from the shore — as if Neptune, pitying their forlorn condition, had stretched forth his trident with a bunch of seaweed upon its prongs, to screen and protect them.

CHAPTER XXX.

THE PURSUERS NONPLUSSED.

NOT a second too soon had they succeeded in making good their entry into this subaqueous asylum. Scarce had their chins come in contact with the water, when the voices of men — accompanied by the baying of dogs, the snorting of maherries, and the neighing of horses — were heard within the gorge, from which they had just issued; and in a few minutes after a straggling crowd, composed of these various creatures, came rushing out of the ravine. Of men, afoot and on horseback, twenty or more were seen pouring forth; all, apparently, in hot haste, as if eager to be in at the death of some object pursued, — that could not possibly escape capture.

Once outside the jaws of the gully, the irregular cavalcade advanced scatteringly over the plain Only for a short distance, however; for, as if by a common understanding rather than in obedience to any command, all came to a halt.

A silence followed this halt,—apparently proceeding from astonishment. It was general,—it might be said universal,—for even the animals appeared to partake of it! At all events, some seconds transpired during which the only sound heard was the sighing of the sea, and the only motion to be observed was the sinking and swelling of the waves.

The Saäran rovers on foot,—as well as those that were mounted,—their horses, dogs, and camels, as they stood upon that smooth plain, seemed to have been suddenly transformed into stone, and set like so many sphinxes in the sand.

In truth it *was* surprise that had so transfixed them,—the men, at least; and their well-trained animals were only acting in obedience to a habit taught them by their masters, who, in the pursuit of their predatory life, can cause these creatures to be both silent and still, whenever the occasion requires it.

For their surprise,—which this exhibition of it proved to be extreme,—the Sons of the Desert had sufficient reason. They had seen the three midshipmen on the crest of the sand-ridge; had even noted the peculiar garb that bedecked their bodies,—all this beyond doubt. Notwithstanding the haste with which they had entered on the pursuit, they had not continued it either in a reckless or improvident manner. Skilled in the ways of the wilderness,—cautious as cats,—they had continued the chase; those in the lead from time to time assuring themselves that the game was still before them. This they had done by glancing occasionally to the ground, where shoe-tracks in the soft sand—three sets of them—leading to and fro, were sufficient evidence that the three mids must have gone back to the *embouchure* of the ravine, and thither emerged upon the open sea-beach.

Where were they now?

Looking up the smooth strand as far as the eye could reach, and down it to a like distance, there was no place where a crab could have screened itself; and these Saärau wreckers, well acquainted with the coast, knew that in neither direction was there any other ravine or gully into which the fugitives could have retreated.

No wonder, then, that the pursuers wondered, even to speechlessness.

Their silence was of short duration, though it was succeeded only by cries expressing their great surprise, among which might have been distinguished their usual invocations to Allah and the Prophet. It was evident that a superstitious feeling had arisen in their minds, not without its usual accompaniment of fear; and although they no longer kept their places, the movement now observable among them was that they gathered closer together, and appeared to enter upon a grave consultation.

This was terminated by some of them once more proceeding to the *embouchure* of the ravine, and betaking themselves to a fresh scrutiny of the tracks made by the shoes of the midshipmen; while the rest sat silently upon their horses and maherries awaiting the result.

The foot-marks of the three mids were still easily traceable — even on the ground already trampled by the Arabs, their horses, and maherries. The "cloots" of a camel would not have been more conspicuous in the mud of an English road, than were the shoe-prints of the three young seamen in the sands of the Saära. The Arab trackers had no difficulty in making them out; and in a few minutes had traced them from the mouth of the gorge, almost in a direct line to the sea. There, however, there was a breadth of wet sea-beach — where the springy sand instantly obliterated any foot-mark that might be made upon it — and there the tracts ended.

But why should they have extended farther? No one could have gone beyond that point, without either walking straight into the water, or keeping along the strip of sea beach, upwards or downwards.

The fugitives could not have escaped in either way — unless they had taken to the water, and committed suicide by drowning themselves! Up the coast, or down it, they would have been seen to a certainty.

Their pursuers, clustering around the place where the tracks terminated, were no wiser than ever. Some of them were ready to believe that drowning had been the fate of the castaways upon their coast, and so stated it to their companions. But they spoke only conjectures, and in tones that told them, like the rest, to be under the influence of some superstitious fear. Despite their confidence in the protection of their boasted Prophet, they felt a natural dread of that wilderness of waters, less known to them than the wilderness of sand.

Ere long they withdrew from its presence, and betook themselves back to their encampment, under a half belief that the three individuals seen and pursued had either drowned themselves in the great deep, or by some mysterious means known to these strange men of the sea, had escaped across its far-reaching waters!

CHAPTER XXXI.

A DOUBLE PREDICAMENT.

SHORT time as their pursuers had stayed upon the strand, it seemed an age to the submerged midshipmen.

On first placing themselves in position, they had chosen a spot where, with their knees resting upon the bottom, they could just hold their chins above water. This would enable them to hold their ground without any great difficulty, and for some time they so maintained it.

5 *

Soon, however, they began to perceive that the water was
rising around them, — a circumstance easily explained by
the influx of the tide. The rise was slow and gradual: but,
for all that, they saw that should they require to remain in
their place of concealment for any length of time, drowning
must be their inevitable destiny.

A means of avoiding this soon presented itself. Inside
the line of breakers, the water shoaled gradually towards
the shore. By advancing in this direction they could still
keep to the same depth. This course they adopted — gliding cautiously forward upon their knees, whenever the tide
admonished them to repeat the manœuvre.

This state of affairs would have been satisfactory enough,
but for a circumstance that, every moment, was making itself more apparent. At each move they were not only approaching nearer to their enemies, scattered along the
strand; but as they receded from the line of the breakers,
the water became comparatively tranquil, and its smooth
surface, less confused by the masses of floating foam, was
more likely to betray them to the spectators on the shore.

To avoid this catastrophe — which would have been fatal
— they moved shoreward, only when it became absolutely
necessary to do so, often permitting the tidal waves to sweep
completely over the crown of their heads, and several times
threaten suffocation.

Under circumstances so trying, so apparently hopeless, most
lads — aye, most men — would have submitted to despair,
and surrendered themselves to a fate apparently unavoidable.
But with that true British pluck — combining the tenacity
of the Scotch terrier, the English bulldog, and the Irish
staghound — the three youthful representatives of the triple
kingdom determined to hold on.

And they held on, with the waves washing against their
cheeks — and at intervals quite over their heads — with the
briny fluid rushing into their ears and up their nostrils, until

one after another began to believe, that there would be no alternative between surrendering to the cruel sea, or to the not less cruel sons of the Saära.

As they were close together, they could hold council, — conversing all the time in something louder than a whisper. There was no risk of their being overheard. Though scarce a cable's length from the shore, the hoarse soughing of the surf would have drowned the sound of their voices, even if uttered in a much louder tone; but being skilled in the acoustics of the ocean, they exchanged their thoughts with due caution; and while encouraging one another to remain firm, they speculated freely upon the chances of escaping from their perilous predicament.

While thus occupied, a *predicament* of an equally perilous, and still more singular kind, was in store for them. They had been hitherto advancing towards the water's edge, — in regular progression with the influx of the tide, — all the while upon their knees. This, as already stated, had enabled them to sustain themselves steadily, without showing anything more than three quarters of the head above the surface.

All at once, however, the water appeared to deepen; and by going upon their knees they could no longer surmount the waves, — even with their eyes. By moving on towards the beach, they might again get into shallow water; but just at this point the commotion caused by the breakers came to a termination, and the flakes of froth, with the surrounding spray of bubbles, here bursting, one after another, left the surface of the sea to its restored tranquillity. Anything beyond — a cork, or the tiniest waif of seaweed — could scarce fail to be seen from the strand, — though the latter was itself constantly receding as the tide flowed inward.

The submerged middies were now in a dilemma they had not dreamed of. By holding their ground, they could not fail to "go under." By advancing further, they would run the risk of being discovered to the enemy.

Their first movement was to get up from their knees, and raise their heads above water by standing in a crouched attitude on their feet. This they had done before, — more than once, — returning to the posture of supplication only when too tired to sustain themselves.

This they attempted again, and determined to continue it to the last moment, — in view of the danger of approaching nearer to the enemy.

To their consternation they now found it would no longer avail them. Scarce had they risen erect before discovering that even in this position they were immersed to the chin, and after plunging a pace or two forward, they were still sinking deeper. They could feel that their feet were not resting on firm bottom, but constantly going down.

"A quicksand!" was the apprehension that rushed simultaneously into the minds of all three!

Fortunately for them, the Arabs at that moment, yielding to their fatalist fears, had faced away from the shore; else the plunging and splashing made by them in their violent endeavors to escape from the quicksand, could not have failed to dissipate these superstitions, and cause their pursuers to complete the capture they had so childlessly relinquished.

As it chanced, the Saäran wreckers saw nothing of all this; and as the splashing sounds, which otherwise might have reached them, were drowned by the louder *sough* of the sea, they returned toward their encampment in a state of perplexity bordering upon bewilderment!

CHAPTER XXXII.

ONCE MORE THE MOCKING LAUGH.

AFTER a good deal of scrambling and struggling, our adventurers succeeded in getting clear of the quicksand, and planting their feet upon firmer bottom, — a little nearer to the water's edge. Though at this point more exposed than they wished to be, they concealed themselves as well as they could, holding their faces under the water up to the eyes.

Though believing that their enemies were gone for good, they dared not as yet wade out upon the beach. The retiring pursuers would naturally be looking back; and as the moon was still shining clearly as ever, they might be seen from a great distance.

They feel that they would not be safe in leaving their place of concealment until the horde had recrossed the ridge, and descended once more into the oasis that contained their encampment.

Making a rough calculation as to the time it would take for the return journey, — and allowing a considerable margin against the eventuality of any unforeseen delay, — the mids remained in their subaqueous retreat, without any material change of position.

When at length it appeared to them that the " coast was clear," they rose to their feet, and commenced wading towards the strand.

Though no longer believing themselves observed, they proceeded silently and with caution, — the only noise made among them being the chattering of their teeth, which were going like three complete sets of castanets.

This they could not help. The night breeze playing upon the saturated garments, — that clung coldly around their bodies, — chilled them to the very bones ; and not only their teeth, but their knees knocked together, as they staggered towards the beach.

Just before reaching it, an incident arose that filled them with fresh forebodings. The strange beast that had threatened to intercept their retreat over the ridge, once more appeared before their eyes. It was either the same, or one of the same kind, — equally ugly, and to all appearance, equally determined to dispute their passage.

It was now patrolling the strand close by the water's edge, — going backwards and forwards, precisely as it had done along the saddle-shaped sand wreath, — all the while keeping its hideous face turned towards them. With the moon behind their backs, they had a better view of it than before ; but this, though enabling them to perceive that it was some strange quadruped, did not in any way improve their opinion of it. They could see that it was covered with a coat of long shaggy hair, of a brindled brown color ; and that from a pair of large orbs, set obliquely in its head, gleamed forth a fierce, sullen light.

How it had come there they knew not ; but there it was. Judging from the experience of their former encounter with it they presumed it would again retreat at their approach ; and, once more drawing their dirks, they advanced boldly towards it.

They were not deceived. Long before they were near, the uncouth creature turned tail ; and, again giving utterance to its unearthly cry, scampered off towards the ravine, — in whose shadowy depths it soon disappeared from their view.

Supposing they had nothing further to fear, our adventurers stepped out upon the strand, and commenced consultation as to their future course.

To keep on down the coast and get as far as possible from the Arab encampment, — was the thought of all three ; and as they were unanimous in this, scarce a moment was wasted in coming to a determination. Once resolved, they faced southward; and started off as briskly as their shivering frames and saturated garments would allow them.

There was not much to cheer them on their way, — only the thought that they had so adroitly extricated themselves from a dread danger. But even this proved only a fanciful consolation; for scarce had they made a score of steps along the strand, when they were brought to a sudden halt, by hearing a noise that appeared to proceed from the ravine behind them.

It was a slight noise, something like a snort, apparently made by some animal; and, for the moment, they supposed it to come from the ugly quadruped that, after saluting them, had retreated up the gorge.

On turning their eyes in that direction, they at once saw that they were mistaken. A quadruped had produced the noise; but one of a very different kind from the hairy brute with which they had parted. Just emerging from the shadow of the sand-hills, they perceived a huge creature, whose uncouth shape proclaimed it to be a camel.

The sight filled them with consternation. Not that it was a camel; but because, at the same time, they discovered that there was a man upon its back, who, brandishing a long weapon, was urging the animal towards them.

The three midshipmen made no effort to continue the journey thus unexpectedly interrupted. They saw that any attempt to escape from such a fast-going creature would be idle. Encumbered as they were with their wet garments, they could not have distanced a lame duck; and, resigning themselves to the chances of destiny, they stood awaiting the encounter.

CHAPTER XXXIII.

A CUNNING SHEIK.

WHEN the camel and its rider first loomed in sight, — indistinctly seen under the shadow of the sand dunes, — our adventurers had conceived a faint hope that it might be Sailor Bill.

It was possible, they thought, that the old man-o-war's-man, left unguarded in the camp, might have laid hands on the maherry that had made away with him, and pressed it into service to assist his escape.

The hope was entertained only for an instant. Bill had encountered no such golden opportunity; but was still a prisoner in the tent of the black sheik, surrounded by his shrewish tormentors.

It was the maherry, however, that was seen coming back. for as it came near the three middies recognized the creature whose intrusion upon their slumbers of the preceding night had been the means, perhaps, of saving their lives.

Instead of a Jack Tar now surmounting its high hunch, they saw a little wizen-faced individual with sharp angular features, and a skin of yellowish hue puckered like parchment. He appeared to be at least sixty years of age; while his costume, equipments, and above all, a certain authoritative bearing, bespoke him to be one of the head men of the horde.

Such in truth was he, — one of the two sheiks, — the old Arab to whom the straying camel belonged; and who was now mounted on his own maherry.

His presence on the strand at this, to our adventurers, most inopportune moment, requires explanation.

He had been on the beach before, along with the others: and had gone away with the rest. But instead of contin-

uing on to the encampment, he had fallen behind in the ravine; where, under the cover of some rocks, and favored by
the obscure light within the gorge, he had succeeded in giving his comrades the slip. There he had remained, — permitting the rest to recross the ridge, and return to the tents.

He had not taken these steps without an object. Less
superstitious than his black brother sheik, he knew there
must be some natural explanation of the disappearance of
the three castaways; and he had determined to seek, and if
possible, to discover it.

It was not mere curiosity that prompted him to this determination. He had been all out of sorts, with himself, since
losing Sailor Bill in the game of *helga;* and he was desirous
of obtaining some compensation for his ill-luck, by capturing the three castaways who had so mysteriously disappeared.

As to their having either drowned themselves, or walked
away over the waste of waters, the old sheik had seen too
many Saäran summers and winters to give credence either
to one tale or the other. He knew they would turn up
again; and though he was not quite certain of the where, he
more than half suspected it. He had kept his suspicions to
himself, — not imparting them even to his own special followers. By the laws of the Saära, a slave taken by any
one of the tribe belongs not to its chief, but to the individual who makes the capture. For this reason, had the cunning sexagenarian kept his thoughts to himself, and fallen
solus into the rear of the returning horde.

It might be supposed that he would have made some of
his following privy to his plan, — for the sake of having
help to effect such a wholesale capture. But no. His experience as a " Barbary wrecker " had taught him that
there would be no danger, — no likelihood of resistance, —
even though the castaways numbered thirty instead of
three.

H

Armed with this confidence, and his long gun, he had returned down the ravine; and laid in wait near its mouth, —
at a point where he commanded a view of the coast line, to
the distance of more than a mile on each side of him.

His vigil was soon rewarded: by seeing the three individuals for whom it had been kept step forth from the sea,
— as if emerging from its profoundest depths, — and stand
conspicuously upon the beach.

He had waited for nothing more; but, giving the word to
his maherry, had ridden out of the ravine, and was now
advancing with all speed upon the tracks of the retreating
mids.

CHAPTER XXXIV.

A QUEER ENCOUNTER.

IN about threescore seconds from the time he was first seen
pursuing them, the old sheik was up to the spot where
our adventurers had awaited him.

His first salute appeared to be some words of menace or
command, — rendered more emphatic by a series of gestures
made with his long gun; which was successively pointed at
the heads of the three. Of course, none of them understood
what was said; but his gesticulations made it clear enough,
that he required their company to the Arab encampment.

Their first impulse was to yield obedience to this command; and Terence had given a sign of assent, which was
acquiesced in by Colin. Not so Master Blount, in whom
the British bull-dog had become aroused even to the showing of his teeth.

" See him hanged first!" cried Harry. " What! yield up
to an old monkey like that, and walk tamely to the camp at

THE SHEIK CAPTURED

the tail of his camel? No such thing! If I am to become a prisoner, it will be to one who can take me."

Terence, rather ashamed at having shown such facile submission, now rushed to the opposite extreme; and drawing his dirk, cried out, —

"By Saint Patrick! I'm with you, Harry! Let's die, rather than yield ourselves prisoners to such a queer old curmudgeon!"

Colin, before declaring himself, glanced sharply around, — carrying his eye towards the *embouchure* of the ravine, to assure himself that the Arab was alone.

As there was nobody else in sight, — and no sound heard that would indicate the proximity of any one, — it was probable enough that the rider of the maherry was the only enemy opposed to them.

"The deil take him!" cried Colin, after making his cautious reconnoissance. "If he take us, he must first fight for it. Come on, old skin-flint! you'll find we're true British tars, — ready for a score of such as you."

The three youths had by this time unsheathed their shining daggers, and thrown themselves into a sort of triangle, the maherry in their midst.

The old sheik — unprepared for such a reception — was altogether taken aback by it; and for some seconds sate upon his high perch seemingly irresolute how to act.

Suddenly his rage appeared to rise to such a pitch, that he could no longer command his actions; and bringing the long gun to his shoulder, he levelled it at Harry Blount, — who had been foremost in braving him.

The stream of smoke, pouring forth from its muzzle, for a moment enveloped the form of the youthful mariner; but from the midst of that sulphury *nimbus* came forth a clear manly voice, pronouncing the word "Missed!"

"Thank God!" cried Terence and Colin, in a breath; "now we have him in our power! He can't load again! Let's on him all together! Heave ho!"

And uttering this nautical phrase of encouragement, the three mids, with naked dirks, rushed simultaneously towards the maherry.

The Arab, old as he may have been, showed no signs either of stiffness or decrepitude. On the contrary he exhibited all the agility of a tiger-cat; along with a fierce determination to continue the combat he had initiated, — notwithstanding the odds that were against him. On discharging his gun, he had flung the useless weapon to the ground; and instead of it now grasped a long curving scimitar, with which he commenced cutting around him in every direction.

Thus armed, he had the advantage of his assailants; for while he might reach any one of them by a quick cut, they with their short dirks could not come within thrusting-distance of him, without imminent danger of having their arms, or perchance their heads, lopped sheer off their shoulders.

Defensively, too, had the rider of the maherry an advantage over his antagonists. While within distance of them, at the point of his curving blade, seated upon his high perch, he was beyond the reach of their weapons. Get close to him as they might, and spring as high as they were able, they could not bring the tips of their daggers in contact with his skin.

In truth, there seemed no chance for them to inflict the slightest wound upon him; while at each fresh " wheel " of the maherry, and each new sweep of the scimitar, one or other of them was in danger of decapitation !

On first entering upon the fight, our adventurers had not taken into account the impregnable position of their antagonist. Soon, however, did they discover the advantages in his favor, with their own proportionate drawbacks. To neutralize these was the question that now occupied them. If something was not done soon, one or other — perhaps all three — would have to succumb to that keen cutting of the scimitar.

" Let's kill the camel!" cried Harry Blount, " that 'll bring him within reach ; and then — "

The idea of the English youth was by no means a bad one ; and perhaps would have been carried out. But before he could finish his speech, another scheme had been conceived by Terence, — who had already taken steps towards its execution.

It was this that had interrupted Harry Blount in the utterance of his counsel.

At school the young Milesian had been distinguished in the exercise of vaulting. " Leap-frog " had been his especial delight ; and no mountebank could bound to a greater height than he. At this crisis he remembered his old accomplishment, and called it to his aid.

Seeking an opportunity, — when the head of the maherry was turned towards his comrades, and its tail to himself, — he made an energetic rush ; sprang half a score of feet from the ground ; and flinging apart his feet, while in the air, came down " stride legs " upon the croup of the camel.

It was fortunate for the old Arab that the effort thus made by the amateur *saltimbanque* had shaken the dirk from his grasp, — else, in another instant, the camel would have ceased to " carry double."

As it was, its two riders continued upon its back ; but in such close juxtaposition, that it would have required sharp eyes and a good light to tell that more than one individual was mounted upon it.

Fast enfolded in the arms of the vigorous young Hibernian, could scarce be distinguished the carcass of the old Arab sheik, — shrunken to half size by the powerful compression ; while the scimitar, so late whistling with perilous impetuosity through the air, was now seen lying upon the sand, — its gleam no longer striking terror into the hearts of those whose heads it had been threatening to lop off !

CHAPTER XXXV.

HOLDING ON TO THE HUMP.

THE struggle between Terence and the sheik still continued, upon the back of the maherry. The object of the young Irishman was to unhorse, or rather *un-camel*, his antagonist, and get him to the ground.

This design the old Arab resisted toughly, and with all his strength, knowing that dismounted he would be no match for the trio of stout lads whom he had calculated on capturing at his ease. Once *à pied* he would be at their mercy, since he was now altogether unarmed. His gun had been unloaded; and the shining scimitar, of which he had made such a dangerous display, was no longer in his grasp. As already stated it had fallen to the ground, and at that precious moment was being picked up by Colin; who in all probability would have used it upon its owner, had not the latter contrived to escape beyond its reach.

The mode of the sheik's escape was singular enough. Still tenaciously holding on to the hump, from which the young Irishman was using every effort to detach him, he saw that his only chance of safety lay in retreating from the spot, and, by this means, separating the antagonist who clutched him from the two others that threatened upon the ground below.

A signal shout to the maherry was sufficient to effect his purpose. On hearing it, the well-trained quadruped wheeled, as upon a pivot, and in a shambling, but quick pace, started back towards the ravine, whence it had late issued.

To their consternation Colin and Harry beheld this unexpected movement; and before either of them could lay hold of the halter, — now trailing along the sand, — the maherry was going at a rate of speed which they vainly endeavored

to surpass They could only follow in its wake, — as they
did so, shouting to Terence to let go his hold of the sheik,
and take his chance of a tumble to the ground.

Their admonitions appeared not to be heeded. They
were not needed, — at least after a short interval had
elapsed.

At first the young Irishman had been so intent on his endeavors to dismount his adversary, that he did not notice the
signal given to the maherry, nor the retrograde movement it
had inaugurated. Not until the camel was re-entering the
ravine, and the steep sides of the sand dunes cast their dark
shadows before him, did he observe that he was being carried away from his companions.

Up to this time he had been vainly striving to detach the
sheik from his hold upon the hump. On perceiving the danger, however, he desisted from this design, and at once entered upon a struggle of a very different kind, — to detach
himself.

In all probability this would have proved equally difficult,
for, struggle as he might, the tough old Arab, no longer
troubling himself about the control of his camel, had twisted
his sinewy fingers under the midshipman's dirk-belt, and
held the latter in juxtaposition to his own body, supported
by the hump of the maherry, as if his very life depended on
not letting go.

A lucky circumstance — and this only — hindered the
young Irishman from being carried to the Arab encampment; a circumstance very similar to that which on the
preceding night had led to the capture of that same camel.

Its halter was again trailing.

Its owner, occupied with the "double" which it had so
unexpectedly been called upon to carry, was conducting it
only by his voice, and had neither thought nor hands for the
halter.

Once again the trailing end got into the split hoof — once

again the maherry was tripped up; and came down neck foremost upon the sand.

Its load was spilled — Bedouin and Hibernian coming together to the ground — both, if not dangerously hurt, at least so shaken, as, for some seconds, to be deprived of their senses.

Neither had quite recovered from the shock, when Harry Blount and Colin, coming up in close pursuit, stooped over the prostrate pair; and neither Arab nor Irishman was very clear in his comprehension, when a crowd of strange creatures closed around them, and took possession of the whole party; as they did so yelling like a cohort of fiends.

In the obfuscation of his "sivin" senses, the young Irishman may have scarcely understood what was passing around him. It was too clear to his companions, — clear as a catastrophe could be to those who are its victims.

The shot fired by the sheik, if failing in the effects intended, had produced a result almost equally fatal to the three fugitives, — it had given warning to the Arabs in their encampment; who, again sallying forth, had arrived just in time to witness the "decadence" of the camel, and now surrounded the group that encircled it.

The courageous representative of England and the cool young Scotchman were both taken by surprise, too much so to give them a chance of thinking either of resistance or flight; while the mind of the Irish middy, from a different cause, was equally in a hopeless "muddle."

It resulted in all three being captured and conducted up the ravine towards the camp of the wreckers.

CHAPTER XXXVI.

OUR ADVENTURERS IN UNDRESS.

OUR adventurers made their approach to the *douar*, — for such is the title of an Arab encampment, — with as much unwillingness as Sailor Bill had done but an hour before. Equally *sans cérémonie*, or even with less ceremony, did they enter among the tents, and certainly in a less becoming costume, — since all three were stark naked with the exception of their shirts.

This was the only article of clothing their captors had left upon their backs; and so far as comfort was concerned, they would have been as well without it: for there was not a thread of the striped cotton that was not saturated with sea-water.

It was a wonder that even these scanty garments were not taken from them; considering the eagerness with which they had been divested of everything else.

On the instant after being laid hold of, they had been stripped with as much rapidity, as if their bodies were about to be submitted to some ignominious chastisement. But they knew it was not that — only a desire on the part of their captors to obtain possession of their clothes — every article of which became the subject of a separate contention, and more than one leading to a dispute that was near terminating in a contest between two scimitars.

In this way their jackets and dreadnought trowsers — their caps and shoes — their dirks, belts, and pocket paraphernalia — were distributed among nearly as many claimants as there were pieces.

You may suppose that modesty interfered to reserve to them their shirts? Such a supposition would be altogether erroneous. There is no such word in the Bedouin vocabulary — no such feeling in the Bedouin breast.

6

In the *douar* to which they were conducted were lads as old as they, and lasses too, without the semblance of clothing upon their nude bodies ; not even a shirt, — not even the orientally famed fig-leaf !

The reason of their being allowed to retain their homely garments had nothing to do with any sentiment of delicacy. For the favor, — if such it could be called, — they were simply indebted to the avarice of the old sheik, who, having recovered from the stunning effects of his tumble, claimed all three as his captives, and *their shirts along with them !*

His claim as to their persons was not disputed ; they were his by Saäran custom. So, too, would their clothing, had his capture been complete ; but as there was a question about this, a distribution of the garments had been demanded and acceded to.

The sheik, however, would not agree to giving up the shirts ; loudly declaring that they belonged to the skin ; and after some discussion on this moot point, his claim was allowed ; and our adventurers were spared the shame of entering the Arab encampment *in puris naturalibus.*

In their shirts did they once more stand face to face with Sailor Bill, not a bit better clad than they : for though the old man-o'-war's-man was still " anchored " by the marquee of the black sheik, his " toggery " had long before been distributed throughout the *douar ;* and scarce a tent but contained some portion of his " belongings."

His youthful comrades saw, but were not permitted to approach him. They were the undisputed property of the rival chieftain, — to whose tent they were taken ; but not until they had " run a muck " among the women and children, very similar to that which Bill had to submit to himself. It terminated in a similar manner : that is, by their *owner* taking them under his protection, — not from any motives of humanity, but simply to save his property from receiving damage at the hands of the incarnate female furies, who seemed to take delight in maltreating them !

The old sheik, after allowing his *fair* followers, with their juvenile *neophites*, for some length of time to indulge in their customary mode of saluting strange captives, with-drew the latter beyond the reach of persecution, to a place assigned them under the shadow of his tent.   There, with a sinewy Arab standing over them, — though as often squatted beside them, — they were permitted to pass the remainder of the night, if not in sleep at least in a state of tranquillity.

CHAPTER XXXVII.

THE CAPTIVES IN CONVERSATION.

THIS tranquillity only related to any disturbance expe rienced from their captors.   There was none.

These had been on the eve of striking their tents, and moving off to some other oasis, — previous to the last inci-dent that had arisen.

As already stated, the two sheiks, by a mutual under-standing, had been about to shake hands, and separate, — the son of Japhet going north, to the markets of Morocco, while the descendant of Ham was to face homeward to his more tropical and appropriate clime, — under the skies of Timbuctoo.

The " windfall " that had so unexpectedly dropped into the douar; first in the shape of Sailor Bill, — and after-wards, in more generous guise, by the capture of the three " young gentlemen " of the gunroom, — had caused some change in the plans of their captors.

By mutual understanding between the two sheiks, some-thing was to be done in the morning; and their design of separating was deferred to another day.

The order to strike tents had been countermanded: and both tribes retired to rest, — as soon as the captives had been disposed of for the night.

The douar was silent, — so far as the children of Ham and Japhet were concerned. Even *their* children had ceased to clamor and squall.

At intervals might be heard the neigh of a Barbary horse, the barking of a dog, the bleating of a goat, or a sound yet more appropriate to the scene, the snorting of a maherry.

In addition to these, human voices were heard. But they proceeded from the throats of the sons of Shem. For the most part they were uttered in a low tone, as the three mid-shipmen conversed seriously and earnestly together; but occasionally they became elevated to a higher pitch, when Sailor Bill, guarded on the opposite side of the encampment — took part in the conversation, and louder speech was necessary to the interchange of thought between him and his fellow-captives.

The Arab watchers offered no interruption. They under-stood not a word of what was being said, and so long as the conversation of their captives did not disturb the douar, they paid no heed to it.

" What have they done to you, Bill?" was the first ques-tion asked by the new comers, after they had been left free to make inquiries.

" Faix!" responded the sailor, for it was Terry who had put the interrogatory: "iverything they cowld think av — iverything to make an old salt as uncomfortable as can be. They 've not left a sound bone in my body; nor a spot on my skin that 's not ayther pricked or scratched wid thar cruel thorns. My carcass must be like an old seventy-four after comin' out av action — as full av holes as a meal sieve."

"But what did they do to you, Bill?" said Colin, almost literally repeating the interrogatory of Terence.

The sailor detailed his experiences since entering the encampment.

"It's very clear," remarked the young Scotchman, "that we need look for nothing but ill-treatment at the hands of these worse than savages. I suppose they intend making slaves of us."

"That at least," quietly assented Harry.

"Sartin," said the sailor. "They've let me know as much a'ready. There be two captains to their crew; one's the smoke-dried old sinner as brought yer in; the other a big nayger, as black as the ace o' spades. You saw the swab? He's inside the tent here. He's my master. The two came nigh quarrelling about which should have me, and settled it by some sort o' a game they played wi' balls of kaymal's dung. The black won me; an' that's why I'm kep by his tent. Mother av Moses! Only to think of a British tar being the slave o' a sooty nayger! I never thought it wud a come to this."

"Where do you think they'll take us, Bill?"

"The Lord only knows, an' whether we're all bound for the same port."

"What! you think we may be separated?"

"Be ma sang, Maister Colin, I ha'e ma fears we wull!"

"What makes you think so?"

"Why, ye see, as I've telt ye, I'm booked to ship wi' the black, — 'sheik' I've heerd them ca' him. Well: from what I ha'e seed and heerd, there's nae doot they're gaein' to separate an' tak different roads. I didna ken muckle o' what they sayed, but I could mak oot two words I hae often heerd while cruisin' in the Gulf o' Guinea. They are the names o' two great toons, a lang way up the kintry, — Tim

buctoo and Sockatoo. They are negro toons; an' for that
reezun I ha'e a suspeshun my master 's bound to one or other o' the two ports."

"But why do you think that we are to be taken elsewhere?" demanded Harry Blount.

"Why, because, Master 'Arry, you belong to the hold
sheik, as is plainly a Harab, an' oose port of hentry lies in a
different direction, — that be to the northart."

"It is all likely enough," said Colin; "Bill's prognostica-
tion is but too probable."

"Why, ye see, Maister Colin, they are only land sharks
who ha'e got hold o' us. They 're too poor to keep us; an'
wull be sure to sell us somewhere, an' to somebody that ha'e
got the tocher to gie for us. That 's what they 'll do wi' us
poor bodies."

"I hope," said Terence, "they 'll not part us. No doubt
slavery will be hard enough to bear under any circumstan
ces; but harder if we have to endure it alone. Together,
we might do something to alleviate one another's lot. I
hope we shall not be separated!"

To this hope all the others made a sincere response; and
the conversation came to an end. They who had been carrying it on, worn out by fatigue, and watchfulness long protracted, — despite the unpleasantness of their situation,—
soon after, and simultaneously, yielded their spirits to the
soothing oblivion of sleep.

CHAPTER XXXVIII.

THE DOUAR AT DAWN.

THEY could have slept for hours, — twenty-four of them, — had they been permitted such indulgence.

But they were not. As the first streaks of daylight became visible over the eastern horizon, the whole douar was up and doing.

The women and children of both hordes were seen flitting like shadows among the tents. Some squatted under camels, or kneeling by the sides of the goats, drew from these animals that lacteal fluid that may be said to form the staple of their food. Others might be observed emptying the precious liquid into skin bottles and sacks, and securing it against spilling in its transport through the deserts.

The matrons of the tribes — hags they looked — were preparing the true *dejeûner*, consisting of *Sangleh*, — a sort of gruel, made with millet meal, boiled over a dull fire of camel's dung.

The *Sangleh* was to be eaten, by such of them as could afford it, mixed with goats' or camels' milk, — unstrained and hairy, — half curdled into a crab-like acidity, the moment it entered its stinking receptacle.

Here and there men were seen milking their mares or maherries, — not a few indulging in the universal beverage by a direct application of their lips to the teats of the animal ; while others, appointed to the task, were preparing the paraphernalia of the douar, for transportation to some distant oasis.

Watching these various movements, were the three mids, — still stripped to their shirts, — and the old man-o'-war's-man, clad with like scantiness; since the only garment that clung to his sinewy frame was a pair of cotton drawers neither very clean nor very sound at the seams.

All four shivered in the chill air of the morning; for hot
as is the Saära under its noonday sun, in the night hours
its thermometer frequently falls almost to the point of freez-
ing!

Their state of discomfort did not hinder them from observing what was passing around them. They could have
slept on; but the discordant noises of the douar, and a belief that they would not be permitted any longer to enjoy
their interrupted slumbers, hindered them from reclosing
their eyes. Still recumbent, and occasionally exchanging
remarks in a low tone of voice, they noted the customs of
their captors.

The young Scotchman had read many books relating to
the *prairies* of America, and their savage denizens. He
was forcibly reminded of these by what he now saw in
this oasis of the sandy Saära; the women treated like dogs,
or worse, — doing all the work that might be termed labor,
— tending the cattle, cooking the meals, pitching or striking
the tents, loading the animals, — and themselves bearing
such portions of the load as exceeded the transport strength
of the tribal quadrupeds, — aided only by such wretched
helots as misfortune had flung in the way of their common
masters. The men, mostly idle, — ludicrously nonchalant, —
reclining on their saddle-pads, or skins, inhaling the narcotic
weed, apparently proud in the possession of that lordship of
wretchedness that surrounded them.

Colin was constrained to compare the savage life of two
continents, separated by an ocean. He came to the conclusion, that under similar circumstances, mankind will ever be
the same. In the Comanche of the *Llano Estacado*, or the
Pawnee of the Platte, he would have found an exact coun-
terpart of the Ishmaelitish wanderer over the sandy plains
of the Saära.

He was allowed but scant time to philosophize upon these
ethnological phenomena. As the douar became stirred into

general activity, he, along with his two companions, was rudely started from his attitude of observation, and ordered to take a share in the toils of the captors.

At an earlier hour, and still more rudely, had Sailor Bill received the commands of his master; who, as the first rays of the Aurora began to dapple the horizon, had ordered the old man-o-war's-man to his feet, at the same time administering to him a cruel kick, that came very near shivering some of his stern timbers.

Had the black sheik been acquainted with the English language, — as spoken in Ratcliff Highway, — he would have better understood Sailor Bill's reply to his rude matutinal salutation; which, along with several not very complimentary wishes, ended by devoting the "nayger's" eyes to eternal perdition.

CHAPTER XXXIX.

AN OBSTINATE DROMEDARY.

THE morning meal was eaten as soon as prepared. Its scantiness surprised our adventurers. Even the more distinguished individuals of the horde partook of only a very small quantity of milk, or sangleh. The two sheiks alone got anything like what might have been deemed an ordinary breakfast; while the more common class, as the half-breeds — *hassanes* — and the negro slaves had to content themselves with less than a pint of sour milk to each, half of which was water — the mixture denominated *cheni*.

Could this meal be meant for breakfast? Harry Blount and Terence thought not. But Colin corrected them, by alleging that it was. He had read of the wonderful ab-

6 *   I

stemiousness of these children of the desert: how they can
live on a single meal a day, and this scarce sufficient to sustain life in a child of six years old; that is, an English child.
Often will they go for several successive days without eating
and when they do eat regularly, a drink of milk is all they
require to satisfy hunger.

Colin was right. It was their ordinary breakfast. He
might have added, their dinner too, for they would not likely
obtain another morsel of food before sundown.

But where was the breakfast of Colin and his fellow-captives? This was the question that interested them far more
than the dietary of the Bedouins. They were all hungering
like hyenas, and yet no-one seemed to think of them — no
one offered them either bite or sup. Filthy as was the mess
made by the Arab women, and filthily as they prepared
it, — boiling it in pots, and serving it up in wooden dishes,
that did not appear to have had a washing for weeks, — the
sight of it increased the hungry cravings of the captives;
and they would fain have been permitted to share the scanty
dejeûner.

They made signs of their desire; piteous appeals for food,
by looks and gestures; but all in vain: not a morsel was
bestowed on them. Their brutal captors only laughed at
them, as though they intended that all four should go without eating.

It soon became clear that they were not to starve in idleness. As soon as they had been started to their feet each
of them was set to a task; one to collect camels' dung for
the cooking fires; another to fetch water from the brackish
muddy pool which had caused the oasis to become a place
of encampment; while the third was called upon to assist
in the loading of the tent equipage, along with the salvage
of the wreck, — an operation entered upon as soon as the
sangleh had been swallowed.

Sailor Bill, in a different part of the douar, was kept

equally upon the alert: and if he, or any of the other three, showed signs of disliking their respective tasks, one of the two sheiks made little ado about striking them with a leathern strap, a knotty stick, or any weapon that chanced to come readiest to hand. They soon discovered that they were under the government of taskmasters not to be trifled with, and that resistance or remonstrance would be alike futile. In short, they saw *that they were slaves!*

While packing the tents, and otherwise preparing for the march, they were witnesses to many customs, curious as new to them. The odd equipages of the animals, — both those of burden and those intended to be ridden, — the oval panniers, placed upon the backs of the camels, to carry the women and younger children; the square pads upon the humps of the maherries; the tawny little piccaninnies strapped upon the backs of their mothers; the kneeling of the camels to receive their loads, — as if consenting to what could not be otherwise than disagreeable to them, — were all sights that might have greatly interested our adventurers, had they been viewing them under different circumstances.

Out of the last mentioned of these sights, an incident arose, illustrating the craft of their captors in the management of their domestic animals.

A refractory camel, that, according to usual habit, had voluntarily humiliated itself to receive its load, after this had been packed upon it, refused to rise to its feet. The beast either deemed the burden inequable and unjust, — for the Arabian camel, like the Peruvian llama, has a very acute perception of fair play in this respect, — or a fit of caprice had entered its mulish head. For one reason or another it exhibited a stern determination *not* to oblige its owner by rising to its feet; but continued its genuflexion in spite of every effort to get it on all-fours.

Coaxing and cajolery were tried to no purpose. Kicking by sandalled feet, scourging with whips, and beating with

cudgels produced no better effect; and to all appearance the
obstinate brute had made up its mind to remain in the oasis
and let the tribe depart without it.

At this crisis an ingenious method of making the camel
change its mind suggested itself to its master; or perhaps he
had practised it on some former occasion.   Maddened by the
obstinacy of the animal, he seized hold of an old burnouse,
and rushing up, threw it over its head.   Then drawing the
rag tightly around its snout, he fastened it in such a manner
as completely to stop up the nostrils.

The camel finding its breathing thus suddenly interrupted,
became terrified; and without further loss of time, scram-
bled to its feet — to the great amusement of the women and
children who were spectators of the scene.

CHAPTER XL.

WATERING THE CAMELS.

IN an incredibly short space of time the tents were down,
and the douar with all its belongings was no longer to be
seen; or only in the shape of sundry packages balanced
upon the backs of the animals.

The last operation before striking out upon the desert
track, was the watering of these; the supply for the journey
having been already dipped up out of the pool, and poured
into goat-skin sacks.

The watering of the camels appeared to be regarded as
the most important matter of all.   In this performance
every precaution was taken, and every attention bestowed,
to ensure to the animals a full supply of the precious fluid,
— perhaps from a presentiment on the part of their owners

that they themselves might some day stand in need of, and make use of, the *same* water!

Whether this was the motive or not, every camel belonging to the horde was compelled to drink till its capacious stomach was quite full; and the quantity consumed by each would be incredible to any other than the owner of an African dromedary. Only a very large cask could have contained it.

At the watering of the animals, our adventurers had an opportunity of observing another incident of the Saära,— quite as curious and original as that already described.

It chanced that the pool that furnished the precious fluid, and which contained the only fresh water to be found within fifty miles, was just then on the eve of being dried up. A long season of drought—that is to say, *three or four years* —had reigned over this particular portion of the desert, and the lagoon, formerly somewhat extensive, had shrunk into the dimensions of a trifling tank, containing little more than two or three hundred gallons. This, during the stay of the two tribes united as wreckers, had been daily diminishing; and had the occupants of the douar not struck tents at the time they did, in another day or so they would have been in danger of suffering from thirst. This was in reality the cause of their projected migration. But for the fear of getting short in the necessary commodity of fresh water, they would have hugged the seashore a little longer, in hopes of picking up a few more "waifs" from the wreck of the English ship.

At the hour of their departure from the encampment, the pool was on the eve of exhaustion. Only a few score gallons of not very pure water remained in it—about enough to fill the capacious stomachs of the camels; whose owners had gauged them too often to be ignorant of the quantity.

It would not do to play with this closely calculated supply. Every pint was precious; and to prove that it was so esteemed, the animals were constrained to swallow it in a fashion, which certainly nature could never have intended.

Instead of taking it in by the mouth the camels of these Saäran rovers were compelled to quench their thirst through the nostrils!

You will wonder in what manner this could be effected? inquiring whether the quadrupeds voluntarily performed this nasal imbibing?

Our adventurers, witnesses of the fact, wondered also — while struck with its quaint peculiarity.

There is a proverb that "one man may take a horse to the water, but twenty cannot compel him to drink." Though this proverb may hold good of an English horse, it has no significance when applied to an African dromedary. Proof. Our adventurers saw the owner of each camel bring his animal to the edge of the pool; but instead of permitting the thirsty creature to step in and drink for itself, its head was held aloft, a wooden funnel was filled, the narrow end inserted into the nostril, and by the respiratory canal the water introduced to the throat and stomach!

You may ask, why this selection of the nostrils instead of the mouth? Our adventurers so interrogated one another. It was only after becoming better acquainted with the customs of the Saära that they acquired a satisfactory explanation of one they had frequent occasion to observe.

Though ordinarily of the most docile disposition, and in most of its movements the most tranquil of creatures, the dromedary, when drinking from a vessel, has the habit of repeatedly shaking its head, and spilling large quantities of the water placed before it. Where water is scarce, — and, as in the Saära, considered the most momentous matter of life, — a waste of it after such a fashion could not be tolerated. To prevent it, therefore, the camel-owner has contrived that this animal, so essential to his own safe existence, should drink through the orifices intended by nature for its respiration.

CHAPTER XLI.

A SQUABBLE BETWEEN THE SHEIKS.

THE process of watering the camels was carried on with the utmost diligence and care. It was too important to be trifled with, or negligently performed. While filling the capacious stomachs of the quadrupeds, their owners were but laying in a stock for themselves.

As Sailor Bill jocularly remarked, " it was like filling the water-casks of a man-of-war previous to weighing anchor for a voyage." In truth, very similar was the purpose for which these ships of the desert were being supplied; for, when filling the capacious stomachs of the quadrupeds, their owners were not without the reflection that the supply might yet pass into their own. Such a contingency was not improbable, neither would it be new.

For this reason the operation was conducted with diligence and care, — no camel being led away from the pool until it was supposed to have had a " surfeit," and this point was settled by seeing the water poured in at its nostrils running out at its mouth.

As each in turn got filled, it was taken back to the tribe to which it belonged; for the united hordes had by this time become separated into two distinct parties, preparatory to starting off on their respective routes.

Our adventurers could now perceive a marked difference between the two bands of Saära wanderers into whose hands they had unfortunately fallen. As already stated, the black sheik was an African of the true negro type, with thick lips, flattened nostrils, woolly hair, and heels projecting several inches to the rear of his ankle-joints. Most of his following were similarly " furnished," though not all of them. There were a few of mixed color, with straight hair, and features almost Caucasian, who submitted to his rule, or rather to his ownership, since these last all appeared to be his slaves.

Those who trooped after the old Arab were mostly of his own race, mixed with a remnant of mongrel Portuguese, — descendants of the peninsular colonists who had fled from the coast settlements after the conquest of Morocco by the victorious " Sheriffs."

Of such mixed races are the tribes who thinly people the Saära, — Arabs, Berbers, Ethiopians of every hue; all equally Bedoweens, — wanderers of the pathless deserts. It did not escape the observation of our adventurers that the slaves of the Arab sheik and his followers were mostly pure negroes from the south, while those of the black chieftain, — as proclaimed by the color of their skin, — showed a Shemitic or Japhetic origin. The philosophic Colin could perceive in this a silent evidence of the retribution of races.

The supply of water being at length laid in, not only in the skins appropriated to the purpose, but also within the stomachs of the camels, the two tribes seemed prepared to exchange with each other the parting salute, — to speak the " Peace be with you!" And yet there was something that caused them to linger in each other's proximity. Their new-made captives could tell this, though ignorant of what it might be.

It was something that had yet to be settled between the two sheiks, who did not appear at this moment of leave-taking to entertain for each other any very cordial sentiment of friendship.

Could their thoughts have found expression in English words, they would have taken shape somewhat as follows : —

" That lubberly nigger," (we are pursuing the train of reflections that passed through the mind of the Arab sheik,) " old Nick burn him ! — thinks I 've got more than my share of this lucky windfall. He wants these boys bad, — I know that. The Sultan of Timbuctoo has given him a commission to procure *white slaves*, — that's clear; and *boy slaves* if he can, — that's equally certain. This lot would suit him to a T. I can tell that he don't care much for the old salt he has tricked me out of by his superior skill at that silly game of helga. No; His Majesty of the mud-walled city don't want such as him. It's boys he's after, — as can wait smartly at his royal table, and give *éclat* to his ceremonial entertainments. Well, he can have these three *at a price*."

"Ay, but a big price," continued the cunning old trafficker in human flesh, after a short reflection, "a wopping big price. The togs we've stripped from them were no common clothing. Good broadcloth in their jackets, and bullion bands on their caps. They must be the sons of great sheiks. At Wedmoon the old Jew will redeem them. So, too, the merchants at Suse; or maybe I had best take them on to Mogador, where the consul of their country will come down handsomely for such as they. Yes, that's the trick!"

At this parting scene the thoughts of Fatima's husband were equally occupied with trading speculations, in which he was assisted by the amiable Fatima herself.

Translated also into English, they would have read as follows: —

"The Sultan would give threescore of his best blacks for those three tripe-colored brats."

"I know it, Fatty dear; he's told me so himself."

"Then why not get them, and bring 'em along?"

"Ah, that's easy to say. How can I? You know they belong to the old Arab by right, — at least, he claims them, though not very fairly, for if we had n't come up in good time they would have taken him instead of his taking them; no matter for that, they're his now by the laws of the Saära.

"Bother the laws of the Saära!" exclaimed Fatima, with a disdainful toss of her head, and a scornful turning up of her two protruding teeth; "all stuff and nonsense! There's no law in the Saära; and if there was, you know we're never coming into it again. The price you'd get for those three hobbledehoys would keep us comfortable for the balance of our lives; and we need never track the Devil's Desert again. Take 'em by force from old Yellow-face, if you can't get 'em otherwise; but you may 'chouse' him out of them at a game of *helga*, — you know you can beat him at that. If he won't play again, try your hand at bargaining against your blacks; offer him two to one."

Thus counselled by the partner of his bosom, the black sheik, instead of bidding the *saleik aloum* to his Arab *confrère*, raised his voice aloud, and demanded from the latter a parley upon business of importance.

CHAPTER XLII.

THE TRIO STAKED.

THE parley that followed was of course unintelligible to our adventurers, the *Boy Slaves*.

But although they did not understand the words that were exchanged between the two sheiks, they were not without having a conjecture as to their import. The gestures made by the two men, and their looks cast frequently towards themselves, led them to believe that the conversation related to their transference from one to the other.

There was not much to choose between the two masters. Both appeared to be unfeeling savages, and so far had treated their captives with much cruelty. They could only hope, in case of a transfer taking place, that it would not be partial, but would extend to the trio, and that they would be kept together. They had been already aware that old Bill was to be parted from them, and this had caused them a painful feeling; but to be themselves separated, perhaps never to meet again, was a thought still more distressing.

The three youths had long been shipmates, — ever since entering the naval service of their country. They had become fast friends; and believed that whatever might be the fate before them, they could better bear it in each other's company. Companionship would at least enable them to cheer one another; mutual sympathy would, to some extent, alleviate the hardest lot; while alone, and under such cruel taskmasters, the prospect was gloomy in the extreme.

With feelings of keen anxiety, therefore, did they listen to the palaver, and watch the countenances of their captors.

After a full half-hour spent in loud talking and gesticulating, some arrangement appeared to have been arrived at between the two sheiks. Those most interested in it could only guess what it was by what followed.

Silence having been partially restored, the old Arab was seen to step up to the spot where the slaves of the black sheik were assembled; and, after carefully scrutinizing them, pick out three of the stoutest, plumpest, and healthiest young negroes in the gang. These were separated from the others, and placed on the plain some distance apart.

"We're to be exchanged," muttered Terence, "we're to belong to the ugly black nagur. Well, perhaps it's better We'll be with old Bill."

"Stay a wee," said Colin; "there's something more to come yet, I think."

The black sheik at this moment coming up, interrupted the conversation of the captives.

What was he going to do? Take them with him, they supposed. The old Arab had himself led out the three young "darkies"; and the black sheik was about to act in like manner with the trio of white captives.

So reasoned they; and, as it was a matter of indifference

to them with which they went, they would offer no opposition.

To their chagrin, however, instead of all three, only one of them was led off; the other two being commanded by gestures to keep their ground.

It was O'Connor to whom this partiality was shown; the black sheik having selected him after a short while spent in scrutinizing and comparing the three. The Irish youth was of stouter build than either of his shipmates; and this, perhaps, guided the black sheik in making his choice. By all appearances, the conditions of the exchange were to be different from what our adventurers had anticipated. It was not to be man for man, or boy for boy; but three for one, — three blacks to a white.

This was, in reality, the terms that had been agreed upon. The avaricious old Arab, not caring very much to part with his share of the spoil, would not take less than three to one; and to this the black sheik, after long and loud bargaining, had consented.

Terence was led up, and placed alongside the three young darkies, who, instead of taking things as seriously as he, were exhibiting their ivories in broad grins of laughter, as if the disposal of their persons was an affair to be treated only as a joke!

Our adventurers were now apprehensive that they were to be separated. Their only hope was that the bargaining would not end there; but would extend to a further exchange of six blacks for the two remaining whites.

Their conjectures were interrupted by their seeing that the " swop " was not yet considered complete.

What followed, in fact, showed them that it was not a regular trade at all; but a little bit of gambling between the two sheiks, in which Terence and the three young blacks were to be the respective stakes.

Old Bill was able to explain the proceedings, from his experience of the preceding night; and as he saw the two sheiks repair to the place where his own proprietorship had been decided, he cried out : —

"Yere goin' to be gambled for, Masther Terry! Och! ye'll be along wid me, — for the black can bate the owld Arab at that game, all hollow."

The holes in which the *helga* had been played on the preceding night were now resorted to. The proper number of dung pellets were procured, and the game proceeded.

It ended as the old man-o'-war's-man had prognosticated, by the black sheik becoming the winner and owner of Terence O'Connor.

The Arab appeared sadly chagrined, and by the way in which he strutted and stormed over the ground, it was evident he would not rest satisfied with his loss. When did gamester ever leave gaming-table so long as a stake was left him to continue the play?

Two of the midshipmen still belonged to the old sheik. With these he might obtain a *revanche*. He made the trial. He was unfortunate, as before. Either the luck was against him, or he was no match at " desert draughts " for his sable antagonist.

It ended in the black sheik becoming the owner of the three midshipmen, who, restored to the companionship of Sailor Bill, in less than twenty minutes after the conclusion of the game, were trudging it across the desert in the direction of Timbuctoo!

CHAPTER XLIII.

GOLAH.

IN their journey over the sea of sand, our four **adven-turers** formed part of a company of sixteen men and women, along with six or seven children.

All were the property of one man, — the huge and dusky sheik who had won Sailor Bill and the three middies at " desert draughts."

It soon became known to his white captives that his name was Golah, a name which Terence suggested might probably be an African abbreviation of the ancient name of Goliah.

Golah was certainly a great man, — not in bone and flesh alone, but in intellect as well.

We do not claim for him the gigantic mind that by **arrang-ing** a few figures and symbols, by the light of a lamp in a garret, could discover a new planet in the solar system, and give its dimensions, weight, and distance from the dome of St. Paul's.   Neither do we claim that the power of his in-tellect, if put forth in a storm of eloquence, could move the masses of his fellow-creatures, as a hurricane stirs up the waters of the sea ; yet for all this Golah had a great intel-lect.   He was born to rule, and not a particle of all the pro-pensities and sentiments constituting his mind was ever in tended to yield to the will of another.

The cunning old sheik, who had the first claim to the three mids, had been anxious to retain them ; but they were also wanted by Golah, and the Arab was compelled to give them up, after having been fairly beaten at the game ; part-ing with his sable competitor in a mood that was anything but agreeable.

The black sheik had three wives, all of whom possessed the gift of eloquence in a high degree.

For all this a simple glance from him was enough to stop any one of them in the middle of a monosyllable.

Even Fatima, the favorite, owed much of her influence to the ability she displayed in studying her lord's wishes to the neglect of her own.

Golah had seven camels, four of which were required for carrying himself and his wives, with their children, trappings, tent utensils, and tents.

The three other camels were laden with the spoils which had been collected from the wreck.

Twelve of the sixteen adults in the company were compelled to walk, being forced to keep up with the camels the best way they could.

One of these was Golah's son, a youth about eighteen years of age. He was armed with a long Moorish musket, a heavy Spanish sword, and the dirk that had been taken from Colin.

He was the principal guard over the slaves, in which duty he was assisted by another youth, whom our adventurers afterwards learnt was a brother of one of Golah's wives.

This second youth was armed with a musket and scimitar, and both he and Golah's son seemed to think that their lives depended on keeping a constant watch over the ten slaves; for there were six others besides Sailor Bill and his young companions. They had all been captured, purchased, or won at play, during Golah's present expedition, and were now on the way to some southern market.

Two of the six were pronounced by Sailor Bill to be Kroomen, — a race of Africans with whose appearance he was somewhat familiar, having often seen them acting as sailors in ships coming from the African coast.

The other slaves were much lighter in complexion, and by the old man-o'-war's-man were called " Portugee blacks." All had the appearance of having spent some time in bondage on the great Saàra.

On the first day of their journey the white captives had learnt the relations existing between the majority of the company and the chief Golah; and each of them felt shame as well as indignation at the humiliating position in which he was placed.

Those feelings were partly excited and greatly strengthened by hunger and thirst, as well as by the painful toil they had to undergo in dragging themselves over the sandy plain beneath a scorching sun.

"I have had enough of this," said Harry Blount to his companions. "We might be able to stand it several days longer, but I 've no curiosity to learn whether we can or not."

"Go on! you are thinking and speaking for me, Harry," said Terence.

"There are four of us," continued Harry, — "four of that nation whose people boast they *never will be slaves;* besides, there are six others, who are our fellow-bondsmen. They 're not much to look at, but still they might count for something in a row. Shall we four British tars, belong to a party of ten, — all enslaved by three men, — black men at that?"

"That 's just what I 've been thinking about for the last hour or two," said Terence. "If we don't kill old Golah, and ride off with his camels, we deserve to pass every day of our lives as we 're doing this one — in slavery."

"Just say the word, — when and how," cried Harry "I 'm waiting. There are seven camels. Let us each take one; but before we go we must eat and drink the other three. I 'm starving."

"Pitch on a plan, and I 'll pitch into it," rejoined Terence. "I 'm ready for anything, — from pitch and toss up to manslaughter."

"Stay, Master Terence," interrupted the old sailor. "Av coorse ye are afther wantin' to do somethin', an' thin to think aftherwards why ye did it. Arry, my lad, yer half out o' yer mind. Master Colin be the only yin o' ye that keeps his seven senses about him. Suppose all av ye, that the big chief was dead, an' that his son was not alive, and that the other nager was a ristin' quietly wid his black heels turned from the place where the daisies hought to grow, — what should we do thin? We 'ave neyther chart nor compass. We could'ner mak oot our reckonin'. Don't ye see a voyage here is just like one at sea, only it be just the revarse. When men are starvin' at sea, they want to find land, but when they are starvin' in the desert the*y* want to find water. The big nager, our captain, can navigate this sea in safety, — we can't. We must let him take us to some port and then do the best we can to escape from him."

"You are quite right," said Colin, "in thinking that we might be unable to find our way from one watering-place to another; but it is well for us to calculate all the chances. After reaching some *port*, as you call it, may we not find ourselves in a position more difficult to escape from, — where we will have to contend with a hundred or more of these negro brutes in place of only three?"

"That 's vary likely," answered the sailor; "but they 're only men, and we 'av a chance of beatin' 'em. We may fight with men, and conquer 'em, an' we may fight with water an' conquer that; but when we fight against no water that will conquer us. Natur is sure to win."

"Bill 's right there," said Terence, "and I feel that Nature is getting the best of me already."

While they were holding this conversation, they noticed that one of the Kroomen kept near them, and seemed listening to all that was said. His sparkling eyes betrayed the greatest interest.

"Do you understand us?" asked old Bill, turning sharply towards the African, and speaking in an angry tone.

"Yus, sa, — a lilly bit," answered the Krooman, without

seeming to notice the unpleasant manner in which the ques
tion had been put.

"And what are you listening for?"

"To hear what you tell um. I like go in Ingleesh ship.
You talk good for me. I go long with you."

With some difficulty the sailor and his companions could
comprehend the Krooman's gibberish. They managed to
learn from him that he had once been in an English ship,
and had made a voyage along the African coast, trading for
palm-oil. While on board he had picked up a smattering
of English. He was afterwards shipwrecked in a Portuguese brig. Cast away on the shores of the Saära, just as
our adventurers had been, and had passed four years in the
desert, — a slave to its denizens.

He gratified our adventurers by telling them that they
were in no danger of having to endure a prolonged period of
captivity, as they would soon be sold into liberty, instead of
slavery. Golah could not afford to keep slaves; and was
only a kidnapper and dealer in the article. He would sell
them to the highest bidder, and that would be some English
consul on the coast.

The Krooman said there was no such hope for him and
his companions, for their country did not redeem its subjects
from slavery.

When he saw that Golah had obtained some English
prisoners, he had been cheered with the hope that he might
be redeemed along with them, as an English subject, to
which right he had some claim from having served on an
English ship!

During the day the black slaves — well knowing the duty
they were expected to perform, had been gathering pieces
of dried camels' dung along the way; this was to supply
fuel for the fire of the douar at night.

Soon after sunset Golah ordered a halt, when the camels
were unloaded and the tents set up.

About one quarter the quantity of *sangleh* that each required, was then served out to the slaves for their dinner, and as they had eaten nothing since morning, this article of food appeared to have greatly improved, both in appearance and flavor. To the palate of our adventurers it seemed delicious.

Golah, after examining his human property, and evidently satisfied with the condition of all, retired to his tent; from which soon after issued sounds that resembled a distant thunder-storm.

The black sheik was snoring!

The two young men — his son and brother-in-law — relieved each other during the night in keeping watch over the slaves.

Their vigil was altogether unnecessary. Weak, and exhausted with hunger and fatigue, the thoughts of the captives were not of the future, but of present repose; which was eagerly sought, and readily found, by all four of them

CHAPTER XLIV.

A DAY OF AGONY.

AN hour before sunrise the next morning, the slaves were given some *cheni* to drink, and then started on their journey.

The sun, as it soared up into a cloudless sky, shot forth its rays much warmer than upon the day before, while not a breath of air fanned the sterile plain. The atmosphere was as hot and motionless as the sands under their feet. They were no longer hungry. Thirst — raging, burning thirst — extinguished or deadened every other sensation.

Streams of perspiration poured from their bodies, as they struggled through the yielding sand; yet, with all this moisture streaming from every pore, their throats, tongues, and lips became so parched that any attempt on their part to hold converse only resulted in producing a series of sounds that resembled a death-rattle.

Golah, with his family, rode in the advance, and seemed not to give himself any concern whether he was followed by others or not. His two relatives brought up the rear of the *kafila,* and any of the slaves exhibiting a disposition to lag behind was admonished to move on with blows administered by a thick stick.

"Tell them I must have water or die," muttered Harry to the Krooman in a hoarse whisper. "I am worth money, and if old Golah lets me die for want of a drop of water, he 's a fool."

The Krooman refused to make the communication —which he declared would only result in bringing ill treatment upon himself.

Colin appealed to Golah's son, and by signs gave him to understand that they must have water. The young black, in answer, simply condescended to sneer at him. He was not suffering himself, and could have no sympathy for another.

The hides of the blacks, besmeared with oil, seemed to repel the scorching beams of the sun; and years of continual practice had no doubt inured them to the endurance of hunger and thirst to a surprising degree. To their white fellow-captives they appeared more like huge reptiles than human beings.

The sand along the route on this, the second day, was less compact than before, and the task of leg-lifting, produced a weariness such as might have arisen from the hardest work. Added to the agony of their thirst, the white sufferers dwelt frequently on thoughts of death — that great antidote to human miseries; yet so constrained were their actions by force of circumstances, that only by following their leader and owner, Golah, could they hope to find relief.

Had he allowed them to turn back to the coast, whence they had started, or even to repose for a few hours on the way, they could not have done so. They were compelled to move on, by a power that could not be resisted.

That power was Hope, — the hope of obtaining some *sangleh* and a little dirty water.

To turn back, or to linger behind, would bring them nothing but more suffering, — perhaps death itself.

A man intent on dying may throw himself into the water to get drowned, and then find himself involuntarily struggling to escape from the death he has courted.

The same irresistible antipathy to death compelled his white captives to follow the black sheik.

They were unwilling to die, — not for the sole reason that they had homes and friends they wished to see again, — not solely for that innate love of life, implanted by Nature in the breasts of all; but there was a pleasure which they desired to experience once more, — aye, yearned to indulge in it: the pleasure of quenching their terrible thirst. To gratify this pleasure they must follow Golah.

One of Golah's wives had three children; and, as each wife was obliged to look after her own offspring, this woman could not pursue her journey without a little more trouble than her less favored companions.

The eldest of her children was too young to walk a long distance; and, most of the time, was carried under her care upon the maherry. Having her three restless imps, to keep balanced upon the back of the camel, requiring her constant vigilance to prevent them from falling off, she found her hands full enough. It was a sort of travelling that did not at all suit her; and she had been casting about for some way of being relieved from at least a portion of her trouble.

The plan she devised was to compel some one of the

slaves to carry her eldest child, a boy about four years of age.

Colin was the victim selected for this duty. All the attempts made by the young Scotchman to avoid the responsibilities thus imposed upon him proved vain. The woman was resolute, and Colin had to yield; although he resisted until she threatened to call Golah to her assistance.

This argument was conclusive; and the young darkey was placed upon Colin's shoulders, with its legs around his neck, and one of its hands grasping him tightly by the hair.

When this arrangement was completed, night had drawn near; and the two young men who acted as guards hastened forward to select a place for the douar.

There was no danger of any of the slaves making an attempt to escape; for all were too anxious to receive the small quantity of food that was to be allowed them at the night halt.

Encumbered with the "piccaninny," and wearied with the long, ceaseless struggle through the sand, Colin lingered behind his companions. The mother of the child, apparently attentive to the welfare of her first-born, checked the progress of her maherry, and rode back to him.

After the camels had been unloaded, and the tents pitched, Golah superintended the serving out of their suppers, which consisted only of *sangleh*. The quantity was even less than had been given the evening before; but it was devoured by the white captives with a pleasure none of them had hitherto experienced.

Sailor Bill declared that the brief time in which he was employed in consuming the few mouthfuls allowed him, was a moment of enjoyment that repaid him for all the sufferings of the day.

"Ah, Master Arry!" said he, "it's only now we are larnin' to live, although I did think, one time to-day, we was just larnin' to die. I never mean to eat again until I'm hungry

Master Terry," he added, turning to the young Irishman, " is n't this foine livin' intirely? and are yez not afther bein' happy?"

" 'T is the most delicious food man ever ate," answered Terence, " and the only fault I can find is that there is not enough of it."

"Then you may have what is left of mine," said Colin, " for I can't say that I fancy it."

Harry, Terence, and the sailor gazed at the young Scotchman with expressions of mingled alarm and surprise. Small as had been the amount of *sangleh* with which Colin had been served, he had not eaten more than one half of it.

"Why, puir Maister Colly, what is wrang wi' ye?" exclaimed Bill, in a tone expressing fear and pity. "If ye d'nna eat, mon, ye 'll dee."

"I 'm quite well," answered Colin, "but I have had plenty, and any of you can take what is left."

Though the hunger of Colin's three companions was not half satisfied, they all refused to finish the remainder of his supper, hoping that he might soon find his appetite, and eat it himself.

The pleasure they had enjoyed in eating the small allowance given them rendered it difficult for them to account for the conduct of their companion. His abstemiousness caused them uneasiness, even alarm.

CHAPTER XLV.

COLIN IN LUCK.

THE next morning, when the caravan started, Colin again had the care of the young black. He did not always have to carry him, as part of the time the boy trotted along by his side.

During the fore-part of the day, the young Scotchman with his charge easily kept up with his companions, and some of the time might be seen a little in advance of them. His kind attentions to the boy were observed by Golah, who showed some sign of human feeling, by exhibiting a contortion of his features intended for a smile.

Towards noon, Colin appeared to become fatigued with the toil of the journey, and then fell back to the rear, as he had done the evening before. Again the anxious mother, ever mindful of the welfare of her offspring, was seen to check her camel, and wait until Colin and the boy overtook her.

Sailor Bill had been much surprised at Colin's conduct the evening before, especially at the patient manner in which the youth had submitted to the task of looking after the child. There was a mystery in the young Scotchman's behavior he could not comprehend, — a mystery that soon became more profound. It had also attracted the attention of Harry and Terence, notwithstanding the many unpleasant circumstances of the journey calculated to abstract their thoughts from him and his charge.

Shortly after noon, the woman was seen driving Colin up to the *kafila*, urging him forward with loud screams, and blows administered with the knotted end of the rope by which she guided her maherry.

After a time Golah, apparently annoyed by her shrill,

scolding voice, ordered her to desist, and permit the slave to continue his journey in peace.

Although unable to understand the meaning of her words, Colin must have known that the woman was not using terms of endearment.

The screaming, angry tone, and the blows of the rope might have told him this; and yet he submitted to her reproaches and chastisements with a meekness and a philosophic resignation which surprised his companions.

When his thoughts were not too much absorbed by painful reveries over the desire for food and water, Harry endeavored to converse with the Krooman already mentioned. He now applied to the man for an interpretation of the words so loudly vociferated by the angry negress, and launched upon the head of the patient young Scotchman.

The Krooman said that she had called the lad a lazy pig, a Christian dog, and an unbelieving fool; and that she threatened to kill him unless he kept up with the *kafila*.

On the third day of their journeying, it chanced not to be quite so hot as on the one preceding it; and consequently the sufferings of the slaves, especially from thirst, were somewhat less severe.

"I shall never endure such agony again," said Harry, speaking of his experience of the previous day. "Perhaps I may die for the want of water, and on this desert; but I can never suffer so much real pain a second time."

"'Ow is that, Master Arry?" asked Bill.

"Because I cannot forget, after my experience of last night, that the greater the desire for water, the more pleasure there is in gratifying it; and the anticipation of such happiness will go far to alleviate anything I may hereafter feel."

"Well, there be summat in that, for sartin," answered the sailor, "for I can't 'elp thinkin' about 'ow nice our supper was last night, and only 'ope it will taste as well to-night again."

7 *

"We have learnt something new," said Terence, "new, at least, to me; and I shall know how to live when I get where there is plenty. Heretofore I have been like a child — eating and drinking half my time, not because I required it, but because I knew no better. There is Colly, now, he don't seem to appreciate the beauty of this Arabian style of living; or he may understand it better than we. Perhaps he is waiting until he acquires a better appetite, so that he may have all the more pleasure in gratifying it. Where is he now?"

They all looked about. They saw that Colin had once more fallen behind; and that the mother of the child was again waiting for him.

Harry and Terence walked on, expecting that they would soon see their companion rudely driven up by the angry negress.

Sailor Bill stopped, as though he was interested in being a witness to the scene thus anticipated.

In a few minutes after, the young Scotchman, with the child, was hurried forward by the enraged hag — who once more seemed in a great rage at his inability or unwillingness to keep up with the others.

"I ken it 'a noo," said Bill, after he had stood for some time witnessing the ill-treatment heaped upon Colin.

"Our freen Colly's in luck. I 've no langer any wonder at his taking a' this tribble wi' the blackey bairn."

"What is it, Bill? what have you learnt now?" asked Terence and Harry in a breath.

"I 've larnt why Colly could not eat bis dinner yesterday."

"Well, why was it?"

"I 've larnt that the nager's anger with Colly is all a pretince, an' that she 's an old she schemer."

"Nonsense, Bill; that is all a fancy of yours," said Colin, who, with the child on his shoulders, was now walking alongside his companions.

It is no fancy of mine, mon," answered Bill, " but a fancy o' the woman for a bra' fair luddie. What is it that she gives you to eat, Maister Colly ? "

Seeing that it was idle to conceal his good fortune any longer, Colin now confessed it, — informing them that the woman, whenever she could do so without being seen, had given him a handful of dried figs, with a drink of camel's milk from a leathern bottle which she carried under her cloak.

Notwithstanding the opinion they had just expressed, on the enjoyment attending prolonged thirst and hunger, Colin's companions congratulated him on his good fortune, — one and all declaring their willingness to take charge of the little darkey, on the condition of being similarly rewarded.

They had no suspicion at that moment that their opinions might soon undergo a change; and that Colin's supposed good fortune would ere long become a source of much uneasiness to all of them.

CHAPTER XLVI.

SAILOR BILL'S EXPERIMENT.

THE afternoon of this day was very warm, yet Golah rode on at such a quick pace, that it required the utmost exertion of the slaves to keep up with him.

This manner of travelling, under the circumstances in which he was required to pursue it, proved too severe for Sailor Bill to endure with any degree of patience.

He became unable, as he thought, to walk any farther; or, if not wholly unable, he was certainly unwilling, and he therefore sat down.

A heavy shower of blows produced no effect in moving him from the spot where he had seated himself, and the two young men who acted as guards, not knowing what else to do, and having exhausted all their arguments, accompanied by a series of kicks, at length appealed to Golah.

The sheik instantly turned his maherry, and rode back.

Before he had reached the place, however, the three mids had used all their influence in an endeavor to get their old companion to move on. In this they had been joined by the Krooman, who entreated Bill, if he placed any value on his life, to get up before Golah should arrive, for he declared the monster would show him no mercy.

"For God's sake," exclaimed Harry Blount, "if it is possible for you to get up and go a little way farther, do so."

"Try to move on, man," said Terence, "and we will help you. Come, Bill, for the sake of your friends try to get up. Golah is close by."

While thus speaking, Terence, assisted by Colin, took hold of Bill and tried to drag him to his feet; but the old sailor obstinately persisted in remaining upon the ground.

"Perhaps I could walk on a bit farther," said he, "but I won't. I've 'ad enough on it. I'm goin' to ride, and let Golah walk awhile. He's better able to do it than I am. Now don't you boys be so foolish as to get yersels into trouble on my account. All ye've got to do is to look on, an' ye'll larn somethin'. If I've no youth an' beauty, like Colly, to bring me good luck, I've age and experience, and I'll get it by schamin'."

On reaching the place where the sailor was sitting, Golah was informed of what had caused the delay, and that the usual remedy had failed of effect.

He did not seem displeased at the communication. On the contrary, his huge features bore an expression that for him might have been considered pleasant.

He quietly ordered the slave to get up, and pursue his journey.

The weary sailor had blistered feet; and, with his strength almost exhausted by hunger and thirst, had reached the point of desperation. Moreover, for the benefit of himself and his young companions, he wished to try an experiment.

He told the Krooman to inform the sheik that he would go on, if allowed to ride one of the camels.

"You want me to kill you?" exclaimed Golah, when this communication was made to him; "you want to cheat me out of the price I have paid for you; but you shall not. You must go on. I, Golah, have said it."

The sailor, in reply, swore there was no possible chance for them to take him any farther, without allowing him to ride.

This answer to the sheik's civil request was communicated by the Krooman; and, for a moment, Golah seemed puzzled as to how he should act.

He would not kill the slave after saying that he must go on; nor would he have him carried, since the man would then gain his point.

He stood for a minute meditating on what was to be done. Then a hideous smile stole over his features. He had mastered the difficulty.

Taking its halter from the camel, he fastened one end of it to the saddle, and the other around the wrists of the sailor. Poor old Bill made resistance to being thus bound, but he was like an infant in the powerful grasp of the black sheik.

The son and brother-in-law of Golah stood by with their muskets on full cock, and the first move any of Bill's companions could have made to assist him, would have been a signal for them to fire.

When the fastenings were completed, the sheik ordered his son to lead the camel forward, and the sailor, suddenly jerked from his attitude of repose, was rudely dragged onward over the sand.

"You are going now!" exclaimed Golah, nearly frantic with delight; "and we are not carrying you, are we? Neither are you riding? *Bismillah!* I am your master!"

The torture of travelling in this manner was too great to be long endured, and Bill had to take to his feet and walk forward as before. He was conquered; but as a punishment for the trouble he had caused, the shiek kept him towing at the tail of the camel for the remainder of that day's journey.

Any one of the white slaves would once have thought that he possessed too much spirit to allow himself or a friend to be subjected to such treatment as Bill had that day endured.

None of them was deficient in true courage; yet the proud spirit, of which each had once thought himself possessed, was now subdued by a power to which, if it be properly applied, all animate things must yield.

That power was the feeling of hunger; and there is no creature so wild and fierce but will tamely submit to the dominion of the man who commands it. It is a power that must be used with discretion, or the victims to it, urged by desperation, may destroy their keeper. Golah had the wisdom to wield it with effect; for by it, with the assistance of two striplings, he easily controlled those who, under other circumstances, would have claimed the right to be free.

CHAPTER XLVII

AN UNJUST REWARD.

THE next morning on resuming the journey Golah condescended to tell his captives that they should reach a well or spring that afternoon, and stay by it for two or three days.

This news was conveyed to Harry by the Krooman; and all were elated at the prospect of rest, with a plentiful supply of water.

Harry had a long conversation with the Krooman as they were pursuing their route. The latter expressed his surprise that the white captives were so contented to go on in the course in which the sheik was conducting them.

This was a subject about which Harry and his companions had given themselves no concern; partly because that they had no idea that Golah was intending to make a very long journey, and partly that they supposed his intentions, whatever they were, could not be changed by anything they might propose.

The Krooman thought different. He told Harry that the route they were following, if continued, would lead them far into the interior of the country — probably to Timbuctoo; and that Golah should be entreated to take them to some port on the coast, where they might be ransomed by an English consul.

Harry perceived the truth of these suggestions; and, after having a conversation with his companions, it was determined between them that they should have a talk with Golah that very night.

The Krooman promised to act as interpreter, and to do all in his power to favor their suit. He might persuade the sheik to change his destination, by telling him that he would find a far better market in taking them to some place where vessels arrive and depart, than by carrying them into the interior of the country.

The man then added, speaking in a mysterious manner, that there was one more subject on which he wished to give them warning. When pressed to mention it, he appeared reluctant to do so.

He was at last prevailed upon to be more communicative; when he proclaimed his opinion, that their companion, Colin, would never leave the desert.

" Why is that?" asked Harry.

" Bom-by he be kill. De sheik kill um."

Although partly surmising his reasons for having formed this opinion, Harry urged him to further explain himself.

" Ef Golah see de moder ob de piccaninny gib dat lad one lilly fig, — one drop ob drink, he kill um, sartin-sure. I see, one, two, — seb'ral more see. Golah no fool. Bom-by he see too, and kill um bof, — de lad an' de piccaninny moder."

Harry promised to warn his companion of the danger, and save him before the suspicions of Golah should be aroused.

" No good, no good," said the Krooman.

In explanation of this assertion, Harry was told that, should the young Scotchman refuse any favor from the woman, her wounded vanity would change her liking to the most bitter hatred, and she would then contrive to bring down upon him the anger of Golah, — an anger that would certainly be fatal to its victim.

" Then what must I do to save him?" asked Harry.

" Noting," answered the Krooman. " You noting can do. Ony bid him be good man, and talk much, — pray to God. Golah wife lub him, and he sure muss die."

Harry informed the sailor and Terence of what the Krooman had told him, and the three took counsel together.

" I believes as how the darkey be right," said Bill.   " Of
course, if the swab Goliarh larns as 'ow one av 'is wives ha'
taken a fancy to Master Colly, 't will be all up wi' the poor
lad.   He will be killed, — and mayhap eaten too, for that
matter."

" Like enough," assented Terence.   " And should he
scorn her very particular attentions, her resentment might
be equally as dangerous as Golah's.   I fear poor Colin has
drifted into trouble."

" What ye be afther sayin' about the woman," said Bill,
' minds me o' a little story I wunce heeard whin I was a
boy.   I read it in a book called the Bible.   It was about a
young man, somethin' like Master Colly, barrin' his name
was Joseph.   A potter's wife tuck a fancy to him; but Joseph, bein' a dacent an' honest youngster, treted her wid
contimpt, an' came to great grief by doin' that same.   You
must 'ave read that story, Master 'Arry," continued Bill,
turning from Terence to the young Englishman, and changing his style of pronunciation.   " Did it not 'appen summers
in this part o' the world ?   Hif I remember rightly, it did.
I know 't was summers in furrin parts."

" Yes," answered Harry, " that little affair did happen in
this part of the world, — since it was in Africa, — and our
comrade has a fair prospect of being more unfortunate than
Joseph.   In truth, I don't see how we shall be able to assist him."

" There he is, about a hundred cable lengths astern," said
Bill, looking back.   " And there 's the old 'oman, too, look-
in' sharp afther him, while Colly is atin' the figs and drinkin'
the camel's milk ; and while I 'm dying for a dhrop of that
same, old Goliarh is no doubt proud wid the great care
she 's takin' of his child.   Bud won't there be a row when
he larns summat more ?   Won't there, Master 'Arry ?"

" There will, indeed," answered Harry.   " Colin will soon
be up with us, and we must talk to him."

Harry was right, for Colin soon after overtook them, — having been driven up as usual by the negress, who seemed in great anger at the trouble he was causing her.

"Colin," said Harry, when their companion a. l the child had joined them, "you must keep that woman away from you. Her partiality for you has already been noticed by others. The Krooman has just been telling us that you will not live much longer; that Golah is neither blind nor foolish; and that, on the slightest suspicion he has of the woman showing you any favor, — even to giving you a fig, — he will kill you."

"But what can I do?" asked Colin. "If the woman should come to you and offer you a handful of figs and a drink of milk, could you refuse them?"

"No, I certainly could not. I only wish such an alternative would present itself; but you must manage in some way or other to keep away from her. You must not linger behind, but remain all the time by us."

"If you knew," asked Colin, "that you could quench your thirst by lagging a few paces behind, would you not do so?"

"That would be a strong temptation, and I should probably yield; but I tell you that you are in danger."

Neither of Colin's companions could blame him. Suffering, as he was, from the ceaseless agony of hunger and thirst, any indiscretion, or even crime, seemed justifiable, for the sake of obtaining relief.

The day became hotter and hotter, until in the afternoon the sufferings of the slaves grew almost unendurable. Sailor Bill appeared to be more severely affected than any of his companions. He had been knocking about the world for many long years, injuring his constitution by dissipation and exposure in many climes; and the siege that thirst and hunger were now making to destroy his strength became each hour more perceptible in its effect.

By the middle of the afternoon it was with the utmost difficulty he could move along; and his tongue was so parched that in an attempt to speak he wholly failed. His hands were stretched forth towards Colin; who, since the warning he had received, had kept up along with the rest.

Colin understood the signal; and placed the boy on the old man's shoulders. Bill wished to learn if the mother would reward him for taking care of her child, as she had his predecessor in the office. To carry out the experiment he allowed himself to be left in the rear of the caravan.

Golah's son and the other guard had noticed the old sailor's suffering condition, and objected to his being incumbered with the child. They pointed to Harry and Terence; but Bill was resolute in holding on to his charge; and cursing him for an unbelieving fool, they allowed him to have his own way.

Not long after, the mother of the child was seen to stop her camel, and the three mids passed by her unnoticed. The old sailor hastened up as fast as his weary limbs would allow to receive the hoped-for reward; but the poor fellow was doomed to a cruel disappointment.

When the woman perceived who had been entrusted with the carrying of her child, she pronounced two or three phrases in a sharp, angry tone. Understanding them, the child dismounted from the sailor's back and ran with all speed towards her.

Bill's reward was a storm of invectives, accompanied by a shower of blows with the knotted end of the halter. He strove to avoid the punishment by increasing his speed; but the camel seemed to understand the relative distance that should be maintained between its rider and the sailor, so that the former might deliver and the latter receive the blows with the most painful effect. This position it kept until Bill had got up to his companions; his naked shoulders bearing crimson evidence of the woman's ability in the handling of a rope's end.

As she rode past Colin, who had again taken charge of the child, she gave the young Scotchman a look that seemed to say, "You have betrayed me!" and without waiting for a look in return, she passed on to join her husband at the head of the caravan.

The black slaves appeared highly amused at the sailor's misfortunes. The incident had aroused their expiring energies, and the journey was pursued by them with more animation than ever.

Bill's disappointment was not without some beneficial effect upon himself. He was so much revived by the beating, that he soon after recovered his tongue; and as he shuffled on alongside his companions, they could hear him muttering curses, some in good English, some in bad, some in a rich Irish brogue, and some in the broadest Scotch.

CHAPTER XLVIII.

THE WATERLESS WELL.

GOLAH expected to reach the watering-place early in the evening; and all the caravan was excited by the anticipation of soon obtaining a plentiful supply of water.

It was well they were inspired by this hope. But for that, long before the sun had set, Sailor Bill and three or four others would have dropped down in despair, physically unable to have moved any further. But the prospect of plenty of water, to be found only a few miles ahead, brought, at the same time, resolution, strength, and life. Faint and feeble, they struggled on, nearly mad with the agony of nature's fierce demands; and soon after sunset they succeeded in reaching the well.

It was dry!

Not a drop of the much desired element was shining in the cavity where they had expected to find it.

Sailor Bill and some of the other slaves sank upon the earth, muttering prayers for immediate death.

Golah was in a great rage with everything, and his wives, children, slaves, and camels, that were most familiar with his moods, rushed here and there to get out of his way.

Suddenly he seemed to decide on a course to be taken in this terrible emergency, and his anger to some extent subsided.

Unbuckling the last goat-skin of water from one of the camels, he poured out a small cup for each individual of the *kafila*. Each was then served with a little *sangleh* and a couple of dried figs.

All were now ordered to move on towards the west, Golah leading the way. The new route was at right angles to the course they had been following during the earlier part of the day.

Some of the slaves who declared that they were unable to go further, found out, after receiving a few ticklings of the stick, that they had been mistaken. The application of Golah's cudgel awakened dormant energies of which they had not deemed themselves possessed.

After proceeding about two miles from the scene of their disappointment, Golah suddenly stopped, — as he did so, giving to his followers some orders in a low tone.

The camels were immediately brought into a circle, forced to kneel down, while their lading was removed from them.

While this was going on, the white captives heard voices, and the trampling of horses' hoofs.

The black sheik, with his highly educated ear, had detected the approach of strangers. This had caused him to order the halt.

When the noises had approached a little nearer Golah called out in Arabic: " Is it peace? "

" It is," was the answer; and as the strangers drew nearer, the salutations of " Peace be with you! " — " Peace be with all here, and with your friends! " were exchanged.

The caravan they had met consisted of between fifteen and twenty men, some horses and camels; and the sheik who commanded it inquired of Golah from whence he came.

" From the west," answered Golah, giving them to understand that he was travelling the same way as themselves.

" Then why did you not keep on to the well? " was the next inquiry.

" It is too far away," answered Golah. " We are very weary."

" It is not far," said the chief, " not more than half a league. You had better go on."

" No. I think it is more than two leagues, and we shall wait till morning."

We shall not. I know the well is not far away, and we shall reach it to-night."

" Very well," said Golah, "go, and may God be with you. But stay, masters, have you a camel to sell? "

" Yes, a good one. It is a little fatigued now, but will be strong in the morning."

Golah was aware that any camel they would sell him that night would be one that could only move with much difficulty, — one that they despaired of getting any further on the way. The black sheik knew his own business best; and was willing they should think they had cheated him in the bargain.

After wrangling for a few minutes, he succeeded in buying their camel, — the price being a pair of blankets, a shirt, and the dirk that had been taken from Terence. The camel had no cargo; and had for some time been forced onward at considerable trouble to its owner.

The strangers soon took their departure, going off in the direction of the dry well. As soon as they were out of sight Golah gave orders to reload the animals, and resume the interrupted march. To excite the slaves to a continuance of the journey, he promised that the camel he had purchased should be slaughtered on the next morning for their breakfast; and that they should have a long rest in the shade of the tents during the following day.

This promise, undoubtedly, had the anticipated effect in revivifying their failing energies, and they managed to move on until near daybreak, when the camel lately purchased laid itself down, and philosophically resisted every attempt at compelling it to continue the journey.

It was worn out with toil and hunger, and could not recover its feet.

The other animals were stopped and unladen, the tents were pitched, and preparations made for resting throughout the day.

After some dry weeds had been collected for fuel, Golah proceeded to fulfil his promise of giving them plenty of food.

A noose was made at the end of a rope, and placed around the camel's lower jaw. Its head was then screwed about, as far as it would reach, and the rope was made fast to the root of its tail, — the long neck of the camel allowing its head to be brought within a few inches of the place where the rope was tied.

Fatima, the favorite, stood by holding a copper kettle; while Golah opened a vein on the side of the animal's neck near the breastbone. The blood gushed forth in a stream; and before the camel had breathed its last. the vessel held to catch it had become filled more than half full.

The kettle was then placed over the fire, and the blood boiled and stirred with a stick until it had become as thick

as porridge. It was then taken off, and when it had cooled
down, it resembled, both in color and consistency, the liver
of a fresh killed bullock.

This food was divided amongst the slaves, and was greed
ily devoured by all.

The heart and liver of the camel, Golah ordered to be
cooked for his own family; and what little flesh was on the
bones, was cut into strips, and hung up in the sun to dry.

In one portion of the camel's stomach was about a gallon
and a half of water, thick and dirty with the vegetation it
had last consumed; but all was carefully poured into a goat's
skin, and preserved for future use.

The intestines were also saved, and hung out in the sun
to get cured by drying, to be afterwards eaten by the
slaves.

During the day Harry and Terence asked for an inter
view with Golah; and, accompanied by the Krooman, were
allowed to sit down by the door of his tent while they conversed with him.

Harry instructed the Krooman to inform their master,
that if they were taken to some seaport, a higher ransom
would be paid for them than any price for which they could
be sold elsewhere.

Golah's reply to this information was, that he doubted its
truth; that he did not like seaport towns; that his business lay
away from the sea; and that he was anxious to reach Timbuctoo as soon as possible. He further stated, that if all his
slaves were Christian dogs, who had reached the country in
ships, it might be worth his while to take them to some port
where they would be redeemed; but as the most of them
were of countries that did not pay ransoms for their subjects, there would be no use in his carrying them to the
coast, — where they might escape from him, and he would
then have had all his trouble for nothing.

He was next asked if he would not try to sell the white

captives along with the two Kroomen, to some slave dealer, who would take them to the coast for a market.

Golah would not promise this. He said, that to do so, he should have to sell them on the desert, where he could not obtain half their value.

The only information they were able to obtain from him was, that they were quite certain of seeing that far-famed city, Timbuctoo, — that was if they should prove strong enough to endure the hardships of the journey.

After thanking Golah for his condescension in listening to their appeal, the Krooman withdrew, followed by the others, who now for the first time began to realize the horror of their position. A plentiful supply of food, along with the day's rest, had caused all the white slaves to turn their thoughts from the present to the future.

Harry Blount and Terence, after their interview with Golah, found Colin and Sailor Bill anxiously awaiting their return.

"Well, what's the news?" asked Bill, as they drew near.

"Very bad," answered Terence. "There is no hope for us : we are going to Timbuctoo."

"No, I'm no going there," said Bill, "if it was in another world I migh* see the place soon enough, but in this, niver, — niver!"

CHAPTER XLIX.

THE WELL.

AT an early hour next morning the caravan started on its journey, still moving westward. This direction Golah was compelled to pursue to obtain a supply of water, although it was taking him no nearer his destination.

Two days' journey was before them ere they could reach another well. While performing it, Golah, vexed at the delay thus occasioned, was in very ill-humor with things in general.

Some of his displeasure was vented upon the camel he was riding, and the animal was usually driven far ahead of the others.

The sheik's wrath also fell upon his wives for lingering behind, and then upon the slaves for not following closer upon the heels of his camel. His son, and brother-in-law, would at intervals be solemnly cursed in the name of the Prophet for not driving the slaves faster.

Before the well had been reached, the four white slaves were in a very wretched condition. Their feet were blistered and roasted by the hot sand, and as the clothing allowed them was insufficient protection against the blazing sun, their necks and legs were inflamed and bleeding.

The intestines and most of the flesh of the slaughtered camel had been long ago consumed, as well as the filthy water taken from its stomach.

Colin had again established himself in the favor of the sheik's wife, and was allowed to have the care of the child; but the little food and drink he received for his attention to it were dearly earned.

The weight of the young negro was a serious incumbrance in a weary journey through what seemed to be a burning plain ; moreover the " darkey," in keeping its seat on the young Scotchman's shoulders, had pulled a quantity of hair out of his head, besides rendering his scalp exceedingly irritable to further treatment of a like kind.

Hungry, thirsty, weak, lame, and weary, the wretched captives struggled on until the well was reached.

On arriving within sight of a small hill on which were growing two or three sickly bushes, Golah pointed towards it, at the same time turning his face to those who were following him. All understood the signal, and seemed suddenly inspired with hope and happiness. The travellers pressed forward with awakened energy, and after passing over the hill came in sight of the well at its foot. —

The eagerness exhibited by the slaves to quench their thirst might have been amusing to any others than those who beheld them; but their master seemed intent on giving them a further lesson in the virtue of patience.

He first ordered the camels to be unladen, and the tents to be pitched. While some were doing this, he directed others to seek for fuel.

Meanwhile, he amused himself by collecting all the dishes and drinking-vessels, and placing them contiguous to the well.

He then attached a rope to a leathern bucket, and, drawing water from the reservoir, he carefully filled the utensils, with the least possible waste of the precious fluid his followers were so anxious to obtain.

When his arrangements were completed, he called his wives and children around him. Then, serving out to each of them about a pint of the water, and giving them a few seconds for swallowing it, he ordered them off.

Each obeyed without a murmur, all apparently satisfied.

The slaves were next called up, and then there was a rush in real earnest. The vessels were eagerly seized, and their contents greedily swallowed. They were presented for more, refilled, and again emptied.

The quantity of water swallowed by Sailor Bill and his three young companions, and the rapacity with which it was gulped down, caused Golah to declare that there was but one God, that Mahomet was his Prophet, and that four of the slaves about him were Christian swine.

After all had satisfied the demands of nature, Golah showed them the quantity of water he deemed sufficient for a thirsty individual by drinking about a pint himself — not more than a fifth of the amount consumed by each of his white slaves.

Long years of short allowance had accustomed the negro sheik to make shift with a limited allowance of the precious commodity, and yet continue strong and active.

About two hours after they had reached the well, and just as they had finished watering the camels, another caravan arrived. Its leader was hailed by Golah with the words, "Is it peace?" — the usual salutation when strangers meet on the desert.

"The answer was, "It is peace"; and the new comers dismounted, and pitched their camp.

Next morning Golah had a long talk with their sheik, after which he returned to his own tents in much apparent uneasiness.

The caravan newly arrived consisted of eleven men, with eight camels and three Saäran horses. The men were all Arabs — none of them being slaves. They were well armed, and carried no merchandise. They had lately come from the north west, for what purpose Golah knew not: since the account the stranger sheik had given of himself was not satisfactory.

Though very short of provisions, Golah resolved not to leave the well that day; and the Krooman learnt that this resolution was caused by his fear of the strangers.

"If he is afraid of them," said Harry, "I should suppose that would make him all the more anxious to get out of their company."

The Krooman, in explanation, stated that if the Arabs were robbers — pirates of the desert — they would not molest Golah so long as he remained at the well.

"In this the Krooman was correct. Highway robbers do not waylay their victims at an inn, but on the road. Pirates do not plunder ships in a harbor, but out on the open ocean. Custom, founded on some good purpose, has established a similar rule on the great sandy ocean of the Saára.

"I wish they were robbers, and would take us from Golah!" said Colin. "We should then perhaps be carried to the north, where we might be ransomed some time or other. As it is, if we are to be taken to Timbuctoo, we shall never escape out of Africa."

"We shall not be taken there," cried Terence. "We shall turn robbers ourselves first. I will for one; and when I do, Golah shall be robbed of *one* of his slaves at least."

"An' that wan will be Misther Terence O'Connor, ov coorse?" said Bill.

"Yes."

"Thin ye will 'ave done no more than Master Colly, who has already robbed 'im ov twa — the haffections ov 'is wife an' bairn."

"That will do, Bill," said Colin, who did not like hearing any allusion made to the woman. "We have something else that should engage our attention. Since we have learnt that they intend taking us to Timbuctoo, it is time we began to act. We must not go there."

"That is understood," said Harry; "but what can we do? Something should be done immediately. Every day we journey southward carries us farther from home, or the chance of ever getting there. Perhaps these Arabs may buy us, and take us north. Suppose we get the Krooman to speak to them?"

All consented to this course. The Krooman was called, and when informed of their wishes he said that he must not be seen speaking to the Arabs, or Golah would be displeased. He also stated — what the white captives had already observed — that Golah and his son were keeping a sharp watch over them, as well as over the strangers; and that an opportunity of talking to the Arab sheik might not be easily obtained.

While he was still speaking, the latter was observed proceeding towards the well to draw some water.

The Krooman instantly arose, and sauntered after.

He was observed by the quick eye of Golah, who called to him to come away; which he did, but not before quenching his thirst, that did not appear to be very great.

On the Krooman's return from the well, he informed Harry that he had spoken to the Arab sheik. He had said, "Buy us. You will get plenty of money for us in Swearah;" and that the reply of the sheik was, "The white slaves are dogs, and not worth buying."

"Then we have no hope from that source!" exclaimed Terence.

The Krooman shook his head; not despondently, but as if he did not agree in the opinion Terence had expressed.

"What! do you think there is any hope?" asked Harry.

The man gave a nod of assent.

"How? In what way?"

The Krooman vouchsafed no explanation, but sauntered silently away.

When the sun was within two or three hours of setting over the Saära, the Arabs struck their tents, and started off in the direction of the dry well — from whence Golah and his caravan had just come. After they had disappeared behind the hill, Golah's son was sent to its top to watch them while his women and slaves were ordered to strike the tents as quickly as possible.

Then waiting till the shades of night had descended over the desert, and the strangers were beyond the reach of vision, Golah gave orders to resume the march once more in a southeasterly direction — which would carry them away from the seacoast — and, as the white slaves believed, from all chances of their ever recovering their freedom.

The Krooman, on the contrary, appeared to be pleased at their taking this direction, notwithstanding the objections he had expressed to going inland.

CHAPTER L.

A MOMENTOUS INQUIRY.

DURING the night's journey Golah still seemed to have some fear of the Arabs; and so great was his desire to place as much ground as possible between himself and them, that he did not halt, until the sun was more than two hours above the horizon.

For some time before a halt had been planned, Fatima, his favorite wife, had been riding by his side, and making, what seemed, from the excited movements of both, an important communication.

After the tents had been pitched, and food was about being served out, Golah commanded the mother of the boy carried by Colin to produce the bag of figs that had been intrusted to her keeping.

Trembling with apprehension, the woman rose to obey. The Krooman glanced at the white captives with an expression of horror; and although they had not understood Golah's command, they saw that something was going wrong.

The woman produced the bag; which was not quite half full. There were in it about two quarts of dried figs.

The figs that had been served out three days before at the

dry well had been taken from another bag kept in the custody of Fatima.

The one now produced by the second wife should have been full: and Golah demanded to know why it was not.

The woman tremblingly asseverated that she and her children had eaten them.

At this confession Fatima uttered a scornful laugh, and spoke a few words that increased the terror of the delinquent mother, — at the same time causing the boy to commence howling with affright.

"I tell you so," said the Krooman, who was standing near the white slaves; "Fatima say to Golah, 'Christian dog eat the figs'; Golah kill him now; he kill da woman too."

In the opinion of those who travel the great desert, about the greatest crime that can be committed is to steal food or drink, and consume either unknown to their companions of the journey.

Articles of food intrusted to the care of any one must be guarded and preserved, — even at the expense of life.

Under no circumstances may a morsel be consumed, until it is produced in the presence of all, and a division, either equitable or otherwise, has been made.

Even had the story told by the woman been true, her crime would have been considered sufficiently great to have endangered her life; but her sin was greater than that.

She had bestowed favor upon a slave, — a Christian dog, — and had aroused the jealousy of her Mahometan lord and master.

Fatima seemed happy; for nothing less than a miracle could, in her opinion, save the life of her fellow-wife, who chanced to be a hated rival.

After drawing his scimitar from its sheath, and cocking his musket, Golah ordered all the slaves to squat themselves on the ground, and in a row.

This order was quickly comprehended and obeyed, — the whites seating themselves together at one end of the line.

Golah's son and the other guard — each with his musket loaded and cocked — were stationed in front of the row : and were ordered by the sheik to shoot any one who attempted to get up from the ground.

The monster then stepped up to Colin, and, seizing the young Scotchman by the auburn locks, dragged him a few paces apart from his companions. There, for a time, he was left alone.

Golah then proceeded to serve out some cheni to every individual on the ground ; but none was given to the woman who had aroused his anger, nor to Colin.

In the sheik's opinion, to have offered them food would have been an act as foolish as to have poured it upon the sands.

Food was intended to sustain life, and it was not designed by him that they should live much longer. And yet it was evident from his manner that he had not quite determined as to how they were to die.

The two guards, with the muskets in their grasp, kept a sharp eye on the slaves, while Golah became engaged in a close consultation with Fatima.

" What shall we do ? " asked Terence ; " the old villain means mischief, and how can we prevent it ? We must not let him kill poor Colly ? "

" We must do something immediately," said Harry. "We have neglected it too long, and shall now have to act under the disadvantage of their being prepared for an attack. Bill, what should we do ? "

" 1 was just thinking," said Bill, " that if we all made a rush at 'em, at the words *One — two — three !* not more 'n two or three of us might be killed afore we grappled with 'em. Now, this might do, if these black fellows would only jine us."

The Krooman here expressed himself as one willing to take his chance in any action they should propose, and believed that his countrymen would do the same. He feared, however, that the other blacks could not be trusted, and that any proposal he might make to them would be in a language the two guards would understand.

"Well, then," said Harry, "there will be six of us against three. Shall I give the word?"

"All right!" said Terence, drawing his feet under his body, by way of preparation for rising suddenly.

The scheme was a desperate one, but all seemed willing to undertake it.

Since leaving the well, they had felt convinced that life and liberty depended on their making a struggle; though circumstances seemed to have forced that struggle upon them when there was the least hope of success.

"Now all make ready," muttered Harry, speaking in a calm voice, so as not to excite the attention of the guards. "One!"

"Stop!" exclaimed Colin, who had been listening attentively to all that was said. "I'm not with you. We should all be killed. Two or three would be shot, and the sheik himself could finish all the rest with his scimitar. It is better for him to kill me, if he really means to do so, than to have all four destroyed in the vain hope of trying to save one."

"It is not for you alone that we are going to act," interposed Harry. "It is as much for ourselves."

"Then act when there is a chance of succeeding," pursued Colin. "You cannot save me, and will only lose your own lives."

"De big black sheik am going to kill someb'dy, dat berry sure," said the Krooman, as he sat with his eyes fixed upon Golah.

The latter was still in consultation with Fatima, his face

wearing an expression that was horrible for all except her-self to behold. Murder by excruciating torture seemed written on every feature of his countenance.

The woman, upon whose manner of death they were de-liberating, was in the act of caressing her children, appar-ently conscious that she had but a few minutes more to re-main in their company. Her features wore an expression of calm and hopeless resignation, as if she had yielded her-self up to the decree of an inevitable fate.

The third wife had retired a short distance from the others. With her child in her arms, she sat upon the ground, con-templating the scene before her with a look of mingled sur-prise, curiosity, and regret.

From the appearance of the whole caravan, a stranger could have divined that some event of thrilling interest was about to transpire.

"Colin," cried Terence, encouragingly, "we won't sit here quietly, and see you meet death. We had better do some-thing while yet we have a chance. Let Harry give the word."

"I tell you it's madness," expostulated Colin. "Wait till we see what he intends doing. Perhaps he'll keep me a while for future vengeance, and ye may have a chance of a rescue when there are not two men standing over us ready to blow our brains out."

Colin's companions saw there was truth in this remark, and for a while they waited in silence, with their eyes fixed upon the tent of the shiek.

They had not long to wait, for, soon after, Golah came forth, having finished his consultation with Fatima.

On his face appeared a hideous smile, — a smile that made most of those who beheld it shudder with a sensation of horror.

CHAPTER LI.

A LIVING GRAVE.

GOLAH'S first act after coming forth was to take some thongs from his saddle. Having done this, he beckoned to the two who guarded the slaves, giving them some admonition in an unknown tongue. The effect was to excite their greater vigilance. The muzzles of their muskets were turned towards the white captives, and they seemed anxiously waiting the order to fire.

Golah then looked towards Terence, and made a sign for the young Irishman to get up and come towards him.

Terence hesitated.

"Go on, Terry," muttered Colin   "He don't mean *you* any harm."

At this instant Fatima stepped at from the tent, armed with her husband's scimitar, and apparently anxious for an opportunity of using it.

Acting under the advice of the others, Terence sprang to his feet: and advanced to the spot where the sheik was standing. The Krooman who spoke English was then called up; and Golah, taking him and the midshipman each by a hand, led them into his tent, — whither they were followed by Fatima.

The sheik now addressed a few words to the Krooman, who then told Terence that his life depended on perfect obedience to Golah's orders. His hands were to be tied: and he must not call out so as to be heard by the others.

"He say," said the Krooman, " if you no make fight, and no make noise, he no kill you."

The man further counselled Terence to submit quietly, — saying that the least resistance would lead to all the white slaves being killed.

Though possessing more than average strength and power for a youth of his age, Terence knew that, in a strife with the gigantic black sheik, he would not have the slightest chance of being victor.

Should he shout to his companions, and have them all act in concert, — as they had already proposed?

No. Such an act would most likely lead to two of them being shot; to the third having his brains knocked out with the butt-end of a musket; and to the fourth, — himself, — being strangled in the powerful grasp of Golah, if not beheaded with the scimitar in the hands of Fatima. On reflection, the young Scotchman yielded, and permitted his hands to be tied behind his back; so, too, did the Krooman.

Golah now stepped out of the tent: and immediately after returned, leading Harry Blount along with him.

On reaching the opening, and seeing Terence and the Krooman lying bound upon the floor, the young Englishman started back, and struggled to free himself from the grasp of the hand that had hold of him. His efforts only resulted in his being instantly flung to the earth, and fast held by his powerful adversary, who at the same time was also employed in protecting his victim from the fury of Fatima.

Terence, Harry, and the Krooman were now conducted back over the ground, and placed in their former position in the row, — from which they had been temporarily taken.

Sailor Bill and Colin were next treated in a similar fashion, — both being fast bound like their companions.

"What does the ould divil mane?" asked Bill when Golah was tying his hands together. "Will he murder us all?"

"No," answered the Krooman. "He no kill but one of your party."

His eyes turned upon Colin as he spoke.

"Colin! Colin!" exclaimed Harry; "see what you have done by opposing our plan! We are all helpless now."

"And so much the better for yourselves," answered Colin "You will now suffer no further harm."

"If he means no harm, why has he bound us?" asked Bill. "It's a queer way of showing friendship."

"Yes, but a safe one," answered Colin. "You cannot now bring yourselves into danger by a foolish resistance to his will"

Terence and Harry understood Colin's meaning; and now, for the first time, comprehended the reason why they had been bound.

It was to prevent them from interfering with Golah's plans for the disposal of his two victims.

Now that the white slaves were secured, no danger was apprehended from the others; and the two who had been guarding them retired to the shade of a tent to refresh themselves with a drink of cheni.

While the brief conversation above related was being held, Golah had become busily engaged in overhauling the lading of one of his camels.

The object of his search was soon discovered : for, the moment after, he came towards them carrying a long Moorish spade.

Two of the black slaves were then called from the line ; the spade was placed in the hands of one, and a wooden dish was given to the other. They were then ordered to make a large hole in the sand, — to accomplish which they at once set to work.

"They are digging a grave for me, or that of the poor woman, — perhaps for both of us?" suggested Colin, as he calmly gazed on the spectacle.

His companions had no doubt but that it was as he had said ; and sat contemplating the scene in melancholy silence.

While the slaves were engaged in scooping up the hole, Golah called the two guards, and gave them some orders about continuing the journey.

The blacks set about the work were but a few minutes in making an excavation in the loose sand of some four feet in depth. They were then directed to dig another.

"It's all over with me,' said Colin; "he intends to kill two, and of course I must be one of them."

"He *should* kill us all," exclaimed Terence. "We de serve it for leaving the well last night. We should have made an effort for our lives, while we had the chance."

"You are right," replied Harry; "we *are* fools, cowardly fools! We deserve neither pity in this world nor happiness in the next. Colly, my friend, if you meet with any harm, I swear to avenge it, whenever my hands are free."

"And I'll be with you," added Terence.

"Never mind me, old comrades," answered Colin, who seemed less excited than the others. "Do the best you can for yourselves, and you may some time escape from this monster."

The attention of Harry was now attracted to Sailor Bill, who had turned his back toward one of the black slaves sitting near him, and was by signs entreating the man to untie his hand.

The man refused, evidently fearing the anger of Golah should he be detected.

The second Krooman, who was unbound, now offered to loose the hands of his countryman; but the latter seemed satisfied with his want of freedom, and refused the proffered aid. He also feared death at the hands of Golah.

If left to divine the ultimate intentions of the black sheik by the knowledge of human nature they had acquired before falling into his hands, the white captives would not have been seriously alarmed for the welfare of any one of their number. But Golah was a specimen of natural history new to them; and their apprehensions were excited to the highest pitch by the conduct of those whom they knew to be better acquainted with his character.

The behavior of the woman who had aroused his anger showed that she was endeavoring to resign herself to some fearful mode of death. The wild lamentations of her children denoted that they were conscious of some impending misfortune.

Fatima seemed about to realize the fulfilment of some long-cherished hope, — the hope of revenge on a detested rival.

The care Golah had taken to hinder any interference with his plans, — the words of the Krooman, the looks and gestures of the guards and of Golah himself, the digging of two graves in the sand, — all gave warning that some fearful tragedy was about to be enacted. Our adventurers were conscious of this, and conscious, also, that they could do nothing to prevent it.

Nearly frantic with the helplessness of their position, they could only wait — "trembling for the birth of Fate."

CHAPTER LII.

THE SHEIK'S PLAN OF REVENGE.

THE second sand-pit was dug a short distance from the first; and when it had been sunk to the depth of about four and a half feet, Golah commanded the blacks to leave off their labor, — one of them being sent back to the line to be seated along with his fellow-slaves.

By this time the tents had been struck, the camels loaded; and all but Golah and Fatima appeared willing and anxious to depart from the spot. These were not: for their business at that camping-place had not yet been completed.

When the two guards had again resumed their former

stations in front of the line, — as before with their muskets at full cock, — Golah advanced towards the woman, who, disengaging herself from her children, stood up at his ap proach.

Then succeeded a moment of intense interest.

Was he going to kill her?

If so, in what manner?

All looked on with painful anticipation of some dire event.

It soon transpired. The woman was seized by Golah himself; dragged towards the pits that had been dug; and thrust into one of them. The slave who wielded the spade was then commanded to fill up the excavation around her.

Terence was the first to speak.

"God help her!" he exclaimed; "the monster is going to bury her alive! Can't we save her?"

"We are not men if we do not try!" exclaimed Harry, as he suddenly sprang to his feet.

His example was immediately followed by his white companions.

The two muskets were instantly directed towards them; but at a shout from Golah their muzzles were as quickly dropped.

The sheik's son then, at his father's command, ran to the pit to secure the woman, while Golah himself rushed forward to meet the helpless men who were advancing towards him.

In an instant the four were thrown prostrate to the earth. With their hands tied, the powerful sheik upset them as easily as though they had been bags of sand.

Raising Harry by the hair of his head with one hand and Terence with the other, he dragged them back to their places in the line where they had been already seated.

Sailor Bill saved himself from like treatment by roiling

over and over until he had regained his former place. Colin
was allowed to lie on the ground where the sheik had
knocked him over.

Golah now returned to the pit where the woman stood
half buried.

She made no resistance — she uttered no complaint — but
seemed calmly to resign herself to a fate that could not be
averted. Golah apparently did not intend to behold her
die, for, when the earth was filled in around her body, her
head still remained above ground. She was to be starved to
death ! As the sheik was turning away to attend to other
matters, the woman spoke. Her words were few. and produced no effect upon him. They did, however, upon the
Krooman, whose eyes were seen to fill with tears that rapidly
chased each other down his mahogany-colored cheeks.

Colin, who seemed to notice everything except the fate
threatening himself, observed the Krooman's excitement,
and inquired its cause.

" She ask him to be kind to her little boy," said the man,
in a voice trembling with emotion.

Are tears unmanly ? — No.

The shining drops that rolled from that man's eyes, and
sparkled adown his dusky cheeks, on hearing the unfortunate woman's prayer for her children, proved that he was
not a brute, but a man, — a man with a soul that millions
might envy.

After leaving the place where the woman was buried,
Golah walked up to Colin ; and. dragging him to his feet,
led him away to the other pit.

His intentions were now evident to all. The two individuals, who had aroused his anger and jealousy, were to be
left near each other, buried alive, to perish in this fearful
fashion.

" Colin ! Colin ! what can we do to save you ? " ex
claimed Harry, in a tone expressing despair and anguish.

"Nothing," answered Colin; "don't attempt it, or you will only bring trouble on yourselves.   Leave me to my fate."

At this moment the speaker was thrown into the pit, and held in an upright attitude by Golah, while the black slave proceeded to fill in the earth around him.

Following the philosophical example set by the woman, Colin made no useless resistance ; and was soon submerged under the sand piled up to his shoulders.   His companions sat gazing with speechless horror, all suffering the combined anguish of shame, regret, and despair.

The sheik was now ready to depart; and ordered the slave who had been assisting him in his diabolical work to mount the camel formerly ridden by the woman who was thus entombed.   The black obeyed, pleased to think that his late task was to be so agreeably rewarded ; but a sudden change came over his features when Golah and Fatima passed up the three children, and placed them under his care.

Golah had but one more act to perform before leaving the spot.   It was an act worthy of himself, although suggested by Fatima.

After filling a bowl about half full of water, he placed it midway between Colin and the woman, but so distant from each that neither could possibly reach it !

This Satanic idea was executed with the design of tantalizing the sufferers in their dying hours with the sight of that element the want of which would soon cause them the most acute anguish.   By the side of the bowl he also placed a handful of figs.

"There," he tauntingly exclaimed ; "I leave you two together, and with more food and drink than you will ever consume.   Am I not kind ?   What more can you ask ? *Bismillah!*   God is great, and Mahomet is his prophet ; and I am Golah, the kind, the just ! "

Saying this, he gave orders to resume the march.

"Don't move!" exclaimed Terence; "we will give him some trouble yet."

"Of course we'll not go, and leave Colin there," said Harry. "The sheik is too avaricious to kill all his slaves. Don't move a step, Bill, and we may have Colly liberated yet."

"I shall do as you say, ov coorse," said Bill; "but I expect we shall 'ave to go. Golah has got a way of making a man travel, whether he be willing or not."

All started forward from the place but the three white slaves and the two whom Golah intended to remain.

"Cheer up, lad," said Bill to Colin; "we'll never go, and leave you there."

"Go on, go on!" exclaimed Colin. "You can do me no good, and will only injure yourselves."

Golah had mounted his camel and ridden forward, leaving to his two guards the task of driving on the slaves; and, as if apprehensive of trouble from them, he had directed Terence, Harry, Bill, and the Krooman to be brought on with their hands tied behind them.

The three refused to move; and when all efforts to get them on had been tried in vain, the guards made a loud appeal to their sheik.

Golah came riding back in a great rage.

Dismounting from his camel he drew the ramrod from his musket; then, rushing up to Terence, who was the nearest to him, administered to him a shower of blows that changed the color of his shirt from an untidy white to the darker hue of blood.

The two guards, following the example of their lord and master, commenced beating Harry and Bill, who, unable to make any resistance, had to endure the torture in silence.

"Go on, my friends!" exclaimed Colin; "for God's sake go, and leave me! You cannot do anything to avert my fate!"

Colin's entreaties, as well as the torture from the blows they received, were alike without effect. His shipmates could not bring themselves to desert their old comrade, and leave him to the terrible death that threatened him.

Rushing up to Bill and Harry, Golah caught hold of each, and hurled them to the gronnd by the side of Terence. Keeping all three together, he now ordered a camel to be led up; and the order was instantly obeyed by one of the guards. The halter was then taken from the head of the animal.

"We 'ave got to go now," said Bill. "He 's going to try the same dodge as beat me the other day. I shall save him the trouble."

Bill tried to rise, but was prevented. He had refused to walk when earnestly urged to do so; and now, when he was willing to go on, he had to wait the pleasure of his owner as to the manner in which his journey should be continued.

While Golah was fastening the rope to Harry's hands, the sharp shrill voice of Fatima called his attention to some of the people who had gone on before.

The two women, who led the camels loaded with articles taken from the wreck, had advanced about three hundred yards from the place; and were now, along with the black slaves, surrounded by a party of men mounted on maherries and horses.

CHAPTER LIII.

CAPTURED AGAIN.

GOLAH'S fear of the Arabs met by the well had not been without a cause. His forced night march, to avoid meeting them again, had not secured the object for which it had been made.

Approaching from the direction of the rising sun, the Arabs had not been discovered in the distance; and Golah, occupied in overcoming the obstinate resistance of the white slaves, had allowed them to come quite near before they had been observed by him.

Leaving his captives, the sheik seized his musket; and, followed by his son and brother-in-law, rushed forward to protect his wives and property.

He was too late. Before he could reach them they were in the possession of others; and as he drew near the spot where they had been captured, he saw a dozen muskets presented towards himself, and heard some one loudly commanding him, in the name of the Prophet, to approach in peace!

Golah had the discretion to yield to a destiny that could not be averted, — the misfortune of being made a prisoner and plundered at the same time.

Calmly saying, "It is the will of God," he sat down, and invited his captors to a conference on the terms of capitulation.

As soon as the caravan had fallen into the possession of the robbers, the Krooman's hands were unbound by his companion, and he hastened to the relief of the white slaves.

"Golah no our massa now," said he, while untying Harry's wrists; "our massa is Arab dat take us norf. We get free. Dat why dis Arab no buy us, — he know us he hab for noting."

The cords were quickly untied, and the attention of the others was now turned to disinterring Colin and the woman from their living graves.

To do this, Harry wanted to use the water-bowl the sheik had left for the purpose of tantalizing his victims with the sight of its contents.

"Here, drink this water," said he, holding the vessel to Colin's lips. "I want to make use of the dish."

"No, no; dig me out without that," answered Colin. "Leave the water as it is; I have a particular use for it when I get free. I wish the old sheik to see me drink it."

Bill, Harry, and the Krooman set to work: and Colin and the woman were soon uncovered and dragged out. Terence was then awakened to consciousness by a few drops of the water poured over his face.

Owing to the cramped position in which he had been placed and so long held, Colin was for a few minutes unable to walk. They waited, to give him time to recover the use of his limbs. The slave who had the care of the woman's children was now seen coming back with them, and the woman ran to meet him.

The delight of the wretched mother at again embracing her offspring was so great, that the gentle-souled Krooman was once more affected to tears.

In the conference with the Arab robbers, Golah was unable to obtain the terms he fancied a sheik should be entitled to.

They offered him two camels and the choice of one wife out of the three, on condition he should go back to his own country, and return to the desert no more.

These terms Golah indignantly refused, and declared that he would rather die in defence of his rights.

Golah was a pure negro, and one of a class of traders

much disliked by the Arabs. He was a lawless intruder on their grounds, — a trespasser upon their special domain, the Great Desert. He had just acquired a large amount of wealth in goods and slaves, that had been cast on their coast; and these they were determined he should not carry back with him to his own country.

Though he was as much a robber as themselves, they had no sympathies with him, and would not be satisfied with merely a share of his plunder. They professed to understand all his doings in the past; and accused him of not being a *fair trader!*

They told him that he never came upon the desert with merchandise to exchange, but only with camels, to be driven away, laden with property justly belonging to them, the real owners of the land.

They denied his being a true believer in the Prophet; and concluded their talk by declaring that he should be thankful for the liberal terms they had offered him.

Golah's opposition to their proposal became so demonstrative, that the Arabs were obliged to disarm and bind him; though this was not accomplished without a fierce struggle, in which several of his adversaries were overthrown.

A blow on the head with the stock of a musket at length reduced him to subjection, after which his hands were fast tied behind his back.

During the struggle, Golah's son was prevented from interfering in behalf of his father, by the black slaves who had been so long the victims of his cruel care; while the brother-in-law, as well as Fatima and the third wife, remained passive spectators of the scene.

On Golah being secured, the white slaves, with old Bill at their head, came up and voluntarily surrendered themselves to their new masters.

Colin had in his hands the bowl of water, and the dried figs that had been placed beside it.

Advancing towards Golah, he held the figs up before his eyes, and then, with a nod and an expression that seemed to say, "Thank you for this," he raised the bowl to his lips with the intention of drinking.

The expression on the sheik's features became Satanic, but suddenly changed into a glance of pleasure, as one of the Arabs snatched the vessel out of Colin's hands, and instantly drank off its contents.

Colin received the lesson meekly, and said not a word.

The Arabs speedily commenced making arrangements for leaving the place. The first move was to establish a communication between Golah and the saddle of one of his camels.

This was accomplished by using a rope as a medium; and the black giant was compelled to walk after the animal with his hands tied behind him, — in the same fashion as he had lately set for Sailor Bill.

His wives and slaves seemed to comprehend the change in their fortunes, and readily adapted their conduct to the circumstances.

The greatest transformation of all was observable in the behavior of the favorite Fatima.

Since his capture she had kept altogether aloof from her late lord, and showed not the slightest sympathy for his misfortunes.

By her actions she seemed to say: "The mighty Golah has fallen, and is no longer worthy of my distinguished regard."

Very different was the behavior of the woman whom the cruel sheik would have left to die a lingering death. Her husband's misfortune seemed to have awakened within her a love for the father of her children: and her features, as she gazed upon the captive, — who, although defeated, was unsubdued in spirit, — wore a mingled expression of pity and grief.

9   M

Hungry, thirsty, weary and bleeding — enslaved on the
Great Desert, still uncertain of what was to be their fate,
and doubtful of surviving much longer the hardships they
might be forced to endure — our adventurers were far from
being happy; but, with all their misery, they felt joyful
when comparing their present prospects with those before
them but an hour ago.

With the exception of Golah, the Arabs had no trouble
with their captives. The white and black slaves knew they
were travelling towards the well; and the prospect of again
having plenty of water was sufficient inducement to make
them put forth all their strength in following the camels.

Early in the evening a short halt was made; when each
of the company was served with about half a pint of water
from the skins. The Arabs, expecting to reach the well
soon after, could afford to be thus liberal; but the favor so
granted, though thankfully received by the slaves was scorn-
fully refused by their late master — the giant-bodied and
strong-minded Golah.

To accept of food and drink from his enemies in his
present humiliating position — bound and dragged along
like a slave — was a degradation to which he scorned to
submit.

On Golah contemptuously refusing the proffered cup of
water, the Arab who offered it simply ejaculated, "Thank
God!" and then drank it himself.

The well was reached about an hour after midnight; and
after quenching their thirst, the slaves were allowed to go
to rest and sleep, — a privilege they stood sorely in need of
having been over thirty hours afoot, upon their cheerless
and arduous journey.

CHAPTER LIV.

AN UNFAITHFUL WIFE.

ON waking up the next morning, our adventurers were gratified with a bit of intelligence communicated by the Krooman: that they were to have a day of rest. A camel was also to be killed for food.

The Arabs were going to divide amongst themselves the slaves taken from Golah; and the opportunity was not to be lost of recruiting their strength for a long journey.

As Sailor Bill reflected upon their sufferings since leaving that same place two days before, he expressed regret that they had not been captured before leaving the well, and thus spared the horrors they had endured.

Stimulated by the remembrance of so much suffering needlessly incurred, he asked the Krooman to explain the conduct of their new masters.

The Krooman's first attempt at satisfying his curiosity was to state, that the Arabs had acted after a manner peculiar to themselves, — in other words, that it was "a way they had."

The old sailor was not satisfied with this answer; and pressed for a further explanation.

He was then told that the robbers on the desert were always in danger of meeting several caravans at a watering-place; and that any act of violence committed there would bring upon the perpetrators everlasting disgrace, as well as the enmity of all desert travellers. The Krooman explained himself by saying, that should a caravan of a hundred men arrive at the well, they would not now interfere in behalf of Golah, but would only recognize him as a slave. On the contrary, had they found him engaged in actual strife with the robbers they would have assisted him.

This was satisfactory to all but Bill. Even Colin, who had been buried alive, and Terence, who had been so unmercifully beaten, were pleased at their change of masters on any terms; but the old sailor, sailor-like, would not have been himself without some cause of complaint.

Before their newly acquired wealth could be divided, the Arabs had to come to some resolution as to the disposal of the black sheik; who still remained so unmanageable that he had to be kept bound, with a guard placed over him.

The Arabs could not agree amongst themselves as to what should be done with him. Some of them urged that, despite the color of his skin, he might be a true believer in the Prophet; and that, notwithstanding his manner of trading and acquiring wealth — a system nearly as dishonest as their own — he was entitled to his liberty, with a certain portion of his property.

Others claimed that they had a perfect right to add him and his large family to the number of their slaves.

He was not an Arab, but an Ethiopian, like most of his following; and, as a slave, would bring a high price in any of the markets where men were bought and sold.

Those who argued thus were in the minority; and Golah was at length offered his wives and their children, with a couple of camels and his scimitar.

This offer the black sheik indignantly refused, — much to the astonishment of those who had been so eloquent in his behalf.

His decision produced another debate; in which the opinions of several of his captors underwent such a change, that it was finally determined to consider him as one of the slaves.

Every article that had been obtained from the wreck was now exposed to view, and a fixed price set upon it.

The slaves were carefully examined and valued, — as well

as the camels, muskets, and everything that had belonged to Golah or his dependants.

When these preliminary arrangements had been completed, the Arabs proceeded to an equitable partition of the property.

This proved a very difficult matter to manage, and occupied their time for the rest of the day. Three or four would covet the same article; and long and noisy discussions would take place before the dispute could be settled to their mutual satisfaction.

The Krooman, who understood the desert language, was attentive to all that transpired; and from time to time informed the white slaves of what was being done.

At an early period in the discussions, he discovered that each of the four was to fall to different masters.

"You and me," said he to Harry, "we no got two massas — only one."

His words were soon after proved to be true. They were carried apart from each other, evidently with the designs of being appropriated by different owners; and the fear that they might also be separated again came over them.

When the slaves, camels, tents, and articles that had been gathered from the wreck were distributed amongst the eleven Arabs, each one took the charge of his own; but there still remained Golah, his wives and their children, to be disposed of.

No one seemed desirous of becoming the owner of the black sheik and his wives. Even those who had said that he would make a valuable slave, appeared unwilling to take him, although induced to do so by the taunts of their companions.

The fact was, that they were afraid of him. He would be too difficult to manage; and none of them wished to be the master of one who obstinately refused both food and drink, and who so defiantly invoked upon the heads of his

captors the curse of Mahomet, and swore by the beard of the
Prophet that the moment his hands were free, he would kill
the man who should dare to own or claim him as a slave.

Golah, with all his faults, was neither cunning nor deceitful, and, having a spirit too great to affect submission, he did
not intend to yield.

He was arrogant, cruel, avaricious, and vindictive; but
the wrongs he did were always accomplished in a plain,
open-handed way, and never by stratagem or treachery.

By accepting the terms the Arabs had offered him, his
strength, courage, and unconquerable will might afterwards
have enabled him to obtain revenge upon his captors, and
regain a portion of his property; but it was not in his nature to sham submission, even for the sake of gaining a
future advantage.

As not one of the Arabs was willing to accept of him, at
the value at which he had been appraised, or to allow another to have him for less, it was finally decided that he
should be retained as the common property of all, until he
could be sold to some other tribe, when a distribution might
be made of the proceeds of the sale. His wives and children
were to be disposed of in like manner.

This arrangement was satisfactory to all but Golah himself, who expressed himself greatly displeased with it. Nev-
ertheless, he seemed a little disposed to yield to circumstances; for, soon after the decision of his captors was made
known to him, he called to Fatima, and commanded her to
bring him a bowl of water.

The favorite refused, under the plea that she had been
forbidden to give him anything.

This was true; for, as he had declined to accept of anything at the hands of those claiming to be his masters, they
had determined to starve him into submission.

Fatima's refusal to obey him caused Golah his greatest
chagrin. Ever accustomed to prompt and slavish obedience

from others, the idea of his own wife — his favorite too — denying his modest request, almost drove him frantic.

"I am your husband," he cried, "and whom should you obey but me? Fatima! I command you to bring me some water!"

"And I command you not to do it," said the Arab sheik, who, standing near by, had heard the order.

Fatima was an artful, selfish woman, who had gained some influence over her husband by flattering his vanity, and professing a love she had never felt.

She had acted with slavish obedience to him when he was all-powerful; but now that he was himself a slave, her submission had been transferred with perfect facility to the chief of the band who had captured him.

It was now that Golah began to realize the fact that he was a conquered man.

His heart was nearly bursting with rage, shame, and disappointment; for nothing could so plainly awaken him to the comprehension of his real position, as the fact that Fatima, his favorite, she who had ever professed for him so much love and obedience, now refused to attend to his simplest request.

After making one more violent and ineffectual effort at breaking his bonds, he sank down upon the earth and remained silent — bitterly contemplating the degraded condition into which he had fallen.

The Krooman, who was a very sharp observer of passing events, and had an extensive knowledge of peculiar specimens of human nature, closely watched the behavior of the black sheik.

"He no like us," he remarked to the whites. ' He nebba be slave. Bom-by you see him go dead."

CHAPTER LV.

TWO FAITHFUL WIVES.

WHILE Golah's mind appeared to be stunned almost to unconsciousness by the refusal of Fatima to obey his orders, his other two wives were moving about, as if engaged in some domestic duty.

Presently the woman he had buried in the sand was seen going towards him with a calabash of water, followed by the other who carried a dish of *sangleh*.

One of the Arabs perceiving their intention, ran up, and, in an angry tone, commanded them to retire to their tents. The two women persisted in their design, and in order to prevent them, without using violence, the Arab offered to serve the food and drink himself.

This they permitted him to do; but when the water was offered to Golah it was again refused.

The black sheik would not receive either food or drink from the hand of a master.

The *sangleh* was then consumed by the Arab with a real or sham profession of gratitude; the water was poured into a bucket, and given to one of the camels; and the two calabashes were returned to the women.

Neither a keen longing for food, nor a burning thirst for water, could divert Golah's thoughts from the contemplation of something that was causing his soul extreme anguish.

His physical tortures seemed, for the time, extinguished by some deep mental agony.

Again the wives — the unloved ones — advanced towards him, bearing water and food; and again the Arab stepped forward to intercept them. The two women persisted in their design, and, while opposing the efforts of the Arab to raru them back, they called on the two youths, the relatives of the black sheik, as also on Fatima, to assist them.

Of the three persons thus appealed to, only Golah's son obeyed their summons; but his attempt to aid the women was immediately frustrated by the Arab, who claimed him as a slave, and who now commanded him to stand aside. His command having no effect, the Arab proceeded to use force. At the risk of his life the youth resisted. He dared to use violence against a master — a crime that on the desert demands the punishment of death.

Aroused from his painful reverie by the commotion going on around him, Golah, seeing the folly of the act, shouted to his son to be calm, and yield obedience ; but the youth, not heeding the command of his father, continued his resistance. He was just on the point of being cut down, when the Krooman ran forward, and pronouncing in Arabic two words signifying " father and son," saved the youth's life. The Arab robber had sufficient respect for the relationship to stay his hand from committing murder; but to prevent any further trouble with the young fellow, he was seized by several others, fast bound, and flung to the ground by the side of his father.

The two women, still persisting in their design to relieve the wants of their unfortunate husband, were then knocked down, kicked, beaten, and finally dragged inside the tents.

This scene was witnessed by Fatima ; who, instead of showing sympathy, appeared highly amused by it, — so much so as even to give way to laughter ! Her unnatural behavior once more roused the indignation of her husband.

The wrong of being robbed — the humiliation of being bound — the knowledge that he himself, along with his children, would be sold into slavery — the torture of hunger and thirst — were sources of misery no longer heeded by him all were forgotten in the contemplation of a far greater anguish.

9 *

Fatima, the favorite, the woman to whom his word should have been law, — the woman who had always pretended to think him something more than mortal, — now not only shunning but despising him in the midst of his misfortunes!

This knowledge did more towards subduing the giant than all his other sufferings combined.

"Old Golah looks very down in the mouth," remarked Terence to his companions. "If it was not for the beating he gave me yesterday, I could almost pity him. I made an oath, at the time he was thwacking me with the ramrod, that if my hands were ever again at liberty, I'd see if it was possible to kill him; but now that they are free, and his are bound, I've not the heart to touch him, bad as he is."

"That is right, Terry," said Bill; "it's only wimin an' bits o' boys as throws wather on a drowned rat, — not as I mane to say the owld rascal is past mischief yet. I believe he'll do some more afore the Devil takes 'im intirely; but I mane that Him as sits up aloft is able to do His own work without your helping Him.

"You speak truth, Bill," said Harry; "I don't think there is any necessity for seeking revenge of Golah for his cruel treatment of us; he is now as ill off as the rest of us."

"What is that you say?" inquired Colin. "Golah like one of us? Nothing of the kind. He has more pluck, endurance, obstinacy, and true manly spirit about him than there is in the four of us combined."

"Was his attempt to starve you dictated by a manly spirit?" asked Harry.

"Perhaps not, but it was the fault of the circumstances under which he has been educated. I don't think of that now; my admiration of the man is too strong. Look at his refusing that drink of water when it had been several times offered him!"

"There is something wonderful about him, certainly," assented Harry; "but I don't see anything in him to admire."

"No more do I," said Bill. "He might be as comfortable now as we are; and I say a man's a fool as won't be 'appy when he can."

"What you call his folly," rejoined Colin, "is but a noble pride that makes him superior to any of us. He has a spirit that will not submit to slavery, and we have not."

"That be truth," remarked the Krooman; "Golah nebbar be slave."

Colin was right. By accepting food and drink from his captors, the black sheik might have satisfied the demands of mere animal nature, but only at the sacrifice of all that was noble in his nature. His self-respect, along with the proud, unyielding spirit by which everything good and great is accomplished, would have been gone from him for ever.

Sailor Bill and his companions, the boy slaves, had been taught from childhood to yield to circumstances, and still retain some moral feeling; but Golah had not.

The only thing he could yield to adverse fate was *his life*.

At this moment the Krooman, by a gesture, called their attention towards the captive sheik, at the same time giving utterance to a sharp ejaculation.

"Look!" exclaimed he, "Golah no stay longer on de Saära. You him see soon die now — look at him!"

At the same instant Golah had risen to his feet, inviting his Arab master to a conference.

"There is but one God," said he, "Mahomet is his prophet; and I am his servant. I will never be a slave. Give me one wife, a camel, and my scimitar, and I will go. I have been robbed; but God is great, and it is his will, and my destiny."

Golah had at length yielded, though not because that he suffered for food and water; not that he feared slavery or death; not that his proud spirit had become weak or given way; but rather that it had grown stronger under the prompting of *Revenge*.

The Arab sheik conferred with his followers; and there arose a brief controversy among them.

The trouble they had with their gigantic captive, the difficulty they anticipated in disposing of him, and their belief that he was a good Mussulman, were arguments in favor of granting his request, and setting him at liberty.

It was therefore decided to let him go — on the condition of his taking his departure at once.

Golah consented; and they proceeded to untie his hands. While this was being done, the Krooman ran up to Colin's master, and cautioned him to protect his slave, until the sheik had departed.

This warning was unnecessary, for Golah had other and more serious thoughts to engage his mind than that of any animosity he might once have felt against the young Scotchman.

"I am free," said Golah, when his hands were untied. "We are equals, and Mussulmen. I claim your hospitality. Give me some food and drink."

He then stepped forward to the well, and quenched his thirst, after which some boiled camel meat was placed before him.

While he was appeasing an appetite that had been two days in gaining strength, Fatima, who had observed a strange expression in his eyes, appeared to be in great consternation. She had believed him doomed to a life of slavery, if not to death; and this belief had influenced her in her late actions.

Gliding up to the Arab sheik, she entreated to be separated from her husband; but the only answer she received was, that Golah should have either of the three wives he chose to take; that he (the sheik) and his companions were men of honor, who would not break the promise they had given.

A goat-skin of water, some barley meal, for making *sany·*

leh, and a few other necessary articles, were placed on a camel, which was delivered over to Golah.

The black sheik then addressed a few words in some African language to his son; and, calling Fatima to follow him, he started off across the desert.

CHAPTER LVI.

FATIMA'S FATE.

A COMPLETE change had come over the fortunes of Fatima. Vain, cruel, and tyrannical but the moment before, she was now humbled to the dust of the desert. In place of commanding her fellow wives, she now approached them with entreaties, begging them to take charge of her child, which she seemed determined to leave behind her Both willingly assented to her wishes.

Our adventurers were puzzled by this circumstance, for there appeared to be no reason that Fatima should leave her offspring behind her. Even the Krooman could not explain it; and as the shades of night descended over the desert, the mother separated from her child, perhaps never more to embrace it in this world of wickedness and woe.

About two hours before daybreak, on the morning after the departure of Golah, there was an alarm in the douar, which created amongst the Arabs a wonderful excitement.

The man who had been keeping guard over the camp was not to be seen; and one of the fleetest camels, as well as a swift desert horse, was also gone.

The slaves were instantly mustered, when it was found that one of them was likewise missing. It was Golah's son.

His absence accounted for the loss of the camel, and perhaps the horse, but what had become of the Arab guard?

He certainly would not have absconded with the slave, for he had left valuable property behind him.

There was no time for exchanging surmises over this mystery. Pursuit must be instantly made for the recovery of slave, camel, and horse.

The Arab sheik detailed four of his followers to this duty, and they hastened to make ready for their departure. They would start as soon as the light of day should enable them to see the course the missing animals had taken.

All believed that the fugitives would have to be sought for in a southerly direction; and therefore the caravan would have to be further delayed in its journey.

While making preparations for the pursuit, another unpleasant discovery was made. Two ship's muskets, that had been taken from Golah's party were also missing.

They had been extracted from a tent in which two of the Arabs had slept, — two of the four who were now preparing to search for the missing property.

The sheik became alarmed. The camp seemed full of traitors; and yet, as the guns were the private property of the two men who slept in the tent, they could not, for losing them, reasonably be accused of anything more than stupidity.

Contrary to the anticipations of all, the tracks of the lost animals were found to lead off in a north-westerly direction; and at about two hundred yards from the camp a dark object was seen lying upon the ground. On examination it proved to be the Arab who had been appointed night-guard over the douar.

He was stone dead; and by his side lay one of the missing muskets, with the stock broken, and covered with his own brains.

The tragedy was not difficult to be explained. The man had seen one or two of the hoppled animals straying from the camp. Not thinking that they were being led gently away, he had, without giv'ng any alarm, gone out to bring them back. Golah's son, who was leading them off, by keeping concealed behind one of the animals, had found an opportunity of giving the guard his death-blow, without any noise to disturb the slumbering denizens of the douar.

No doubt he had gone to rejoin his father, and the adroit manner in which he had made his departure, taking with him a musket, a camel, and a horse, not only excited the wonder, but the admiration of those from whom he had stolen them.

In the division of the slaves, young Harry Blount and the Krooman had become the property of the Arab sheik. The Krooman having some knowledge of the Arabic language, soon established himself in the good opinion of his new master. While the Arabs were discussing the most available mode to obtain revenge for the murder of their companion, as well as to regain possession of the property they had lost, the Krooman, skilled in Golah's character, volunteered to assist them by a little advice.

Pointing to the south, he suggested to them that, by going in that direction, they would certainly see or hear something of Golah and his son.

The sheik could the more readily believe this, since the country of the black chief lay to the southward, and Golah, on leaving the douar, had gone in that direction.

" But why did his dog of a son not go south ? " inquired the Arabs, pointing to the tracks of the stolen horse, which still appeared to lead towards the northwest.

" If you go north," replied the Krooman, " you will be sure to see Golah; or if you stay here, you will learn something of him ? "

" What ! will he be in both directions at the same time, and here likewise ? "

" No, not that; but he will follow you."

The Arabs were willing to believe that there was a chance of recovering their property on the road they had been intending to follow, especially as the stolen horse and camel had been taken in that direction.

They determined, therefore, to continue their journey.

Too late they perceived their folly in treating Golah as they had done. He was now beyond their reach, and, in all likelihood, had been rejoined by his son. He was an enemy against whom they would have to keep a constant watch; and the thought of this caused the old Arab sheik to swear by the Prophet's beard that he would never again show mercy to a man whom he had plundered.

For about an hour after resuming their march, the footprints of the camel could be traced in the direction they wished to go; but gradually they became less perceptible, until at length they were lost altogether. A smart breeze had been blowing, which had filled the tracks with sand, which was light and easily disturbed.

Trusting to chance, and still with some hope of recovering the stolen property, they continued on in the same direction, and, not long after losing the tracks, they found some fresh evidence that they were going the right way.

The old sheik, who was riding in advance of the others, on looking to the right, perceived an object on the sand that demanded a closer inspection. He turned and rode towards it, closely followed by the people of his party.

On drawing near to the object it proved to be the body of a human being, lying back upwards, and yet with the face turned full towards the heavens. The features were at once recognized as those of Fatima, the favorite!

The head of the unfortunate woman had been severed from her body, and then placed contiguous to it, with the face in an inverted position.

The ghastly spectacle was instructive. It proved that Golah, although going off southward, must have turned back again, and was now not far off, hovering about the track he believed his enemies would be likely to take. His son, moreover, was, in all likelihood, along with him.

When departing along with her husband, Fatima had probably anticipated the terrible fate that awaited her; and, for that reason, had left her child in the care of the other wives.

Neither of these seemed in the least surprised on discovering the body. Both had surmised that such would be Fatima's fate; and it was for that reason they had so willingly taken charge of her child.

The caravan made a short halt, which was taken advantage of by the two women to cover the body with sand.

The journey was then resumed.

CHAPTER LVII.

FURTHER DEFECTION.

NOTWITHSTANDING that Golah's brother-in-law, who had formerly been a freeman, was now a slave, he seemed well satisfied with the change in his circumstances.

He made himself very useful to his new masters in looking after the camel, and doing all the other necessary work which his knowledge of Saäran life enabled him effectually to execute.

When the Arab caravan came to a halt on the evening of his first day's journey along with it, he assisted in unloading the camels, putting the hopples on them, pitching the tents, and doing anything else which was required to be done.

While the other slaves were eating the small portion of
food allowed them, one of the camels formerly belonging to
Golah — a young and fleet maherry that had been ridden by
Fatima, strayed a short distance from the douar. Seeing it
the black sheik's brother-in-law, who had been making him
self so useful, ran after the animal as if to fetch it back. He
was seen passing beyond the camel, as though he intended
turning it toward the camp; but in another instant it was
discovered that he had no such design. The youth was
seen to spring to the back of the maherry, lay hold of its
hump, and ride rapidly away. Accustomed to hearing the
sound of his voice, the faithful and intelligent animal obeyed
his words of command. Its neck was suddenly craned out
towards the north; and its feet were flung forward in long
strides that bore its rider rapidly away from the rest. The
incident caused a tremendous commotion in the caravan. It
was so wholly unexpected, that none of the Arabs were prepared to intercept the fugitive. The guard for the night
had not been appointed. They were all seated on the
ground, engaged in devouring their evening repast, and before a musket could be discharged at the runaway, he had
got so far into the glimmering twilight that the only effect of
two or three shots fired after him was to quicken the pace of
the maherry on which he was fleeing.

Two fleet horses were instantly saddled and mounted, one
by the owner of the camel that had been stolen, and the
other by the owner of the slave who had stolen it.

Each, arming himself with musket and scimitar, felt sure
of recapturing the runaway. Their only doubt arose from
the knowledge of the swiftness of the maherry, and that its
rider was favored by the approaching darkness.

The whole encampment was by this time under arms
and after the departure of the pursuers, the sheik gathered
all the slaves together, and swore by the beard of the
Prophet that they should all be killed, and that he would

set the example by killing the two belonging to himself, which were Harry Blount and the Krooman. Several of his followers proceeded to relieve their excitement by each beating the slave or slaves that were his own property, and amongst these irate slave-owners was the master of Sailor Bill. The old man-o-war's-man was cudgelled till his objections to involuntary servitude were loudly expressed, and in the strongest terms that English, Scotch, and Irish could furnish for the purpose.

When the rage of the old sheik had to some extent subsided, he procured a leathern thong, and declared that his two slaves should be fast bound, and never released as long as they remained in his possession.

" Talk to him," exclaimed Harry to the Krooman; " tell him, in his own language, that God is great, and that he is a fool! We don't wish to escape, — certainly not at present."

Thus counselled, the Krooman explained to the sheik that the white slaves, as well as himself, who had sailed in English ships, had no intention of running away, but wished to be taken north, where they might be ransomed; and that they were not such fools as to part from him in a place where they would certainly starve. The Krooman also informed the sheik that they were all very glad at being taken out of the hands of Golah, who would have carried them to Timbuctoo, whence they never could have returned, but must have ended their days in slavery.

While the Krooman was talking to the sheik, several of the others came up and listened. The black further informed them that the white slaves had friends living in Agadeer and Swearah (Santa Cruz and Mogador), — friends who would pay a large price to ransom them. Why, then, should they try to escape while journeying towards the place where those friends were living?

The Krooman went on to say that the young man who

had just made off was Golah's brother-in-law; that, unlike themselves, in going north he would not be seeking freedom but perpetual slavery, and for that reason he had gone to rejoin Golah and his son.

This explanation seemed so reasonable to the Arabs, that their fears for the safety of their slaves soon subsided, and the latter were permitted to repose in peace.

As a precautionary measure, however, two men were kept moving in a circle around the douar throughout the whole of the night; but no disturbance arose, and morning returned without bringing back the two men who had gone in pursuit of the cunning runaway.

The distance to the next watering-place was too great to admit of any delay being made; and the journey was resumed, in the hope that the two missing men would be met on the way.

This hope was realized.

All along the route the old sheik, who rode in advance, kept scanning the horizon, not only ahead, but to the right and left of their course. About ten miles from their night's halting-place he was seen to swerve suddenly from his course, and advance towards something that had attracted his attention. His followers hastened after him, — all except the two women and their children, who lingered a long way behind.

Lying on the ground, their bodies contiguous to each other, were the two Arabs who had gone in pursuit of the runaway.

They were both dead.

One of them had been shot with a musket ball that had penetrated his skull, entering directly between his temples. The other had been cut down with a scimitar, his body being almost severed in twain.

The youth who had fled the night before, had evidently come up with Golah and his son; and the two men who

had pursued him had lost their lives, their animals, muskets, and scimitars.

Golah now had two accomplices, and the three were well
mounted and well armed.

The anger of the Arabs was frightful to behold. They
turned towards the two women whom they knew to be Golah's wives. The latter had thrown themselves on their
knees and were screaming and supplicating for mercy.

Some of the Arabs would have killed them on the instant;
but were prevented by the old sheik, who, although himself
wild with rage, had still sufficient reason left to tell him that
the unfortunate women were not answerable for the acts of
their husband. Our adventurers found reason to regret the
misfortune that had befallen their new masters; for they
could not but regard with alarm the returning power of Golah.

"We shall fall into his hands again," exclaimed Terence.
" He will kill all these Arabs one after another, and obtain
all he has lost, ourselves included. We shall yet be driven
to Timbuctoo."

"Then we should deserve it," cried Harry, "for it will
partly be our own fault, if ever we fall into Golah's power
again."

"I don't think so," said Bill, " Golah is a wondersome
man, and as got somethin' more nor human natur' to 'elp 'im.
I think as 'ow if we should see 'im 'alf a mile off, signalizin'
for us to follow 'im, we should 'ave to go. I've tried my
hand at disobeyin' his orders, and don't do it again, — not if
I knows it."

The expressions of anger hitherto portrayed on the countenances of the Arabs, had given place to those of anxiety.
They knew that an enemy was hovering around them, — an
enemy whom they had wronged, — whose power they had
undervalued, and whom they had foolishly restored to liberty.

The bodies of their companions were hastily interred in the sand, and their journey northward was once more resumed.

CHAPTER LVIII.

A CALL FOR TWO MORE.

THE sufferings of the slaves for water and food again commenced, while the pace at which they were compelled to travel, to keep up with the camels, soon exhausted the little strength they had acquired from the rest by the well.

During the long afternoon following the burial of the two Arabs, each of the boy slaves at different times declared his utter inability to proceed any farther.

They were mistaken; and had yet to learn something of the power which love of life exerts over the body.

They knew that to linger behind would be death. They did not desire to die, and therefore struggled on.

Like men upon a treadmill, they were compelled to keep on moving, although neither able nor willing.

The hour of sunset found them wading through sand that had lately been stirred by a storm. It was nearly as light and loose as snow; and the toil of moving through it was so wearisome, that the mounted Arabs, having some pity on those who had walked, halted early for the night. Two men were appointed to guard the camp in the same manner as upon the night before; and with the feelings of hunger and thirst partly appeased, weary with the toils of day, our adventurers were soon in a sound slumber. Around them, and half-buried in the soft sard, lay stretched the other denizens of the douar, all slumbering likewise.

Their rest remained undisturbed until that darkest hour of the night, just before the dawning of day. They were then startled from sleep by the report of a musket, — a report that was immediately followed by another in the opposite direction. The douar was instantly in wild confusion.

The Arabs seized their weapons, and rushed forth from among the tents.

One of the party that ran in the direction in which the first shot was heard, seeing a man coming towards them, in the excitement of the moment fired his musket, and shot the individual who was advancing, who proved to be one of those entrusted with the guard of the camp.

No enemies could be discovered. They had fled, leaving the two camp-guards in the agonies of death.

Some of the Arabs would have rushed wildly hither and thither, in search of the unseen foe, but were prevented by the sheik, who, fearing that all would be lost, should the douar be deserted by the armed men, shouted the signal for all his followers to gather around him.

The two wounded men were brought into a tent, where, in a few minutes, one of them — the man who had been shot by one of his companions — breathed his last. He had also received a wound from the first shot that had been heard, his right arm having been shattered by a musket-ball.

The spine of the other guard had been broken by a bullet, so that recovery was clearly impossible.

He had evidently heard the first shot fired at his companion from the opposite side of the camp: and was turning his back upon the foe that had attacked himself.

The light of day soon shone upon the scene, and they were able to perceive how their enemies had approached so near the camp without being observed.

About a hundred paces from where the guards had been standing at the time the first two shots were fired, was a furrow or ravine running through the soft sand.

This ravine branched into two lesser ones, including within their angle the Arab camp, as also the sentinels stationed to guard it.

Up the branches the midnight murderers had silently stolen, each taking a side; and in this way had got within easy distance of the unsuspecting sentries.

In the bottom of one of the furrows, where the sand was more firmly compacted, was found the impression of human footsteps.

The tracks had been made by some person hurriedly leaving the spot.

" Dis be de track ob Golah," said the Krooman to Harry, after he had examined it. " He made um when runnin' 'way after he fire da musket."

" Very likely," said Harry; " but how do you know it is Golah's track?"

" 'Cause Golah hab largess feet in all de world, and no feet but his make dat mark."

" I tell you again," said Terence, who overheard the Krooman's remark, " we shall have to go with Golah to Timbuctoo. We belong to him. These Arabs are only keeping us for a few days, but they will all be killed yet, and we shall have to follow the black sheik in the opposite direction."

Harry made no reply to this prophetic speech. Certainly, there was a prospect of its proving true.

Four Arabs out of the eleven of which their party was originally composed, were already dead, while still another was dying!

Sailor Bill pronounced Golah, with his son and brother-in-law, quite a match for the six who were left. The black sheik, he thought, was equal to any four of their present masters in strength, cunning, and determination.

" But the Arabs have us to help them," remarked Colin. " We should count for something."

" So we do, — as merchandise," replied Harry; " we have

hitherto been helpless as children in protecting ourselves. What can we do? The boasted superiority of our race or country cannot be true here in the desert. We are out of our element."

"Yes, that's sartain!" exclaimed Bill; "but we're not far from it. Shiver my timbers if I don't smell salt water Be Jabers! if we go on towards the west we shall see the say afore night."

During this dialogue the Arabs were holding a consultation as to what they should do.

To divide the camp, and send some after their enemies, was pronounced impolitic: the party sent in pursuit, and that left to guard the caravan, — either would be too weak if attacked by their truculent enemy.

In union alone was strength, and they resolved to remain together, believing that they should have a visit from Golah again, while better prepared to receive him.

The footprints leading out from the two ravines were traced for about a mile in the direction they wished to follow.

The tracks of camels and horses were there found; and they could tell by the signs that their enemies had mounted and ridden off towards the west.

They possibly might have avoided meeting Golah again by going eastward; but, from their knowledge of the desert, no water was to be found in that direction in less than five days' journey.

Moreover, they did not yet wish to avoid him. They thirsted for revenge, and were impatient to move on; for a journey of two days was still before them before they could hope to arrive at the nearest water.

When every preparation had been made to resume their route, there was one obstacle in the way of their taking an immediate departure.

Their wounded companion was not yet defunct. They

10

saw it would be impossible for him to live much longer; for
the lower part of his body, — all below the shattered portion
of the spine, — appeared already without life. A few hours
at most would terminate his sufferings; but for the expira-
tion of those few hours, — or minutes, as fate should decide,
— his companions seemed unwilling to wait!

They dug a hole in the sand near where the wounded
man was lying. This was but the work of a few minutes.
As soon as the grave was completed, the eyes of all were
once more turned upon the wretched sufferer.

He was still alive, and by piteous moans expressing the
agony he was enduring.

"Bismillah!" exclaimed the old sheik, "why do you not
die, my friend? We are waiting for the fulfilment of your
destiny"

"I am dead," ejaculated the sufferer, speaking in a faint
voice, and apparently with great difficulty.

Having said this, he relapsed into silence, and remained
motionless as a corpse.

The sheik then placed one hand upon his temples. "Yes!"
he exclaimed, "the words of our friend are those of truth and
wisdom. He is dead."

The wounded man was then rolled into the cavity which
had been scooped out, and they hastily proceeded to cover
him with sand.

As they did so, his hands were repeatedly uplifted, while
a low moaning came from his lips; but his movements were
apparently unseen, and his cries of agony unnoticed!

His companions remained both deaf and blind to any
evidence that might refute his own assertion that he was
dead.

The sand was at length heaped up, so as completely to
cover his body, when, by an order from the old sheik, his
followers turned away from the spot and the Kafila moved
on!

CHAPTER LIX.

ONCE MORE BY THE SEA.

SAILOR BILL'S conjecture that they were not far from the sea proved correct.

On the evening of that same day they saw the sun sink down into a shining horizon, which they knew was not that of the burning sand-plain over which they had been so long moving.

That faint and distant view of his favorite element was a joyful moment for the old sailor.

" We are in sight of home ! " he exclaimed. " Shiver my timbers if I ever lose sight of it again ! I shan't be buried in the sand. If I must go under alive, it shall be under water, like a Christyun. If I could swim, I'd start right off for Hold Hingland as soon as we get to yonder shore."

The boy slaves were alike inspired with hope and joy at the distant view.

The sea was still too far off to be reached that night, and the douar was pitched about five miles from the shore.

During this night, three of the Arabs were kept constantly on guard ; but the camp was not disturbed, and next morning they resumed their journey, some with the hope, and others with the fear, that Golah would trouble them no more.

The Arabs wished to meet him during the hours of daylight, and secure the property they had lost ; and from their knowledge of the part of the desert they were now traversing, they were in hopes of doing this. They knew there was but one place within two days' journey where fresh water could be obtained ; and should they succeed in reaching this place before Golah, they could lie in wait for his arrival. They were certain he must visit this watering place to save his animals from perishing with thirst.

At noonday a halt was made not far from the beach.
It was only for a short while; for they were anxious to
reach the well as soon as possible. The few minutes spent
at the halting-place were well employed by the boy slaves
in gathering shell-fish and bathing their bodies in the surf.

Refreshed by this luxurious food, as well as by the washing, of which they were greatly in need, they were able to
proceed at a better pace; so that about an hour before sun
set the caravan arrived at the well.

Just before reaching it, the old sheik and one of his com
panions had dismounted and walked forward to examine
such tracks as might be found about the place. They were
chagrined to find that Golah had been before. He had been
to the well, and obtained a supply of water. His footmarks
were easily identified. They were fresh, having been made
but an hour or two before the arrival of the caravan; and
in place of their having to wait for Golah, he was undoubtedly waiting for them. They felt sure that the black sheik
was not far off, watching for a favorable opportunity of again
paying them a nocturnal visit. They could now understand
why he had not attempted to molest them on the preceding
night. He had been hastening forward, in order to reach
the well in advance of them.

The apprehensions of the Arabs became keener and
keener after this discovery. They were also much puzzled
as to what they should do; and a diversity of opinion arose
as to the best plan for guarding the camp against their implacable foe. Some were in favor of staying by the well
for several days, until the supply of water which their enemy had taken with him should be exhausted. Golah would
then have to revisit the well, or perish of thirst upon the
desert. The idea was an ingenious one, but unfortunately
their stock of provisions would not admit of any delay, and
it was resolved that the journey should be resumed at
once.

Just as they were preparing to move away from the well, a caravan of traders arrived from the south, and the old sheik made anxious inquiries as to whether the new-comers had seen any one on their route. The traders, to whom the caravan belonged, had that morning met three men who answered to the description of Golah and his companions. They were journeying south, and had purchased a small supply of food from the caravan.

Could it be that Golah had given up the hope of recover ing his lost property? relinquished his deadly purpose of revenge? The Arabs professed much unwillingness to believe it. Some of them loudly proposed starting southward in pursuit. But this proposition was overruled, and it was evident that the old sheik, as well as most of his followers, were in reality pleased to think that Golah would trouble them no more.

The sheik decreed that the property of those who had perished should be divided amongst those who survived. This giving universal satisfaction, the Arab Kafila took its departure, leaving the caravan of the traders by the well, where they were intending to remain for some time longer.

Shortly after leaving the well, the old sheik ordered a halt by the seashore, where he stopped long enough for his slaves to gather some shell-fish, enough to satisfy the hunger of all his followers.

A majority of the Arabs were under the belief that the black sheik had started at last for his own country — satisfied with the revenge he had already taken. They seemed to think that keeping watch over the camp would no longer be necessary.

With this opinion their Krooman captive did not agree; and, fearing to fall again into the possession of Golah, he labored to convince his new master that they were as likely that night to receive a visit from the black sheik as they had ever been before.

He argued that, if Golah had entertained a hope of de-
feating his foes — eleven in number — when alone, and
armed only with a scimitar, he certainly would not be likely
to relinquish that hope after having succeeded in killing
nearly half of them, and being strengthened by a couple of
able assistants.

The Krooman believed that Golah's going south, — as
reported by the party met at the well, — was proof that
he really intended proceeding north; and he urged the
Arab sheik to set a good guard over the douar through the
night.

"Tell him," said Harry, "if they are not inclined to keep
guard for themselves, that we will stand it, if they will only
allow us to have weapons of some kind or other."

The Krooman made this communication to the Arab sheik,
who smiled only in reply.

The idea of allowing slaves to guard an Arab douar, especially to furnish them with fire-arms, was very amusing to
the old chieftain of the Saära.

Harry understood the meaning of his smile. It meant
refusal; but the young Englishman had also become impressed with the danger suggested by Terence, that Golah
would yet kill the Arabs, and take the boy slaves back to
Timbuctoo.

"Tell the sheik that he is an old fool," said he to the interpreter; "tell him that we have a greater objection to falling into the hands of Golah than he has of losing either us
or his own life. Tell him that we wish to go north, where
we can be redeemed; and that for this reason alone we
should be far more careful than any of his own people in
guarding the camp against surprise."

When this communication was made to the old sheik it
seemed to strike him as having some reason in it; and, convinced by the Krooman's arguments that there was still danger to be apprehended from Golah's vengeance, he directed

that the douar should be strictly guarded, and that the white slaves might take part in the duty.

"You shall be taken north, and sold to your countrymen," promised he, "if you give us no trouble in the transit. There are but few of my people left now, and it is hard for us to travel all day and keep watch all night. If you are really afraid of falling into the hands of this Prophet-accursed negro, and will help us in guarding against his murderous attacks, you are welcome to do so; but if any one of you attempt to play traitor, the whole four of you shall lose your heads. I swear it by the beard of the Prophet!"

The Krooman assured him that none of the white slaves had any desire to deceive him, adding that self-interest, if nothing else, would cause them to be true to those who would take them to a place where they would have a chance of being ransomed out of slavery.

Darkness having by this time descended over the desert, the sheik set about appointing the guard for the night. He was too suspicious of his white slaves to allow all the four of them to act as guards at the same time, while he and his companions were asleep. He was willing, however, that one of them should be allowed to keep watch in company with one of his own followers.

In choosing the individual for this duty, he inquired from the Krooman which of the four had been most ill-used by the black shiek. Sailor Bill was pointed out as the man, and the interpreter gave some details of the cruel treatment to which the old man-o'-war's-man had been subjected at the hands of Golah.

"Bismillah! that is well," said the sheik. "Let him keep the watch. After what you say, revenge should hinder him from closing his eyes in sleep for a whole moon. There's no fear that he will betray us."

CHAPTER LX.

GOLAH CALLS AGAIN.

IN setting the watch for the night one of the sentinels was stationed on the shore about a hundred yards north of the douar. His instructions were to walk a round of about two hundred paces, extending inward from the beach.

Another was placed about the same distance south of the camp, and was to pace backwards and forwards after a similar fashion.

Sailor Bill was stationed on the land side of the camp, where he was to move to and fro between the beats of the two Arab guards, each of whom, on discovering him at the termination of his round, was to utter the word "*Akka*," so that the sailor should distinguish them from an enemy.

The Arabs themselves were supposed to be sufficiently intelligent to tell a friend from a foe without requiring any countersign.

Before Bill was sent upon his beat, the old sheik went into a tent, and soon after reappeared with a large pistol, bearing a strong likeness to a blunderbuss. This weapon he placed in the sailor's hand, with the injunction — translated to him by the interpreter — not to discharge it until he should be certain of killing either Golah or one of his companions.

The old sailor, although sorely fatigued with the toil of the day's journey, had so great a horror of again becoming the property of the black sheik, that he cheerfully promised to "walk the deck all night, and keep a good lookout for breakers," and his young companions sought repose in full confidence that the promise would be faithfully kept.

Any one of the boy slaves would willingly have taken his place, and allowed their old comrade to rest for the night; but Bill had been selected by the old sheik, and from his decree there was no appeal.

The two Arabs doing duty as sentinels knew, from past experience, that if the Kafila was still followed by Golah, they would be the individuals most exposed to danger; and this knowledge was sufficient to stimulate them to the most faithful discharge of their trust.

Neither of them wished to become victims to the fate which had befallen their predecessors in office.

For two or three hours both paced slowly to and fro; and Bill, each time he approached the end of his beat, could hear distinctly pronounced the word "*Akka*," which proved that his co-sentinels were fully on the alert.

It so chanced that one of them had no faith in the general belief that the enemy had relinquished his purposes sanguinary of vengeance.

He drew his deductions from Golah's conduct in the past, and during the long silent hours of the night his fancy was constantly dwelling on the manner in which the dreaded enemy had approached the douar on former occasions.

This sentry was the one stationed to the south of the douar; and with eyes constantly striving to pierce the darkness that shrouded the sand plain, the water, on which a better light was reflected, received no attention from him. He believed the douar well protected on the side of the sea, for he had no idea that danger could come from that direction.

He was mistaken.

Had their enemies been, like himself and his companions, true children of the Saära, his plan of watching for their approach might have answered well enough; but the latter chanced to be the offspring of a different country and race.

About three hours after the watch had been established, the sentinel placed on the southern side of the douar was being closely observed by the black sheik, yet knew it not.

Golah had chosen a singular plan to secure himself against being observed, similar to that selected by the three mids for the like purpose soon after their being cast away upon the coast.

He had stolen into the water, and with only his woolly occiput above the surface, had approached within a few yards of the spot where the Arab sentry turned upon his round.

In the darkness of the night, at the distance of twelve or fifteen paces, he might have been discovered, had a close survey been made of the shining surface. But there was no such survey, and Golah watched the sentinel, himself unseen.

The attention of the Arab was wholly occupied in looking for the approach of a foe from the land side; and while he was in continual fear of hearing the report of a musket, or feeling the stroke of its bullet.

This disagreeable surprise he never expected could come from the sea, but was so fully anticipated from the land, that he paid but little or no attention to the restless waves that were breaking with low moans against the beach.

As he turned his back upon the water for the hundredth time, with the intention of walking to the other end of his beat, Golah crept gently out of the water and hastened after him.

The deep sighing of the waves against the shingly shore hindered the sound of footsteps from being heard.

Golah was only armed with a scimitar; but it was a weapon that, in his hands, was sure to fall with deadly effect. It was a weapon of great size and weight, having been made expressly for himself; and with this upraised, he silently but swiftly glided after the unconscious Arab.

Adding the whole strength of his powerful arm to the weight of the weapon, the black sheik brought its sharp edge slantingly down upon the neck of the unsuspecting sentinel.

With a low moan, that sounded in perfect harmony with the sighing of the waves, the Arab fell to the earth, leaving his musket in the huge hand his assassin had stretched forth to grasp it. Putting the gun to full cock, Golah walked on in the direction in which the sentry had been going. He intended next to encounter the man who was guarding the eastern side of the douar. Walking boldy on, he took no trouble to avoid the sound of his footsteps being heard, believing that he would be taken for the sentry he had just slain. After going about a hundred paces without seeing any one, he paused, and with his large fiercely gleaming eyes strove to penetrate the surrounding gloom. Still no one was to be seen, and he laid himself along the earth to listen for footfalls.

Nothing could be heard; but after glancing for some moments along the ground, he saw a dark object outlined above the surface. Unable, from the distance, to form a correct idea of what it was, he cautiously advanced towards it, keeping on all fours, till he could see that the object was a human being, prostrate on the ground, and apparently listening, like himself. Why should the man be listening? Not to note the approach of his companion, for that should be expected without suspicion, as his attitude would indicate. He might be asleep, reasoned Golah. If so, Fortune seemed to favor him, and with this reflection he steadily moved on towards the prostrate form.

Though the latter moved not, still Golah was not quite sure that the sentry was asleep. Again he paused, and for a moment fixed his eyes on the body with a piercing gaze. If the man was not sleeping, why should he allow an enemy to approach so near? Why lie so quietly, without showing any sign or giving an alarm? If Golah could despatch this sentinel as he had done the other, without making any noise.

he would, along with his two relatives (who were waiting the result of his adventure), afterwards steal into the douar, and all he had lost might be again recovered.

The chance was worth the risk, so thought Golah, and silently moved on.

As he drew nearer, he saw that the man was lying on his side, with his face turned towards him, and partly concealed by one arm.

The black sheik could see no gun in his hands, and consequently there would be but little danger in an encounter with him, if such should chance to arise.

Golah grasped the heavy scimitar in his right hand, evidently intending to despatch his victim as he had done the other, with a single blow.

The head could be severed from the body at one stroke, and no alarm would be given to the slumbering camp.

The heavy blade of shining steel was raised aloft; and the gripe of the powerful hand clutching its hilt became more firm and determined.

Sailor Bill! has your promise to keep a sharp lookout been broken so soon?

Beware! Golah is near with strength in his arm, and murder in his mind!

CHAPTER LXI.

SAILOR BILL STANDING SENTRY.

AFTER two hours had been passed in moving slowly to and fro, hearing the word "*Akka*," and seeing nothing but gray sand, Sailor Bill began to feel weary, and now regretted that the old sheik had honored him with his confidence.

For the first hour of his watch he had kept a good look-out to the eastward, and had given the whole of his attention to his sentinel's duty.

Gradually his intense alertness forsook him, and he began to think of the past and future.

Themes connected with these subjects seldom troubled Bill, — his thoughts generally dwelling upon the present; but, in the darkness and solitude in which he was now placed, there was but little of the present to arrest his attention. For the want of something else to amuse his mind, it was turned to the small cannon he was carrying in his hand.

"This 'ere thing," thought he, " aint o' much use as a pistol, though it might be used as a war-club at close quarters. I hope I shan't 'ave to fire it hoff. The barrel is thin, and the bullet hinside it must be a'most as large as an 'en's heg. It ud be like enough to bust. Preaps 't aint loaded, and may 'ave been given to me for amusement. I may as well make sure about that."

After groping about for some time, the sailor succeeded in finding a small piece of stick, with which he measured the length of the barrel on the outside; then, by inserting the stick into the muzzle, he found that the depth of the barrel was not quite equal to its length.

There must be something inside therefore, but he was positive there was no ball. He next examined the pan, and found the priming all right.

"I see 'ow 't is," muttered he, " the old sheik only wants me to make a row with it, in case I sees anything as is suspicious. He was afeard to put a ball in it lest I should be killin' one of themselves. That 's his confidence. He on'y wants me to bark without being able to bite. But this don't suit me at all, at all. Faix, I 'll find a bit of a stone and ram it into the barrel."

Saying this he groped about the ground in search of a pebble of the proper size; but for some time could find none to his liking. He could lay his hand on nothing but the finest sand.

While engaged in this search he fancied he heard some one approaching from the side opposite to that in which he was expecting to hear the word " *Akka*."

He looked in that direction, but could see nothing save the gray surface of the sea-beach.

Since being on the desert Bill had several times observed the Arabs lay themselves along the earth to listen for the sound of footsteps. This plan he now tried himself.

With his eyes close to the ground, the old sailor fancied he was able to see to a greater distance than when standing upright. There seemed to be more light on the surface of the earth than at four or five feet above it; and objects in the distance were placed more directly between his eyes and the horizon.

While thus lying extended along the sand, he heard footsteps approaching from the shore; but, believing they were those of the sentinel, he paid no attention to them. He only listened for a repetition of those sounds he fancied to have come from the opposite direction.

But nothing was now heard to the eastward; and he came to the conclusion that he had been deceived by an excited fancy.

Of one thing, however, he soon became certain. It was, that the footsteps which he supposed to be those of the Arab who kept, what Bill called, the "larboard watch," were drawing nearer than usual, and that the word "*Akka*" was not pronounced as before.

The old sailor slewed himself around, and directed his gaze towards the shore.

The sound of footsteps was no longer heard, but the figure of a man was perceived at no great distance from the spot.

He was not advancing nearer, but standing erect, and apparently gazing sharply about him.

Could this man be the Arab sentinel?

The latter was known to be short and of slight frame, while the man now seen appeared tall and of stout build. Instead of remaining in his upright attitude, and uttering, as the sentry should have done, the word "*Akka*," the stranger was seen to stoop down, and place his ear close to the earth as if to listen.

During a moment or two while the man's eyes appeared to be turned away from him, the sailor took the precaution to fill the barrel of his pistol with sand.

Should he give the alarm by firing off the pistol, and then run towards the camp?

No! he might have been deceived by an excited imagination. The individual before him might possibly be the Arab guard trying to discover his presence before giving the sign.

While the sailor was thus undecided, the huge form drew nearer, approaching on all fours. It came within eight or ten paces of the spot, and then slowly assumed an upright position. Bill now saw it was not the sentinel but the black sheik!

The old man-o'-war's-man was never more frightened in his life. He thought of discharging the pistol, and running back to the douar; but then came the thought that he would certainly be shot down the instant he should rise to his feet; and fear held him motionless.

Golah drew nearer and nearer, and the sailor seeing the scimitar uplifted suddenly formed the resolution to act.

Projecting the muzzle of his huge pistol towards the black, he pulled the trigger, and at the same instant sprang to his feet.

There was a loud deafening report, followed by a yell of wild agony.

Bill stayed not to note the effect of his fire: but ran as

fast as his legs would carry him towards the camp, — already alarmed by the report of the pistol.

The Arabs were running to and fro in terrible fear and confusion, shouting as they ran.

Amidst these shouts was heard, — in the direction from which the sailor had fled, — a loud voice frantically calling, " Muley! Muley!"

" 'T is the voice of Golah!" exclaimed the Krooman in Arabic. " He is calling for his son, — Muley is his son's name!"

" They are going to attack the douar," shouted the Arab sheik, and his words were followed by a scene of the wildest terror.

The Arabs rushed here and there, mingling their cries with those of the slaves; while women shrieked, children screamed, dogs barked, horses neighed, and even the quiet camels gave voice to their alarm.

In the confusion the two wives of Golah, taking their children along with them, hurried away from the camp, and escaped undiscovered in the darkness.

They had heard the voice of the father of their children, and understood that accent of anguish in which he had called out the name of his son.

They were women, — women who, although dreading their tyrant husband in his day of power, now pitied him in his hour of misfortune.

The Arabs, anxiously expecting the appearance of their enemy, in great haste made ready to meet him; but they were left unmolested.

In a few minutes all was quiet: not a sound was heard in the vicinity of the douar; and the late alarm might have appeared only a panic of groundless fear.

The light of day was gradually gathering in the east when the Arab sheik, recovering from his excitement, ventured to make an examination of the douar and its denizens.

Two important facts presented themselves as evidence, that the fright they had experienced was not without a cause. The sentry who had been stationed to guard the camp on its southern side was not present, and Golah's two wives and their children were also absent!

There could be no mystery about the disappearance of the women. They had gone to rejoin the man whose voice had been heard calling "Muley."

But where was the Arab sentry? Had another of the party fallen a victim to the vengeance of Golah?

CHAPTER LXII.

GOLAH FULFILS HIS DESTINY.

TAKING the Krooman by one arm, the Arab sheik led him up to the old man-o'-war's-man, who, sailor-like having finished his watch, had gone to sleep.

After being awakened by the sheik, the Krooman was told to ask the white man why he fired his pistol.

"Why, to kill Golah, — the big nager!" answered Bill; 'an' I'm mighty desaved if I 'ave not done it."

This answer was communicated to the sheik, who had the art of expressing unbelief with a peculiar smile, which he now practised.

Bill was asked if he had seen the black sheik.

"Seen him! sartinly I did," answered the sailor. "He was not more nor four paces from me at the time I peppered 'im. I tell you he is gone and done for."

The sheik shook his head, and again smiled incrediously.

Further inquiries were interrupted by the discovery of

the body of the Arab sentinel whom Golah had killed, and all clustered around it.

The man's head was nearly severed from his body; and the blow — which must have caused instant death — had evidently been given by the black sheik. Near the corpse, tracks were observed in the sand such as no other human being but Golah could have made.

It was now broad daylight; and the Arabs, glancing along the shore to southward, made another discovery.

Two camels with a horse were seen upon the beach about half a mile off; and, leaving one of their number to guard the douar, the old sheik with his followers started off in the hope of recovering some of the property they had lost.

They were followed by most of the slaves; who, by the misfortunes of their master, were under less restraint.

On arriving near the place where the camels were, the young man we have described as Golah's brother-in-law, was found to be in charge of them. He was lying on the ground; but on the approach of the Arabs, he sprang to his feet, at the same time holding up both his hands.

He carried no weapon; and the gesture signified, " It is peace."

The two women, surrounded by their children, were near by, sitting silent and sorrowful on the sea-beach. They took no heed of the approach of the Arabs; and did not even look up as the latter drew near.

The muskets and other weapons were lying about. One of the camels was down upon the sand. It was dead; and the young negro was in the act of eating a large piece of raw flesh he had severed from its hump.

The Arab sheik inquired after Golah. He to whom the inquiry was directed pointed to the sea, where two dark bodies were seen tumbling about in the surf as it broke against the shingle of the beach.

The three midshipmen, at the command of the sheik, waded in, and dragged the bodies out of the water.

They were recognized as those of Golah and his son, Muley.

Golah's face appeared to have been frightfully lacerated; and his once large fierce eyes were altogether gone.

The brother-in-law was called on to explain the mysterious death of the black sheik and his son.

His explanation was as follows:—

"I heard Golah calling for Muley after hearing the report of a gun. From that I knew that he was wounded. Muley ran to assist him, while I stayed behind with the horse and camels. I am starving! Very soon Muley came running back, followed by his father, who seemed possessed of an evil spirit. He ran this way and that way, swinging his scimitar about, and trying to kill us both as well as the camels. He could not see, and we managed to keep out of his way. I am starving!"

The young negro here paused, and, once more picking up the piece of camel's flesh, proceeded to devour it with an alacrity that proved the truth of his assertion.

"Pig!" exclaimed the sheik, "tell your story first, and eat afterwards."

"Praise be to Allah!" said the youth, as he resumed his narrative, "Golah ran against one of the camels and killed it."

His listeners looked towards the dead camel. They saw that the body bore the marks of Golah's great scimitar.

"After killing the camel," continued the young man, "the sheik became quiet. The evil spirit had passed out of him; and he sat down upon the sand. Then his wives came up to him; and he talked to them kindly, and put his hands on each of the children, and called them by name. They screamed when they looked at him, and Golah told them not to be frightened; that he would wash his face and

frighten them no more. The little boy led him to the water
and he rushed into the sea as far as he could wade. He
went there to die. Muley ran after to bring him out, and
they were both drowned. I could not help them, for I was
starving!"

The emaciated appearance of the narrator gave strong
evidence of the truth of the concluding words of his story.
For nearly a week he had been travelling night and day,
and the want of sleep and food could not have been much
longer endured.

At the command of the Arab chief, the slaves now buried
the bodies of Golah and his son.

Gratified at his good fortune, in being relieved from all
further trouble with his implacable foeman, the sheik determined to have a day of rest, which to his slaves was very
welcome, as was also the flesh of the dead camel, now given
them to eat.

About the death of Golah there was still a mystery the
Arabs could not comprehend; and the services of the Krooman as interpreter were again called into requisition.

When the sheik learnt what the sailor had done, — how
the pistol had been made an effective weapon by filling the
barrel with sand, — he expressed much satisfaction at the
manner in which the old man-o'-war's-man had performed
his duty.

Full of gratitude for the service thus rendered him, he
promised that not only the sailor himself, but the boy slaves,
his companions, should be taken to Mogador, and restored to
their friends.

CHAPTER LXIII.

ON THE EDGE OF THE SAÃRA.

AFTER a journey of two long dreary days — days that were to the boy slaves periods of agonizing torture, from fatigue, hunger, thirst, and exposure to a burning sun — the kafila arrived at another watering-place.

As they drew near the place, our adventurers perceived that it was the same where they had first fallen into the hands of Golah.

"May God help us!" exclaimed Harry Blount, as they approached the place. "We have been here before. We shall find no water, I fear. We did not leave more than two bucketfuls in the hole; and as there has been no rain since, that must be dried up, long ago.

An expression of hopeless despair came over the countenances of his companions. They had seen, but a few days before, nearly all the water drawn out of the pool, and given to the camels.

Their fears were soon removed, and followed by the real gratification of a desire they had long been indulging — the desire to quench their thirst. There was plenty of water in the pool — a heavy deluge of rain having fallen over the little valley since they had left it.

The small supply of food possessed by the travellers would not admit of their making any delay at this watering-place; and the next morning the journey was resumed.

The Arabs appeared to bear no animosity towards the young man who had assisted Golah in killing their companions; and now that the black sheik was dead, they had no fear that the former would try to escape. The negro was one of those human beings who cannot own themselves, and who never feel at home unless with some one to control

them. He quietly took his place along with the other
slaves, — apparently resigned to his fate, — a fate that
doomed him to perpetual slavery, though a condition but little lower than that he had occupied with his brother-in-law.

Eight days were now passed in journeying in a direction
that led a little to the east of north.

To the white slaves they were days of indescribable agony, from those two terrible evils that assail all travellers
through the Saära, — hunger and thirst. Within the distance passed during these eight days they found but one
watering-place, where the supply was not only small in
quantity but bad in quality.

It was a well, nearly dried up, containing a little water,
offensive to sight and smell, and only rendered endurable to
taste by the irresistible power of thirst.

The surface of the pool was covered nearly an inch thick
with dead insects, which had to be removed to reach the
discolored element beneath. They were not only compelled
to use, but were even thankful to obtain, this impure beverage.

The route followed during these eight days was not along
the seashore; and they were therefore deprived of the
opportunity of satisfying their hunger with shell-fish. The
Arabs were in haste to reach some place where they could
procure food for their animals, and at the pace at which
they rode forward, it required the utmost exertion on the
part of their slaves to keep up with them.

The old man-o'-war's-man, unused to land travelling, could
never have held out, had not the Arabs allowed him, part of
the time, to ride on a camel. The feat he had performed, in
ridding them of that enemy who had troubled them so much
— and who, had he not been thwarted in his attack upon the
camp, would probably have killed them all — had inspired
his masters with some slight gratitude. The sailor, therefore, was permitted to ride, when they saw that otherwise

they would have to leave him behind to die upon the desert.

During the last two days of the eight, our adventurers noticed something in the appearance of the country, over which they were moving, that inspired them with hope. The face of the landscape became more uneven; while here and there stunted bushes and weeds were seen, as if struggling between life and death.

The kafila had arrived on the northern border of the great Saära; and a few days more would bring them to green fields, shady groves, and streams of sparkling water.

Something resembling the latter was soon after discovered. At the close of the eighth day they reached the bed of what appeared to be a river recently dried up. Although there was no current they found some pools of stagnant water: and beside one of these the douar was established.

On a hill to the north were growing some green shrubs to which the camels were driven; and upon these they immediately commenced browsing. Not only the leaves, but the twigs and branches were rapidly twisted off by the long prehensile lips of the animals, and as greedily devoured.

It was twilight as the camp had been fairly pitched; and just then two men were seen coming towards them leading a camel. They were making for the pools of water, for the purpose of filling some goat skins which were carried on their camel. They appeared both surprised and annoyed to find the pools in possession of strangers.

Seeing they could not escape observation, the men came boldly forward, and commenced filling their goat-skins. While thus engaged they told the Arab sheik that they belonged to a caravan near at hand that was journeying southward; and that they should continue their journey early the next morning.

After the departure of the two men the Arabs held a consultation.

"They have told us a lie," remarked the old sheik, "they
are not on a journey, or they would have halted here by
the water. By the beard of our Prophet they have spoken
falsely!"

With this opinion his followers agreed; and it was suggested that the two men they had seen were of some party
encamped by the seashore, and undoubtedly amusing themselves with a wreck, or gathering wealth in some other un-
usual way.

Here was an opportunity not to be lost; and the Arabs
determined to have a share in whatever good fortune Provi-
dence might have thrown in the way of those already upon
the ground. If it should prove to be a wreck there might
be serious difficulty with those already in possession; it was
resolved, therefore, to wait for the morning, when they could
form a better opinion of their chances of success, should a
conflict be necessary to secure it.

CHAPTER LXIV.

THE RIVAL WRECKERS.

EARLY next morning the kafila was *en route* for the
seashore, which was discovered not far distant. On
coming near a douar of seven tents was seen standing
upon the beach: and several men stepped forward to receive them.

The usual salutations were exchanged, and the new comers began to look about them. Several pieces of timber
lying along the shore gave evidence that their conjecture,
as to a wreck having taken place, had been a correct one.

"There is but one God, and He is kind to us all," said

the old sheik; "He casts the ships of unbelievers on cur shores, and we have come to claim a share of His favors."

"You are welcome to all you can justly claim," answered a tall man, who appeared to be the leader of the party of wreckers. "Mahomet is the prophet of Him who sends favors to all, both good and bad. If he has sent anything for you, look along the sea-beach and find it."

On this invitation the camels of the kafila were unloaded, and the tents pitched. The new-comers then set about searching for the *débris* of the wrecked vessel.

They discovered only some spars, and other pieces of ship-timbers, which were of no value to either party.

A consultation now took place between the old sheik and his followers. They were unanimous in the belief that a sunken ship was near them, and that they had only to watch the rival wreckers, and learn where she was submerged.

Desisting from their search, they resolved to keep a look-out.

When this determination became known to the other party, its chief, after conferring with his companions, came forward, and, announcing himself as the representative of his people, proposed a conference.

"I am Sidi Hamet," said he, "and the others you see here are my friends and relatives. We are all members of the same family, and faithful followers of the Prophet. God is great, and has been kind to us. He has sent us a prize. We are about to gather the gifts of His mercy. Go your way, and leave us in peace."

"I am Rias Abdallah Yezzed," answered the old sheik, "and neither my companions nor myself are so bad but that we, too, may be numbered among those who are entitled to God's favor, when it pleases Him to cast on our shores the ships of the infidel."

In rejoinder Sidi Hamet entered upon a long harangue; in which he informed the old sheik that in the event of a ves-

11   P

sel having gone to pieces, and the coast having been strown
with merchandise, each party would have been entitled to
all it could gather; but unfortunately for both, those pleasant circumstances did not now exist; although it was true,
that the hulk of a vessel, containing a cargo that could not
wash ashore was lying under water near by. They had discovered it, and therefore laid claim to all that it contained.

Sidi Hamet's party was a strong one, consisting of seventeen men; and therefore could afford to be communicative
without the least danger of being disturbed in their plans
and prospects.

They acknowledged that they had been working ten days
in clearing the cargo out of the sunken vessel, and that their
work was not yet half done — the goods being very difficult
to get at.

The old sheik inquired of what the cargo consisted; but
could obtain no satisfactory answer.

Here was a mystery. Seventeen men had been fourteen
days unloading the hulk of a wrecked ship, and yet no articles of merchandise were to be seen near the spot!

A few casks, some pieces of old sail, with a number of
cooking utensils that had belonged to a ship's galley, lay
upon the beach; but these could not be regarded as forming
any portion of the cargo of a ship.

The old sheik and his followers were in a quandary.

They had often heard of boxes full of money having been
obtained from wrecked ships.

Sailors cast away upon their coast had been known to
bury such commodities, and afterwards under torture to re-
veal the spot where the interment had been made.

Had this vessel, on which the wreckers were engaged,
been freighted with money, and had the boxes been buried
as soon as brought ashore?

It was possible, thought the new comers. They must
wait and learn; and if there was any means by which they

could claim a share in the good fortune of those who had first discovered the wreck, those means must be adopted.

The original discoverers were too impatient to stay proceedings till their departure; and feeling secure in the superiority of numbers, they recommenced their task of discharging the submerged hulk.

They advanced to the water's edge, taking along with them a long rope that had been found attached to the spars. At one end of this rope they had made a running noose, which was made fast to a man, who swam out with it to the distance of about a hundred yards.

The swimmer then dived out of sight. He had gone below to visit the wreck, and attach the rope to a portion of the cargo.

A minute after his head was seen above the surface, and a shout was sent forth. Some of his companions on the beach now commenced hauling in the rope, the other end of which had been left in their hands.

When the noose was pulled ashore, it was found to embrace a large block of sandstone, weighing about twenty-five or thirty pounds !

The Krooman had already informed Harry Blount and his companions of something he had learnt from the conversation of the wreckers; and the three mids had been watching with considerable interest the movements of the diver and his assistants.

When the block of sandstone was dragged up on the beach, they stared at each other with expressions of profound astonishment.

No wonder : the wreckers were employed in clearing the ballast out of a sunken ship !

What could be their object ? Our adventurers could not guess. Nor, indeed, could the wreckers themselves have given a good reason for undgergoing such an amount of ludicrous labor

Why they had not told the old sheik what sort of cargo they were saving from the wreck, was because they had no certain knowledge of its value, or what in reality it was they were taking so much time and trouble to get safely ashore.

As they believed that the white slaves must have a perfect knowledge of the subject upon which they were themselves so ignorant, they closely scanned the countenances of the latter as the block of ballast was drawn out upon the dry sand.

They were rewarded for their scrutiny.

The surprise exhibited by Sailor Bill and the three mids confirmed the wreckers in their belief that they were saving something of grand value; for, in fact, had the block of sandstone been a monstrous nugget of gold, the boy slaves could not have been more astonished at beholding it.

Their behavior increased the ardor of the salvors in the pursuit in which they were engaged, along with the envy of the rival party, who, by the laws of the Saäran coast, were not allowed to participate in their toil.

The Krooman now endeavored to undeceive his master as to the value of the "salvage," — telling him that what their rivals were taking out of the sunken ship was nothing but worthless stone.

But his statement was met with a smile of incredulity. Those engaged in getting the ballast ashore regarded the Krooman's statements with equal contempt. He was either a liar or a fool, and therefore unworthy of the least attention. With this reflection they went on with their work.

After some time spent in reconsidering the subject, the old sheik called the Krooman aside; and when out of hearing of the wreckers, asked him to give an explanation of the real nature of what he himself pers'sted in calling the "cargo" of the wreck, — as well as a true statement of its value.

The slave did as he was desired; but the old sheik only shook his head, once more declaring his incredulity.

He had never heard of a ship that did not carry a cargo of something valuable. He thought that no men would be so stupid and foolish as to go from one country to another in ships loaded only with worthless stones.

As nothing else in the shape of cargo was found aboard the wreck, the stones must be of some value. So argued the Arab.

While the Krooman was trying to explain the real purpose for which the stones had been placed in the hold of the vessel, one of the wreckers came up and informed him that a white man was in one of their tents, that he was ill, and wished to see and converse with the infidel slaves, of whose arrival he had just heard.

The Krooman communicated this piece of intelligence to our adventurers; and the tent that contained the sick white man having been pointed out to them, they at once started towards it, expecting to see some unfortunate countryman, who, like themselves, had been cast away on the inhospitable shores of the Saära.

CHAPTER LXV.

ANOTHER WHITE SLAVE.

ON entering within the tent to which they had been directed, they found, lying upon the ground, a man about forty years of age. Although he appeared a mere skeleton, consisting of little more than skin and bones, he did not present the general aspect of a man suffering from ill health; nor yet would he have passed for a *white* man anywhere out of Africa.

"You are the first English people I've seen f r ovei thirty years," said he, as they entered the tent: "for I car tell by your looks that every one of you are English. You are my countrymen. I was white once myself; and you will be as black as I am when you have been sun-scorched here for forty-three years, as I have been."

"What!" exclaimed Terence; "have you been a slave in the Saära so long as that? If so, God help us! What hope is there of our ever getting free?"

The young Irishman spoke in a tone of despair.

"Very little chance of your ever seeing home again, my lad," answered the invalid; "but *I* have a chance now, if you and your comrades don't spoil it. For God's sake don't tell these Arabs that they are the fools they are for making salvage of the ballast. If you do, they'll be sure to make an end of me. It's all my doing. I've made them believe the stones are valuable, so that they may take them to some place where I can escape. It is the only chance I have had for years, — don't destroy it, as you value the life of a fellow-countryman."

From further conversation with the man, our adventurers learned that he had been shipwrecked on the coast many years before, and had ever since been trying to get transported to some place where he might be ransomed. He declared that he had been backward and forward across the desert forty or fifty times; and that he had belonged to not less than fifty masters!

"I have only been with these fellows a few weeks," said he, "and fortunately when we came this way we were able to tell where the sunken ship was by seeing her foremast then sticking out of the water. The vessel was in ballast; and the crew probably put out to sea in their boats, without being discovered. It was the first ship my masters had ever heard of without a cargo; and they would not believe but what the stones were such, and must be worth something —

else why should they be carried about the world in a ship. I told them it was a kind of stone from which gold was obtained; but that it must be taken to some place where there was plenty of coal or wood, before the gold could be melted out of it, and then intrusted to white men who understood the art of extracting the precious metal from the rocks.

"They believe all this; for they can see shining particles in the sandstone which they think is really gold, or something that can be converted into it. For four days they forced me to toil, at diving and assisting them; but that didn't suit my purpose; and I've at length succeeded in making them believe that I am not able to work any longer."

"But do you really think," asked Harry Blount, "that they will carry the ballast any distance without learning its real value?"

"Yes; I did think that they might take it to Mogador, and that they would let me go along with them."

"But some one will meet them, and tell them that their lading is worthless?" suggested Colin.

"No, I think that fear of losing their valuable freight will keep them from letting any one know what they've got. They are hiding it in the sand now, as fast as they get it ashore, for fear some party stronger than themselves should come along and take it away from them. I intend to tell them after they have started on their journey, not to let any one see or know what they have, until they are safe within the walls of Mogador, where they will be under the protection of the governor. They have promised to take me along with them, and if I once get within sight of a seaport, not all the Arabs in Africa will hinder me from recovering my liberty."

While the pretended invalid was talking to them, Sailor Bill had been watching him, apparently with eager interest.

"Beg pardon for aving a small taste o' difference wi'

you in the mather ov your age," said the sailor, as soon as the man had ceased speaking; "but I'll never belave you 've been about 'ere for forty years. It can't be so long as that."

The two men, after staring at each other for a moment, uttered the words "Jim!" "Bill!" and then, springing forward, each grasped the hand of the other. Two brothers had met!

The three mids remembered that Bill had told them of a brother, who, when last heard from, was a slave somewhere in the Saära, and they needed no explanation of the scene now presented to them.

The two brothers were left alone; and after the others had gone out of the tent they returned to the Krooman — who had just succeeded in convincing the sheik, that the stones being fished out of the sunken ship were, at that time and place, of no value whatever.

All attempts on the part of the old sheik to convince the wreckers, as he had been convinced himself, proved fruitless.

The arguments he used to them were repeated to the sailor, Bill's brother; and by him were easily upset with a few words.

"Of course they will try to make you believe the cargo is no good," retorted Jim. "They wish you to leave it, so that they can have it all to themselves. Does not common sense tell you that they are liars?"

This was conclusive; and the wreckers continued their toil, extracting stone after stone out of the hold of the submerged ship.

Sailor Bill, at his brother's request, then summoned his companions to the tent.

"Which of you have been trying to do me an injury?" inquired Jim. "I told you not to say that the stones were worthless."

It was explained to him how the Krooman had been enlightening his master.

"Call the Krooman," said Jim, "and I 'll enlighten him. If these Arabs find out that they have been deceived, I shall be killed, and your master — the old sheik — will certainly lose all his property. Tell him to come here also. I must talk to him. Something must be done immediately, or I shall be killed."

The Krooman and the old sheik were conducted into the tent; and Jim talked to them in the Arabic language.

"Leave my masters alone to their folly," said he to the sheik; "and they will be so busy that you can depart in peace. If not, and you convince them that they have been deceived, they will rob you of all you have got. You have already said enough to excite their suspicions, and they will in time learn that I have been humbugging them. My life is no longer safe in their company. You buy me, then; and let us all take our departure immediately."

"Are the stones in the wreck really worth nothing?" asked the sheik.

"No more than the sand on the shore; and when they find out that such is the case, some one will be robbed. They have come to the sea-coast to seek wealth, and they will have it one way or the other. They are a tribe of bad men. Buy me, and leave them to continue the task they have so ignorantly undertaken."

"You are not well," replied the sheik; "and if I buy you, you cannot walk."

"Let me ride on a camel until I get out of sight of these my masters," answered Jim; "you will then see whether I can walk or not. They will sell me cheap; for they think I am done up. But I am not; I was only weary of diving after worthless stones."

The old sheik promised to follow Jim's advice; and or-

dered his companions to prepare immediately for the contin-
nance of their journey.

Sidi Hamet was called, and asked by Rias Abdallah if
he would sell some of the stones they had saved from the infidel ship.—

"Bismillah! No!" exclaimed the wrecker. "You say
they are of no value, and I do not wish to cheat any true
believer of the prophet."

"Will you *give* me some of them, then?"

"No! Allah forbid that Sidi Hamet should ever make a
worthless present to a friend!"

"I am a merchant," rejoined the old sheik; "and wish to
do business. Have you any slaves, or other property you
can sell me?"

"Yes! You see that Christian dog," replied the wrecker, pointing to Sailor Bill's brother; "I will sell him."

"You have promised to take me to Swearah," interrupted
Jim. "Do not sell me, master; I think I shall get well
some time, and will then work for you as hard as I can."

Sidi Hamet cast upon his infidel slave a look of contempt
at this allusion to his illness; but Jim's remark, and the
angry glance, were both unheeded by the Arab sheik.

The slave's pretended wishes not to be sold were disre-
garded; and for the consideration of an old shirt and a small
camel-hair tent, he became the property of Rias Abdallah
Yezzed.

The old sheik and his followers then betook themselves to
their camels; and the kafila was hurried up the dry bed of
the river, — leaving the wreckers to continue their toilsome
and unprofitable task.

CHAPTER LXVI.

SAILOR BILL'S BROTHER.

AFTER leaving the coast, the travellers kept at a quick pace, and Sailor Bill and his brother had but little opportunity of holding converse together. When the douar had been pitched for the night, the old salt and the "young gentlemen," his companions, gathered around the man whose experience in the miseries of Saäran slavery so far exceeded their own.

"Now, Jim," began the old man-o'-war's-man, "you must spin us the yarn of all your cruising since you 've been here. We 've seen somethin' o' the elephant since we 've been cast ashore, and that 's not long. I don't wonder at you sayin' you 'ave been aboard this craft forty-three years."

"Yes, that is the correct time according to my reckoning," interrupted Jim; "but, Bill, you don't look much older than when I saw you last. How long ago was it?"

"About eleven years."

"Eleven years! I tell you that I 've been here over forty."

"'Ow can that be?" asked Bill. "Daze it, man, you 'll not be forty years old till the fourteenth o' the next month. You 'ave lost yer senses, an' in troth, it an't no wonder!"

"That is true, for there is nothing in the Saära to help a man keep his reckoning. There are no seasons; and every day is as like another as two seconds in the same minute. But surely I must have been here for more than eleven years."

"No," answered Bill, "ye 'ave no been here only a wee bit langer than tin; but afther all ye must 'ave suffered in that time, it is quare that ye should a know'd me at all, at all."

"I did not know you until you spoke," rejoined Jim "Then I could n't doubt that it was you who stood before me, when I heard our father's broad Scotch, our mother's Irish brogue, and the talk of the cockneys amongst whom your earliest days were passed, all mingled together."

"You see, Master Colly," said Bill, turning to the young Scotchman. "My brother Jim has had the advantage of being twelve years younger than I ; and when he was old enough to go to school, I was doing something to help kape 'im there, and for all that I believe he is plased to see me."

"Pleased to see you!" exclaimed Jim. "Of course I am."

"I 'm sure av it," said Bill.

"Well, then, brother, go ahead, an' spin us your yarn."

"I have no one yarn to spin," replied Jim, "for a narrative of my adventures in the desert would consist of a thousand yarns, each giving a description of some severe suffering or disappointment. I can only tell you that it seems to me that I have passed many years in travelling through the sands of the Saära, years in cultivating barley on its borders, years in digging wells, and years in attending flocks of goats, sheep, and other animals. I have had many masters, — all bad, and some worse, — and I have had many cruel disappointments about regaining my liberty. I was once within a single day's journey of Mogador, and was then sold again and carried back into the very heart of the desert. I have attempted two or three times to escape; but was recaptured each time, and nearly killed for the unpardonable dishonesty of trying to rob my master of my own person. I have often been tempted to commit suicide; but a sort of womanly curiosity and stubbornness has prevented me. I wished to see how long Fortune would persecute me, and I was determined not to thwart her plans by putting myself beyond their reach. I did not like to give in, for any one who tries to escape from trouble by killing himself, shows that he has come off sadly worsted in the war of life."

"You are quite right," said Harry Blount; but I hope that your hardest battles in that war are now over. Our masters have promised to carry us to some place where we may be ransomed by our countrymen, and you of course will be taken along with us."

"Do not flatter yourselves with that hope," said Jim. "I was amused with it for several years. Every master I have had gave me the same promise, and here I am yet. I did think when my late owners were saving the stones from the wreck, that I could get them to enter the walls of some seaport town, and that possibly they might take me along with them. But that hope has proved as delusive as all others I have entertained since shipwrecked on the shore of this accursed country. I believe there are a few who are fortunate enough to regain their liberty; but the majority of sailors cast away on the Saäran coast never have the good fortune to get away from it. They die under the hardships and ill-treatment to which they are exposed upon the desert — without leaving a trace of their existence any more than the dogs or camels belonging to their common masters.

"You have asked me to give an account of my life since I have been shipwrecked. I cannot do that; but I shall give you an easy rule by which you may know all about it. We will suppose you have all been three months in the Saära, and Bill here says that I have been here ten years; therefore I have experienced about forty times as long a period of slavery as one of yourselves. Now, multiply the sum total of your sufferings by forty, and you will have some idea of what I have undergone.

"You have probably witnessed some scenes of heartless cruelty — scenes that shocked and wounded the most sensitive feelings of your nature. I have witnessed forty times as many. While suffering the agonies of thirst and hunger, you may have prayed for death as a relief to your anguish. Where such have been your circumstances once, they have been mine for forty times.

"You may have had some bright hopes of escaping, and once more revisiting your native land; and then have experienced the bitterness of disappointment. In this way I have suffered forty times as much as any one of you."

Sailor Bill and the young gentlemen, — who had been for several days under the pleasant hallucination that they were on the high road to freedom, — were again awakened to a true sense of their situation by the words of a man far more experienced than they in the deceitful ways of the desert.

Before separating for the night, the three mids learnt from Bill and his brother that the latter had been first officer of the ship that had brought him to the coast. They could perceive by his conversation that he was an intelligent man, — one whose natural abilities and artificial acquirements were far superior to those of their shipmate, — the old man-of-war's-man.

"If such an accomplished individual," reasoned they, "has been for ten years a slave in the Saära, unable to escape or reach any place where his liberty might be restored, what hope is there for us?"

CHAPTER LXVII.

A LIVING STREAM.

EVERY hour of the journey presented some additional evidence that the kafila was leaving the great desert behind, and drawing near a land that might be considered fertile.

On the day after parting from the wreckers a walled town was reached, and near it, on the sides of some of the hills, were seen growing a few patches of barley.

At this place the caravan rested for the remainder of the day. The camels and horses were furnished with a good supply of food, and water drawn from deep wells. It was the best our adventurers had drunk since being cast away on the African coast.

Next morning the journey was continued.

After they had been on the road about two hours, the old sheik and a companion, riding in advance of the others, stopped before what seemed, in the distance, a broad stream of water.

All hastened forward, and the Boy Slaves beheld a sight that filled them with much surprise and considerable alarm. It was a stream, — a stream of living creatures moving over the plain.

It was a migration of insects, — the famed locusts of Africa.

They were young ones, — not yet able to fly; and for some reason, unknown perhaps even to themselves, they were taking this grand journey.

Their march seemed conducted in regular order, and under strict discipline.

They formed a living moving belt of considerable breadth, the sides of which appeared as straight as any line mathematical science could have drawn.

Not one could be seen straggling from the main body, which was moving along a track too narrow for their numbers, — scarce half of them having room on the sand, while the other half were crawling along on the backs of their *compagnons du voyage*.

Even the Arabs appeared interested in this African mystery, and paused for a few minutes to watch the progress of the glittering stream presented by these singular insects.

The old sheik dismounted from his camel; and with his scimitar broke the straight line formed by the border of the moving mass — sweeping them off to one side.

The space was instantly filled up again by those advancing from behind, and the straight edge restored, the insects crawling onward without the slightest deviation.

The sight was not new to Sailor Bill's brother. He informed his companions that should a fire be kindled on their line of march, the insects, instead of attempting to pass around it, would move right into its midst until it should become extinguished with their dead bodies.

After amusing himself for a few moments in observing these insects, the sheik mounted his camel, and, followed by the kafila, commenced moving through the living stream.

A hoof could not be put down without crushing a score of the creatures; but immediately on the hoof being lifted, the space was filled with as many as had been destroyed!

Some of the slaves, with their naked feet, did not like wading through this living crawling stream. It was necessary to use force to compel them to pass over it.

After looking right and left, and seeing no end to the column of insects, our adventurers made a rush, and ran clear across it.

At every step their feet fell with a crunching sound, and were raised again, streaming with the blood of the mangled locusts.

The belt of the migratory insects was about sixty yards in breadth; yet, short as was the distance, the Boy Slaves declared that it was more disagreeable to pass over than any ten miles of the desert they had previously traversed.

One of the blacks, determined to make the crossing as brief as possible, started in a rapid run. When about half way through, his foot slipped, and he fell full length amidst the crowd of creepers.

Before he could regain his feet, hundreds of the disgusting insects had mounted upon him, clinging to his clothes, and almost smothering him by their numbers.

Overcome by disgust, horror, and fear, he was unable to rise; and two of his black companions were ordered to drag him out of the disagreeable company into which he had stumbled.

After being rescued and delivered from the clutch of the locusts, it was many minutes before he recovered his composure of mind, along with sufficient nerve to resume his journey.

Sailor Bill had not made the crossing along with the others; and for some time resisted all the attempts of the Arabs to force him over the insect stream.

Two of them at length laid hold of him; and, after dragging him some paces into the crawling crowd, left him to himself.

Being thus brought in actual contact with the insects, the old sailor saw that the quickest way of getting out of the scrape was to cross over to the other side.

This he proceeded to do in the least time, and with the greatest possible noise. His paces were long, and made with wonderful rapidity; and each time his foot came to the ground, he uttered a horrible yell, as though it had been planted upon a sheet of red-hot iron.

Bill's brother had now so far recovered from his feigned illness, that he was able to walk along with the Boy Slaves.

Naturally conversing about the locusts, he informed his companions, that the year before he had been upon a part of the Saäran coast where a cloud of these insects had been driven out to sea by a storm, and drowned. They were afterwards washed ashore in heaps; the effluvia from which became so offensive that the fields of barley near the shore could not be harvested, and many hundred acres of the crop were wholly lost to the owners

CHAPTER LXVIII.

THE ARABS AT HOME.

SOON after encountering the locusts, the kafila came upon a well-beaten road, running through a fertile country, where hundreds of acres of barley could be seen growing on both sides.

That evening, for some reason unknown to the slaves, their masters did not halt at the usual hour. They saw many walled villages, where dwelt the proprietors of the barley fields; but hurried past them without stopping either for water or food — although their slaves were sadly in need of both.

In vain the latter complained of thirst, and begged for water. The only reply to their entreaties was a harsh command to move on faster, frequently followed by a blow.

Towards midnight, when the hopes and strength of all were nearly exhausted, the kafila arrived at a walled village, where a gate was opened to admit his slaves. The old sheik then informed them that they should have plenty of food and drink, and would be allowed to rest for two or three days in the village.

A quantity of water was then thickened with barley meal; and of this diet they were permitted to have as much as they could consume.

It was after night when they entered the gate of the village, and nothing could be seen. Next morning they found themselves in the centre of a square enclosure surrounded by about twenty houses, standing within a high wall. Flocks of sheep and goats, with a number of horses, camels, and donkeys, were also within the inclosure.

Jim informed his companions that most of the Saäran Arabs have fixed habitations, where they dwell the greater part of the year, — generally walled towns, such as the one they had now entered.

The wall is intended for a protection against robbers, at the same time that it serves as a pen to keep their flocks from straying or trespassing on the cultivated fields during the night time.

It was soon discovered that the Arabs had arrived at their home; for as soon as day broke, they were seen in company with their wives and families. This accounted for their not making halt at any of the other villages. Being so near their own, they had made an effort to reach it without extending their journey into another day.

"I fear we are in the hands of the wrong masters for obtaining our freedom," said Jim to his companions. "If they were traders, they might take us farther north and sell us; but it's clear they are not! They are graziers, farmers, and robbers, when the chance arises, — that's what they be! While waiting for their barley to ripen, they have been on a raiding expedition to the desert, in the hope of capturing a few slaves, to assist them in reaping their harvest."

Jim's conjecture was soon after found to be correct. On the old sheik being asked when he intended taking his slaves ton to Swearah, he answered: —

"Our barley is now ripe, and we must not leave it to spoil. You must help us in the harvest, and that will enable us to go to Swearah all the sooner."

"Do you really intend to take your slaves to Swearah?" asked the Krooman.

"Certainly!" replied the sheik. Have we not promised? But we cannot leave our fields now. Bismillah! our grain must be gathered."

"It is just as I supposed," said Jim. "They will promise anything. They do not intend taking us to Mogador at all. The same promise has been made to me by the same sort of people a score of times."

"What shall we do?" asked Terence.

"We must do nothing," answered Jim. "We must not assist them in any way, for the more useful we are to them the more reluctant they will be to part with us. I should have obtained my liberty years ago, had I not tried to gain the good-will of my Arab masters, by trying to make myself useful to them. That was a mistake, and I can see it now. We must not give them the slightest assistance in their barley-cutting."

"But they will compel us to help them?" suggested Colin.

"They cannot do that if we remain resolute; and I tell you all that you had better be killed at once than submit. If we assist in their harvest, they will find something else for us to do, and your best days, as mine have been, will be passed in slavery! Each of you must make himself a burden and expense to whoever owns him, and then we may be passed over to some trader who has been to Mogador, and knows that he can make money by taking us there to be redeemed. That is our only chance. These Arabs don't know that we are sure to be purchased for a good price in any large seaport town, and they will not run any risk in taking us there. Furthermore, these men are outlaws, desert robbers, and I don't believe that they dare enter the Moorish dominions. We must get transferred to other hands, and the only way to do that is to refuse work."

Our adventurers agreed to be guided by Jim's counsels, although confident that they would experience much difficulty in following them.

Early on the morning of the second day after the Arabs reached their home, all the slaves, both white and black, were roused from their slumbers; and after a spare breakfast of barley-gruel, were commanded to follow their masters to the grain fields, outside the walls of the town.

"Do you want us to work?" asked Jim, addressing himself directly to the old sheik.

Bismillah! Yes!" exclaimed the Arab. "We have kept you too long in idleness. What have you done, or who are you, that we should maintain you? You must work for your living, as we do ourselves!"

"We cannot do anything on land," said Jim. "We are sailors, and have only learnt to work on board a ship."

"By Allah, you will soon learn! Come, follow us to the barley fields!"

"No; we have all agreed to die rather than work for you! You promised to take us to Swearah; and we will go there or die. We will not be slaves any longer!"

Most of the Arabs, with their wives and children, had now assembled around the white men, who were ordered instantly to move on.

"It will not do for us to say we will not or can't move on," said Jim, speaking to his companions in English. "We must go to the field. They can make us do that; but they can't make us work. Go quietly to the field; but don't make yourselves useful when you get there."

This advice was followed; and the Boy Slaves soon found themselves by the side of a large patch of barley, ready for the reaping-hook. A sickle of French manufacture was then placed in the hands of each, and they were instructed how to use them.

"Never mind," said Jim. "Go to work with a will, mates! We'll show them a specimen of how reaping is done aboard ship!"

Jim proceeded to set an example by cutting the grain in a careless manner — letting the heads fall in every direction, and then trampling them under foot as he moved on.

The same plan was pursued by his brother Bill, the Krooman, and Harry Blount.

In the first attempt to use the sickle, Terence was so awkward as to fall forward and break the implement into two pieces.

Colin behaved no better: since he managed to cut one of his fingers, and then apparently fainted away at the sight of the blood.

The forenoon was passed by the Arabs in trying to train their slaves to the work, but in this they were sadly unsuccessful.

Curses, threats, and blows were expended upon them to no purpose, for the Christian dogs seemed only capable of doing much harm and no good. During the afternoon they were allowed to lie idle upon the ground, and watch their masters cutting the barley; although this indulgence was purchased at the expense of lacerated skins and aching bones. Nor was this triumph without the cost of further suffering: for they were not allowed a mouthful of food or a drop of water, although an abundance of both had been distributed to the other laborers in the field.

All five, however, remained obstinate; withstanding hunger and thirst, threats, cursings, and stripes,—each one disdaining to be the first to yield to the wishes of their Arab masters.

CHAPTER LXIX.

WORK OR DIE.

THAT night, after being driven within the walls of the town, the white slaves, along with their guard and the Krooman, were fastened in a large stone building partly in ruins, that had been recently used as a goat-pen.

They were not allowed a mouthful of food nor a drop of water, and sentinels walked around all night to prevent them from breaking out of their prison.

No longer targets for the beams of a blazing sun, they

were partly relieved from their sufferings; but a few hand fuls of barley they had managed to secrete and bring in from the field, proved only sufficient to sharpen an appetite which they could devise no means of appeasing.

A raging thirst prevented them from having much sleep; and, on being turned out next morning, and ordered back to the barley fields, weak with hunger and want of sleep, they were strongly tempted to yield obedience to their masters.

The black slaves had worked well the day before; and, having satisfied their masters, had received plenty of food and drink.

Their white companions in misery saw them eating their breakfast before being ordered to the field.

"Jim," said Sailor Bill, "I've 'alf a mind to give in. I must 'ave somethin' to heat an' drink. I'm starvin' all over."

"Don't think of it, William," said his brother. "Unless you wish to remain for years in slavery, as I have done, you must not yield. Our only hope of obtaining liberty is to give the Arabs but one chance of making anything by us,— the chance of selling us to our countrymen. They won't let us die,— don't think it! We are worth too much for that. They will try to make us work if they can; but we are fools if we let them succeed."

Again being driven to the field, another attempt was made by the Arabs to get some service out of them.

"We can do nothing now," said Jim to the old sheik; "we are dying with hunger and thirst. Our life has always been on the sea, and we can do nothing on land."

"There is plenty of food for those who earn it," rejoined the sheik; "and we cannot give those food who do not deserve it."

"Then give us some water."

"Allah forbid! We are not your servants to carry water for you"

All attempts to make the white slaves perform their task having failed, they were ordered to sit down in the hot sun, where they were tantalized with the sight of the food and water of which they were not permitted to taste.

During the forenoon of the day, all the eloquence Jim could command was required to prevent his brother from yielding. The old man-o'-war's-man was tortured by extreme thirst, and was once or twice on the eve of selling himself in exchange for a cooling draught.

Long years of suffering on the desert had inured Jim to its hardships; and not so strongly tempted as the others, it was easier for him to remain firm.

Since falling into the company of his countrymen, his hope of freedom had revived, and he was determined to make a grand effort to regain it.

He knew that five white captives were worth the trouble of taking to some seaport frequented by English ships; and he believed, if they refrained from making themselves useful, there was a prospect of their being thus disposed of.

Through his influence, therefore, the refractory slaves remained stanch in their resolution to abstain from work.

Their masters now saw that they were better off in the field than in the prison. They could not be prevented from obtaining a few heads of the barley, which they greedily ate, nor from obtaining a little moisture by chewing the roots of the weeds growing around them.

As soon as this was noticed, two of the Arabs were sent to conduct them back to the place where they had been confined on the night before.

It was with the utmost exertion that Sailor Bill and Colin were able to reach the town; while the others, with the exception of Jim, were in a very weak and exhausted state. Hunger and thirst were fast subduing them — in body, if not in spirit.

On reaching the door of the goat-pen, they refused to go n, all clamoring loudly for food and water.

Their entreaties were met with the declaration: that it was the will of God that those who would not work should suffer starvation.

"Idleness," argued their masters, "is always punished by ill-health"; and they wound up by expressing their thanks that such was the case.

It was not until the two Arabs had obtained the assistance of several of the women and boys of the village that they succeeded in getting the white slaves within the goat-pen.

"Jim, I tell you I can't stand this any longer," said Sailor Bill. "Call an' say to 'em as I gives in, and will work to-morrow, if they will let me have water."

"And so will I," said Terence. "There is nothing in the future to compensate for this suffering, and I can endure it no longer."

"Nor will I," exclaimed Harry; "I must have something to eat and drink immediately. We shall all be punished in the next world for self-murder in this unless we yield.

"Courage! patience!" exclaimed Jim. "It is better to suffer for a few hours more than to remain all our lives in slavery."

"What do I care for the future?" muttered Terence; "the present is everything. He is a fool who kills himself to-day to keep from being hungry ten years after. I will try to work to-morrow, if I live so long."

"Yes, call an' tell 'em, Jem, as 'ow we gives in, an' they 'll send us some refreshment," entreated the old sailor. "It ain't in human natur to die of starvation if one can 'elp it."

But neither Jim nor the Krooman would communicate to the Arabs the wishes of their companions; and the words and signals the old sailor made to attract the attention of those outside were unheeded.

12

Early in the evening, both Colin and the Krooman also expressed themselves willing to sacrifice the future for the present.

"We have nothing to do with the future," said Colin; in answer to Jim's entreaties that they should remain firm. "The future is the care of God, and we are only concerned with the present. We ought to promise anything if we can obtain food by it."

"I tink so too now," said the Krooman; "for it am worse than sure dat if we starve now we no be slaves bom by."

"They will not quite starve us to death," said Jim. "I have told you before that we are worth too much for that. If we will not work they will sell us, and we may reach Mogador. If we do work, we may stay here for years. I entreat you to hold out one day longer."

"I cannot," answered one.

"Nor I," exclaimed another.

"Let us first get something to eat, and then take our liberty by force," said Terence, "I fancy that if I had a drink of water, I could whip all the Arabs on earth."

"And so could I," said Colin.

"And I, too," added Harry Blount.

Sailor Bill had sunk upon the floor, hardly conscious of what the others were saying; but, partly aroused by the word water, repeated it, muttering, in a hoarse whisper, "Water! Water!"

The Krooman and the three youths joined in the cry; and then all, as loudly as their parched throats would permit, shouted the word, "Water! Water!"

The call for water was apparently unheeded by the Arab men, but it was evidently music to many of the children of the village, for it attracted them to the door of the goat-pen, around which they clustered, listening with strong expressions of delight.

Through a long night of indescribable agony, the cry of

" Water ! Water ! " was often repeated in the pen, and at each time in tones fainter and more supplicating than before.

The cry at length became changed from a demand to a piteous prayer.

CHAPTER LXX.

VICTORY !

NEXT morning, when the Arabs opened the door of the prison, Sailor Bill and Colin were found unable to rise ; and the old salt seemed quite unconscious of all efforts made to awaken his attention.

Not till then did Jim's resolution begin to give way. He would now submit to save them from further suffering ; but although knowing it was the wish of all that he should tender their submission on the terms the Arabs required, for a while he delayed doing so, in order to discover the course their masters designed adopting towards them.

" Are you Christian dogs willing to earn your food now ? " inquired the old sheik, as he entered the goat-pen.

Faint and weak with hunger, nearly mad with thirst, alarmed for the condition of his brother, and pitying the agony of the others, Jim was about to answer the sheik's question in the affirmative ; but there was something in the tone in which the question had been put, that determined him to refrain for a little longer.

The earthly happiness of six men might depend upon the next word he should utter, and that word he should not speak without some deliberation.

With an intellect sharpened by torture, Jim turned his

gaze from the old sheik upon several other Arabs that had
come near.

He could see that they had arrived at some decision
amongst themselves, as to what they should do, and that
they did not seem much interested in the ultimatum demanded by the sheik's inquiry.

This lack of excitement or interest did not look like further starvation and death; and in place of telling the Arabs
that they were willing to submit, Jim informed the old sheik
that all were determined to die rather than remain slaves.

"There is not one of us that wishes to live," he added,
"except for the purpose of seeing our native land again.
Our bodies are now weak, but our spirits are still strong.
We will die!"

On receiving this answer, the Arabs departed, leaving the
Christians in the pen.

The Krooman, who had been listening during the interview, then faintly called after them to return; but he was
stopped by Jim, who still entertained the hope that his firmness would yet be rewarded.

Half an hour passed, and Jim began to doubt again. He
might not have correctly interpreted the expressions he had
noted upon the faces of the Arabs.

"What did you tell them?" muttered Terence. "Did
you tell them that we were willing to work, if they would
give us water?"

"Yes — certainly!" answered Jim, now beginning to
regret that he had not tendered their submission before it
might be too late.

"Then why do they not come and relieve us?" asked
Terence, in a whisper — hoarse from despair.

Jim vouchsafed no answer; and the Krooman seemed in
too much mental and bodily anguish to heed what had been
said.

Shortly after, Jim could hear the flocks being driven out

of the town; and looking through a small opening in the wall of the pen, he could see some of the Arabs going out towards the barley fields.

Could it be that he had been mistaken — that the Arabs were going to apply the screw of starvation for another day? Alarmed by this conjecture, he strove to hail them, and bring them back; but the effort only resulted in a hoarse whisper.

"May God forgive me!" thought he. "My brother, as well as all the others, will die before night! I have murdered them, and perhaps myself!"

Driven frantic with the thought, frenzy furnished him with the will and strength to speak out.

His voice could now be heard, for the walls of the stone building rang with the shouts of a madman!

He assailed the door with such force that the structure gave way, and Jim rushed out, prepared to make any promises or terms with their masters, to save the lives he had endangered by his obstinacy.

His submission was not required: for on looking out, two men and three or four boys were seen coming towards the pen, bearing bowls of water, and dishes filled with barley-gruel.

Jim had conquered in the strife between master and man. The old sheik had given orders for the white slaves to be fed.

Jim's frenzy immediately subsided into an excitement of a different nature.

Seizing a calabash of water, he ran to his brother Bill; and raising him into a sitting posture, he applied the vessel to the man-o'-war's-man's lips.

Bill had not strength even to drink, and the water had to be poured down his throat.

Not until all of his companions had drunk, and swallowed a few mouthfuls of the barley-gruel, did Jim himself partake of anything.

The effect of food and water in restoring the energies of a starving man is almost miraculous; and he now congratulated his companions on the success of his scheme.

"It is all right!" he exclaimed. "We have conquered them! We shall not have to reap their harvest! We shall be fed, fattened, and sold; and perhaps be taken to Mogador. We should thank God for bringing us all safely through the trial. Had we yielded, there would have been no hope of ever regaining our liberty!"

CHAPTER LXXI.

SOLD AGAIN.

TWO days elapsed, during which time our adventurers were served with barley-gruel twice a day. They were allowed a sufficient quantity of water, with only the trouble of bringing it from the well, and enduring a good deal of insult and abuse from the women and children whom they chanced to meet on their way.

The second Krooman, who, in a moment of weakness inspired by the torture of thirst, had assisted the other slaves at their task, now tried in vain to get off from working. He came each evening to the pen to converse with his countryman; and at these meetings bitterly expressed his regret that he had submitted.

There was no hope for him now, for he had given proof that he could be made useful to his owners.

On the evening of the second day after they had been relieved from starvation, the white slaves were visited in their place of confinement by three Arabs they had not before seen.

These were well-armed, well-dressed, fine-looking fellows, having altogether a more respectable appearance than any inhabitants of the desert they had yet encountered.

Jim immediately entered into conversation with them, and learned that they were merchants, travelling with a caravan; and that they had claimed the hospitality of the town for that night.

They were willing to purchase slaves; and had visited the pen to examine those their hosts were offering for sale.

"You are just the men we are most anxious to see," said Jim, in the Arabic language, which, during his long residence in the country, he had become acquainted with, and could speak fluently. "We want some merchant to buy us, and take us to Mogador, where we may find friends to ransom us."

"I once bought two slaves," rejoined one of the merchants, "and at great expense took them to Mogador. They told me that their consul would be sure to redeem them; but I found that they had no consul there. They were not redeemed; and I had to bring them away again, — having all the trouble and expense of a long journey."

"Were they Englishmen?" asked Jim.

"No: Spaniards."

"I thought so. Englishmen would certainly have been ransomed."

"That is not so certain," replied the merchant; "the English may not always have a consul in Mogador to buy up his countrymen."

"We do not care whether there is one or not!" answered Jim. "One of the young fellows you see here has an uncle — a rich merchant in Mogador, who will ransom not only him, but all of his friends. The three young men you see are officers of an English ship-of-war. They have rich fathers in England, — all of them grand sheiks, — and they

were learning to be captains of war-ships, when they were
lost on this coast. The uncle of one of them in Mogador
will redeem the whole party of us."

"Which is he who has the rich uncle?" inquired one of
the Arabs.

Jim pointed to Harry Blount, saying, "That is the youngster. His uncle owns many great vessels, that come every
year to Swearah, laden with rich cargoes."

"What is the name of this uncle?"

To give an appearance of truth to his story, Jim knew
that it was necessary for some of the others to say something that would confirm it; and turning towards Harry,
he muttered, "Master Blount, you are expected to say
something — only two or three words — any thing you
like!"

"For God's sake, get them to buy us!" said Harry, in
complying with the singular request made to him.

Believing that the name he must give to the Arabs should
something resemble in sound the words Harry had spoken,
Jim told them that the name of the Mogador merchant was
"For God's sake buy us."

After repeating these words two or three times, the Arabs
were able to pronounce them — after a fashion.

"Ask the young man," commanded one of them, "if he is
sure the merchant 'For God's sake bias' will ransom you
all?"

"When I am done speaking to you," said Jim, whisper-
ing to Harry, "say Yes! nod your head, and then utter
some words!"

"Yes!" exclaimed Harry, giving his head an abrupt inclination. "I think I know what you are trying to do, Jim.
All right!"

"Yes!" said Jim, turning to the Arab; "the young fellow says that he is quite certain his uncle will buy us all.
Our friends at home will repay him."

"But how about the black man?" asked one of the merchants. "He is not an Englishman?"

"No; but he speaks English. He has sailed in English ships, and will certainly be redeemed with the rest."

The Arabs now retired from the pen, after promising to call and see our adventurers early in the morning.

After their departure, Jim related the whole of the conversation to his companions, which had the effect of inspiring them with renewed hope.

"Tell them anything," said Harry, "and promise anything; for I think there is no doubt of our being ransomed, if taken to Mogador, although I'm sure I have no uncle there, and don't know whether there's any English consul at that port."

"To get to Mogador is our only chance," said Jim; "and I wish I were guilty of no worse crime than using deception, to induce some one to take us there. I have a hope that these men will buy us on speculation; and if lies will induce them to do so, they shall have plenty of them from me. And you," continued he, turning to the Krooman, "you must not let them know that you speak their language, or they will not give a dollar for you. When they come here in the morning, you must converse with the rest of us in English, — so that they may have reason to think that you will also be redeemed."

Next morning, the merchants again came to the pen, and the slaves, at their request, arose and walked out to the open space in front, where they could be better examined.

After becoming satisfied that all were capable of travelling, one of the Arabs, addressing Jim, said : —

"We are going to purchase you, if you satisfy us that you are not trying to deceive us, and agree to the terms we offer. Tell the nephew of the English merchant that we must be paid one hundred and fifty Spanish dollars for each of you."

Jim made the communication to Harry; who at once con
sented that this sum should be paid.

"What is the name of his uncle?" asked one of the
Arabs. "Let the young man tell us."

"They wish to know the name of your uncle," said Jim,
turning to Harry. "The name I told you yesterday. You
must try and remember it; for I must not be heard repeating it to you."

"For God's sake buy us!" exclaimed Harry.

The Arabs looked at each other with an expression that
seemed to say, "It 's all right!"

"Now," said one of the party, "I must tell you what will
be the penalty, if we be deceived. If we take you to
Mogador, and find that there is no one there to redeem you,
if the young man, who says he has an uncle, be not telling
the truth, then we shall cut his throat, and bring the rest
of you back to the desert, to be sold into perpetual slavery.
Tell him that."

"They are going to buy us," said Jim to Harry Blount;
"but if we are not redeemed in Mogador, you are to have
your throat cut for deceiving them."

"All right!" said Harry, smiling at the threat, "that will
be better than living any longer a slave in the Saära."

"Now look at the Krooman"; suggested Sailor Bill, "and
say something about him."

Harry taking the hint, turned towards the African.

"I hope," said he, "that they will purchase the poor fellow; and that we may get him redeemed. After the many
services he has rendered us, I should not like to leave him
behind."

"He consents that you may kill the Krooman, if we are
not ransomed"; said Jim, speaking to the Arab merchants,
"but he does not like to promise more than one hundred
dollars for a negro. His uncle might refuse to pay more."

For some minutes the Arabs conversed with each other

m a low tone; and then one of them replied, "It is well We will take one hundred dollars for the negro. And now get ready for the road. We shall start with you to-morrow morning by daybreak."

The merchants then went off to complete their bargain with the old sheik, and make other arrangements for their departure.

For a few minutes the white slaves kept uttering exclamations of delight at the prospect of being once more restored to liberty. Jim then gave them a translation of what he had said about the Krooman.

"I know the Arab character so well," said he, "that I did not wish to agree to all their terms without a little haggling, which prevents them from entertaining the suspicion that we are trying to deceive them. Besides, as the Krooman is not an English subject, there may be great difficulty in getting him redeemed; and we should therefore bargain for him as cheaply as possible."

Not long after the Arab merchants had taken their departure from the pen, a supply of food and drink was served out to them: which, from its copiousness, proved that it was provided at the expense of their new owners.

This beginning augured well for their future treatment; and that night was spent by the Boy Slaves in a state of contentment and repose, greater than they had experienced since first setting foot on the inhospitable shores of the Saära.

CHAPTER LXXII.

ONWARD ONCE MORE.

EARLY next morning our adventurers were awakened, and ordered to prepare for the road.

The Arab merchants had purchased from their late hosts three donkeys, upon which the white slaves were allowed to ride in turns. Harry Blount, however, was distinguished from the rest. As the nephew of the rich merchant, "For God's sake buy us!" he was deemed worthy of higher favor, and was permitted to have a camel.

In vain he protested against being thus *elevated* above his companions. The Arabs did not heed his remonstrances, and at a few words from Jim he discontinued them.

"They think that we are to be released from slavery by the money of your relative," said Jim, "and you must do nothing to undeceive them. Not to humor them might awaken their suspicions. Besides, as you are the responsible person of the party, — the one whose throat is to be cut if the money be not found, — you are entitled to a little distinction, as a compensation for extra anxiety.

The Krooman, who had joined the slaves in cutting the grain, was in the field at work when the merchants moved off, and was not present to bid farewell to his more fortunate countryman.

After travelling about twelve miles through a fertile country, much of which was in cultivation, the Arab merchants arrived at a large reservoir of water, where they encamped for the night.

The water was in a stone tank, placed so as to catch all the rain that fell in a long narrow valley, gradually descending from some hills to the northward.

Jim had visited the place before, and told his companions

that the tank had been constructed by a man whose memory was much respected, and who had died nearly a hundred years ago.

During the night the Krooman, who had been left behind, entered the encampment, confident in the belief that he had escaped from his taskmasters.

At sunset he had contrived to conceal himself among the barley sheaves until his masters were out of sight, when he had started off on the track taken by the Arab merchants.

He was not allowed long indulgence in his dream of liberty. On the following morning, as the kafila was about to continue its journey, three men were seen approaching on swift camels; and shortly after Rias Abdallah Yessed, and two of his followers rode up.

They were in pursuit of the runaway Krooman, and in great rage at the trouble which he had caused them. So anxious were the Boy Slaves that the poor fellow should continue along with them, that, for their sake, the Arab merchants made a strenuous effort to purchase him; but Rias Abdallah obstinately refused to sell him at anything like a reasonable price. The Krooman had given proof that he could be very useful in the harvest-field; and a sum much greater than had been paid for any of the others, was demanded for him. He was worth more to his present owners than what the Arab merchants could afford to give; and was therefore dragged back to the servitude from which he had hoped to escape.

"You can see now, that I was right," said Jim. "Had we consented to cut their harvest, we should never have had an opportunity of regaining our liberty. Our labor for a single year would have been worth as much to them as the price they received for us, and we should have been held in perpetual bondage."

Jim's companions could perceive the truth of this observation, but not without being conscious that their good

fortune was, on their part, wholly undeserved, and that **had**
it not been for him, they would have yielded to the **wishes**
cf their late masters.

After another march, the merchants made halt near **some**
wells, around which a large Arab encampment was found
already established, — the flocks and herds wandering over
the adjacent plain.   Here our adventurers had an opportunity of observing some of the manners and customs of **this**
nomadic people.

Here, for the first time, they witnessed the Arab method
of making butter.

A goat's skin, nearly filled with the milk of camels, **asses,**
sheep, and goats, all mixed together, was suspended to the
ridge pole of a tent, and then swung to and fro by a child,
until the butter was produced.   The milk was then poured
off, and the butter clawed out of the skin by the black dirty
fingers of the women.

The Arabs allege that they were the first people who discovered the art of making butter, — though the discovery
does not entitle them to any great credit, since they could
scarce have avoided making it.   The necessity of carrying
milk in these skin bags, on a journey, must have conducted
them to the discovery.   The agitation of the fluid, while being transported on the backs of the camels, producing the
result, naturally suggested the idea of bringing it about by
similar means when they were not travelling.

At this place the slaves were treated to some barley-cakes,
and were allowed a little of the butter; and this, notwithstanding the filthy mode in which it had been prepared, appeared to them the most delicious they had ever tasted.

During the evening, the three merchants, along with several other Arabs, seated themselves in a circle; when a pipe
was lit and passed round from one to another.   Each would
take a long draw, and then hand the pipe to his left-hand
neighbor.

While thus occupied, they kept up an animated conversation, in which the word "Swearah" was often pronounced. Swearah of course meant "Mogador."

"They are talking about us," said Jim, "and we must learn for what purpose. I am afraid there is something wrong. Krooman!" he continued, addressing himself to the black, "they don't know that you understand their language. Lie down near them, and pretend to be asleep; but take note of every word they say. If I go up to them they will drive me away."

The Krooman did as desired; and carelessly sauntering near the circle, appeared to be searching for a soft place on which to lay himself for the night.

This he discovered some seven or eight paces from the spot where the Arabs were seated.

"I have been disappointed about obtaining my freedom so many times," muttered Jim, "that I can scarce believe I shall ever succeed. Those fellows are talking about Mogador; and I don't like their looks. Hark! what is that about 'more than you can get in Swearah!' I believe these new Arabs are making an offer to buy us. If so, may their prophets curse them!"

CHAPTER LXXIII.

ANOTHER BARGAIN.

THE conversation amongst the Arabs was kept up until a late hour; and during the time it continued, our adventurers were impatiently awaiting the return of the Krooman.

He came at length, after the Arabs had retired to their

tents; and all gathered around him, eager to learn what he had heard.

"I find out too much," said he, in answer to their inquiries; "too much, and no much good."

"What was it?"

"Two of you be sold to morrow."

"What two?"

"No one know. One man examine us all in the morning, but take only two."

After suffering a long lesson teaching the virtue of patience, they learnt from the Krooman that one of those who had been conversing with their masters was a grazier, owning large droves of cattle; and that he had lately been to Swearah.

. He had told the merchants that they would not be able to get a large price for their slaves in that place; and that the chances were much against their making more than the actual expenses incurred in so long a journey. He assured the Arab merchants that no Christian consul or foreign merchant in Mogador would pay a dollar more for redeeming six slaves than what they could be made to pay for two or three; that they were not always willing or prepared to pay anything; and that whenever they did redeem a slave, they did not consider his value, but only the time and expense that had been incurred in bringing him to the place.

Under the influence of these representations, the Arab merchants had agreed to sell two of their white slaves to the grazier, — thinking they would get as much for the remaining four as they would by taking all six to the end of the journey.

The owner of the herds was to make his choice in the morning.

"I thought there was a breaker ahead," exclaimed Jim, after the Krooman had concluded his report. "We must not be separated except by liberty or death. Our masters must take us all to Mogador. There is trouble before us yet; but we must be firm, and overcome it. Firmness has saved us once, and may do so again."

After all had promised to be guided in the coming emergency by Jim, they laid themselves along the ground, and sought rest in sleep.

Next morning, while they were eating their breakfast, they were visited by the grazier who was expected to make choice of two of their number.

"Which is the one who speaks Arabic?" he inquired from one of the merchants.

Jim was pointed out, and was at once selected as one of the two to be purchased.

"Tell 'im to buy me, too, Jim," said Bill, "We'll sail in company, you and I, though I don't much like partin' with the young gentlemen here."

"You shall not part either with them or me, if I can help it," answered Jim; "but we must expect some torture. Let all bear it like devils; and don't give in. That's our only chance!"

Glancing his eyes over the other slaves, the grazier selected Terence as the second for whom he was willing to pay a price.

His terms having been accepted by the merchants, they were about concluding the bargain, when they were accosted by Jim.

He assured them that he and his companions were determined to die, before they should be separated, — that none of them would do any work if retained in slavery, — and that all were determined to be taken to Swearah.

The merchants and the buyer only smiled at this interruption; and went on with the negotiation.

In vain did Jim appeal to their cupidity, — reminding them that the merchant, "for God's sake bias," would pay a far higher price for himself and his companions.

His arguments and entreaties failed to change their determination, — the bargain was concluded; and Jim and Terence were made over to their new master.

The merchants then mounted their camels, and ordered the other four to follow them.

Harry Blount, Colin, and Sailor Bill answered this command by sulkily sitting down upon the sand.

Another command from the merchants was given in sharp tones that betrayed their rising wrath.

"Obey them!" exclaimed Jim. "Go on; and Master Terence and I will follow you. We'll stand the brunt of the battle. They shall not hold me here alive!"

Colin and Bill each mounted a donkey, and Harry his camel — the Arab merchants seeming quite satisfied at the result of their slight exhibition of anger.

Jim and Terence attempted to follow them; but their new master was prepared for this; and, at a word of command, several of his followers seized hold of and fast bound both of them.

Jim's threat that they should not hold him alive, had thus proved but an idle boast.

Harry, Colin, and Bill, now turned back, dismounted, and showed their determination to remain with their companions, by sitting down alongside of them.

"These Christian dogs do not wish for liberty!" exclaimed one of the merchants. "Allah forbid that we should force them to accept it. Who will buy them?"

These words completely upset all Jim's plans. He saw that he was depriving the others of the only opportunity they might ever have of obtaining their liberty.

"Go on, go on!" he exclaimed. "Make no further resistance. It is possible they may take you to Mogador. Do not throw away the chance."

"We are not goin' to lave you, Jim," said Bill, "not even for liberty, — leastways, I'm not. Don't you be afeerd o that!"

"Of course we will not, unless we are forced to do so," added Harry. "Have you not said that we must keep together?"

"Have you not all promised to be guided by me?" replied Jim. "I tell you now to make no more resistance Go on with them if you wish ever to be free!"

"Jim knows what he is about," interposed Colin; "let us obey him."

With some reluctance, Harry and Bill were induced to mount again; but just as they were moving away, they were recalled by Jim, who told them not to leave; and that all must persevere in the determination not to be separated.

"The man has certainly gone mad," reflected Harry Blount, as he turned back once more. "We must no longer be controlled by him; but Terence must not be left behind. We cannot forsake *him*."

Again the three dismounted, and returning to the spot where Jim and Terence lay fast bound along the sand, sat determinedly down beside them.

CHAPTER LXXIV.

MORE TORTURE.

THE sudden change of purpose and the counter-orders given by Jim were caused by something he had just heard while listening to the conversation of the Arabs.

Seeing that the merchants, rather than have any unnecessary trouble with them, were disposed to sell them all, Jim had been unwilling to deprive his brother and the others of an opportunity of obtaining their freedom. For this reason had he entreated them to leave Terence and himself to their fate.

But just as he had prevailed on Harry and his companion to go quietly, he learnt from the Arabs that the man who had purchased Terence and himself refused to have any more of them; and also that the other Arabs present were either unable or unwilling to buy them.

The merchants, therefore, would have to take them farther before they could dispose of them.

In Jim's mind then revived the hope that, by opposing the wishes of his late masters, he and Terence might be bought back again and taken on to Mogador.

It was this hope that had induced him to recall his companions after urging them to depart.

A few words explained his apparently strange conduct to Harry and Colin, and they promised to resist every attempt made to take them any farther unless all should go in company.

The merchants in vain commanded and entreated that the Christian dogs should move on. They used threats, and then resorted to blows.

Harry, to whom they had hitherto shown much respect, was beaten until his scanty garments were saturated with blood.

Unwilling to see others suffering so much torture unsupported by any selfish desire, Jim again counselled Harry and the others to yield obedience to their masters.

In this counsel he was warmly seconded by Terence.

But Harry declared his determination not to desert his old shipmate Colin, and Bill remained equally firm under the torture; while the Krooman, knowing that his only chance of liberty depended on remaining true to the white slaves, and keeping in their company, could not be made to yield.

Perceiving that all his entreaties — addressed to his brother, Harry, and Colin — could not put an end to the painful scene he was compelled to witness, Jim strove to effect some purpose by making an appeal to his late masters.

" Buy us back, and take us all to Swearah as you promised," said he. " If you do so, we will go cheerfully as we were doing before. I tell you, you will be well paid for your trouble."

One of the merchants, placing some confidence in the truth of this representation, now offered to buy Jim and Terence on his own account; but their new master refused to part with his newly-acquired property.

A crowd of men, women, and children had now gathered around the spot; and from all sides were heard shouts of " Kill the obstinate Christian 'dogs.' How dare they resist the will of true believers ! "

This advice was given by those who had no pecuniary interest in the chattels in question; but the merchants, who had invested a large sum in the purchase of the white slaves, had no idea. of making such a sacrifice for the gratification of a mere passion.

There was but one way for them to overcome the difficulty that had so unexpectedly presented itself. This was to separate the slaves by force, taking the four along with them; and leaving the other two to the purchaser who would not revoke his bargain.

To accomplish this, the assistance of the bystanders was required and readily obtained.

Harry was first seized and placed on the back of his camel, to which he was firmly bound.

Colin, Bill, and the Krooman were each set astride of a donkey, and then made fast by having their feet tied under the animal's belly.

For a small sum the merchants then engaged two of the Arabs to accompany them and guard the white slaves to the frontier of the Moorish empire, a distance of two days' jour ney

While the party was about to move away from the spot, one of the merchants, addressing himself to Jim, made the following observations.

"Tell the young man, the nephew of the merchant, 'For God's sake bias,' that since we have started for Swearah in the belief that his story is true, we shall now take him there whether he is willing or not, and if he has in anyway deceived us, he shall surely die."

"He has not deceived you," said Jim, "take him and the others there, and you will certainly be paid."

"Then why do they not go willingly?"

"Because they do not wish to leave their friends."

"Ungrateful dogs! cannot they be thankful for their own good fortune? Do they take us for slaves, that we should do their will?"

While the conversation was going on, the other two merchants had headed their animals to the road; and in a minute after Harry Blount and Colin had parted with their old messmate Terence, without a hope of ever meeting him again.

CHAPTER LXXV.

EN ROUTE.

AND now away for the Moorish frontier.

Away, — trusting that the last hasty promise of the merchant to test their earnest story, and yield to the importunate desires which they had so long cherished, might not be unfulfilled.

Away, — out into the desert again; into that broad, barren wilderness of sand, stretching wearily on as far as eye could reach, and beyond the utmost limit of human steps, where the wild beasts almost fear to tread.

Away, — under the glare of the tropic sun, whose torrid beams fall from heavens that glow like hot walls of brass, and beat down through an atmosphere whose faint undulations in the breath of the desert wind ebb and flow over the parched travellers, like waves of a fiery sea; under a sun that seems to grow ever larger and brighter as the tired eyes, sick with beholding its yellow splendor overflowing all the world, yet turn toward it their fascinated gaze, and faint into burning dryness at its sight.

Away, — from the coolness of city walls, and the dark shadows of narrow, high-built streets, where the sunlight comes only at the height of noon, where men hide within doors as the hot hours draw nigh, and rest in silent chambers, or drowse away the time with *tchibouque* or *narghileh*, whose softened odor of the rich Eastern tobacco floats up through perfumed waters and tubes of aromatic woods to leisurely lips, and curls in dim wreaths before restful eyelids half dropping to repose.

Away, — from the association of men in street, lane, bazaar, and market-place. No very profitable or happy association for the poor captives, one might think; and yet not so. For in every group of bystanders, or bevy of passers, they perchance might see him who should prove their angel of deliverance, — a kindly merchant, a new speculator, or even, by some event of gracious fortune, a countryman or a friend.

Away, — from all that they had borne and hoped, and borne and seen and suffered, into the desert whose paths lay invisible to them, mapped out in the keen intellects of their guides and guards, who read the streaming sand of Saära as sailors read the wilds of sweeping seas, but whose dusky faces, as inscrutable as the barren wastes, revealed no trace of the secret of the path they led, — whether indeed the great Moorish Empire were their destination, or whether they turned their steps to some unknown and untried goal.

Away,—from the hum of business, from the gossip of idlers and the staid speech of a city into the silence of the vast desolation wherein they moved, the only reasoning, thinking beings it contained. Silence all around, unbroken save by the smothered tread of the beasts in their little train, the shouts of the drivers, the chattering of the attendants, the rattling of harness and burdens, and the soft sough of the sand as it sank back into the hot level from which the passing hoofs had disturbed it.

Away, away,—and who shall attempt to paint the feelings of the captives as their wanderings began again? It would need a brilliant pen to convey the sensations with which the *voyageur*, eager for scenes of adventure and fresh from the hived-up haunts of civilization, would enter upon a desert jaunt, to whom all was full of novelty and interest, whose companions were subjects for curious study, speaking in accents the unfamiliar Oriental cadence of which fell pleasantly upon his ear, and who found in every hour some fresh cause for wonder or pleasure. But a pen of marvellous power and pathos must be invoked to portray the mingled emotions that swayed in swift succession the minds of our Boy Slaves! No charm existed for them in the strangeness of desert scenery, Arab comradeship, and the murmur of Eastern tongues; they had long passed the time for that, while their bitter familiarity with all these made even a deep revulsion of feeling in their sorely tried souls. Hope, fear, doubt, fatigue, anxious yearning, and vague despair, —all in turn swept through their thoughts, even as the dust of their pitiless pathway swept over their scorched faces, and covered with effacing monotony every vestige of their passage. Mine is no such potent pen, and so let us leave them, bound to their beasts of burden, going down from the abodes of men into the depths again; and so let us leave them, journeying ever onward,—away, away!

CHAPTER LXXVI.

HOPE DEFERRED.

FOR the first hour of their journey, Harry, Colin, and Sailor Bill, were borne along fast bound upon the backs of their animals. So disagreeable did they find this mode of locomotion, that the Krooman was requested to inform their masters, that they were willing to accompany them without further opposition, if allowed the freedom of their limbs, this was the first occasion on which the Krooman had made known to the Arab merchants that he could speak their language.

After receiving a few curses and blows for having so long concealed his knowledge of it, the slaves were unbound, and the animals they bestrode were driven along in advance of the others, while the two hired guards were ordered to keep a short watch over them.

The journey was continued until a late hour of the night; when they reached the gate of a high wall enclosing a small town.

Here a long parley ensued, and at first the party seemed likely to be turned back upon their steps to pass the night in the desert, but at last the guardians of the village, being satisfied with the representations of the Arabs, unbarred the portals and let them enter.

After the slaves had been conducted inside, and the gate fastened behind them, their masters, relieved of all anxiety about losing their property, accepted the hospitality of the sheik of the village, and took their departure for his house, directing only that the white slaves should be fed.

After the latter had eaten a hearty meal, consisting of barley-bread and milk; they were conducted to a pen, which

13   ⁹

they were told was to be their sleeping-place, and there they passed the greater part of the night in fighting fleas.

Never before had either of them encountered these insects, either so large in size or of so keen appetites.

It was but at the hour at which their journey should have been resumed, that they forgot their hopes and cares in the repose of sleep. Weary in body and soul, they slept on till a late hour; and when aroused to consciousness by an Arab bringing some food, they were surprised to see that the sun was high up in the heavens.

Why had they not been awakened before?

Why this delay?

In the mind of each was an instinctive fear that there must be something wrong, — that some other obstacle had arisen, blocking up their road to freedom. Hours passed, and their masters came not near them.

They remained in much anxiety, vainly endeavoring to surmise what had caused the interruption to their journey.

Knowing that the merchants had expressed an intention to conduct them to Mogador as soon as possible, they could not doubt but what the delay arose from some cause affecting their own welfare.

Late in the afternoon they were visited by their masters; and in that interview their worst fears were more than realized.

By the aid of the Krooman, one of the merchants informed Harry that they had been deceived, — that the sheik, of whose hospitality they had been partaking, had often visited Swearah, and was acquainted with all the foreign residents there. He had told them that there was no one of the name "For God sake byas."

He had assured them that they were being imposed upon; and that by taking the white slaves to Swearah, they would certainly lose them.

"We shall not kill you," said one of the masters to Har

ry, "for we have not had the trouble of carrying you the whole distance; and besides, we should be injuring ourselves. We shall take you all to the borders of the desert, and there sell you for what you will fetch."

Harry told the Krooman to inform his masters that he had freely pledged his existence on the truth of the story he had told them; that he certainly had an uncle and friend in Mogador, who would redeem them all; but that, should his uncle not be in Swearah at the time they should arrive there, it would make no difference, as they would certainly be ransomed by the English Consul. "Tell them," added Harry, "that if they will take us to Swearah, and we are not ransomed as I promised, they shall be welcome to take my life. I will then willingly die. Tell them not to sell us until they have proved my words false; and not to injure themselves and us by trusting too much to the words of another.

To this communication the merchants made reply:— That they had been told that slaves brought from the desert into the Empire of Morocco could, and sometimes did, claim the protection of the government, which set them free without paying anything; and those who were at the expense of bringing them obtained nothing for their trouble.

One of the merchants, whose name was Bo Musem, seemed inclined to listen with some favor to the representations of Harry; but he was overruled by the other two, so that all his assertions about the wealth of his parents at home, and the immense worth he and his comrades were to this country, as officers in its navy, failed to convince his masters that they would be redeemed.

The merchants at length went away, leaving Harry and Colin in an agony of despair; while Sailor Bill and the Krooman seemed wholly indifferent as to their future fate. The prospect of being again taken to the desert, seemed to have so benumbed the intellect of both, as to leave them incapable of emotion.

Hope, fear, and energy seemed to have forsaken the old sailor, who, usually so fond of thinking aloud, had not now sufficient spirit left, even for the anathematizing of his enemies.

CHAPTER LXXVII.

EL HAJJI.

LATE in the evening of the second night spent within the walls of the town, two travellers knocked at the gate for admittance.

One of them gave a name which created quite a commotion in the village, all seeming eager to receive the owner with some show of hospitality.

The merchants sat up to a late hour in company with these strangers and the sheik of the place. Kids were caught and killed, and a savory stew was soon served up for their guests, while, with coffee, pipes, and many customary civilities, the time slipped quickly by.

Notwithstanding this, they were astir upon the following morning before daybreak, busied in making preparations for their journey.

The slaves, on being allowed some breakfast, were commanded to eat it in all haste, and then assist in preparing the animals for the road.

They were also informed that they were to be taken south, and sold.

"Shall we go, or die?" asked Colin. "I, for one, had rather die than again pass through the hardships of a journey in the desert."

Neither of the others made any reply to this. The spirit of despair had taken too strong a hold upon them.

The merchants themselves were obliged to caparison their animals; and just as they were about to use some strong arguments to induce their refractory slaves to mount, they were told that " El Hajji " (" the pilgrim ") wished to see the Christians.

Soon after, one of the strangers who had entered the town so late on the night before was seen slowly approaching.

He was a tall, venerable-looking Arab, with a long white beard reaching down to the middle of his breast. His costume, by its neatness and the general costliness of the articles of which it was composed, bespoke him a man of the better class, and his bearing was nowise inferior to his guise.

Having performed the pilgrimage to the Prophet's Tomb, ne commanded the respect and hospitality of all good Mussulmans whithersoever he wandered.

With the Krooman as interpreter, he asked many questions, and seemed to be much interested in the fate of the miserable-looking objects before him.

After his curiosity had been satisfied as to the name of the vessel in which they had reached the country, the time they had passed in slavery, and the manner of their treatment which had produced their emaciated and wretched appearance, he made inquiries about their friends and relatives at home.

Harry informed him that Colin and himself had parents, brothers, and sisters, who were now probably mourning them as lost: that they and their two companions were sure to be ransomed, could they find some one who would take them to Mogador. He also added, that their present masters had promised to take them to that place, but were now prevented from doing so through the fear that they would not be rewarded for their trouble.

" I will do all I can to assist you," said El Hajji, after the Krooman had given the interpretation of Harry's speech. " I owe a debt of gratitude to one of your countrymen, and

I shall try to repay it. When in Cairo I was unwell, and starving for the want of food. An officer of an English ship of war gave me a coin of gold. That piece of money proved both life and fortune to me; for with it I was able to continue my journey, and reach my friends. We are all the children of the true God; and it is our duty to assist one another. I will have a talk with your masters."

The old pilgrim then turning to the three merchants, said, —

" My friends, you have promised to take these Christian slaves to Swearah, where they will be redeemed. Are you bad men who fear not God, that your promise should be thus broken ? "

" We think they have deceived us," answered one of the merchants, " and we are afraid to carry them within the emperor's dominions for fear they will be taken from us without our receiving anything. We are poor men, and nearly all our merchandise we have given for these slaves. We cannot afford to lose them.

" You will not lose the value of them," said the old man, " if you take them to Swearah. They belong to a country the government of which will not allow its subjects to remain in bondage ; and there is not an English merchant in Swearah that would not redeem them. A merchant who should refuse to do so would scarce dare return to his own country again. You will make more by taking them to Swearah than anywhere else."

" But they can give themselves up to the governor when they reach Swearah," urged one of the merchants, " and we may be ordered out of the country without receiving a single cowrie for all. Such has been done before. The good sheik here knows of an Arab merchant who was treated so. He lost all, while the governor got the ransom, and put it in his own pocket."

This was an argument El Hajji was unable to answer

but he was not long in finding a plan for removing the difficulty thus presented.

"Do not take them within the Empire of Morocco," said he, "until after you have been paid for them. Two of you can stay with them here, while the other goes to Swearah with a letter from this young man to his friends. You have as yet no proof that he is trying to deceive you; and therefore, as true men, have no excuse for breaking your promise to him. Take a letter to Swearah; and if the money be not paid, then do with them as you please, and the wrong will not rest upon you."

Bo Muzem, one of the merchants, immediately seconded the pilgrim's proposal, and spoke energetically in its favor.

He said that they were but one day's journey from Agadeez, a frontier town of Morocco; and that from there Swearah could be reached in three days.

The merchants for a few minutes held consultation apart, and then one of them announced that they had resolved upon following El Hajji's advice. Bo Muzem should go to Swearah as the bearer of a letter from Harry to his uncle.

"Tell the young man," said one of the merchants, addressing himself to the interpreter, "tell him, from me, that if the ransom be not paid, he shall surely die on Bo Muzem's return. Tell him that."

The Krooman made the communication, and Harry accepted the terms.

A piece of dirty crumpled paper, a reed, and some ink was then placed before Harry; and while the letter was being written, Bo Muzem commenced making preparations for his journey.

Knowing that their only hope of liberty depended on their situation being made known to some countrymen resident in Mogador, Harry took up the pen, and, with much difficulty, succeeded in scribbling the following letter: —

"Sir, — Two midshipmen of H. M. S. —— (lost a few weeks ago north of Cape Blanco), and two seamen are now held in slavery at a small town one day's journey from Santa Cruz. The bearer of this note is one of our masters His business in Mogador is to learn if we will be ransomed · and if he is unsuccessful in finding any one who will pay the money to redeem us, the writer of this note is to be killed. If you cannot or will not pay the money they require (one hundred and fifty dollars for each slave), direct the bearer to some one whom you think will do so.

"There is a midshipman from the same vessel, and another English sailor one day's journey south of this place.

"Perhaps the bearer of this note, Bo Muzem, may be induced to obtain them, so that they also may be ransomed.

"HENRY BLOUNT."

This letter Harry folded, and directed to "Any English merchant in Mogador."

By the time it was written, Bo Muzem was mounted, and ready for the road.

After receiving the letter, he wished Harry to be informed once more, that, should the journey to Swearah be fruitless, nothing but his (Harry's) life would compensate him for the disappointment.

After promising to be back in eight days, and enjoining upon his partners to look well after their property during his absence, Bo Muzem took his departure from the town.

CHAPTER LXXVIII.

BO MUZEM'S JOURNEY.

ALTHOUGH an Arab merchant, Bo Muzem was an honest man, — one who in all business transactions told the truth, and expected to hear it from others.

He pursued his journey towards Mogador with but a faint hope that the representations made by Harry Blount would prove true, and with the determination of taking the life of the latter, should he find himself deceived. He placed more faith in the story told him by the sheik, than in the mere supposition of the pilgrim, that the white slaves would find some one to ransom them. For often, — alas too often! — the hopes which captives have dwelt on for tedious months, until they have believed them true, have proved, when put to the test, but empty and fallacious dreams.

His journey was partly undertaken through a sense of duty. After the promise made to the slaves, he thought it but right to become fully convinced that they would not be redeemed before the idea of taking them to Mogador should be relinquished.

He pressed forward on his journey with the perseverance and self-denial so peculiar to the race. After crossing the spurs of the Atlas Mountain near Santa Cruz, he reached, on the evening of the third day, a small walled town, within three hours ride of Mogador.

Here he stopped for the night, intending to proceed to the city early on the next morning. Immediately after entering the town, Bo Muzem met a person whose face wore a familiar look.

It was the man to whom but a few days before, he had sold Terence and Jim.

"Ah! my friend, you have ruined me, exclaimed the

13 *

Arab grazier, after their first salutations had passed. "I have lost those two useless Christian dogs you sold me, and I am ruined."

Bo Muzem asked him to explain.

"After your departure," said the grazier, "I tried to get some work out of the infidels; but they would not obey, and I believe they would have died before doing anything to make themselves useful. As I am a poor man, I could not afford to keep them in idleness, nor to kill them, which I had a strong inclination to do. The day after you left me, I received intelligence from Swearah which commanded me to go there immediately on business of importance; and thinking that possibly some Christian fool in that place might give something for their infidel countrymen, I took the slaves along with me.

"They promised that if I would take them to the English Consul, he would pay a large price for their ransom. When we entered Mogador, and reached the Consul's house, the dogs told me that they were free, and defied me trying to take them out of the city, or obtaining anything for my trouble or expense. The governor of Swearah and the Emperor of Morocco are on good terms with the infidel's government, and they also hate us Arabs of the desert. There is no justice there for us. If you take your slaves into the city you will lose them."

"I shall not take them into the empire of Morocco," said Bo Muzem, "until I have first received the money for them."

"You will never get it in Swearah. Their consul will not pay a dollar, but will try to get them liberated without giving you anything."

"But I have a letter from one of my slaves to his uncle, — a nut merchant in Swearah. The uncle must pay the money."

"The slave has lied to you. He has no uncle there, and

I can soon convince you that such is the case. There is lying in this place a Mogador Jew, who is acquainted with every infidel merchant in that place, and he also understands the languages they speak. Let him see the letter."

Anxious to be convinced as to whether he was being deceived or not, Bo Muzem readily agreed to this proposition; and in company with the graziers, he repaired to the house where the Jew was staying for the night.

The Jew, on being shown the letter, and asked to whom it was addressed, replied, —

"To any English merchant in Mogador."

"*Bismillah!*" exclaimed Bo Muzem. "All English merchants cannot be uncles to the young dog who wrote this letter."

"Tell me," added he, "did you ever hear of an English merchant in Swearah named 'For God sake byas?'"

The Jew smiled, and with some difficulty restraining an inclination to laugh outright at the question, gave the Arab a translation of the words, "For God's sake buy us."

Bo Muzem was now satisfied that he had been "sold."

"I shall go no farther," said he, after they had parted with the Jew. "I shall return to my partners. We will kill the Christian dog who wrote the letter, and sell the rest for what we can get for them."

"That is your best plan," rejoined the grazier. "They do not deserve freedom, and may Allah forbid that hereafter any true believers should try to help them to it."

Early the next morning Bo Muzem set out on his return journey, thankful for the good fortune that had enabled him so early to detect the imposture that was being practised upon him.

He was accompanied by the grazier, who chanced to be journeying in the same direction.

"The next Christian slaves I see for sale I intend to buy them," remarked the latter, as they journeyed along.

" Bismallah ! " exclaimed Bo Muzem, " that is strange
I thought you had had enough of them ? "

" So I have," answered the grazier ; " but that 's just why
I want more of them. I want revenge on the unbelieving
dogs ; and will buy them for the purpose of obtaining it. I
work them until they are too old to do anything and then
let them die of hunger."

" Then buy those we have for sale," proposed Bo Muzem.
We are willing to sell them cheap, all but one. The one
who wrote this letter I shall kill. I have sworn it by the
prophet's beard."

As both parties appeared anxious for a bargain, they soon
came to an understanding as to the terms ; and the grazier
promised to give ten dollars in money, and four head of
horses for each of the slaves that were for sale. He also
agreed that one of his herdsmen should assist in driving the
cattle to any Arab settlement where a market might be
found for them.

The simple Bo Muzem had now in reality been " sold,"
for the story he had been told about the escape of the two
slaves, Terence and Jim, was wholly and entirely false.

CHAPTER LXXIX

RAIS MOURAD.

SIX days passed, during which the white slaves were
comparatively well treated, far better than at any other
time since their shipwreck. They were not allowed to suffer
with thirst, and were supplied with nearly as much food as
they required.

On the sixth day after the departure of Bo Muzem, they

were visited by their masters, accompanied by a stranger, who was a Moor.

They were commanded to get upon their feet; and were then examined by the Moor in a manner that awakened suspicion that he was about to buy them.

The Moor wore a caftan richly embroidered on the breast and sleeves; and confined around the waist with a silken vest or girdle.

A pair of small yellow Morocco-leather boots were seen beneath trowsers of great width, made of the finest satin, and on his head was worn a turban of scarlet silk.

Judging from the respect shown to him by the merchants, he was an individual of much importance. This was also evident from the number of his followers, all of whom were mounted on beautiful Arabian horses, the trappings of which were made from the finest and most delicately shaded leathers, bestudded beautifully with precious metals and stones.

The appearance of his whole retinue gave evidence that he was some personage of wealth and influence.

After he had examined the slaves, he retired with the two merchants; and shortly afterwards the Krooman learnt from one of the followers that the white slaves had become the property of the wealthy Moor.

The bright anticipations of liberty that had filled their souls for the last few days, vanished at this intelligence. Each felt a shock of pain, — of hopeless despair, — that for some moments stunned them almost to speechlessness.

Harry Blount was the first to awaken to the necessity of action.

"Where are our masters the merchants?" he exclaimed. "They cannot — they shall not sell us. Come, all of you follow me!"

Reaching forth from the pens that had been allowed them for a residence, the young Englishman, followed by his com panions, started towards the dwelling of the sheik, to which the merchants and the Moor had retired.

All were now excited with disappointment and despair; and on reaching the sheik's house, the two Arab merchants were called out to witness a scene of anger and grief.

"Why have you sold us?" asked the Krooman when the merchant came forth. "Have you not promised that we should be taken to Swearah, and has not one gone there to obtain the money for our ransom?"

The merchants were on good terms with themselves and all the world besides. They had made what they believed to be a good bargain; and were in a humor for being agreeable.

Moreover they did not wish to be thought guilty of a wrong, even by Christian slaves, and they therefore condescended to give some explanation.

"Suppose," said one of them, "that our master Bo Muzem should find a man in Swearah who is willing to ransom you, how much are we to get for you?"

"One hundred dollars for me," answered the Krooman, "and one hundred and fifty for each of the others."

"True; and for that we should have to take you to Swearah, and be at the expense of feeding you along the road?"

"Yes."

"Well, Rais Mourad, a wealthy Moor, has paid us one hundred and fifty dollars for each of you; and would we not be fools to take you all the way to Swearah for less money? Besides we might never get paid at Swearah, — whereas we have received it in cash from Rais Mourad. You are no longer our slaves, but his."

When the Krooman had made this communication to the others, they saw that all further parley with the Arab merchants was useless; and that their fate was now in the hands of Rais Mourad.

At Harry's request, the Krooman endeavored to ascertain in what direction the Moor was going to take them; but the only information they received was that Rais Mourad knew his own business, and was not in the habit of conferring with his slaves as to what he should do with them.

Some of the followers of the Moor now came forward; and the slaves were ordered back to their pen, where they found some food awaiting them. They were commanded to eat it immediately, as they were soon to set forth upon a long journey.

Not one of them, after their cruel disappointment, had any appetite for eating; and Sailor Bill doggedly declared that he would never taste food again.

"Don't despair, Bill," said Harry; "there is yet hope for us."

"Where? — where is it?" exclaimed Colin; "I can't perceive it."

"If we are constantly changing owners," argued Harry, 'we may yet fall into the hands of some one who will take us to Mogador."

"Is that your only hope?" asked Colin, in a tone of disappointment.

"Think of poor Jim," added Bill; he's 'ad fifty masters, — been ten years in slavery, and not free yet; and no hope in it neyther."

"Shall we go quietly with our new master?" asked Colin.

"Yes," answered Harry; "I have had quite enough of resistance, and the beating that is sure to follow it. My back is raw at this moment. The next time I make any resistance, it shall be when there is a chance of gaining something by it, besides a sound thrashing."

Rias Mourad being unprovided with animals for his slaves to ride upon, and wishing to travel at a greater speed than they could walk, purchased four small horses from the sheik, and it was during the time these horses were being caught and made ready for the road, that the slaves were allowed to eat their dinner.

Although Harry, as well as the others, had determined on making no opposition to going away with Rias Mourad, they were very anxious to learn where he intended to take them.

All the inquiries made by the Krooman for the purpose of gratifying their curiosity, only produced the answer, " God knows, and will not tell you. Why should we do more than Him ?"

Just as the horses were brought out, and all were nearly ready for a start, there was heard a commotion at the gate of the town ; and next moment Bo Muzem, accompanied by three other Arabs, rode in through the gateway.

CHAPTER LXXX.

BO MUZEM BACK AGAIN.

AS soon as the white slaves recognized Bo Muzem, they all rushed forward to meet him.

"Speak, Krooman !" exclaimed Harry. " Ask him if the money for our ransom will be paid ? If so, we are free, and they dare not sell us again."

" Here, — here !" exclaimed Bill, pointing to one of the Arabs who came with Bo Muzem. " Ax this man where be brother Jim an' Master Terence ?"

Harry and Colin turned towards the man from whom Bill desired this inquiry to be made, and recognized in him the grazier, to whom Terence and Jim had been sold.

The Krooman had no opportunity for putting the question; for Bo Muzem, on drawing near to the gate of the town, had allowed his passion to mount into a violent rage; and as he beheld the slaves, shouted out, " Christian dogs! you have deceived me. Let every man, woman, and child, in this town assemble, and be witnesses of the fate that this lying Christian so richly deserves. Let all witness the death of this young infidel, who has falsely declared he has an uncle in Swearah, named ' For God's sake buy us.' Let all witness the revenge Bo Muzem will take on the unbelieving dog who has deceived him."

As soon as Bo Muzem's tongue was stopped sufficiently to enable him to hear the voices of those around him, he was informed that the slaves were all sold, — the nephew of " For God's sake buy us," among the rest, and on better terms than he and his partners had expected to get at Swearah.

Had Harry Blount been rescued, Bo Muzem would have been much pleased at this news; but he now declared that his partners had no right to sell without his concurrence, — that he owned an interest in them; and that the one who had deceived him should not be sold, but should suffer the penalty incurred, by sending him on his long and fruitless journey.

Rais Mourad now came upon the ground. The Moor was not long in comprehending all the circumstances connected with the affair. He ordered his followers to gather around the white slaves and escort them outside the walls of the town.

Bo Muzem attempted to prevent this order from being executed. He was opposed by everybody, not only by the Moor, but his own partners, as well as the sheik of the town, who declared that there should be no blood spilled among those partaking of his hospitality.

The slaves were mounted on the horses that had been provided for them, and then conducted through the gateway leaving Bo Muzem half frantic with impotent rage.

r

There was but one man to sympathize with him in his disappointment, the grazier to whom Terence and Jim had been sold, and who had made arrangements for the purchase of the others.

Riding up to the Moor, this man declared that the slaves were his property; that he had purchased them the day before, and had given four horses and ten dollars in money for each.

He loudly protested against being robbed of his property, and declared that he would bring two hundred men, if necessary, for the purpose of taking possession of his own.

Rais Mourad, paying no attention to this threat, gave orders to his followers to move on; and, although it was now almost night, started off in the direction of Santa Cruz.

Before they had proceeded far, they perceived the Arab grazier riding at full speed in the opposite direction, and towards his own home.

"I wish that we had made some inquiries of that fellow about Jim and Terence," said Colin; "but it's too late now."

"Yes, too late," echoed Harry, "and I wish that he had obtained possession of us instead of our present master. We should then have all come together again. But what are we to think of this last turn of Fortune's wheel?"

"I am rather pleased at it," answered Colin. "A while ago we were in despair, because the Moor had bought us. That was a mistake. If he had not done so, you Harry would have been killed."

"Bill!" added the young Scotchman, turning to the old sailor, "what are you dreaming about?"

"Nothing," answered Bill, "I'm no goin to drame or think any mair."

"We ah gwine straight for Swearah," observed the Krooman as he spoke, glancing towards the northwest.

"That is true," exclaimed Harry, looking in the same direction. "Can it be that we are to be taken into the empire of Morocco? If so, there is hope for us yet."

"But Bo Muzem could find no one who would pay the money for our ransom," interposed Colin.

"He nebba go thar," said the Krooman. "He nebba had de time."

"I believe the Krooman is right," said Harry. "We have been told that Mogador is four days' journey from here, and the Arab was gone but six days."

The conversation of the slaves was interrupted by the Moors, who kept constantly urging them to greater speed.

The night came on very dark, but Rais Mourad would not allow them to move at a slower pace.

Sailor Bill, being as he declared unused to "navigate any sort o' land craft," could only keep his seat on the animal he bestrode, by allowing it to follow the others, while he clutched its mane with a firm grasp of both hands.

The journey was continued until near midnight, when the old sailor, unable any longer to endure the fatigue, managed to check the pace of his horse, and dismount.

The Moors endeavored to make him proceed, but were unsuccessful.

Bill declared that should he again be placed on the horse, he should probably fall off and break his neck.

This was communicated to Rais Mourad, who had turned back in a rage to inquire the cause of the delay. It was the Krooman who acted as interpreter.

The Moor's anger immediately subsided on learning that one of the slaves could speak Arabic.

"Do you and your companions wish for freedom?" asked the Moor, addressing himself to the Krooman.

"We pray for it every hour."

"Then tell that foolish man that freedom is not found here — that to obtain it he must move on with me."

The Krooman made the communication as desired.

" I don't want to hear any more about freedom,' answered
Bill; "I've 'eard enough ov it. If any on 'em is goin' to
give us a chance for liberty, let 'em do it without so many
promises."

The old sailor remained obstinate.

Neither entreaties nor threats could induce him to go
farther; and Rais Mourad gave orders to his followers to
halt upon the spot, as he intended to stay there for the remainder of the night. The halt was accordingly made, and
a temporary camp established.

Although exhausted with their long, rough ride, Harry
and Colin could not sleep. The hope of liberty was glowing
too brightly within their bosoms.

This hope had not been inspired by anything that had
been said or done by Rais Mourad; for they now placed no
trust in the promises of any one.

Their hopes were simply based upon the belief that they
were now going towards Mogador, that the Moor, their master, was an intelligent man — a man who might know that
he would not lose his money by taking English subjects to a
place where they would be sure of being ransomed.

CHAPTER LXXXI.

A PURSUIT.

AT the first appearance of day, Rais Mourad ordered
the march to be resumed, over a long ridge of sand.
The sun soon after rising, on a high hill about four leagues
distant were seen the white walls of the city of Santa Cruz,
or, as it is called by the Arabs, Agadez. Descending the
sand ridge, the cavalcade moved over a level plain covered

with grain crops, and dotted here and there with small walled villages surrounded by plantations of vines and date-trees.

At one of the villages near the road the cavalcade made a halt, and was admitted within the walls. Throwing them selves down in the shade of some date-trees, the white slaves soon fell into a sound slumber.

Three hours after they were awakened to eat a small compound of hot barley-cakes and honey.

Before they had finished their repast, Rais Mourad came up to the spot, and began a conversation with the Krooman.

" What does the Moor say ? " inquired Harry.

" He say dat if we be no bad, and we no cheat him, he take us to Sweareh, to de English Consul."

" Of course we will promise that, or anything else," assented Harry, " and keep the promise too, if we can. He will be sure to be well paid for us. Tell him that ! "

The Krooman obeyed: and the Moor, in reply, said that he was well aware that he would be paid something by the Consul, but that he required a written promise from the slaves themselves as to the amount.

He wanted them to sign an agreement that he should be paid two hundred dollars for each one of them.

This they readily assented to, and the Moor then produced a piece of paper, a reed, and some ink.

Rais Mourad wrote the agreement himself in Arabic, on one side of the paper, and then, reading it sentence by sentence, requested the Krooman to translate it to his companions.

The translation given by the Krooman was —

" To English Consul, —

" We be four Christian slave. Rais Mourad buy us of Arab. We promise to gib him two hundred dollar for one, or eight hundred dollar for four, if he take us to you. Please pay him quick."

Harry and Colin signed the paper without any hesitation, and it was then handed with the pen to Sailor Bill.

The old sailor took the paper; and, after carefully surveying every object around him, walked up to one of the saddles lying on the ground a few paces off.

Spreading the paper on the saddle, he sat down, and very deliberately set about the task of making his autograph.

Slowly as the hand of a clock moving over the face of a dial, Bill's hand passed over the paper, while his head oscillated from side to side as each letter was formed.

After Bill had succeeded in painting a few characters which, in his opinion, expressed the name of William Mc-Neal, Harry was requested to write a similar agreement on the other side of the paper, which they were also to sign.

Rais Mourad was determined on being certain that his slaves had put their names to such an agreement as he wished, and therefore had written it himself, so that he might not be deceived.

About two hours before sunset all were again in the saddle; and, riding out of the gateway, took a path leading up the mountain on which stands the city of Santa Cruz.

When about half-way up, a party of horsemen, between twenty and thirty in number, was seen coming after them at full speed.

Rais Mourad remembered the threat made by the grazier who claimed the slaves as his property, and every exertion was made to reach the city before his party could be overtaken.

The horses ridden by the white slaves were small animals, in poor condition, and were unable to move up the hill with much speed, although their riders had been reduced by starvation to the very lightest of weights.

Before reaching the level plain on the top of the hill, the pursuers gained on them rapidly, and had lessened the distance between the two parties by nearly half a mile. The nearest gate of the city was still more than a mile ahead, and towards it the Moors urged their horses with all the energy that could be inspired by oaths, kicks, and blows.

As they neared the gate the herds of their pursuers were seen just rising over the crest of the hill behind them. But as Rais Mourad saw that his slaves were now safe, he checked his steed, and the few yards that remained of the journey were performed at a slow pace, for the Moor did not wish to enter the gate of a strange city in a hasty or undig-nified manner.

No delay on passing the sentinels, and in five minutes more the weary slaves dismounted from their nearly ex-hausted steeds, and were commanded by Rais Mourad to thank God that they had arrived safe in the Empire of Morocco.

In less than a quarter of an hour after Bo Muzem and the grazier rode through the gateway, accompanied by a troop of fierce-looking Arab horsemen.

The wrath of the merchant seemed to have waxed greater in the interval, and he appeared as if about to make an im-mediate attack upon Harry Blount, the chief object of his spiteful vengeance.

In this he was prevented by Rais Mourad, who appealed to an officer of the city guard to protect him.

The officer informed the merchant that while within the walls of the city he must not molest other people, and Bo Muzem was compelled to give his word that he would not do so : that is to say, he was bound over to keep the peace.

The other Arabs, in whose company they had come, were also given to understand that they were in a Moorish city ; and, as they saw that they were powerless to do harm with-out meeting with punishment, their fierce deportment soon gave way to a demeanor more befitting the streets of a civilized town.

Both pursued and pursuers were cautioned against any

infringement of the laws of the place; and as a different quarter was assigned to each party, all chances of a conflict were,
for the time, happily frustrated.

CHAPTER LXXXII.

MOORISH JUSTICE.

THE next morning, Rais Mourad was summoned to
appear before the governor of the city. He was ordered, also, to bring his slaves along with him. He had no
reluctance in obeying these orders, and a soldier conducted
him and his followers to the governor's house.

Bo Muzem and the grazier were there before them; and
the governor soon after made his appearance in the room
where both parties were waiting.

He was a fine-looking man, of venerable aspect, about six-
ty-five years of age, and, from his appearance, Harry and
Colin had but little fear of the result of his decision in an
appeal that might be made against them.

Bo Muzem was the first to speak. He stated that, in
partnership with two other merchants, he had purchased the
four slaves then present. He had never given his consent
to the sale made by his partners to the Moor; and there
was one of them whom it had been distinctly understood
was not to be sold at all. That slave he now claimed as his
own property. He had been commissioned by his partners
to go to Swearah, and there dispose of the slaves. He had
sold the other two to his friend Mahommed, who was present. He had no claim on them. Mahommed, the grazier
was their present owner.

The grazier was now called upon to make his statement.

This was soon done. All he had to say was, that he had purchased three Christian slaves from his friend, Bo Muzem, and had given four horses and ten dollars in money for each of them. They had been taken away by force by the Moor, Rais Mourad, from whom he now claimed them.

Rais Mourad was next called upon to answer the accusation. The question was put, why he retained possession of another man's property.

In reply, he stated that he had purchased them of two Arab merchants, and had paid for them on the spot; giving one hundred and fifty silver dollars for each.

After the Moor had finished his statement, the governor remained silent for an interval of two or three minutes.

Presently, turning to Bo Muzem, he asked, "Did your partners offer you a share of the money they received for the slaves?"

"Yes," answered the merchant, "but I would not accept it."

"Have you, or your partners, received from the man, who claims three of the slaves, twelve horses and thirty dollars?"

After some hesitation, Bo Muzem answered in the negative.

"The slaves belong to the Moor, Rais Mourad, who has paid the money for them," said the governor, "and they shall not be taken from him here. Depart from my presence, all of you."

All retired, and, as they did so, the grazier was heard to mutter that there was no justice for Arabs in Morocco.

Rais Mourad gave orders to his followers to prepare for the road; and just as they were ready to start, he requested Bo Muzem to accompany him outside the walls of the city.

The merchant consented, on condition that his friend Mahommed the grazier should go along with them.

14

"My friend," said Rais Mourad, addressing Bo Muzem,
"you have been deceived. Had you taken these Christians
to Swearah, as you promised, you would have certainly been
paid for them all that you could reasonably have asked. I
live in Swearah, and was obliged to make a journey to the
south upon urgent business. Fortunately, on my return, I
met with your partners, and bought their slaves from them.
The profit I shall make on them will more than repay me
all the expenses of my journey. The man Mahommed,
whom you call your friend, has bought two other Christians.
He has sold them to the English Consul. Having made
two hundred dollars by that transaction, he was anxious to
trade you out of these others, and make a few hundred more.
He was deceiving you for the purpose of obtaining them.
There is but one God, Mahomet is his prophet, and you are
a fool ! "

Bo Muzem required no further evidence in confirmation
of the truth of this statement. He could not doubt that the
Moor was an intelligent man, who knew what he was about
when buying the slaves. The grazier Mahommed had certainly purchased the two slaves spoken of, had acknowledged
having carried them to Swearah, and was now anxious to
obtain the others.

All was clear to him now ; and for a moment he stood
mute and motionless, under a sense of shame at his own
stupidity.

This feeling was succeeded by one of wild rage against
the man who had so craftily outwitted him.

Drawing his scimitar, he rushed towards the grazier, who,
having been attentive to all that was said, was not wholly
unprepared for the attack.

The Arabs never acquire much skill in the use of the
scimitar, and an affair between them with these weapons is
soon decided.

The contest between the merchant and his antagonist was

not an exception to other affrays between their countrymen. It was a strife for life or death, witnessed by the slaves who felt no sympathy for either of the combatants.

A mussulman in a quarrel generally places more dependence on the justice of his cause than either on his strength or skill; and when such is not the case much of his natural prowess is lost to him.

Confident in the rectitude of his indignation, Bo Muzem, with his Mohammedan ideas of fatalism, was certain that the hour had not yet arrived for him to die; nor was he mistaken.

His impetuous onset could not be resisted by a man unfortified with the belief that he had acted justly: and Mahommed the grazier was soon sent to the ground, rolling in the dust in the agonies of death.

" There's one less on 'em anyhow," exclaimed Sailor Bill, as he saw the Arab cease to live. " I wish he had brought brother Jem and Master Terence here. I wonder what he has done wi' 'em?"

" We should learn, if possible," answered Harry, " and before we get any farther away from them. Suppose we speak to the Moor about them? He may be able to obtain them in some way."

At Harry's request, the Krooman proceeded to make the desired communication, but was prevented by Rais Mourad ordering the slaves into their places for the purpose of continuing the journey which this tragic incident had interrupted.

After cautioning Bo Muzem to beware of the followers of Mahommed, who now lay dead at their feet, the Moor, at the head of his kafila, moved off in the direction of Mogador.

CHAPTER LXXXIII.

THE JEW'S LEAP.

THE road followed by Rais Mourad on the day after leaving Santa Cruz was through a country of very uneven surface.

Part of the time the kafila would be in a narrow valley by the sea-shore, and in the next hour following a zigzag path on the side of some precipitous mountain.

In such places the kafila would have to proceed in single file, while the Moors would be constantly cautioning the slaves against falling from the backs of their animals.

While stopping for an hour at noon for the horses to rest, the Krooman turned over a flat stone, and underneath it found a large scorpion.

After making a hole in the sand about six inches deep, and five or six in diameter, he put the reptile into it.

He then went in search of a few more scorpions to keep the prisoner company. Under nearly every stone he turned over, one or two of these reptiles were found, all of which were cast into the hole where he had placed the first.

When he had secured about a dozen within the prison from which they could not escape, he began teasing them with a stick.

Enraged at this treatment the reptiles commenced a mortal combat among themselves, a sight which was witnessed by the white slaves with about the same interest as that between the two Arabs in the morning. In other words, they did not care which got the worst of it.

A battle between two scorpions would commence with much active skirmishing on both sides, each seeking to fasten its claws on the other.

When one of the reptiles would succeed in getting a fair

grip, its adversary would exhibit every disposition to surrender, apparently begging for its life, but all to no purpose, as
no quarter would be given.

The champion would inflict the fatal sting; and the
unfortunate reptile receiving it would die immediately
after.

After all the scorpions had been killed except one, the
Krooman himself finished the survivor with a blow of his
stick.

When rebuked by Harry for what the latter regarded as
an act of wanton cruelty, he answered that it was the duty
of every man to kill scorpions.

In the afternoon they reached a place called the Jew's
Leap. It was a narrow path along the side of a mountain,
the base of which was washed by the sea.

The path was about half a mile long and not more than
four or five feet broad. The right hand side was bounded
by a wall of rocks, in some places perpendicular and rising
to a height of several hundred feet.

On the left hand side was the sea, about four hundred feet
below the level of the path.

There was no hope for any one who should fall from this
path, — no hope but heaven.

Not a bush, tree, or any obstacle was seen to offer the
slightest resistance to the downward course of a falling
body.

The Krooman had passed this way before, and informed
his companions that no one ever ventured on the path in
wet weather; that it was at all times considered dangerous;
but that, as it saved a tiresome journey of seven miles around
the mountain, it was generally taken in dry weather. He
also told them that the name of "Jew's Leap" was given
to the precipice, from a party of Jews having once been
forced over it.

It was in the night-time. They had met a numerous

party of Moors coming in the opposite direction. Neither party could turn back, a contest arose, and several on both sides were hurled over the precipice into the sea.

On this occasion as many Moors as Jews had been thrown from the path; but it had pleased the former to give the spot the name of the "Jew's Leap," which it still bears.

Before venturing upon this dangerous road, Rais Mourad was careful to see that no one was coming from the opposite direction.

After shouting at the top of his voice, and hearing no reply, he led the way, bidding his followers to trust more to their animals than to themselves.

As the white slaves entered on the pass, two Moors were left behind to follow them, and when all had proceeded a short distance along the ledge, the horse ridden by Harry Blount became frightened. It was a young animal, and having been reared on the plains of the desert, was unused to mountain-road.

While the other horses were walking along very cautiously, Harry's steed suddenly stopped, and refused to go any farther.

In such a place a rider has good cause to be alarmed at any eccentricity of behavior in the animal he bestrides, and Harry was just preparing to dismount, when the animal commenced making a retrogade movement, as if determined to turn about.

Harry was behind his companions, and closely followed by one of the Moors. The latter becoming alarmed for his own safety, struck the young Englishman's horse a blow with his musket to make it move forward.

The next instant the hind legs of the refractory animal were over the edge of the precipice, and its body, with the weight of its rider clinging to his neck, was about evenly balanced as on the brink. The horse made a violent struggle to avoid going over, with its nose and fore feet laid close along the path, and vainly striving to regain the position from which it had so imprudently parted.

At this moment its rider determined to make a desperate exertion for his life.

Seizing the horse by the ears, and drawing himself up, he placed one foot on the brink of the precipice, and then sprang clear over the horse's head, just as the animal relinquished its hold! In another instant the unfortunate quadruped was precipitated into the sea, its body striking the water with a dull plunge, as if the life had already gone out of it.

The remainder of the ledge was traversed without any difficulty; and after all had got safely over, Harry's companions were loud in congratulating him upon his narrow escape.

The youth remained silent.

His soul was too full of gratitude to God to give any heed to the words of man.

CHAPTER LXXXIV.

CONCLUSION.

ON the evening of the second day after passing the Jew's Leap, Rais Mourad, with his following, reached the city of Mogador; but too late to enter its gates, which were closed for the night.

For a great part of the night, Harry, Colin, and Sailor Bill were unable to sleep.

They were kept awake by the memory of the sufferings they had endured in slavery, but more by the anticipation of liberty, which they believed to be now near.

They arose with the sun call, impatient to enter the city, and learn their fate. Rais Mourad, knowing that no business could be done until three or four hours later, would not permit them to pass into the gate.

For three hours they waited with the greatest impatience. So strongly had their minds been elated with the prospect of getting free, that the delay was creating the opposite extreme of despair, when they were again elated at the sight of Rais Mourad returning to them.

Giving the command to his followers, he led the way into the city.

After passing through several narrow streets, on turning a corner, they saw waving over the roof of one of the houses a sight that filled them with joy inexpressible. It was the flag of Old England!

It indicated the residence of the English consul. On seeing it all three gave forth a loud simultaneous cheer, and hastened forward, in the midst of a crowd of Moorish men, women, and children.

Rais Mourad knocked at the gate of the consulate, which was opened; and the white slaves were ushered into the court-yard. At the same instant two individuals came running forth from the house. They were Terence and Jim!

A fine looking man about fifty years of age, now stepped forward; and taking Harry and Colin by the hand, congratulated them on the certainty of soon recovering their liberty.

The presence of Terence and Jim in the consulate at Mogador, was soon explained. The Arab grazier, after buying them, had started immediately for Swearah, taking his slaves with him. On bringing them to the English consul he was paid a ransom, and they were at once set free. At the same time he had given his promise to purchase the other slaves and bring them to Mogador.

The consul made no hesitation in paying the price that had been promised for Harry, Colin, and Bill; but he did not consider himself justified in expending the money of his government in the redemption of the Krooman, who was not an English subject.

The poor fellow was overwhelmed with despair at the prospect of being restored to a life of slavery.

His old companions in misfortune could not remain tranquil spectators of his grief. They promised he should be free. Each of the middies had wealthy friends on whom he could draw for money, and they were in hopes that some English merchant in the city would advance the amount.

They were not disappointed. On the very next day the Krooman's difficulty was settled to his satisfaction.

The consul having mentioned his case to several foreign merchants, a subscription-list was opened, and the amount necessary to the purchase of his freedom was easily obtained.

The three mids were furnished with plenty of everything they required, and only waited the arrival of some English ship to carry them back to the shores of their native land.

They had not long to wait; for shortly after, the tall masts of a British man-of-war threw their shadows athwart the waters of Mogador Bay.

The three middies were once more installed in quarters that befitted them: while Sailor Bill and his brother, as well as their Krooman comrade, found a welcome in the forecastle of the man-of-war.

All three of the young officers rose to rank and distinction in the naval service of their country. It was their good fortune often to come in contact with each other, and talk laughingly of that terrible time, no longer viewed with dread or aversion, when all three of them were serving their apprenticeship as Boy Slaves in the Saära.